"Have you ever been in love?" he asked, without blinking.

In her head she saw a young man in uniform with red hair. She blinked the image away. "No," she said. "Not really. How about you?"

"I loved a woman who died."

"I'm sorry." She looked away, gulped from her cocktail.

"Don't be. She wasn't."

It was such an odd thing to say that it made her wonder if he'd made it up to shock her.

"It was a long time ago."

"And there hasn't been anyone since?" He seemed to invite this kind of talk—flirtatious in its frankness.

"Of course. I'm perpetually in love. It's a grand way to be. You should try it some time. You might like it."

Grace shook her head. "You talk about love the way other people talk about ice cream."

He shrugged. "One is hot, the other cold. Both taste good."

"Love isn't something you can just choose to try."

"Tell that to her." Again he indicated the woman in gray. Her face wore an expression that was exquisitely sad. The man in the hat had hold of her hand.

"She doesn't look like she's having a 'grand' time of it," said Grace.

Critical acclaim for Anna Davis's previous historical novel,

THE SHOE QUEEN

"A wonderfully realistic denouement. . . . Touching."
—*Publishers Weekly*

"Fiction at its best: fast-paced and dramatic with characters whose motives are rewardingly complex. . . . A fantastical version of a bohemian reality in which it is a joy to lose yourself." —*Telegraph* (UK)

"An enjoyable whirlwind of beauty and seduction, with a satisfying dark undercurrent." —*Psychologies* (UK)

THE
JEWEL
BOX

ANNA DAVIS

POCKET BOOKS
New York London Toronto Sydney

Pocket Books
A Division of Simon & Schuster, Inc.
1230 Avenue of the Americas
New York, NY 10020

First Pocket Books trade paperback edition June 2009

For information about special discounts for bulk purchases, please contact Simon & Schuster Special Sales at 1-866-506-1949 or business@simonandschuster.com.

The Simon & Schuster Speakers Bureau can bring authors to your live event. For more information or to book an event contact the Simon & Schuster Speakers Bureau at 1-866-248-3049 or visit our website at www.simonspeakers.com.

Designed by Aline C. Pace

Manufactured in the United States of America

10 9 8 7 6 5 4 3 2 1

Library of Congress Cataloging-in-Publication Data

Davis, Anna, 1971-
The jewel box / by Anna Davis.
p. cm.
1. Woman journalists—Fiction. 2. Women—England—Fiction. 3. London (England)—History—1800-1950—Fiction. I Title.
PR6054.A89156J49 2009
823'.914—dc22
2008045263

ISBN: 978-1-4165-3736-6

For Rhidian and Leo,

with love

I.

The Dance

The West-Ender
April 4, 1927

Last night, at the newly opened Salamander Dinner-Dance Club on Coventry Street (they serve one of London's better steaks au poivre accompanied by brisk, stirring jazz), a louche gentleman in a top hat wreaked violent Charleston on me, and simply would not be shaken off. Today I am officially "In Recovery"—the kind that necessitates a night at home with a fish-paste sandwich and a mug of cocoa. For it's not merely my head that's aching— it's not just the usual ringing of the ears, rasping of the throat and churning of the stomach. No, today my lily-white tootsies are black and blue, too. Reader, I can barely walk!

As you know, it's been over a year since the Charleston stepped off the boat and took up residence in our better nightclubs. They dance it dandily in Paris and New York. So how much longer is it going to be before the Londoner learns how to do it properly? Men are generally the worst. There's something, frankly, convulsive about those kicking, flailing legs. At the Salamander, you take your life in your hands when you step onto the dance floor. In fact, I wouldn't even advise taking a table *beside* the dance floor. But many of the fairer sex are not so much better—really, there are a lot of farmyard hens strutting about the West End, pecking and flapping.

The solution? Lessons, of course. Trust me, girls, it's a sound investment. I suggest any of you with a nagging suspicion that your Charleston may be of the feathered, clucking sort should seek out, posthaste, Miss Leticia (known to her friends as "Teenie Weenie") Harrison, of Mayfair. Take heed: This might change your life. In an ideal world, one would of course take the hubby or boyfriend along to Teenie Weenie's—but if he thinks he's too fine and manly for classes, you'll have to teach him yourself. Let's face it, we've been educating our men in so many departments since long before we—that is, those of us over thirty—got the vote (NB: the under-thirties

would have my sympathy were it not for the fact that I covet your tender youth), and we'll be doing so for as long as men are men and women are women. Embrace your fate.

Two irritating comments that I regularly encounter, of an evening, now my fame is spreading:

"Miss Sharp, where do you find the stamina to go out all night every night? Your job must be the hardest in London."

—and—

"What an easy job you have, Miss Sharp. All you have to do is go out and enjoy yourself and then tell us all about it."

Also, I am outraged at the reports of various pretenders claiming to be me in order to bag good tables and complimentary cocktails. Doormen, if ever in doubt, ask "Diamond" to blow you a smoke ring. This is a very particular talent of mine, and should instantly reveal any fake gems. Oh, and by the way, I have never in my life had to *ask* for a free drink!

Diamond Sharp

One

The photograph shows a woman with flirtatious eyes and sharply bobbed hair. She is seated alone at a restaurant table with an empty champagne glass in front of her. Resting between the first two fingers of her gloved hand is a lit cigarette in a long ebony holder. From her lipsticked mouth, slightly open, issues a perfect smoke ring. The slogan above the photograph is simply, "Dare You?" The small print beneath the image explains that the tobacco in Baker's Lights is toasted and does not aggravate the throat.

Mr. Aubrey Pearson tossed the proof onto the desk and leaned back against creaky leather upholstery. "Well?"

Grace Rutherford, from the hard wooden seat on the other side of the table, cleared her throat. "Well, Mr. Pearson, I was thinking . . ."

"Were you? Were you *really*?" The eyebrows moved toward each other in a deep frown. "Did you think for one moment about how our client would react to this?" He indicated the proof.

Grace took a breath. If only she was having this discussion with Mr. Henry Pearson, the older brother. He was altogether more freethinking. "I believe this campaign could increase Baker's sales by about a third. Maybe more. We've never targeted women before—not for cigarettes—and it's about time we did. This year, London girls are wearing their hair and dresses shorter than ever, copying the Hollywood flapper look. They want the life that goes with it too—dancing the Charleston all night, having romances with dashing young men. It's the dream. Living life just a little bit wild. Doing things their mothers wouldn't have done. They all smoke, you know, the Hollywood actresses."

Mr. Pearson rubbed his head, where the hair was thinning. Perhaps it was thinning *because* he always rubbed it there, in just that spot. "Miss Rutherford, we absolutely cannot have an image of a girl smoking a cigarette in this advertising campaign. We have a reputation to uphold."

"Oh, sir, that's such bunkum. It's about time Pearson and Pearson joined the modern age."

"A word of warning." Pearson's voice was quiet now. "If I were you, I should think very carefully about what you plan to say next."

"All right." Grace swallowed. "Forget about the image. We don't have to show a woman smoking. Imagine a dance floor full of couples. In the foreground a man extends a hand to a girl, inviting her to step out. The copy reads, 'Will You? Won't You?' Here's another: The girl is seated beside her beau in an open-top car. The line is, 'How Fast are You?'"

Pearson pulled open a desk drawer and began to rummage about inside. Slamming it shut, he bellowed for his secretary, Gloria, to fetch an aspirin.

"Sir?"

"How long have you been with us, Miss Rutherford?"

"Almost ten years."

He proffered a smile. It looked all wrong on his face—as though someone had glued it there. "You might well think, my dear, that London has changed considerably in those ten years."

"Oh, it has."

"But I would put it to you that not all of those changes are for the better. There are many people out there—*many*—who take that view. And at the heart of this ever-changing city, there is a fundamental core of values which remain unchanged, and which must remain so. A still, stable core, around which whirls a lot of flux and chaos. Pearson and Pearson is part of that core. That's why we're able to hold on to clients like Baker's in the face of all the competition."

"Sir, with respect—"

"Respect—yes, that's a part of it, Miss Rutherford. Do you think it demonstrates respect for your employers and their clients when you arrive at the office an hour late, and visibly bleary? Or when you sit about the place, smoking cigarettes and exchanging jokes? Do you think it sets a good example to the typists and the secretaries?"

"But the other copywriters do just the same. And nobody seems to mind."

Another of those glued-on smiles. "You're an intelligent

girl. I shouldn't need to spell it out for you. And what the devil possessed you to put *yourself* in that blessed photograph? Stanley Baker'd laugh himself all the way down the road to Benson's if I let him see that proof."

The secretary appeared with two aspirin and a glass of water, set them down on the desk and retreated. In her wake came a distinctly uncomfortable silence.

"So," said Grace. "Shall I hand in my notice?"

A chuckle. "My, what drama! You have spirit, that's for certain. Go back and do some more thinking. You did hit on something with your idea about targeting women. But not this way. See if you can come up with something more . . . domestic. And as to the rest of it—"

"I know, sir. I understand."

Ten minutes later, in her tiny office, Grace picked up the telephone and asked to be connected to Richard Sedgwick, the editor of the *Piccadilly Herald* newspaper.

"Dickie, I want you to meet me for dinner tonight."

"Grace? Is that you?"

"Of course it's me. Seven o'clock? I don't much care where."

"Sorry, old thing. Busy tonight."

Grace drummed her fingernails impatiently on the desk. "What sort of busy? Work?"

Something that might have been a sigh but could easily have been a crackle on the line. "I'm not sure that's any of your—"

"So it's a girl. Not that dreadful Patsy again? It's *not* her, is it, Dickie?"

"Grace. You know how fond of you I am, but—"

"That lisp is an affectation. Didn't you realize? And the nose wrinkling. She's playing the *little girl*. She thinks that's what men want." A frown. "It's not, is it, Dickie?"

"I'm not seeing Patsy this evening."

"Then who?" Becoming aware of an unusual silence among the typists outside the room, Grace extended her right leg and gave the door a sharp kick so that it slammed shut.

"I have to go and see that German picture. You know—the one that cost all the money. It's on at the Pavilion."

"Oh, that. Nobody's going to *Metropolis*, Dickie. It's depressing and preposterous. Evil machines and virgin girls—or was it the other way around? Quite, quite silly."

"Thank you for your enlightened and knowledgeable view, dearest."

"Not at all." Grace slid a cigarette from the box on her desk and searched about for a book of matches. "What say we eat at the Tour Eiffel? You know how I hate it there, but I'd go anywhere for you, darling."

"My, how selfless we are."

"Then we could round the night off with a little party that Diamond's been invited to."

"So we're going dancing now, too?"

Grace found her matches and struck one, the receiver wedged between ear and shoulder. "Seriously, Dickie. There's something I need to talk to you about."

Coming up Tottenham Court Road half an hour late, Grace was caught in an April downpour with no umbrella. There were no taxis, trams or buses in sight, and so she was obliged to scurry inelegantly through the end-of-day hordes; gutter water splattering up her ankles; gray rain soaking through her clothes in smeary patches; the scent of wet builders' dust rank in her nostrils. As she hurried, she silently cursed her timekeeping (Grace was always half an hour late); her employers (for locating their offices on Piccadilly—simply not close enough to Percy Street, home of the Tour Eiffel); the weather (this was London, after all. Who didn't curse the weather occasionally?); God (in whom she didn't believe); and Dickie Sedgwick (for agreeing to meet her, and for liking the Tour Eiffel).

By the time she arrived at the restaurant the rain was heavier still. Running, head down, for the door, Grace collided, hard enough to make her teeth rattle, with a very solid person. A hand closed around her forearm, and she looked up into pale, blue eyes set wide apart in a broad face. The mouth was smiling—or perhaps it was just one of those mouths that's shaped so that it always appears to smile.

"Are you married?" The voice was smoothly American.

"No." The word was out before she could stop it. The hand still held her forearm.

"Good." When he spoke, he seemed to be looking past her. She became aware of a taxi parked nearby, its motor running. The man had perhaps just got out of it. The driver would be watching.

"Excuse me." She jerked free and moved haughtily toward the restaurant.

"Thirty-two, I should think." His smile, reflected in the glass, was distorted. Jagged. "There's a poignancy in your face." He was delving in his pocket for change, stepping back to pay the driver. "Liquid and lovely."

"I'm thirty, actually. Not that it's any of your business."

"It'll ice over in a year or two," said the man. "Always does."

✳　✳　✳

Before the war, the Tour Eiffel had been a haunt for the more avant-garde artists and writers; Augustus John, Wyndham Lewis, Ezra Pound. Later on the sketches and notes in the visitors' book were added to by Charles Chaplin, Ronald Firbank and George Gershwin—and the restaurant became the favorite of a more glitzy, fashionable crowd. By 1927, it was a monument to itself, with prices to match. The paintings and etchings of varying quality which crowded its walls put Grace in mind of gravestones, albeit higgledy-piggledy crazily colored gravestones. This place traded on its Bohemian past. One could perhaps order an hors d'oeuvre of coddled memories followed by a main course of stewed nostalgia. Certainly, Dickie Sedgwick was quite at home here.

"Punctual as ever." Dickie stood up to kiss her on the cheek. "Gracie, darling, you're absolutely soaking!"

"It's nothing. I shall be dry again directly." Grace sat on a carved walnut chair. "Meanwhile you can amuse yourself by watching great clouds of steam rising off me."

"Well, if you're sure." Dickie sat down. "I feel I should *do* something for you."

"Just get me a drink, will you?"

"Try some of this." He turned the wine bottle on the table so she could see its label. "It's from the Rhône Valley, so Joe tells me. Frightfully good."

"I'm sure it is, but I'm lacking a glass. Be a good fellow, and get Joe's attention?"

He was still talking about the wine, and she was dabbing with her napkin at the damp patches on her black silk-crêpe dinner dress, when glancing up, she saw the broad-shouldered man from the street enter the dining room. He was wearing a white starched evening shirt and bow tie. Rudolph Stulik, the proprietor, was instantly at his side, leading him to the best corner table, fussing about over his comfort, lighting his cigarette. The pale blue eyes turned suddenly in Grace's direction, and she looked away—down at the beaded jet buckle on her dress—and back up at Dickie. He had a crumpled weariness about him this evening. Not at all his dapper, ebullient self.

"You seem tired, Dickie. Is everything all right at the *Herald*?"

A flicker of irritation. "It's not all about the newspaper, you know, Grace."

"I know." An awkward moment. It was best not to draw him out further. Grace chanced another little gaze across the room. Stulik was explaining the menu to the American in the greatest detail, then pointing out a few paintings by the better known of his art clientele. The man appeared interested, but as Stulik looked away he shot a glance directly at Grace.

"Pig of a day." Grace made herself look at Dickie, and only Dickie. "I handed in my notice." She took a sip from her glass. "I say, you're right about the wine. Very crisp."

"*Did* you?"

"Well, I tried to. Pearson didn't take me seriously, though. Aubrey Pearson, that is. And I suppose I didn't take myself seriously either. I can't afford to lose my job, not really. But they're such dinosaurs, they drive one to distraction."

"So you're always saying. Shall we both have the fish? They've lemon sole today. With new potatoes."

"Dickie, you have no idea what it's like for a girl, working in a place like that. The men can do just whatever they like, so long as they get their copy written on time. But me—one hint of a laugh, one whiff of ciggie smoke and I'm for it. I'm supposed to be grateful to them, don't you see? For *letting* me work there. That's why I wanted to talk to you. I was wondering . . ."

Sedgwick chuckled. "You were wondering what it would be like to work at the *Herald.* D'you honestly think it's any better on a newspaper? Do you think you'd be treated just like any other fellow? It's the world we live in, my darling. But it's getting better—slowly." He nodded to the waiter. "Joe, two fish, please."

"Too slow for me." Grace looked across the room without meaning to. The American was staring at his wristwatch, frowning . . . She dragged her attention back to Dickie's freckled face—back to the matter in hand. "I've been thinking. What if Diamond were to start writing more than just her column? She could do book reviews, political comment, horoscopes even!"

He shook his head. "It wouldn't work."

"But *why*? Diamond is a huge success, you're always saying so. Who else on your silly paper gets sacks of letters? Who else gets gossiped about by *other* newspapers? Do you know what Harold Grimes came up with yesterday in the *Mail*? He thinks Rebecca West is Diamond Sharp. *Rebecca West!*"

"Man's an idiot." Dickie spoke under his breath, then cleared his throat. "Look. I couldn't be more pleased with the way it's all going. I can hardly believe it, to be truthful. But reading Diamond is like eating liquorice. You only want the tiniest bit."

A huff. "Well, I needn't be Diamond all the time."

His hand came across the table to take hold of hers. Gently. "Grace, you *are* Diamond. *All* the time. You couldn't be anyone else if you wanted to. I wouldn't *want* you to be anyone else."

The American was looking over again. At her hand, held in Dickie's.

"Though sometimes I feel like Victor Frankenstein," Dickie muttered.

"Well, then." She freed her hand. "I shall have to do what

any right-thinking monster would, and demand that you double my fee."

"Now, now, Miss Sulky. You'd better watch out—that frown of yours is carving permanent lines in your forehead. Ages you by a good ten years, I'd say."

"Oh, Dickie, you're so beastly! There's simply no use in talking to you about anything serious." She cast about in vain for their waiter. "Where's Joe? We need some more wine."

The American was gone from his table.

A bottle and a half later, Dickie and Grace hailed a taxi to Ciro's on Orange Street. The rain had set in. Coupled with the darkness, it blurred the city. Grace gazed out of the window at bright shop fronts and the streaks of light reflected on the wet pavements. Figures scuttled beneath umbrellas or huddled together at bus stops, but for the most part London had gone home to bed.

"Who the devil goes to a party on a *Tuesday*?" Dickie said. "It simply isn't civilized. Whose party is it, anyway?"

"I can't remember." Grace was vague as the wet night. "I've lost the invitation."

"Splendid. *Now* she tells me. And you *could* have mentioned it's at Ciro's. I'd assumed it was a little jazz party at someone's house. I'd have changed my suit if I'd known. Put on a bow tie."

Grace opened her bag, drew out a black silk tie and passed it across. "Don't fret. Diamond is always prepared for emergencies. And do cheer up—the invitation said champagne. It's bound to be jolly."

Toying with the tie, Dickie started on a story about Ciro's—another night, another party—but Grace had stopped listening; awed, as always, by Piccadilly Circus at night. Here was the Big New World that left the likes of Pearson & Pearson lagging far behind in the gentle past. The Circus, most famous convergence point of London's great thoroughfares, was illuminated now by huge bold brand names picked out in colored lights. London County Council's strenuous efforts to legislate against these advertisements had succeeded only in strengthening the determination of retailers to cash in on their location. Down at ground level, however, all was shabby, temporary and makeshift during the construction of an enormous new Underground station. The seminal statue of Eros had been removed while the works were in progress, and at first it had seemed that the Circus's soul had gone with it. By now, though, Eros had been gone for so long that Grace could barely remember what it looked like. The soul of Piccadilly seemed instead to inhabit the new adverts. While ostensibly they yelled "Schweppes," "Bovril," "Gordon's Gin," they might really have been shouting, "I Am London. I Am the Future."

Tonight the rain was so heavy that the spectacle appeared smeary and dreamlike. Raindrops, lit in bright colors, ran ceaselessly across the window, so that it appeared to Grace as if the Circus was crying. Through the tears she glimpsed the dry interiors of other taxis carrying girls with laughing mouths, tired ladies in hats, young men with a look of hunter or hunted. The insides of other motorcars like tiny, complete worlds. And she, with Dickie, in their own little world, drifting through it all in a kind of trance . . .

Until a taxi pulled momentarily alongside theirs, and she saw someone in profile. A clean jaw, a Roman nose . . .

"It's that man!"

"What man? What are you talking about?"

"Oh." The other taxi had turned right. It had been the most fleeting of glimpses. Had it really been the American?

Or was it just that she was still thinking about him, somewhere behind it all?

"Grace?"

"It's nothing. Look, we're here. Let me help you with that tie."

Double doors opened to reveal Ciro's famous glass dance floor like a sheet of ice, over which the dancers appeared to skate. Jean Lensen and his Ciro's Club Dance Orchestra were in full swing. White suits, slicked-down hair, gleaming brass. The air was smoky and heady with the mingled perfume of a great many women, undercut by a bitter edge of perspiration.

"No wonder the streets were empty," Grace muttered. "Everyone's in here." And indeed it did feel as though every fashionable man and woman in London was collected here under one roof. Vivacious flappers rattling with beads and rhinestones, gazellelike women in silks and feather plumes, immaculate men in dress shirts.

"Well, you were right about the champagne," said Dickie. Waiters threaded back and forth, bearing trays laden with glasses. He lifted one for Grace and one for himself. "Look over there."

By the long bar stood a precarious pyramid of glasses. A barman mounted a stepladder and proceeded to pour from the largest champagne bottle Grace had ever seen. Glittering liquid flowed and frothed its way down the pyramid, filling the glasses in a Möet et Chandon fountain, while nearby onlookers applauded.

Dickie, who was clearly still feeling underdressed and underconfident, brightened when someone called out to him. Grace recognized Ronnie Hazelton from the *Times,* along with a group of tiresome cronies. Still getting her measure of the room, and wanting to explore further, she made as if to follow Dickie but then slipped off through the crowd.

Farther away from the dance floor, seated at tables and, for the most part, talking intently, was a less shiny bunch of people: balding gray men with spectacles, squat little men with beards. Book people, thought Grace, spotting Samuel Woolton, the well-known publisher who'd just set up his own company. Editors, novelists, poets, hiding behind all the pretty boys and girls with titles and private incomes who liked to play at having a job. This must be a literary party—well, notionally anyway.

"Dried off now, I see." He was standing right behind her. Too close.

"Have you been following me?" She spoke without turning around, directing her gaze out at the dance floor. A spotlight was on one of the trumpeters, as he launched into a flashy solo.

"I was going to ask you the same question."

She turned to face him, and as she looked at him something flickered in her stomach and made her want to giggle. An excited girlish giggle—the sort of giggle which she absolutely mustn't give in to.

He was such a broad person—those shoulders, that neck. There was an overwhelming maleness to him. She wanted to know how it would feel to dance with him—to feel the large hands resting heavy on her shoulders, her back.

"Come, now." She wagged a finger at him. "Confess."

He smiled. "I saw you come in with your friend fifteen minutes ago. I've been here two hours."

"Rubbish! Your taxi pulled alongside ours on Regent Street."

A raised eyebrow. "How flattering. I've obviously made quite an impression on you."

"Well, I think you left a bruise on my foot earlier, if that's what you mean by an *impression*."

He took the empty champagne glass from her hand, replacing it with a filled one. "What I mean," he said, "is that when you're thinking about someone—when you can't get them out of your mind—you see them everywhere."

Grace allowed herself a chuckle. He was the sort who used verbal combat as a seduction technique. "Thirty-eight," she said, looking him up and down.

"Pardon me?"

"Years old. Or maybe forty. And divorced. It's the done thing in America, isn't it? You might even be divorced *twice*."

Now he was the one to laugh. "I suppose I deserved that, Miss . . ."

"You can call me Sapphire."

"Can I now?" He reached out to clink glasses with her.

"And you? Who are you?"

"Me?" He shrugged. "I'm a typical Irishman. Full of blarney."

She rolled her eyes. "That accent is about the least Irish I've ever heard. I suppose you have a great-grandfather from Skibbereen or Ballydehob or something. Isn't it enough to be American?"

She didn't know quite how it came about—it was hot and she was a little dizzy—but his right hand was against her cheek now. Just resting there, holding her face so that she couldn't but look into his pale, humorous eyes. "I guess I enjoy a little romance," he said. "Don't you?"

✳ ✳ ✳

It was almost 4:00 A.M. when the taxi pulled up at the end of Tofts Walk, Hampstead. As Grace got out, her right heel stuck in a manhole cover. Muttering words which would have caused consternation at Pearson's, she righted herself, paid the driver and half limped her way up the steep slope to number 9—a Victorian terraced house of the thin, tapering sort. She was still fussing with her keys, trying to open the stiff door without making too much noise, when it was opened from the inside by a man she'd never seen before. A tall man in tweed with glossy brown hair and a mustache. Disconcertingly good-looking. Good-looking enough so that the important question of why a complete stranger should be answering her door in the middle of the night was overtaken by Grace's anxieties over whether her makeup was a fright and whether she was drunk to an extent that was ugly or merely garrulous.

"Miss Rutherford?" He was American. *Another* one. He had his shirtsleeves rolled up, showing tanned, sinewy forearms. He stood back to let her by. The tight space in the hallway forced her to brush against him.

"I'm sorry, but . . ."

"John Cramer." He put his hand out to shake hers. Strong grip. Soft voice. "I live just across the road. I came over to help out."

Sobriety returned in a rush—and panic. "Where's Nancy? And my mother? Where's she?" She threw her jacket over the coat stand and opened the door to the lounge. The lights were all on. At *4:00 A.M.*

"Your mother's gone to bed. Your sister's sitting with the baby."

Grace wheeled around. "What's going on?"

"Felix is unwell," said the man. "He's sleeping now, but the doctor said he shouldn't be left alone." He laid a hand on her shoulder. "Can I get you a hot drink?"

"No, thanks. Excuse me." *Felix.* As she made for the stairs, her head was filled with awful thoughts. Her beautiful little nephew—her golden boy . . .

"Wait a second," called the man, from the bottom of the stairs.

As Grace reached the landing, Felix's door opened and Nancy slipped out, a finger to her lips. Her eyes were red and puffy, her thick blond hair hanging in rat's tails.

"I'm so glad you're home." Her voice was tired and strained. "I've missed you so."

"Come here." Grace opened her arms and folded her little sister in. Nancy was smaller than Grace. She allowed herself to be held tight, her head inclined so that it tucked under Grace's chin. They had always held each other in this way, for as long as either could remember. Grace stroked Nancy's hair, smoothing it behind her ear. "Now, tell me what's happened."

"He had a fever. I thought it was just the teething—you know how he gets. I let Edna go home at the usual time after the children's dinner." She pulled herself free of Grace, so she could face her. "But after she'd left, he was very sick. His forehead was *burning* and he was pouring sweat. I gave him a cool bath, but that didn't seem to help. I was *so* worried, Grace. Poor little Tilly—she had to put herself to bed, pretty much. No stories, no cuddles. Mummy was out, too, you see—at her bridge night. Tilly was such a lamb . . . And then Felix started going all limp."

"Why didn't you ring me at the office?" Grace wanted to shake Nancy—had to work hard not to. "You should have called me as soon as the fever started. I'd have come straight home, you know I would."

"I did try to ring you but there was something wrong with the telephone. Then—this was so dreadful—Felix had a sort of fit. I'd left him on the couch for a moment, and there was a bang. I rushed in, of course, and he'd fallen to the floor and was thrashing about and shaking and I couldn't rouse him. It was so frightening, Grace."

"I'm sure it was. How long did it go on for?"

"I suppose it was only a minute or two but it felt like an age." Nancy's pupils had dilated, and she was trembling. "When it was over, I picked him up in my arms and ran across the road to bang on John's door. He was *wonderful.* He telephoned for the doctor, and then he came over and helped me put Felix to bed. And he's stayed all evening—all *night,* I suppose. Even after Mummy got home, he insisted on staying on to wait for you."

"So what did the doctor say?" A nerve was twitching in Grace's face. The thought of little Felix fitting on the floor was just too awful. "How's Felix now?"

"He said the fit was probably caused by the fever. The temperature had already dropped a bit by the time he got here, and he thought Felix was over the worst of it. But he said we should keep him cool and give him water if he wakes and watch him till the morning just to be sure. He's going to come back tomorrow."

"Right." Grace realized her hands were clenched into fists. She had to make an effort to loosen them.

There was a creak below. Cramer, the neighbor, was climbing the stairs, bearing two cups of cocoa. "Here. I wasn't sure whether to sugar them, but still . . ."

"Thank you." Grace took her cup. Nancy appeared oddly bashful as she took hers. Coquettish, even. She'd referred to him as "John." . . .

"Would you like me to stay on and sit with Felix?" he asked. "I probably won't manage to sleep now anyway. Insomnia has its uses, so feel free to take advantage."

Grace felt the heat in her face even as she glanced at Nancy and saw her cheeks flush pink. "Thank you, Mr. Cramer," she said, with an effort. "You're very kind. But I'm quite happy to sit with Felix."

A shrug and a smile. "Well, if you're sure." His eyes were brown but very dark. Deliciously murky.

The rising sun forced its way through Felix's flimsy curtains, casting a pale glow over his sleeping face. At eleven months old, he was turning from baby to little boy—not quite one or the other. This moment of transition had rendered him especially vulnerable, and especially beautiful. Fluffy golden-duckling hair haloed around his head. His eyes—deep blue when open—were closed now, and fringed with long, thick lashes. The breath came softly from his pink lips, slightly open. His face was cool, the fever gone, and Grace could safely have left him alone—but still she sat on, watching over him, so relieved he was all right that she couldn't quite tear herself away from him. Not yet.

People often said Felix looked the image of Nancy. But they hadn't seen the photographs of Grace as a child, before her hair turned dark. On closer examination Felix's features were much more like his aunt's than his mother's. He had Grace's eyes, Grace's mischievous smile, Grace's pale, almost-transparent skin. It was Felix's four-year-old sister Tilly who resembled Nancy more—with her doll-like face, cute turned-up nose and dimpled cheeks.

Felix lay on his side, with one hand up by his face, the fingers gently curled. Deliciously pudgy little fingers. The other arm was down by his side. Watching him, listening to his breathing and to the dawn chorus outside, Grace thought there was nowhere in the world she would rather be than here. Sitting by her boy. She allowed herself to think of him in that way—as her boy—without feeling it was disloyal to her sister. It was Grace who had looked after Nancy while she was pregnant with Felix—Grace who helped her to go on after the death of her husband, George. Grace had been there at the protracted, almost-disastrous birth, rubbing the small of Nancy's back, holding her up. Holding her together. More often than not, these days, it was Grace who got up when Felix cried at night. With Daddy and George both dead there were no men left at 9 Tofts Walk. Nancy was fragile, struggling to cope with the demands of motherhood. And Catherine, their mother, was eccentric and impractical—full of theories about how the world should function without the least idea of how even her own household did. So it was Grace, inevitably, who had to step up and become the head of the family. Grace was Felix's substitute father.

It wasn't wrong, she told herself, as she sat in the rocking chair looking at her boy—to think of him as her own. It was becoming less and less likely, after all, that she'd ever have children. Not now, at thirty, with no husband and none in prospect. Why should she want a husband, anyway? She was used to being in charge of things—there was no good reason for her to need to surrender that control to a man. And when you're on your own, there's nobody to let you down and disappoint you.

The dawn chorus was over. Felix gave a sweet little sigh

in his sleep. The rocking chair creaked gently. Grace's eyes were closing, her head nodding. Her mind was filled with last night—memories slipping into half-crazy dreams. She was dancing with the fair-haired American or Irishman or whatever he was. It was what she'd wanted, last night—to dance with him—and it hadn't happened. They had still been talking when both had been spotted by people they knew—people who'd dragged them apart. She'd looked for him later, but couldn't find him anywhere.

His hands were on her back, her arms were around his neck. She looked up into his face, only to discover she was dancing with the other American—John Cramer from across the road.

The West-Ender

April 11, 1927

Ladies, ladies, what on earth are you doing with your hair? I have observed, just lately, a marked deterioration in the quality of bobs. Has Mother been tending to your coiffure with the pudding bowl and kitchen scissors? Those heavy, crooked clumps to either side of the face are simply unforgivable! Hie thee to a proficient hairdresser posthaste and do not show your face again at Kit-Cat Club, Ciro's, the Cave of Harmony or 55-Club until you have remedied the situation. If you must go out at all, please confine yourself to the Hammersmith Palais and other suburban venues where such matters may be overlooked.

Really, there is no excuse, as there are plenty of places that do admirable and geometrically satisfying bobs: Steffani's on Jermyn Street, William Jones on Brewer Street and the wonderfully named Angular Salon behind Selfridges, to list but a few. I shan't reveal here the identity of my own, much-treasured bob cutter, as such advertising may prove to my disadvantage next time I call up for a last-minute appointment (though if you write in and appear truly desperate I may take pity on you). As it is, he's becoming just a tad starry (I've hitherto spotted such luminaries as Isadora Duncan, Constance Talmadge and Louise Brooks stepping out from his chair). They come from far and wide for that masterful trigonometry that flows from his fingertips and which simply cannot be matched anywhere outside of Paris. As I sat in his chair yesterday in a half swoon, he whispered into my ear that he moonlights as a magician, sawing ladies in half before select gatherings and occasionally making them vanish. I advised him that in future it would be a public service to vanish only those with badly bobbed hair and leave the rest of us untouched.

Now, children: Spring is with us, the daylight is lingering on and stretching out—and with it, our dancing feet. The newly reopened Silvestra Club is particularly seasonal right now, all hung with pink and green garlands, and the walls sporting an array of tiny turquoise birds. I suggest ye gather ye rosebuds . . . A small request for Dan Cramen's new orchestra, however: Could you play a tiny bit faster? Thank you.

Now, as to last Tuesday: I must beseech the management of Ciro's *not* to offer their splendid venue to dusty old publishers for any more strange literary gatherings. Those glistening champagne fountains were an expensively bought mirage, for I absolutely will not concede that the world of books has about it any real glamour. Mr. Samuel Woolton, you are trying too hard.

Finally, a personal appeal on behalf of my little sister Sapphire: Would a certain broad-shouldered Irish American gentleman please step forward and reveal his identity? Poor Sapphire is smitten and will not rest easy until she knows who this devil-in-a-dinner-suit is.

Diamond Sharp

Two

One week after the Ciro's party, Dickie telephoned Grace to invite her for lunch at Katarina's, a much-lauded Russian restaurant in Kensington.

At the time of the call, Grace was at work on the new campaign for Stewards' Breath-Freshening Elixir with Oscar Cato-Ferguson, a fellow copywriter whom she thought rather oily.

Cato-Ferguson's contention was that they should plug Stewards' as being a new and unbeatable health tonic: "Fresh Breath for Life."

Grace had a pencil between her teeth in place of the habitual cigarette. "I don't like it."

"Why?" Ferguson was lounging back in his chair, his feet up on Grace's desk. "Perhaps because it was *my* idea?"

"Don't be ridiculous." Grace regarded the soles of Ferguson's shoes with pure loathing. "It just doesn't *speak* to me.

Sour breath is more of a social problem than a health problem. It undermines the confidence. That's where Stewards'
can help."

Ferguson glanced at his watch and made as if to suppress
a yawn.

"Kissing." Grace laid particular emphasis on the word—
watched for its effect. Yes, he was sitting up a little now.

That was when the telephone rang.

"Ever tried borscht, Gracie?"

Beneath the swirl of sour cream, the borscht was a deep, intense pink. To the taste, it was thickly sweet.

"What is this stuff?" Grace peered at her spoon.

"Beetroot," said Dickie. "With a dash of vodka, I think.
It's about to be very fashionable. Diamond should take an
interest."

"We'll see about that."

"About your last-but-one column." Dickie sipped his beer.
"I've had a complaint."

"What was it this time? Innuendo? I was *genuinely* talking
about the Charleston, you know."

"Female suffrage, actually. You expressed sympathy for
women under thirty because they don't have the vote."

"No, I didn't. Not exactly. I said I *would* sympathize if it
wasn't for the fact that they're so fearfully young and lovely."

Dickie's expression was reproving. "Exactly how old are
you?"

"Thirty. You know that."

He dispatched the last of his borscht. "The *Piccadilly Herald*
doesn't have a stated position on the extension of the franchise. *You* know that."

"I don't care about the paper's position, stated or unstated.

That's your problem. I'll write what I like. It's up to you whether or not to print it."

"You infuriating bloody woman." He dropped his spoon into his empty dish with a clatter. But then he smiled. "On another subject, when do I get the much-vaunted Hampstead supper? I haven't seen Nancy in ages. And as to the children— they'll be grown up by the time you ladies get around to inviting me over again."

"Seize the Moment with Stewards'." Grace couldn't help but think of the time Cato-Ferguson had tried to "seize the moment" with her. It was at an after-work do—she couldn't remember which one, now—and he'd come staggering around the corner as she emerged from the ladies' room. He was half cut, and tripped over his own feet. She'd reached out to help him regain his balance, and in seconds he had hold of her and was grabbing her all over with his long hands. She'd slapped him hard in the face and he hadn't come near her since.

"The image," said Grace, "is of a man and a woman about to kiss. Their eyes are closed. They are entirely lost in the moment."

"Thinking of putting yourself in the photograph again, are you?" Ferguson's smile was contemptuous. "Fancy yourself as a romantic heroine?"

"Get your feet off my desk, Cato."

They don't come much nicer than you, Grace thought, as she and Dickie tucked into a shared plate of dumplings.

Dickie was one of the rare sort who just might take her whole family on board if she let him. And he'd loved her, really loved her, not so long ago. How many other men had genuinely loved her? Perhaps only one. The good-looking boys she'd flirted with years ago were all taken now, by other women—or else were long dead in the trenches. Those who were still available were the Cato-Fergusons of the world. Opportunists, liars, lounge lizards.

If only she could feel more for Dickie. If only she could feel *that* for him.

"I've got something for you." Dickie tossed an envelope across the table. "It came this morning. I'm not in the habit of opening your mail, but for some reason it was sent care of my office."

Trouble was, Grace could remember how it was, being with Dickie. Why she'd ended it. *There's nothing more lonely than being with the wrong man.*

She reached for the envelope.

Savoy Hotel

London WC2

April 15, 1927

Miss Diamond Sharp
Piccadilly Herald

Dear Miss Sharp,

Would you kindly pass on the following message to your charming sister?

I should be most honored if Miss Sapphire Sharp would consent to step out tomorrow evening from the no-doubt tricky little jewel box in which you sisters reside, to have a drink with me at 7:00 P.M. in the American Bar at the Savoy.

Do entreat Miss Sharp to accept my invitation, as I too am utterly smitten. Tell her that in the event she declines, I shall have to dine alone, once again, on overcooked steak at a dreary London grill, and possibly end my solo evening at the much garlanded Silvestra's where, for lack of anything better to do, I shall sit and admire the small turquoise birds.

I do hope her bruised foot is now completely healed.

Most sincerely,
Your Devil-in-a-Dinner-Suit

"You seem to have hooked your fish." Dickie's voice had a forced casual note. "Will you be writing the date up in your next column?"

It was as Grace moved through the revolving doors and into the Strand foyer, her reflection jumping out at her from gleaming glass and brass, that the panic set in. Her insides started churning and her breath caught in her throat so that she skittered through the great front hall beneath opulent chandeliers, to retreat to the nearest ladies' room and fuss about at the mirror with hair and lipstick; her hands aflutter to the extent that the lipstick dropped through her fingers into the sink and snapped in two.

What if he didn't turn up?

She'd be sitting in the American Bar, alone, with her cigarettes and her cocktail and her disappointment, and a waiter would come across, with sympathy in his face, perhaps suggesting ingratiatingly that the gentleman—whoever he was—must be mad to stand up such a beautiful woman. And she'd find herself admitting that she didn't actually *know* who he was—the gentleman in question—though she believed him to be a guest at the hotel. And the waiter would look confused and a little disapproving—and she'd decide that perhaps it was time to leave and take the bus back to Hampstead.

What if he *did* turn up?

As she entered the bar, fifteen minutes late (frankly this was *early*, by Grace's standards), she made herself close her eyes, holding on to the moment that comes before you look and know. And then she braced herself, opened her eyes and looked around.

She'd forgotten how masculine this place was. Dark wood and model ships. She felt herself rendered girlie and insubstantial by it. There were plenty of people in, this evening, and most of the tables were taken—none of them by him.

A broad-shouldered man with fair hair in a good suit was sitting up at the bar on a high stool, smoking, his back to her. She felt the smile light up on her face and was about to slip across to tap him on the shoulder when she caught the sound of his voice over the general hubbub—and it was thin and English—and glimpsed his face in profile . . . And the nose and chin were all wrong.

Fifteen minutes late. No right-thinking man would be fifteen minutes late to meet a girl like her. He wasn't coming. Something must have come up—some piece of inconsequential business—just significant enough to ruin her evening and dash all her hopes. Or maybe he hadn't intended to meet her at all. Perhaps he'd never set foot in the Savoy and was even now in some other bar, scrutinizing the women and laughing a little at the thought of her sitting alone, waiting and watching for him.

And suddenly there was a hand on *her* shoulder, and the familiar American voice that sounded slightly as though he might be laughing somewhere beneath it all, was saying, "So, shall I call you Diamond or Sapphire? Which is it to be tonight?"

Grace's smile—suitably pleased to see him but not *too* excited, not *too* relieved—was already carefully in place as she turned around and said, "You can call me what you like, so long as you get me a drink."

A corner table had come free. The waiter brought their drinks over—White Ladies for both of them. Served with ice, American-style, this was the latest of the many cocktail innovations of Harry Craddock, the Savoy's famous head barman, who was himself specially imported from America.

They eyed each other over the cocktails. He was both less and more than she remembered. Less perfect, but somehow more real. It was as though she'd come to know him since last seeing him, even though she knew nothing whatever about him. Tonight that seemed an enjoyable contradiction—the not-knowing and the knowing. He was toying with his glass. She was toying with hers.

"So, tell me about your column," he said.

"What is there to say? It's an insider's view of the West End. I tell people where to eat, dance, buy their clothes. And I tell them where not to go."

His finger ran around the rim of his glass, dipped into the cocktail. He licked it. "Come on. I don't read your column every week to find out whether I should buy my shirts at Selfridges or Liberty, whether the house orchestra is better at Ciro's or the Salamander."

"You read my column every week?"

"It's more personal than you're letting on. It's the story of an unusual woman leading a very new London life. A life that would only be possible *now*—this year, today."

"Ah. So you think I'm all parties and champagne and perfectly bobbed hair."

"Well, the bob looks pretty sharp from where I'm sitting."

She smiled down into her glass. "So, what's *your* life like? What are you doing in London?"

"Me?" He shrugged. "I have an interest in people. That's why I'm here."

"People?"

"I like to watch them. Think about what makes them tick. What makes them individual . . . special. You might say I'm a collector."

"How so? Are you going to cram a load of interesting specimens into your suitcase to take back home with you?"

"In a manner of speaking." He took out a packet of Baker's Lights and offered them across. His hands, as he reached over to light her cigarette, were absolutely steady.

"Take a look at the woman in the gray dress just over there." He inclined his head subtly, and Grace glanced across. The woman was about forty or so. Attractive but too thin. Nervy-looking.

"She's married, but not to her companion in the tall hat," he continued. "He doesn't know she's married and she doesn't want him to know."

"How did you divine all that?"

"She had rings when she first sat down. When he went

to the bar, she slipped them off and put them in her purse. She looks a little nervous, don't you think? Just as one should when there's a lot at stake."

"So do you think she's in love with the man in the hat?"

"She'd like to be. But actually she hardly knows him."

She looked up, wanting to study his face while he was still focused on the married woman and her companion—but now his pale eyes were turned on hers.

"Have you ever been in love?" he asked, without blinking.

In her head she saw a young man in uniform with red hair. She blinked the image away. "No," she said. "Not really. How about you?"

"I loved a woman who died."

"I'm sorry." She looked away, gulped from her cocktail.

"Don't be. She wasn't."

It was such an odd thing to say that it made her wonder if he'd made it up to shock her.

"It was a long time ago."

"And has there been anyone since?" He seemed to invite this kind of talk—flirtatious in its frankness.

"Of course. I'm perpetually in love. It's a grand way to be. You should try it some time. You might like it."

Grace shook her head. "You talk about love the way other people talk about ice cream."

He shrugged. "One is hot, the other cold. Both taste good."

"Love isn't something you can just choose to try."

"Tell that to her." Again he indicated the woman in gray. Her face wore an expression that was exquisitely sad. The man in the hat had hold of her hand.

"She doesn't look like she's having a 'grand' time of it," said Grace. "I'm not sure that people do when they're in love."

"Maybe not. But it's love that splits you open, lays bare all that soft, raw stuff that's inside. And that's something you just have to do if you don't want to dry up. Love reminds you that you're alive, Miss Sharp."

"That is, if it doesn't kill you."

"Indeed."

"Excuse me, sir . . ." It was their waiter, with someone clerical-looking in a suit, perhaps from the hotel reception.

"What is it?" He looked them up and down.

"There's a gentleman, sir—out at reception." This from the clerk.

"What of it?" His tone was curt, irritable. "I have company, as you can see."

The clerk nodded at Grace. "Begging your pardon, madam. Sir, he says he's here to speak to you."

"What's his name, this *gentleman*? Did he give you his card?"

"No, sir." The clerk looked embarrassed. "I did ask for his name, of course, but he declined to tell me."

"For God's sake." The American rolled his eyes. "Go tell him I'm otherwise engaged. Or that I'm not here—you couldn't find me. Tell him what the hell you like. Just get rid of him." His volume had risen. People at neighboring tables were looking round at them. Grace dipped her head a little and swallowed some White Lady.

"Very good, sir." The clerk looked as though he was about to say something further but seemingly changed his mind, bit his lower lip. Then he turned and walked away, followed by the waiter.

The American took out another cigarette.

"What was all that about?" asked Grace.

"I'm not sure, though I have my suspicions." He lit up. "I just hope that's the end of it. Now, where shall we dine? I can get us a table in the restaurant here. Or is there someplace else you'd like to take me?"

"I don't know." Grace had noticed the woman in gray was still looking at them. She had bent her head to whisper to the man in the top hat. "I'm not so very hungry. Don't you think that was a bit strange?"

The pale eyes had turned cold. "Nothing surprises me, Miss Sharp. Not anymore. I think we should finish our drinks and get out of here."

"Yes, perhaps so. But . . ."

"I'm sorry, sir." He was back—the clerk—and looking distinctly uncomfortable. "The gentleman is refusing to leave. He says he needs to speak to you urgently. He says you know who he is."

He pushed back his chair and got to his feet. He was a good six inches taller than the clerk. "I've told you, I'm otherwise engaged and I don't wish to speak to this man. Don't you have security in this place?"

"Well, sir—"

"Have your doormen throw him out!"

The clerk took a step back and seemed to gather his confidence before speaking again. "We would prefer to avoid any unnecessary unpleasantness, sir, if at all possible. The management would greatly appreciate it if you would step out to reception and speak to the gentleman. It appears to us that this is a personal matter that has nothing whatever to do with this establishment."

The American sighed and rubbed at his forehead. "Oh, it's that all right. Have him wait out front, will you?" He tipped the retreating clerk and forced his face into an expression that was almost a smile but not quite.

"So?" Grace drained her glass.

"I'm sorry." He rubbed again at his forehead and whispered, "Damn it," under his breath. "This could take some time, I'm afraid."

"Well, that's it, then." Her disappointment was out of proportion to what was happening. This was more than merely the curtailing of a pleasant evening. It was as though someone had just sucked all the color out of her world.

"No, that's not *it*." He took her hand, raised it to his lips and kissed it. "Not by a very long way. How shall I reach you again?"

"At the *Herald*." She felt shaky. "You can send me another note."

"All right. If that's what you want, that's what I'll do. So long, Diamond. Until we meet again."

"Until then, Devil."

Walking out into the foyer, Grace felt flimsy, sketchy—as though she was hardly there. Perhaps the real Grace—the substance—was still sitting there in the bar with him. Or perhaps she hadn't been here at all this evening. The carpet swallowed the sounds of her feet. The reflections in the glass and the brass were fragments only—glimpses of a thin person with an anxious face.

Reception was buzzing. Men in unseasonably heavy overcoats tipping porters to carry enormous cases. Large women with pearls and feathers. Shriveled old ladies with small dogs. Laughing children. And one man, standing with his back to her at the reception desk—very still—obviously waiting for someone. For the Devil. A man she instantly recognized—even just in passing quickly by.

Three

The Past

The Rutherford sisters, at seventeen and almost sixteen, respectively, were famous and infamous in their Hampstead neighborhood. Having been brought up by a radical suffragette mother and Darwinist father to think freely and speak their thoughts openly, they rarely saw the necessity to hold anything back. They came and went when they liked, with whom they liked.

"The girls are undeniably bright," said Miss Stennet, the headmistress of the North London Collegiate School, smiling tensely across her desk at Mr. and Mrs. Rutherford. "They are popular, vivacious and rather charming. So bright and charming, in fact, that this school has tolerated too much from them. It's time, now, for us to join forces in reining them in a little."

"And what, exactly, is the nature of their misdemeanors?" asked Harold Rutherford.

Miss Stennet sighed. "Therein lies the difficulty. It's more about an overall attitude, but I will try to say something further about it. Take their hair, for instance. The school rule is that hair should at all times be tied back."

"Both girls wear their hair too short for tying back." Catherine Rutherford folded her arms.

"Quite so. But why did they cut their hair in the first place? They both had such beautiful hair. And once your girls had started snipping away at each other, the whole school was suddenly at it. Some of them look quite dreadful—and it's all happened while the girls are here in my care. You wouldn't believe the number of complaints I've had from parents."

"Are you telling me that it's my daughters' fault if some of your pupils can't cut hair straight?" asked Catherine. "Are we to take them to task for having strong personalities? For finding their own way rather than following like sheep?"

"The bobbed hair . . ." Miss Stennet was struggling now, "it's symbolic. There's a particular way of being . . . a state of mind that goes with it. Has either of you, by any chance, read *The Vision,* by Dexter O'Connell?"

Confused faces from across the desk.

"Well, I can assure you that your daughters have."

"So are we to limit their reading now?" Harold Rutherford glanced at his watch. "That book's had rather good reviews, hasn't it? I believe O'Connell has won a big prize?"

"'That book' has caused no end of trouble in America for its portrait of a girl of a certain tender age. A girl with bobbed hair and short dresses who lies and drinks and breaks the hearts of vulnerable young men, as have many of the girls who have taken her as their inspiration. That book has been banned in three of America's Southern states. And there are campaigns afoot to ban it in five more."

"Well, Miss Stennet." Catherine got to her feet. "This family does not believe in censorship, and I'm rather shocked to discover that you do. I understood this school to be a modern-thinking establishment. I'm certain that my girls are not liars or drinkers. I'm not so sure about the heartbreaking, but it seems to me one isn't responsible for the intactness or otherwise of another person's internal organs. What right-thinking boy wouldn't fall for Grace or Nancy, after all?"

"I suggest you work out your argument more thoroughly before complaining about our girls again." Harold took his wife's arm. "Is it your contention that they're the headstrong sort who lead others astray? Or are you saying they're the weak, simple-minded sort who ape a lot of silly behavior that they've read in the latest novel? You need to get your story straight, it seems to me."

"I'm saying . . ." The headmistress felt suddenly tired. "I wanted to tell you that I'm a little worried about them. I thought perhaps you might be, too."

On the evening this interview was taking place, the Rutherford sisters were sitting at the dining table at home. Grace was shuffling a pack of playing cards:

"Supposing I spread the cards facedown"—which she did, in the shape of a fan. "What say we both take a card, and then whoever's card is the highest chooses first?"

"All right." Nancy reached out and took a card. It was the jack of diamonds.

"Good card. Pretty boy, too." Now Grace took hers. "Jack of spades. Ha! Which suit is worth more? I can't remember how it works."

"Neither can I. Perhaps we should both take another card. Mind if I shuffle?"

"Be my guest."

Nancy scooped up the cards and began shuffling adeptly. Grace traced the knots in the wood of the table with a long fingernail. "My trouble is," she said, "I'm not sure which of them I prefer. I mean, if you'd asked me half an hour ago I'd have said Steven, without question. But now we come to it, I find I'm rather attached to George, too. So perhaps you'd better just choose and I'll have whichever you don't want."

"Actually"—Nancy set the cards down—"I find I'm in something of the same predicament. I'd definitely have said George if you'd asked me yesterday. But Steven . . . well, he's Steven, isn't he?"

"Dash it all!" Grace bit the fingernail. "There has to be a way to resolve this."

"We could let *them* choose . . ." Nancy shrugged—and for a moment, both girls seemed deep in thought. Then—

"No!" came their voices, in unison, before both collapsed in giggles.

"Seriously, though." Grace struggled to regain composure. "We have to settle this properly. If we let it carry on, they'll get themselves so tangled up they'll go off us altogether!"

"Surely not," said Nancy. "Although . . . I see what you mean."

"George is the cleverer," said Grace. "He's probably going to end up earning the most money. I'd say he's stronger too—physically, I mean. And probably morally. But Steven . . ."

"Steven's the unpredictable one," said Nancy. "The lovable rogue."

"That makes George the better husband," concluded Grace. "But Steven the most fun."

"Oh dear." Nancy shook her head. "We both want Steven for now and George for later."

"Just so," said Grace. "I'm tired of this now. Fancy a game of rummy?"

In the end it was the war that settled it. The war whipped up the emotions, exerting peculiar pressure on relationships. Even the most unromantic of men found themselves declaring their love with poignant eloquence on the eve of separation. The swooning majority fervently believed in the Glorious Return but also sensed tragedy just around the corner. They danced closer, kissed harder, made promises aplenty, and in some cases shed clothes that might not otherwise have been shed.

In the summer of 1915, almost a year after the night the Rutherford sisters spread out their cards, they were still deliberating between the Wilkins brothers—George and Steven. Usually the four went about together. Strolls on the Heath, trips to the pictures and the dance hall. They knew there was speculation, from acquaintances and onlookers, as to which brother was courting which sister, and they relished being talked about. Mr. and Mrs. Rutherford were fond of both boys, and perhaps realized that while all four stuck together, neither girl could easily do something she might later regret. But the foursome couldn't stick together forever.

Grace had been walking alone on the Heath one midmorning, and was sitting on a favored bench on top of Parliament Hill, thinking. She'd been offered a place to read English literature at University College, London, and until recently had been keen. But now it didn't seem right that she should be about to enter into such an essentially selfish pursuit during wartime, while most of the men and boys she knew headed off to Do Their Bit. She thought about the Wilkins brothers, who'd landed commissions in the Royal Welch

Fusiliers, thanks to an uncle in Chester and a bit of time spent as cadets at school. Their impending departure made her feel differently about them, intensified her feelings for them both. She couldn't conceive of her life, and Nancy's, going on without George and Steven being here. They'd *always* been here. It was as she sat, thinking of this, that she heard a "halloo" from down the path, and spotted George making his way up toward her, the sun catching the blond strands in that auburn hair of his, so that it seemed shot through with gold.

"I knew I'd find you here." He sat down beside her.

"Clever boy."

"I have to talk to you, Gracie." There was a breathiness in his voice. Had he been running or something?

"Couldn't wait till tonight, eh?" They were going to a party, the four of them. It was to be their last evening out before the boys left for their regiment.

"No."

She was contemplating the view. Her favorite view in all the world. The city laid wide open, spread out before her as if displaying itself just for her personal amusement. The fresh morning air smelled vaguely metallic. The scent would be gone in an hour or so—it would sweeten and ripen. She looked at George. He was nervous, she realized. Nervous of *her*.

"It's like this, Grace."

She tried to look into his face, but the sun was bright and she found she was squinting. He'd apparently run out of words. "We're leaving on Monday. *Monday*. I almost can't believe it."

"Me neither." Grace's voice was small and quiet, belying the fact that inside her, everything was huge.

He looked so lost. She wanted to put her arm around him. Dare she put her arm around him?

"Grace . . ."

"Will you be together? In France, I mean. You and Steven?"

He frowned, as though she'd said something very odd. "We'll be together at Wrexham. As to later on . . . Well, I don't know."

"I like to think of you together," she said. "I can't imagine you without each other. Buoying each other up. You must think about Nancy and me in that way, too."

"Yes," he said. And then, "Well, no, actually."

"Really?" This was interesting. "You mean, you think of us *apart* from each other? Separated?"

"I think of *you.* Just you."

She focused on the dome of St. Paul's in the distance. Kept her gaze there, fixed on that dome, as her breath quickened.

"George? Are you saying . . ."

"You *know* what I'm saying. It's how I've always felt about you. Always."

She swallowed. Stiffened. "Say it then. Make it real."

"I'm going away, Grace. And I can't go away without knowing . . ." His voice trailed off.

"Say it. I can't believe in it until I hear you say it."

"Hello, you two." A large person stood close by, partially blocking the sun.

"Mother." Grace felt it all ebb away—the tension, the heat in her. "Where did you spring from?"

"*Spring?*" Mrs. Rutherford gave a snort. "I'm not the 'springing' sort. Now, come and walk with me, both of you. George, dear, you can help me persuade my daughter that she should go to university, as planned. Did she tell you she's thinking of passing up her place? No, I didn't think so. Can you credit it, after all the battles fought by women like me so that silly girls like her could get a decent education? She says she wants to do something 'useful,' and yet she didn't even come with me to the big march about the Right to Serve. Neither she nor her sister. Honestly, these girls of mine . . ."

Grace watched George get to his feet. As he took her mother's arm he shot her a look—a look full of *such* longing. A look that made her feel the bench might give way under her.

The party was a farewell dance, held at the home of the supremely wealthy Perry-Johnsons, in honor of their son Frederick, who was also heading off to a commission. No expense had been spared. A full dance orchestra was playing in the lacquered ballroom, where many a black tie, starched shirt, flouncy dress and uniform were spinning about, watched hawkishly or enviously by elder types seated at card tables on the fringes of the room, sipping punch. Mr. and Mrs. Rutherford, who preferred to spend their evenings reading in quiet companionship at home, were not present. As ever, their unchaperoned daughters were trusted to conduct themselves sensibly in the company of George and Steven. And as ever, the girls—one dark, one fair—were in the midst of the dancing throng but detached from the generality of the crowd: the switching of partners, the constant cutting-in. No boy would dare to cut in on the Rutherford girls when they were dancing with those redheaded Wilkins boys. That foursome was private, somehow, and had become increasingly untouchable over time. These days they cut in only on each other.

Spirits were high among the four. The laughter verged on hysteria. Their arms, thrown about necks and around waists, were tight and needy. Grace, dancing with George, marveled at the solidity of his body, the deftness of his steps. His hazel eyes had their usual tranquil quality, but she thrilled at her newfound knowledge of what lay behind that tranquility. She wanted to be alone with him, and yet the postponing of that moment, the drawing-out of the day was in itself delicious. An instant later there was a deliberate collision. Nancy's pretty mess of giggles and girlish blond curls were for a moment brushing against Grace's face, before she found herself whirled away by the leaner, longer and more waspish Steven— who laughed and whispered something unintelligible in her ear, and then led her off, away from the dance floor, out through the French doors and into the humid green darkness of the gardens.

"I love this place," said Grace. They were walking, arm in arm, between elegant trees—weeping willow, cedar and oak, the leaves rustling just slightly. Here and there were little clearings with statues of Greek gods at their center—or fountains, stilled for the night. "It has a quality. I can't explain it."

"It's all silvery and magical," said Steven. "Anything could happen out here. Don't you think?"

"Yes."

And then his mouth was on hers, and she was pressing her body to his—really pressing. She'd been kissed before—by other boys, by George, and even by Steven himself—but not like this. She could feel him, through their clothes, pressing against her—that bit of him that she wasn't supposed to know about, but couldn't ignore. Her mouth was open to his, their tongues working against each other. She could smell him, fresh and metallic, like the grass on the Heath that morning. His hands had been on her back, but now he was touching her breasts through the dress—and she was letting him do it. And then she thought she glimpsed someone standing among the trees, watching—and finally she broke away.

"Well, well." Steven raked a hand through his hair, and

stood smiling, gazing openly at her body. "Who'd have thought it, after all this time? Was that my going-away present?"

Grace was looking about her—looking off, into the trees. If someone had been there at all, they'd gone. "I don't under-stand," she said eventually.

"What is there to understand? I wanted to kiss you. You wanted to kiss me." His eyes were almost the same color as his brother's, but without that tranquil quality. There was some-thing animal about Steven's eyes.

"But what about George? I thought . . ."

"You thought what?"

"I thought you'd decided between us, you and George. I thought . . ."

He frowned, but still appeared amused, beneath that frown. "Oh, Gracie. We've never been able to decide between you. Just as you've never been able to decide between us. That's been our predicament for a long time now, hasn't it?"

A breeze had whipped up out of nowhere. Grace shivered. "There's something you don't know."

"Oh, I doubt that." He made to put an arm around her again, but she drew away from him.

"I saw George today," she said. "On Parliament Hill. He was trying to say something to me. He was trying to . . ."

"Trying to what? Propose to you?"

She felt herself blush, through the darkness.

"Well, that sly old—" he began.

"He didn't actually propose," Grace said quickly. "But he'd decided between us. He made that clear. Tonight, watch-ing you dancing with Nancy, I thought perhaps you'd agreed something together."

"Gracie, darling." He pushed a stray few strands of her hair behind her ears. "We hadn't agreed anything. If we had, do you think I'd have been kissing you that way? Eh? Come here."

They were kissing again. She couldn't help herself—it was just too delicious. But when their mouths finally came apart, she blurted out, "What about Nancy?"

"What *about* her?" His arms were still tight around her. "Are you asking me whether I'd have kissed her like this?"

"No, that's not what I meant."

"I'll be honest with you, Grace. I'd have kissed her too if she was out here instead of you. You're beautiful girls, and you're so alike and so different—and each of you is more special, more valuable, for the existence of the other one. Like a pair of paintings or vases or something. Any man in his right mind would want you both."

"Let go of me!" She had started to struggle against his arms, and now she broke away. "You're utterly immoral, Steven Wilkins. And you're trying to say that George is the same way as you."

He put his head to one side. "But so are *you*, Grace. Admit it to yourself. Where are you going?"

She'd started to stride off, twigs cracking beneath her feet—and he had to run to catch up with her.

"You'd never have kissed me if you weren't going away. What a liberty!"

"But I *am* going away." He drew alongside her. "And if you want me to choose you over your sister—if you want to be my sweetheart and send me perfumed letters and little locks of hair, and miss me and long for me—well, I couldn't be more honored, Grace. And I'd miss you right back and long for you."

"If you think I could *ever* long for *you!*" They'd arrived back at the house. Some men were standing about on the terrace smoking cigars and drinking brandy. Among them was George.

"Hey, big brother," Steven called.

"Excuse me." Grace didn't want to look at them—either of them. Stepping quickly through the French doors and into the dazzle of the ballroom, she cut a path straight through the dancers, and out into the hall.

Tears were blurring her vision as she blundered for the bathroom. She didn't know what to think or believe anymore. She could barely begin to unscramble her own emotions. They were torrid—she knew this much. And probably horrid, too. Was she really so shallow?

"Grace!" The bathroom door opened to reveal Nancy, who immediately flung her arms around Grace and squeezed her in a tight embrace. "I have something to tell you—but don't you *dare* tell Mummy and Daddy—"

"Oh, Nancy, listen . . ."

But Nancy was flushed and excited—too excited even to hear Grace. "George wants to marry me, Grace. It's a secret for now but—oh my darling, isn't it just the most fabulous news!"

The West-Ender
April 18, 1927

Since my Paris trip last year (Oh, what a glorious heaven of fashion, food and frippery—can life ever be so brightly lit again?), you'll recall that I have been searching in vain for a London café which serves really good patisserie. Actually, even *adequate* patisserie would be enough to bring a smile to this West-Ender's wan little face on a damp spring morning. Well, fellow pastry devotees, I finally have news. A whisper reached me earlier this week of an estab-lishment on Baker Street with the colorful name "the Morning Glory," alleged to be serving croissants "as good as you'd get on the Rue de Rivoli." What could I do but scuttle straight over with watering mouth?

It's a funny little place, the Morning Glory. The light is a touch bright, the tables rather close together, and the cutlery—let's be honest—not the cleanest. But the pastries—the *pastries* . . . Best of the selection I tried (and I *did* try a selection, and fear that my hip bones may vanish henceforth beneath a layer of blubber) were some Danish concoctions. The croissants weren't quite up to Right or Left Bank standards but did, at least, have Gallic aspirations. Also available were a startling array of egg dishes, served up by a truly fearsome woman with a mustache.

To nighttime: An almost-reliable rumor says Ben Bernie, the undisputed King of New York's Dance Orchestras, is about to cross the pond for another short season at the Kit-Cat Club. You simply must go, whether you caught him last year or not. Nobody, but nobody, makes my feet fly like that man.

Now, indulge me a moment. Let me hurl myself upon your tender mercies. The fact is, I have had enough of being an Intelligent Woman. What's the use of having a well-oiled brain in this great "modern" city of ours? One doesn't get adequate recognition at the office even when one is constantly outdazzling the utter mediocrities one

works with. Neither can one put this great organ to the purpose of registering one's views in the election of a government until one begins one's fourth decade (less than a year ago, in my case, so no voting yet). And perhaps most bruisingly, men—the sort of men one might like to receive a certain kind of attention from—simply want to talk. *Talk.* I'm witty, you see. I'm a woman of experience and culture, and they want my *views* on things: the latest hit theater play, the dinner at Tour Eiffel, the right way to wear a scarf or possibly what they should do to attract the dim girl they're hopelessly in love with. What good is *conversation*, I ask you? If I was dull, they might be forced to find a more exciting way of passing their time with me.

That is all. Or, actually—no, it's not.

Last week I was entertained briefly (very briefly, as it turned out) at the Savoy by a certain Devil-in-a-Dinner-Suit. Yes, for those of you who pay close attention to this column, I did previously try to pretend that it was my sister, not me, who encountered this person. Apologies for misleading you, dear reader (my wrist is duly slapped), but a girl has to consider the small matter of her dignity. Anyway, said gentleman was called abruptly away from the Savoy, before the ice in our cocktails could so much as begin to melt (by the way, do try the White Lady, should you happen to stray into the Savoy's American Bar), but promised that he would hunt me down via this newspaper. Reader, no missive has been received. Now, sir, I don't take kindly to people who disturb my dignity unduly. If you don't reveal yourself again posthaste, then I shall be the one doing the hunting down—and let me tell you, Devil, that my temper is as sharp as my bob!

Diamond Sharp

Four

It was Sunday morning, presumably. The headache was worse than usual, the throat very raspy from all those ciggies ("the tobacco is toasted and does not aggravate the throat"—oh, *please*). The mirror showed a drawn, squinting figure in long cotton wrap with pallid skin and wine-stained mouth.

"Dear God," said Grace, in an unrecognizable (even to her) and otherworldly voice, and made gingerly for the door.

Outside her room, all was far too hectic. Tilly was playing with two girls who belonged to some neighbor or other. She had dragged forth practically every toy she and Felix possessed, and had lined them up in rows on the stairs for a game of toy shop. The girls were currently fighting over who was to be the shopgirl and who the customers (all of them wanting to be shopgirl). Felix was not in evidence but could be heard screaming from some distant room, his screams overlaid by the occasional, "No, Felix. That was a *no*," in the familiar Irish voice of Edna, their "domestic" and the children's unofficial nanny. More distant, but shrill, were the uneven tones of Grace's mother practicing the alto part from bits of Handel's *Messiah*.

"Auntie Grace, Leticia's being beastly. Tell her to stop it." Tilly's upturned face had round, pink doll cheeks painted on, possibly in lipstick purloined from aunt or mother. The other two girls had identical doll cheeks.

"Not now, sweetie." Grace, clutching at the banister, picked her way down between toys. "Auntie Grace is indisposed."

"But—"

"Remember our agreement about Sunday mornings, Tilly . . ."

The girl huffed and folded her arms in a sulky manner. Grace flapped a limp hand to swat this vision away, and then pressed on to the foot of the stairs, and beyond to the dining-room door.

"Behold. It has risen." Nancy, fresh-faced and shiny-haired, was seated at the table with a cup of tea and a piece of Victoria sponge. Opposite, pouring from the best silver teapot, was their American neighbor, John Cramer. He too was glossy and healthy-looking. His eyes were the rich, shiny brown of the conkers she'd gathered with Tilly last autumn.

"Dear God!" Grace drew the cotton robe together at the neck. If only she could shrink, dwindling away to nothing inside the wrap.

"Charming," said Nancy.

"So nice to see you again, Miss Rutherford."

"Do call her Grace," said Nancy. "She's always found 'Miss Rutherford' aging and spinsterly, isn't that so, Sis?"

"I'm sorry. I . . . Would you excuse me?" Grace turned for

the door, but Cramer was pushing a plate toward the nearest empty chair, saying,

"It's very good cake. And there's way too much for two people."

"Well, thank you. But I can always have some later. I'm rather . . ." She turned to Nancy. "Have I missed breakfast?"

Nancy raised her eyebrows. "Darling, it's almost three."

"Ah." That explained Tilly's contempt when she'd mentioned their Sunday morning "agreement." Hunger was overcoming her squeamishness at being caught in her dressing gown. And anyway, Nancy had clearly already staked her claim to John Cramer. So why should it matter if she looked a wreck? "Perhaps I'd better have some cake, then."

It was Cramer who cut her a slice, and Cramer who filled her cup. In doing so, he dribbled tea onto the white cloth and, with a muttered apology, rushed out for something to mop it up with.

"So, *this* is interesting." Grace took a mouthful of cake. "It's not *every* morning that I find you cozying up in here with a ridiculously handsome man. He certainly seems to have his feet under the table."

Nancy frowned. "He came over to see how Felix is. I do hope you're not about to embarrass me."

"Me embarrass *you*? If anyone should be embarrassed around here, it's me. Just look at the state of me!"

"Indeed." Nancy's mouth shrank up, becoming pinched and pursed, the way it always did when she was angry. "What time did you come in?"

"Oh, I don't know. Does it matter?"

Cramer reappeared with a towel, and dabbed ineffectually at the spilled tea.

"Don't worry about it, John," said Nancy. "It was due for a wash anyway." This was a lie.

"All right." Smiling across from one sister to the other, he slid back onto his seat. "So where d'you go last night, Grace?"

"Café Royal and Cave of Harmony." Grace had to work hard not to care about her appearance. It felt strange, stepping back to let Nancy have first dibs on a man. Nonetheless, it was the right thing to do. While she was telling herself this, she could hear her own voice chuntering on about her night out. "Then off to a party in an artist's studio in Bloomsbury. Terrible paintings but some good gramophone jazz and a rather interesting statue of a mythical god thing with antlers and six arms. Made a jolly good coat stand, actually. Later still, a few of us headed off to Hyde Park. There was some specific reason for that, but I can't recall what it was. I don't suppose it would make any sense in the cold light of day anyway, do you?" She turned to Nancy. "Lovely cake, sis. Did you make it yourself or is it one of Edna's?"

"John brought it over."

"How kind of you, John."

"Not at all," said Cramer. "It's nice to have some friendly neighbors to share it with. I'm stuck in the house on my own so much that I'm worried I'm losing the ability to make conversation. And to tell the truth, my housekeeper bakes so much I'm thinking of padlocking the oven."

Outside the room, the cacophony was growing louder.

"Do you work at home, then?" asked Grace. "What do you do?"

"I'm a journalist. The England correspondent for the *New York Times*, but I do bits and pieces for other papers, too. On the side, as it were."

"How fascinating. Are you planning on staying long in London?"

"I don't know. I'll stay as long as it remains interesting."

Grace sipped her tea and let her gaze meet his. "Do you find lots to interest you here, then?"

"So far, yes." His stare intensified. She felt as though he was rifling through her thoughts. "As to the future, who knows?"

"How about your friend at the Savoy? Is he of interest?"

Nancy seemed about to say something, but then there were screams and cries from the hall—violence breaking out among the four-year-olds. With an "excuse me a moment," she got up and went out to restore peace.

Alone together, Cramer and Grace looked at each other across the table. She shouldn't have mentioned it, of course, but she hadn't been able to resist it. Really, it was too intriguing. She'd been wondering what Cramer's business with the Devil was, and why he'd been so put out when Cramer turned up. Now it seemed likely that it had to do with newspaper journalism. This made her even more curious as to who her Devil might be . . .

"What exactly do you know?" asked Cramer, quietly.

Grace eyed him. Weighed things up. "Everything."

At this he seemed to relax. "I doubt that very much." And with that, he got to his feet. "Nice seeing the two of you, but I have to be going. I have a piece to write by five o'clock."

He reached for the door handle, then hesitated, and looked back at Grace. "I'd steer clear of him if I were you."

"Why?"

Cramer shrugged. "If you already know everything, you won't need me to tell you."

* * *

Later, when the children were in bed and Catherine sat with her friend Clementine playing rummy at the dining room table, Grace persuaded Nancy to take an evening stroll with her through the quiet streets of Hampstead, and then coaxed her into the Mitre. Nancy, who was rarely out and about without the children, feigned reluctance to enter the public house but then became quite giggly at the prospect.

"Here." Grace set two gin fizzes on the table. Her hang-over had cleared remarkably well—and after all, bubbles were a sort of restorative, weren't they? All the same, her nose was oddly sensitive. She was acutely aware of the smell of the room. A cloying, damp smell. The beer-soaked carpet, never properly cleaned. The stench of wet dog.

"I should warn you"—Nancy took a first sip—"Mummy's on the warpath."

"Concerning what?" Grace was busy surveying the lounge bar. She'd chosen a good corner seat from where she could see everyone who came in or out.

"Your column."

"What about it?"

"I don't know. She was reading it this morning—last week's—muttering all the while, and then she threw the paper down and went off, still muttering and cursing. You know what that sort of carry-on leads to."

"Thanks for the warning." Grace's smile slipped slightly. "I wonder what she found so objectionable?"

Nancy shrugged.

Grace played for time, drawing her ebony cigarette holder out of her bag and fussing over the lighting up. "I'm supposed to review restaurants and nightclubs. But I'd like to think I do rather more than that."

"You do."

"But?"

"There isn't a 'but.' Not exactly. And I honestly don't know what upset Mummy." The pupils in Nancy's blue eyes contracted slightly. "But maybe . . ."

"Yes?"

"Well, you write as though you assume everyone is like you. Going out every night to the best places, wearing all the latest fashions, and *worrying* about it all. You write as though these things are the most important things in life, and you seem to be saying that people who don't live that sort of life are . . . well . . . worthless, pretty much."

Grace felt stung. "I don't think that. You surely don't believe that of me?"

"Darling, you can take a little criticism, can't you? Your column's so popular—you're doing so well . . . I suppose I have just the smallest suspicion that most of your readers *don't* lead the sort of life you do. They read your column at the end of a long, hard day, when the children have gone to bed and they finally have a chance to put their feet up. They're on the outside looking in. Reading Diamond Sharp is like going to the theater. Or perhaps to a zoo."

"Nancy." She reached out and took her sister's hand. "Please don't talk that way. I'd change places with you in a second if I could. Tilly and Felix . . ."

"I know. Really, I do know." A heavy glum look crept across her face, and she pulled her hand free. She was clearly thinking about George.

Grace searched about for a distraction. "Hey, Nancy, take a look at those two chaps at the bar. No, *don't* turn around so obviously."

"What about them?" Nancy was all wide-eyed innocence.

"Gosh, you're such a sap. Haven't you noticed how nice-looking they are? I haven't seen them in here before."

"Grace, you're incorrigible."

"Well, they've looked over at us a few times. It's not so often you get *two* that are halfway decent. Not in the same room at the same time, let alone actually together."

Nancy was becoming a touch panicky. "Don't do anything. Please. We're having a quiet drink. That's enough for me."

Grace sniffed. "Please yourself. Just don't let it be said that I don't do my best for you."

"I'd never say that. You're a darling. I'm just not . . ."

"I know." Grace was still watching the two men on stools at the bar. Well-dressed men in their mid-thirties deep in conversation together. "So, what about our new friend John Cramer?"

"What about him?"

"Come *on*, Nancy."

"He's a neighbor. He's been kind to me."

"For goodness' sakes!"

"He likes being around the children. He has a daughter at boarding school in the States and he misses her. His wife died years ago." But she was blushing as she said it. She had always been a blusher. She'd never been able to lie convincingly or keep secrets. Not like Grace.

"Got to know him quite well, haven't you? Just how much time have you spent with him?"

Nancy's mouth pinched up—the embarrassment turning to anger. "Why shouldn't I spend time with him? I'm stuck in the house all day every day with Mummy and the children—and for *once* there's actually been someone around who I can have a nice walk with now and then, and a bit of intelligent conversation. John Cramer has shown me nothing but courtesy and respect. We're both lonely."

"I see."

"Don't look at me like that!"

"Like what?"

Nancy gestured wildly. "All . . . knowing and superior. Grace, you look like Mummy on a bad day."

"That," said Grace, "is possibly the meanest thing you've ever said to me."

"Well, you deserved it." Nancy gulped down the rest of her drink. "You have hundreds of gentlemen friends who are just friends. Can't I have even *one* without all these raised eyebrows and suggestive comments? Is it because you go out to work and I don't? Does one need to move about in the world of men and business in order to be allowed platonic acquaintances? I need friends just as much as you do."

"Oh, Nancy, I was only teasing."

"Well, just so long as you understand. There is nothing more than friendship between John Cramer and me." She was cheering up again. The storm had blown over. "But what about you? Who's the mystery man you keep on about in your column?"

"I don't *keep* on about him. I've mentioned him twice. Anyway, I don't really know who he is. Just about the only concrete thing I know about him is that he and John Cramer don't get on with each other."

"Really? Why on earth is that?"

"I've absolutely no idea." She drained her drink and smacked the glass down on the table.

"Gracie, I do hope you're not going to get yourself tangled up with someone horrid. You need a nice man to settle you down. What's wrong with dear old Dickie? He's thoroughly adorable and we never see him these days."

Grace considered her reply but then decided not to

bother. Nancy probably didn't expect a coherent response in any case. Glancing up at the bar, she saw two empty stools where the nice-looking men had been. "They've gone and left," she said. "Typical! Men just don't know a good thing when they see it, do they? Shall we have another drink?"

Five

"*Gracie,* have you ever read *The Vision?*"

Dickie had chosen a bad time to call. Mondays were always frenetic at Pearson's, and this Monday morning had been more so than usual. Grace had just emerged from a long meeting with all of the copywriting department and the two Mr. Pearsons—a "buck your ideas up" meeting, the sort which took place every time another advertising agency seemed to be running ahead of them. On this occasion they'd lost a long-standing client—Potter's meat spread—to a rival. They'd sat in the boardroom with the air of a bunch of skulking school-boys waiting to be given a good thrashing. All but Grace, the only female copywriter, who made it her habit to be perversely chirpy at such meetings—giving her best, brightest smiles to the slightly doddery Mr. Henry Pearson, while insisting to Mr. Aubrey Pearson that the problem, in the case of Potter's, was not their advertising campaigns, but the name of the product itself.

"What does 'meat spread' conjure up in one's mind?" she'd asked the room at large. "Brown stuff in a jar, that's what. It's a lot of meaty nothing. We should have come up with a new name for the product—something to make it sound exciting and give it an identity all its own. Something like . . . Wonderlunch."

"This is all very well, Miss Rutherford," said Mr. Aubrey. "But it's not our job to come up with new names for the products we advertise. And what's the use of inventing a new name for an account we've lost?"

"The point is to work out how we could do better next time. How we can avoid losing any more accounts."

But they weren't interested, of course. They never were.

After the meeting, Grace called Margaret, her favorite of the typists, into her office, and closed the door.

"Take this down, would you? 'Dear Frank, We are very disappointed to have lost your account, not least because we were just about to put forward a new idea to relaunch your product. We are confident that we can do a better job for you than Benson's, and suggest you reconsider before it is too late.'" She paused to think. "'Our confidence is such that I shall confide our idea' . . . Hmm—is *confide* right, do you think?"

"Not after two mentions of 'confidence.'" Margaret brushed invisible fluff from her immaculate white sleeves. "How about *divulge*?"

"Divulge . . . yes, why not? Where was I? 'Our confidence is such that I shall divulge our idea. Your product needs a new name—Wonderlunch. We feel certain you will agree that this name bestows a new identity on a, frankly, tired brand,

and opens up the possibility for a whole new approach to the advertising. I beseech you to think again and come back to Pearson's—'"

"No, Miss Rutherford." Margaret patted at her thickly coiled black hair, not a strand of which was loose. "Pardon me, but you don't want 'beseech.' Sounds like you're begging."

Grace smiled. This was why she liked Margaret. "You're right, of course. 'I *urge* you to think again and come back to Pearson's. Our door is always open.'" She paused. "I like that bit about the door," she added.

At that moment the telephone rang. Grace nodded to Margaret to answer it.

"Grace Rutherford's office." She put a hand over the receiver. "A Richard Sedgwick for you?"

"Gracie, have you ever read *The Vision*?"

"Hasn't everyone? Why?"

"I'd like you to interview Dexter O'Connell for the *Herald*."

Grace sat up straighter. "You want *me* to interview *Dexter O'Connell*?"

"It's to be written up as a conversation between O'Connell and Diamond Sharp. All the usual Sharpisms. I don't want you to spare him. Got it?"

"Yes. Of course." Grace was smiling all over her face. "How marvelous."

"He's in London. The rumor is he's just finished a new book—the masterpiece he's been threatening for years."

"You want me to ask him?"

"Don't mess it up. He almost never gives interviews. It's an exclusive. How well do you remember *The Vision*?"

Grace scratched her head. "Well, I'll reread it, of course. It's been years. I was still at school—"

"There won't be time for that. You're meeting him tonight."

"Tonight! I can't possibly . . . I have plans and . . ." But Grace was already rethinking her evening, adjusting her priorities. "All right. Tonight it is. I just wish I could remember the book better."

Margaret was mouthing something. Grace turned away from her, vaguely annoyed.

"Tour Eiffel at eight," said Dickie. "The table's booked in his name."

"Tour Eiffel again . . . You're obsessed with the place, Sedgwick."

"His choice. I'll need your copy by the end of tomorrow. Two thousand words should do it."

"Crikey—you don't ask much, do you!"

Margaret was mouthing to her again—tapping her on the shoulder to try to get her attention. Grace scowled and brushed her off.

"Charm him." Dickie sounded oddly sheepish. "All your feminine wiles. I want the piece to be personal. Intimate."

"Goodness, Dickie, what do you think I am?"

"I know what you are, Grace." His voice was softer now. "And I know how you can get the best out of him. I'll have a boy run a copy of *The Vision* around to your office just in case you have a little reading time this afternoon. That and anything else we have on file about O'Connell."

"Very good." Grace attempted a clipped, businesslike tone. "Oh—and Dickie, thanks for giving me a chance at this."

"It's not me you have to thank." There was an edge to his

voice. "It's O'Connell that wanted you. Good luck. And be careful. He has quite a reputation."

"Bye, Dickie."

Grace placed the receiver back in its cradle and turned to face Margaret.

"Miss Rutherford—"

"Let's just finish this letter before I lose my thread, shall we?" She cleared her throat. "Now, where was I?"

Margaret read from her dictation pad.

"Ah, we'd pretty much finished. Sign off from Mr. Aubrey Pearson: All the best, or whatever he usually says."

Margaret gaped. "You're sending this in Mr. Pearson's name?"

"That's right." Grace looked her straight in the eye. "Our secret—right? Don't worry. If there's any trouble, I'll take full responsibility. It won't rebound on you."

"But, Miss Rutherford . . ."

"Yes?"

Margaret chewed the end of her pencil. "The letter would be better as coming from Mr. Henry Pearson. He's closer to Potter. And if it works—well—I think he'll just be pleased. Mr. Aubrey—he's likely to go off at the deep end whether it works or not."

Grace stared at the inscrutable face: the thick, black-rimmed glasses. "You're quite right."

"Grace." Margaret had seemingly forgotten her place. "Why are you doing this? You could lose your job."

Grace decided to tell the truth. "Because I'm someone who has lots of responsibilities—too many. Sometimes they weigh heavily on me. And it's then, when I should be extra careful about doing the right thing, that a little devil pops up in me and just won't stay quiet. Now and then, every so often, up it comes to make trouble. And when it does, there's nothing I can do to stop it."

Margaret seemed to consider this for a moment and nodded silently. Then she said, "I've read *The Vision* eight times. I've read everything Dexter O'Connell has ever written. His novels, his short stories and essays. I've heard him read aloud from his work on three occasions. If you'll take me for a nice lunch at one o'clock, I'll tell you everything I know."

Six

Piccadilly Herald

Diamond Sharp Meets
Dexter O'Connell
April 25, 1927

A Piccadilly Herald World Exclusive

Every once in a while, I meet a man who is truly, head-turningly, staggeringly, and yes, mouth-wateringly handsome. To all you girls who bit your nails to the quick and went goggle-eyed late into the night devouring *The Vision* a few years back, I now confirm that its infamous author, Dexter O'Connell, is one such marvel of American manhood. Yes, *American* is quite the right label here. For when did you last spot one of our nice English boys with shoulders and chest of such remarkable broadness? The body—dare one comment, even in these enlightened days, in print, on the *body* of a man?—well, the body is the sort one simply can't ignore. Yes, it benefited from being clad in the very best of bespoke suits (a silk and cotton blend in a delicate dove-gray, no doubt from Savile Row, or whatever the New York equivalent calls itself), the kind of suit that would certainly make the best of any body, however run-of-the-mill, and disguise its more saggy aspects with expensive cunning. But the sheer, tall, athletic overwhelmingness wasn't due to the suit, I promise you, girls.

This particular body, I would suggest, is the end result of all that sport they play in the American college education (O'Connell went to Yale). Also from a brief but physically demanding stint in the Ambulance Corps during the war (yes, he was one of those good eggs who came to Europe early on to do his bit alongside our men). And from a wholesome southern upbringing involving home-cooked foods with names like "grits" and "succotash" and "meat loaf" (how unappetizing they sound, but there must be something to it).

One shouldn't forget to mention the face, either. The easy smilingness of the mouth; the Roman fineness of the cheekbones and the nose. The flirtatious flyawayness of the fair hair; the clear, cold cleverness of those blue eyes that don't seem to want to meet yours except when you're doing your best to evade their glintingly perceptive gaze.

Trouble is, I don't much like good-looking men. I don't trust 'em as far as I can throw 'em.

He was seated at the best corner table—the table where he'd sat on the night she first met him. She spotted him a few seconds before he looked up and saw her. Just a very few seconds but it was long enough for her to compose herself and arrange her face into a suitably cool expression. Long enough, she felt, to give her the advantage in that instant of discovery—so that when he did look up, it was he and not she who seemed, albeit ever so fleetingly, unsettled.

"Miss Sharp." He'd stood up for her, and he took her hand and kissed it with a gallantry that struck her as ludicrous—then continued to stand there, sizing her up in an overtly male way that made her sense the advantage sliding in his direction. Her dress—a loose chiffon number with floral print, ever so slightly transparent, hinting at the presence of the simple silk shift beneath—was too floaty for the occasion. If she'd had time to go home and change, she'd have put on her plain black Chanel suit and some chunky glass beads.

"Good evening, Mr. O'Connell. I suppose I'm meant to feel flattered by all the subterfuge?"

"Meaning that you don't?"

She sat down, and he did likewise.

"You've contrived a situation in which the focus is absolutely on you, and in which I'm forced to be diminutive and servile. Why on earth should I be flattered by that?"

"Well, that's one way of looking at it. Maybe I just wanted to see you again. Are you going to tell me your real name now?"

Without replying, she began searching about in her bag for her notebook and pen, producing them with a flourish.

"All right, then." He sighed. "But don't you find this kind of combat a little wearying?"

"Poor Dexter. Are you *terribly* weary?" She flipped open the notebook.

He shook his head. "Miss Sharp, this isn't how it's going to work."

"Isn't it?"

"No." He reached across the table and took the notebook and pen out of her hands. Joe, the waiter, had come across while they were talking, and was standing beside them.

"Good evening, Mr. O'Connell. Miss Sharp. May I be so bold as to suggest you share the Chateaubriand? It comes with potatoes and green beans."

"Sounds perfect," said O'Connell. "And bring us a bottle of red, would you, Joe? Your selection—make it a really good one."

"Excuse me," said Grace. "Do I have any say whatsoever in this?"

"No. You're to be diminutive and servile, remember? We'll have it medium rare, Joe. And would you be so kind as to look after these, please?" He handed over Grace's notebook and pen.

"Now," he continued, as the waiter disappeared, "if you won't tell me your name, could you at least tell me something interesting about yourself?"

"Such as?"

"Such as, the reason you haven't married."

[From "Diamond Sharp Meets Dexter O'Connell"]

"Writers are ugly," O'Connell announces, over a leathery Chateaubriand at Tour Eiffel. (Sorry, Mr. Stulik, but it was leathery. Your chef should stop making allowances for the bien-cuit English, and reacquaint himself with the Cuisine Française. The potatoes, conversely, were slightly underdone. Forgivable in the case of certain other vegetables, but in a potato?) "We do nasty things to people in novels," O'Connell says. "We watch them carefully, and then we twist them into the shapes that suit our purposes. They end up like reflections in fairground mirrors. Writing is a cruel business."

I ask him if this was true of the creation of Veronique in *The Vision*, whether O'Connell's first and original flapper was a horribly distorted version of someone he'd once known.

"Of course," he says. "She was a girl I was in love with—a girl who broke my heart. There was much more passion in *The Vision* than in anything else I've written. That's why it's my best novel. It was horrible passion, of course. Hatred, even. But it was passion, all the same."

I ask what's become of the girl who broke his heart.

He shrugs. "It doesn't matter anymore." His face, when he says this, is more ugly than handsome.

"I don't believe that nobody's asked you." O'Connell forked a pile of beans into his mouth without bothering to cut them up.

"It's of no concern to me whether you believe it or not. It's the truth." Grace was struggling with her beef. Her mouth was terribly dry, no matter how much wine she drank. She could barely swallow and felt she must be chewing and chewing, like a cow, having to swill each troublesome mouthful down with yet more wine. She hated being so nervous.

O'Connell seemed determined to pursue this to its bitter end. "There must be somebody. What about your editor? Sedgwick, isn't it?"

"We're just friends."

"Do you think he sees it that way?"

"I don't know. So long as he keeps his feelings to himself, I don't have to think about it."

A smile that worked only the bottom half of O'Connell's face, leaving his eyes untouched. "I've seen you together, don't forget. You should have heard the change in his voice when I told him I wanted *you* to interview me."

"Well, if you're right, that's his misfortune."

He speared a piece of beef, but just sat there with it stuck on the end of his fork, so that she found her gaze attracted to the hand that held the fork. He had a plain silver ring on his little finger. A sprinkling of golden hairs on his skin. "You're a hard woman," he said now. "What made you so hard?"

"There was someone who died. But that's not exactly unusual, is it? Not at the moment. Not in this country. Everyone has lost someone, and it's no real reason for being 'hard,' as you put it. Perhaps I've always been that way."

"Are you trying to present me with a challenge?" That chunk of beef was still suspended there, on his fork.

"What do you mean?"

"You want that I should prize my way into your armor? Open you up like a can of sardines?"

"Can't you find a more lyrical simile? You're a writer, after all. If you're attempting to romance me, you could try to be a little more poetic about it."

He leaned forward very slightly. "Come on. You're not interested in all that flannel, are you? It's something else that you want from me."

"Really? What is it that I want from you?"

"You want to be known. Really *known*."

"Oh. I thought you were going to say something interesting then."

O'Connell chuckled lightly, before putting the forkful of beef into his mouth and beginning to chew. Grace watched his mouth. Thought about his mouth. How it might taste.

"He went a bit wild after *The Vision* came out," said Margaret, over her lunch of curried haddock at the Carlton. "All that money. You know how it is." (As if either of them could possibly know, Grace thought, toying with a limp salad.)

"Cars. Women. Parties. Fights. He was always being thrown out of hotels. He got himself banned from a small town in

Pennsylvania in—oh, I think that must have been about 1920. And he was arrested once, in France. Down on the Riviera. First there was a fight with the proprietor of a restaurant. Fists flying, plates thrown. Then, when they threw him and his friends out, he climbed up on top of a statue of a horse and started shouting and singing. Refused to come down. In the end the police had to fetch a ladder and *drag* him down. He bought his way out of trouble, of course."

"Of course."

"There was a woman called . . . Henrietta, I think her name was. She was with him in France that summer. She was married . . . to a senator, if I'm remembering correctly. That was quite a scandal. She was the basis for Helena Doherty in *Hell and Helena*, his third novel. Have you read that one?"

"I've only read *The Vision*," said Grace. "What happened to Henrietta?"

"She went back to her husband," said Margaret. "He got quite a lashing in the papers about all that. People were jealous, you see. Of his money—the way he was living. All of it. But then he went quiet."

She'd finished her curried haddock and was eyeing the dessert trolley. Grace called the waiter over, but it took a long time for her to decide between some profiteroles, a chocolate and cream gâteau and an apple pie. In the end the gâteau prevailed.

"You say he went quiet? What do you mean?"

"Just that. People said he was burned out. You know, in the newspapers and all that. *Unruly Son* and *Hell and Helena*—they just didn't do very well. Not compared with *The Vision*. The critics didn't like them much and they didn't sell so many copies. *I* liked them, of course, but then I'm not most people. Everybody wanted him to write another like *The Vision*. Perhaps, in the end, it started getting to him. Or perhaps he just ran out of money—I don't know. But he sort of vanished. All those stories—the playboy antics—it all stopped. Nobody really knows what he's been up to these last few years. Every now and then there's a rumor that he's written something new. That's what they're all waiting for. People want him to fulfill his potential and come up with the Great Magnum Opus. We all hope that's what he's been doing. And now *you're* going to find out. You're going to meet him—to be alone with him!"

[From "Diamond Sharp Meets Dexter O'Connell"]

For the last five years, since the publication of his third novel, *Hell and Helena*, Dexter O'Connell has been uncharacteristically silent. No novels, no short stories, not even an article or a book review. For almost a decade, barely a week would pass without O'Connell saying something loud and sparkly and stylish in a prominent publication. Barely a month without a protest against his "demonic" work from the Wisconsin League of Motherhood or the Texan Church of the Lost Children, or some other bunch of crackpots.

Some have imagined him written out, spent out and gone to seed, resting his flabby arms on the bar of a cheap French hotel, sighing for his lost splendor. Others have him closeted away in a garret, bashing out the Great Magnum Opus in monastic isolation. Perhaps bashing his head repeatedly on the desk when he can't summon it up, that ungraspable magical energy that once made writing as easy as laughing.

And now here he is. Eating overcooked beef with Yours Truly. He has about him an air of contentment and ease. His hands don't shake. He doesn't seem at all like a man "back from the brink." But will he whisper a single word into my sympathetic ear about what he's been up to all this time? Will he, heck!

"Yes, I'm writing a new novel," he says reluctantly, after I have expended considerable charm in coaxing and cajoling him (and I *am* charming, let me tell you). "No, it's not finished. It will be, though—probably in a few months' time. I'm over here to work on a section that's set in London. I suppose you could say it's a sequel to *The Vision*, though the word "sequel" is a belittling one somehow. They've stayed with me, those characters. Stanley's gotten a few gray hairs at the same time as me—" (Fret not, girls. I couldn't spot a single gray thread on his head and am positive its particular golden hue doesn't come from a bottle. Put this reference to the aging process down to poetic license.)—"Veronique's acquired a kind of polish and poise that one sees in the slightly older but still beautiful woman. That wicked mischief of hers has evolved into something altogether more calculated. Question is whether there's anything soft under all the brittle shine and cleverness. That's what fascinates me about Veronique."

It's taken him this long, he says, to feel ready to say something more about Stanley and Veronique. Their story has had to sit and mature in his mind as his own life story has gone rolling on. They've been growing up, with him, but have had to wait for him to develop a new perspective—on their experiences and on his own. Now, after all this time, after the bad-boy behavior and the silence, he's finally about to give us the book we've all wanted for such a long time.

* * *

The bottle of good red cast its usual spell, and Grace found herself beginning to relax. By the time they'd arrived at the Armagnac, she was entirely at ease and more than a little garrulous. She'd been telling him how men, in novels, were more attractive than men on the big screen.

"They're limited, you see, by reality." She gestured expansively with her cigarette holder. "When you read a book, you can make of the main man whatever you like. You can mold him to suit your own personal tastes. The camera works to transform an actor into a hero, but it can go only so far in its transformation. I might be able to make a sponge cake from some flour, eggs, sugar and butter, but I couldn't possibly produce the perfect French croissant, no matter how hard I try."

"And you're fond of croissants, as any regular reader of your column will know."

"Shush, shush." Another wave of the cigarette. "I haven't finished. In a year or two, the actors will all be speaking. So even their *voices* won't be left to the imagination. That will make them all the more ordinary."

"Do you think it'll take off? Talking pictures?"

"Oh, certainly," said Grace. "Mark my words. And just watch for the careers that will come crashing down. Talking pictures will require an entirely different sort of acting. The big stars of the future will be our best English theater actors, you wait and see."

"You have it all worked out, don't you?" O'Connell put a fat cigar into his mouth.

"I'm not afraid to speak out. It's the way I was brought up. Mummy and Daddy always encouraged us to question assumptions, form our own views."

"Us?"

"Me and my sister."

"Ah yes, that whole routine. Diamond and Sapphire . . ."

But Grace had wandered off on her own train of thought. "Perhaps *that's* why I'm not married. I'm argumentative. I won't let any man push me around or tell me what to think. I suppose that makes me a bit of a handful."

"Well, I don't know about *pushing* you around. How about we get out of here now and I *dance* you around a little at some fashionable establishment? Might that appeal to your idiosyncratic and thoroughly single-minded self?"

"Oh, rather!" And before she could get control of it, the excitement lit up her face like a child's.

"He has the nicest voice." Margaret had cream on the end of her nose, from the gâteau. Grace was trying to signal its presence to her but she seemed oblivious—giving attention only to her own story. "Musical—you know what I mean? Writers aren't always good readers. The two things don't necessarily go together. But O'Connell . . . he has a quality. You could imagine him on the stage. He's very obviously somebody. If he wasn't a writer, he'd be famous for something else."

"I'd better get the bill." Grace checked her watch. "We have to get back."

"I'm so jealous of you!" Margaret was all eyes—*huge* eyes—behind those glasses of hers. "I've often imagined bumping into him somewhere. Just, you know, bumping into him. And he'd look down at me and he'd say—"

"That's what happened to me." Grace smiled. "I bumped into him."

But Margaret wasn't listening. "I suppose this is the closest I'll ever get to being alone with him. This lunch with you, I mean. When I come to read your interview, I'll recognize my own questions, the things I've told you. It'll be as though I'm talking to him myself, but through you. As though you were some sort of medium for our two spirits."

"Steady on." Grace glanced again at her watch.

"Sorry, Grace." There it was again—that overfamiliarity . . . "His books mean the world to me, that's all."

"Oh, good." The bill had arrived and Grace went fumbling in her purse.

"When does it come out? The article? It'll be funny, seeing your name in the newspaper. 'Interview by Grace Rutherford.' Imagine what they'll say at Pearson's!"

"Ah." Grace emerged from her handbag. "There's something I shall have to tell you on that front. It's quite a secret."

"Really? Do tell. You can trust me."

"Well, the thing is, I write a column for the *Herald* under a fake name . . ."

Margaret still had that blob of cream on her nose. Perhaps it would be there for the rest of the day.

His Charleston was impressive—but then, how would it ever have been anything else? He, the inventor of the flapper, the bad boy of American literature, dancing companion of all those bejeweled lovelies with the fat husbands who'd no doubt have lurked in corners, watching jealously. She couldn't imagine him needing lessons with Teenie Weenie. He fairly whirled her about the Lido Club so that she felt her feet were hardly touching the floor. He made her feel she weighed nothing—inside as well as out, for her emotions were spinning all about her so that she laughed and laughed as they danced. He had a grin on his face, too, that made him look like the young boy he must have been when first he conjured up Veronique.

When finally they staggered, dizzy and disheveled, from the dance floor to their prime table (Manny Hopkins, the proprietor, had actually cleared some people off it on spotting them come in together), with a good view of the orchestra and tonight's special guest singer, Violet Lamore, fresh from a season at the Montmartre in New York, O'Connell called to their waiter for champagne. On impulse Grace turned to him and said, "Are we celebrating something? Have you finished your new novel?"

His face clouded over.

"Dexter, I'm interviewing you for a newspaper. I have to ask you about the novel."

"Oh yes," he said. "The interview. I'd forgotten about the interview."

"It was your idea."

"Not one of my best."

"Dickie thought you might have finished the novel."

"Did he now?" They fell quiet as the waiter brought the champagne.

A crackle of applause. Violet Lamore had taken her position at the microphone. She was tiny and stick-thin, but her voice, when she began to sing, was amazingly deep and resonant, with a hint of tragedy to it. O'Connell sat gazing across, seemingly moved.

Sipping her champagne, Grace watched O'Connell watching the singer. She'd been with him for five hours now. All too soon the evening would be over and she'd be on her way back to Hampstead. Back to the family, to her life of hectic dullness. Somehow she'd have to find the time, in between a few snatched hours of sleep and a day's work at Pearson's, to cull a coherent newspaper interview out of what would surely end up as an evening of flirtation and verbal dueling, underscored by an odd intensity—a sense that, at some deeper level, they had an understanding. That they both knew they were dancing the necessary dance.

Or was it only in her imagination—the understanding between them? Was it just wishful thinking?

"These last few years—your silent years—"

"Ah. Back to the interview again." He rolled his eyes. "I should have just asked you out on a date like any normal person."

"You've been hiding from the world because you don't want to be owned by it. You felt trapped being the Big Writer. Trapped being the Bad Boy. Everyone knew who you were and at first you enjoyed that, but then you found you didn't want that anymore. You had to escape just so you could be yourself. I don't know where you've been all this time, and what you've done, but that's what it was all about."

His face softened. Her hand was resting on the table, and now he reached across for it—laid his hand against it so that just their fingers were touching. Only their fingers. "You're as clever as you are beautiful."

A groan. "How disappointing to hear a line like that from *you* of all people."

"Sorry to disappoint you." His fingers still rested against hers. Only the tips. But that was enough. "I'm just a man."

"Anyway, I'm not beautiful. I'm too pointy. Too knobbly. I dress well. I know how to make the best of myself, where to get my hair cut. I'm *much* more clever than I am beautiful." A sigh escaped her. She wanted, very much, to lay her head down— to let it rest for a moment on his arm. To feel his hand stroke the back of her hair.

"You asked about the novel. Well, there isn't one. There's not much left of me right now. Not after . . . well, not after the last few years."

"So, is it a sort of writer's block?"

"Not exactly. It's something else, with me. I need to know another kind of life now. Something very different than I've experienced before. That would act as a kind of fuel for my writing."

Violet Lamore had started another song. A dark, velvety song about a never-ending night.

"What shall I say in the interview? About the novel?"

"Say whatever you like." Now his hand was closing over hers, holding it tight. "Say what your readers will want to hear. You never know—maybe, in time, it'll turn out to be the truth."

The heat of his hand. The melancholy singing. The fug of the drink. His clear eyes and something present but not quite visible behind his eyes.

"I don't want this evening to end," she said, without thinking. "I don't want to go home."

He smiled. "So don't."

[From "Diamond Sharp Meets Dexter O'Connell"]

Eating dessert with Dexter O'Connell, I realize I'm feeling rather odd. He's not just a writer of novels. He's the creator of a phenomenon. I am the Monster dining with Dr. Frankenstein (albeit an extremely well-dressed monster with immaculate table manners). Don't get me wrong: there were flappers before *The Vision*—of course there were. O'Connell isn't responsible for the fact that I'm out dancing every night, just as it isn't the fault of Louise Brooks or Clara Bow or Coco Chanel and the Ready-to-Wear Revolution (though, I'm sure you'll all agree, girls, that the clothes in our High Streets and catalogues are *so* much more stylish these days). But it was O'Connell who came up with the word "flapper" in his very first short story. It was O'Connell who first brought the flapper to the wider scrutiny of all those buttoned-up types who liked to disapprove but were secretly fascinated. They reveled in rebellious, duplicitous Veronique. Helena, too, with her unhappy marriage and her devilish streak. And impetuous Georgia, in *Unruly Son.* Then there are the heroines of his short stories: the girls who played off their suitors against each other, who bobbed their hair and outshone their peers with their feminine wiles, who danced all night and smoked and drank. Those girls had fun. That's what so many of us long for, isn't it, girls? Before we settle down and start breeding (those of us who can find a husband, that is)? A life lived just a tiny bit fast.

As I chisel my way into my Pavlova (for those of you not in the know, this is a new antipodean dessert which resembles a snow-capped mountain. Named after the prima ballerina, it's made from whipped-up egg whites and lots of sugar), it begins to dawn on me that without Dexter O'Connell, there might be no Diamond Sharp. What a strange thought that is. Perhaps it's the reason why he specifically requested Little Me to do this interview.

When we take our leave of each other outside the restaurant, he shakes my hand in a businesslike manner. His handshake at least is dependable and solid.

Trust him? Not a bit of it. But that's not the point with men like Dexter O'Connell. It's not what we want from him nor what he offers. He is the embodiment of the kind of sumptuous, glamorous decadence which resonates from all his stories. Some of us might dream of living that way, if only we had the chance—but perhaps we shouldn't forget that O'Connell's stories rarely have happy endings. The legend of O'Connell's "lost" five years, and the hint of sadness behind his eyes, tells us that the dream is just that. A vision.

He kissed her in the street. In the rain and the dark. It was after 3:00 A.M. and they'd gone roaming about looking for a taxi. They were somewhere in Bloomsbury, sheltering under a shop awning from the rain—suddenly heavier—when he grabbed her by the shoulders and pulled her to him.

She'd wanted this all evening—this closeness. His body against hers. She'd wanted it long before this evening. She closed her eyes and gave herself up to it, needing it to become everything; to make the rest of her world fade away, even if just for now. His hands were strong and real on her back. His mouth . . . but he'd broken away.

"You know, I shall never know what it feels like to kiss a girl without having to bend down to do it. That's the trouble with being so tall."

"I'd stand on a step if we could only find one."

He laughed. "Never mind steps. Let's go to my hotel room. You can stand on the bed."

He moved to kiss her again, and this time it was she who broke away.

"I can't, Dexter."

"Why not?" He looked annoyed. Or perhaps disappointed. It was hard to make out what was happening in those eyes.

"I have to get home."

He pushed his hands deep into his pockets. "Somebody waiting for you there?"

"Yes . . . no. Not in the way you mean. I live with my sister and her two children. And my mother."

"You mean to say, they can't manage without you for one night? Half a night, really?"

"I have work in the morning. I have the interview to write by the end of the day. I'm just . . ."

"Not that kind of girl?" His voice was mocking. "Well, you sure had me fooled, Diamond Sharp."

"My name is Grace. Grace Rutherford. In the daytime I'm an advertising copywriter. And I'm in charge of a noisy family."

"Well, well. I do believe we have a moment of truth. I guess we'd better find you a cab, Grace. We'll step out again just as soon as this rain eases off."

She was already regretting it—her disclosure. It had broken the spell. He wouldn't be interested now, without that element of mystery to draw him on. Ducking out from under the awning, she walked quickly down the street, oily rain pelting down on her hair, splashing up her legs.

Footsteps behind her. "Grace, wait! What's wrong?"

"You know what's wrong." She wheeled around. "You're . . . you're *you*."

"And you wonder why I disappeared for five years? You're not the only one who was hiding their name. Come on. At least let me help you find a taxi."

He took her hand, muttering something about the weather in this goddamn country, and they walked together toward Tottenham Court Road.

"There's something I have to ask you," she said, as the rain began to slacken off.

"That darned interview!"

"No. It's not for the interview. Dexter . . ."

"Now you have me *really* worried."

"What is John Cramer to you?"

He stopped dead and pulled away from her. "Did you just speak that man's name? Did I hear you right?"

"He was the man at the Savoy, wasn't he? The one who broke up our little date."

"Jesus! Will I never be free of that bastard?" He rubbed at his head, and his shoulders slumped. He looked exhausted.

"He's a neighbor of ours. He's pretty friendly with my sister. I think he might be in love with her."

"Jesus!"

"He warned me to steer clear of you. Why did he do that?"

"Look . . . We go way back, Cramer and I. It's a messy business. I'd thought it was all over, but here he is again—right here in London when we should have the Atlantic Ocean between us. And so, on it goes. And on. I'll be an old man on my deathbed, and I'll look up and he'll be there. Right alongside the Grim-Goddamn-Reaper."

"Are you saying he has some sort of vendetta against you? That he followed you to London?"

"Look, there's a cab." O'Connell stuck his arm out and a taxi pulled up.

"Dexter?"

"Only my mother calls me Dexter." He opened the door for her and stood to one side to let her climb in. "The lady's going to Hampstead," he called to the driver.

"Don't you want a lift?"

"You're going north. I'm headed south to the Savoy."

"Well, I suppose it's good night then."

"I suppose it is. I'll be seeing you, Grace Rutherford. Oh, and watch out for Cramer. Don't let him dally with your sister. Or with you."

And before she could say anything further he'd closed the door and the taxi had pulled out into the road. She held her hand up to wave to him, but he'd turned and was walking away.

Seven

Grace telephoned in sick to the office on the morning after, the better to focus on the writing of the interview. Wanting to revel in it. In spite of her sore head, the usual noisiness of the house, a lack of any notes—and indeed, in spite of her not even having interviewed O'Connell in the usual sense of the word—the piece almost wrote itself.

On days two and three Grace walked around with a gormless smile on her face. At home she was absentminded: losing things, giving omelettes to the children one suppertime even though both hated eggs, failing to pay attention to the mealtime conversation of Nancy and Mother. At work she was unable to focus, and mistakenly sent down for approval an out-of-date draft of the latest Baker's newspaper advertisement—one which had already been rejected—resulting in her being hauled over the coals yet again by Aubrey Pearson. She didn't care. Her head was full of O'Connell. The kissing, of course, and the dancing—but the little things, too. The look of his big hand holding the slender stem of his champagne glass, that enticing mixture of strength and delicacy. A remark he'd made about how, when staying in Europe, he (perversely, so he thought) liked February, best of all months. February, with its crazy chaotic mix of freezing winds, darkness and snow, on the one hand; but, on the other, early spring flowers— pearly snowdrops, purple and gold crocuses perhaps peeping through the snow—and those odd days of clear, dazzling sunshine when you least expected them.

"You never know where you are with February," he'd said. "I like the not knowing. I like life to be unpredictable."

The more time she spent in mentally replaying their evening, the more details she remembered. Until she reached an almost too-perfect state of awareness of it all—her memory tightening, tautening, like a violin being tuned and then overtuned so that the strings were almost snapping. She shook herself then—actually *physically* gave herself a good shaking— and told herself she must stop it right away and pay attention to the very real, pressing things in her life: Felix's dirty nappy, her mother's loneliness, Diamond's attendance at the opening of a new French restaurant on Great Portland Street, Cato-Ferguson's attempts to pass off the successful Stewards' Breath-Freshening Elixir campaign as being entirely his idea (this made easier for him by Grace's "sick" day).

By the end of day three her flights of fancy had moved on apace. She was thinking not so much, now, about what had already taken place between Dexter O'Connell and herself, but more about what would happen next. She saw herself out dancing with him again—perhaps at the Salamander, or at the Kit-Cat Club, where Ben Bernie's Orchestra was playing a short season. Would she abandon her scruples and go back to the Savoy with him next time? She knew she shouldn't, of course—a girl shouldn't give her "all" so easily. But how long would he be prepared to wait and how long could she manage to hold out? He was no ordinary man, and she wasn't exactly a conventional girl. Popular wisdom had it, of course, that a man lost interest when he'd "had his way"—but Grace wanted to believe that there was more *to* her than was the case with the average girl. Inexhaustible new territory that a man would want to go on and on exploring.

There was the small issue that he hadn't yet contacted her. But he would. She knew he would.

On day four—a Saturday (and still no word from O'Connell)—she began to conjure scenes both awkward and magnificent: herself explaining to O'Connell that she couldn't marry him and go to live in America because of her enduring responsibility for Nancy, Tilly and Felix—trying to elicit from him a promise that they might all live together in the Hampstead house, and receiving, instead, a declaration that he would export the entire family to a suitably spacious apartment in New York, perhaps looking out over Central Park so the children wouldn't miss the Heath too much. She'd breeze into a writing job at *The New Yorker*. He'd dedicate his new novel to her. They'd rapidly have two children—twins, perhaps. The fantasies were reaching a hysterical pitch, and Grace was having to shake herself more and more. Mother had invited some old family friends over for lunch, and Grace was obliged to excuse herself several times and go up to her room, purely so she could give herself a good talking-to.

On the Sunday, Grace woke to find doubts creeping right across her sunny hysteria, black clouds inching across the hot blue sky. The fact was, it had been five days. She tried to make allowances for him: He didn't have her telephone number or address—but he knew he could reach her at the *Herald* and he conspicuously hadn't done so. Or *had* he? Perhaps Dickie, in a fit of jealousy, was failing to pass on notes and telephone messages. She should telephone Dickie and confront him. But he'd only deny it, and then what could she do? Instead of accosting Dickie, she should telephone his secretary and get her to look into it—but no, he'd already have primed her. So, what then? It would all be all right, of course. O'Connell would realize that Dickie couldn't be relied on. She had told him she worked for an advertising agency—so he'd telephone his way from agency to agency until he found the right one. She'd arrive at work on Monday morning to discover him sitting in her office, waiting for her . . .

Monday arrived. As Grace pushed through the revolving door into the Pearson's building, something was clenched tight inside her stomach. She almost couldn't bear to look into her office—and when she *did* look, it was empty. Of course it was. The idea that he would be in there, first thing in the morning, was a ludicrous one. The post was brought around at 9:30, and there was nothing from O'Connell.

She was playing ridiculous games with herself, inside her own head. She had been, all week. The fantasies had gathered momentum and gone rolling off on their own. A pram that someone had let go of, careering down steps, like Battleship *Potemkin*.

Knowledge and Despond landed on her shoulders with a great, sickening weight. He would not appear. He would not telephone. He had not sent and would not send a note. The interview was done and dusted. She was no longer the mythical Diamond Sharp to him. She had told him who she really was. And she had told him about her connection to John Cramer. It was all over before it had even begun.

II.
The Rivals

One

The Past

Nancy had already written three letters to George by the time Grace even attempted a letter to Steven. It wasn't that she didn't *want* to write to him. It was just that she didn't know what to say or how to say it. Everything had changed so much and she couldn't decipher her own feelings. And her awareness of the great screes of stuff that Nancy was sending to George only made it harder.

"Dearest Steven,"

This greeting had taken over an hour one Sunday after lunch. She'd switched from "Dear" (too formal) to "Darling" (the opposite) to "My dear" (fond maiden aunt), all with much scrumpling of paper, before settling on "Dearest." This exhausting internal struggle—plus the writing of the date, "September 10, 1915"—was the limit of the afternoon's productivity.

In the evening, Grace returned to her desk to try a little further.

"I hope this letter finds you well. I think of you often and wonder how you are getting along."
(*Maiden aunt again.*)

"Hampstead is dull and gray without you. Nancy and I have no company at the pictures and are forced to partner each other for dancing."
(*Too moany—and when it came to the dancing, not entirely true.*)

"I miss you so much, my brave one, and pray each night for your safe return."
(*Heavens!*)

She gave up, and another week passed. A week of dull university lectures and essays. A week during which Nancy fired off two more letters to George. By the following Sunday the guilt was weighing heavily on her. What sort of a person was she, to leave poor Steven languishing without so much as a hello, when surely all and sundry were reveling in their missives from home? It wasn't as if she didn't like him, after all. It was just . . . But could one in all fairness call it writer's block (as she was beginning to) when the block concerned the writing of a mere letter?

Sick of the inside of her own head, she waited for the

household to go to bed, and then tiptoed into the living room and took out the bottle of dry sherry from the drinks cabinet. Helped herself to a good large glassful, gulped it down and poured a second to take upstairs with her. If that didn't do the trick, then nothing would.

Dearest Steven,

I'm drunk on Daddy's sherry—believe me, it's the only way I shall ever succeed in getting this out. The thing is, you've turned me frightfully shy. I thought I knew you, both of you, but suddenly there's a different you and a different George, and even a different Nancy. I feel I'm the only one of us who is still clinging to the past, to the idea of us as a foursome. The rest of you have moved on. I know that doesn't make sense and I apologize for that (I shall blame the sherry!), but there you have it. I have been tongue-tied when it comes to letter writing, but I promise you I've been thinking of you all the time.

Steven, whatever happens, I want you to know that I shall never forget that night in the garden. I know I was rather cross with you at the time, but that was just because of the surprise of it, and a degree of confusion. Truly, it was a very special night. And you are quite the best kisser I've ever kissed.

I'm not saying this very well (again, the sherry). I think about you when I'm alone. I feel a lot for you—the sort of feelings I can't talk about, even with the sherry.

There. I hope that makes you smile. Steven, I have no idea what you're living, and I'm sorry if this is all just awfully trivial to you. I can't pretend that I remotely understand this war, or what it must be like to fight in it.

I've been unforgivably slow in writing to you, but I hope you'll forgive me all the same. Write back when you can, and take good care of yourself and George. I want you to come back soon to kiss me again.

With all my love,
Gracie

The following morning, after breakfast, a much refreshed Grace (with not the slightest trace of a headache) headed upstairs to fetch the letter, intending to take it to the post office before she could change her mind.

I shan't read it again, she told herself—but then of course she did. And blushed. Then she read it again and blushed some more and stood procrastinating.

Buck up and think of Steven, she told herself. You've written it and now you must send it.

So she placed the letter in an envelope, sealed and addressed it, and went downstairs to fetch her coat and keys.

But in the few minutes she'd spent upstairs, the doorbell had rung and the world had moved on. Through the open doorway to the living room, she saw Mrs. Wilkins sitting in a chair, her face in her hands, and Mr. Wilkins over by the mantel, staring into the empty fireplace. Daddy was delving in his drinks cabinet—a look of surprise flitting briefly across his face when he held up the sherry bottle and saw how little was left.

"Here's Grace." Mummy had spotted her, and was advancing toward the door. There were tears on her face. "Come in here a moment, darling. Where's your sister?"

Grace's heart began to pound. Her hand opened and the letter fell to the floor. She heard her own voice say, "Which of them is it?"

Steven had been killed in shelling at the Loos Battle. His death changed everything. The Rutherford girls had been in a bubble while the war went on somewhere else. They knew people who'd died, of course. But nobody crucial had been snatched away from them until now. Nobody intrinsic.

Grace went on at university for a time but it all seemed so irrelevant, with Steven dead and George still out there. There had to be something more useful she could do. Despite her parents' protests she dropped out and got a job at a munitions factory, in the belief that the most direct and effective way to contribute was to build weapons with her own lily-white hands. Weapons to kill the men who'd murdered Steven.

It was good to be an automaton, working hard and with no time for moping about. But the other women, all of whom came from less-privileged backgrounds, looked on her with an odd mixture of awe and contempt. Unable to comprehend why someone of Grace's means should have *chosen* to work alongside them, handling the TNT that caused jaundice and led to them being nicknamed "Canary Girls" rather than taking an easier, loftier sort of job, they treated her with suspicion, and kept away from her. The only other well-to-do type was the Welfare Supervisor, whom Grace quickly realized had landed her senior role purely as an accident of birth. This woman's personal style was to attempt to conceal her incompetence and inarticulacy beneath a façade of refined delicacy— rather as one might disguise an ugly mess in the corner of a room by throwing a lace cloth over it. The supervisor, Emily, made friendly but condescending overtures to Grace—her particular brand of friendliness being far more objectionable than the mild hostility of the other women. More intolerable still were Emily's whispers of a plan to elevate Grace "off the production line" to work alongside her.

"It was always a silly idea," said Harold. "Such a waste of a good brain. You should give it up and go back to university. If you're bothered about doing your bit, you could do something voluntary like your mother and sister." Nancy, who had taken an office job by day, was fund-raising for war-widowed families in dire financial straits. Catherine, along with many others in the WSPU, had joined the Women's Police Service, and spent her evenings patrolling the Heath in a uniform, giving wayward girls a jolly good talking-to, and routing out the couples with a big stick.

In the end, it was a second family tragedy that made Grace give up her factory work, though not to go back to university. In February 1917, Harold died of influenza, plunging the family into a profound state of shock that lasted way beyond the funeral. Through the period of acute loss, each of them tried and failed to stifle a private realization that persistently nagged: that bronchial Harold had been quietly ill for ages, and none of them had so much as acknowledged it, he least of all. With so much war bereavement going on around them, they'd lost track of the fact that they were vulnerable at home, too. For a while the household was the proverbial chicken that continues to run about after its head has been cut off. Grace and Nancy went out to work as before, and Catherine continued to tread her beat. But the fires were not lit in the evening because Harold had always been the one to light them. Nobody considered what tasks might be left undone because Daddy wasn't there to do them, nor what further tasks might need to be tackled as a result of his death. Nobody so much as entered his study.

Chance dictated that it was Grace who happened to be at home on the day when the maid awkwardly announced that while she understood the family were having a hard time, so was she without her weekly wages. It was Grace who answered the door when the milkman stopped by to say he would have to stop delivering if they didn't settle on the spot. It was Grace who took the telephone call from the family solicitor who wanted to know what the devil was happening about Harold's affairs. And so Grace was the one to finally sit down in the dusty study and start searching through files.

The factory work had been a sort of game, she realized. She'd been motivated primarily by a sense of duty and patriotism, but she now saw that her first duty was to her family. Catherine might be presenting a cheerful coping exterior but Grace could see beyond that. Mummy was in a kind of frozen state—unable to step into Daddy's shoes in any meaningful way, unable to comprehend even her own emotions. And Nancy dragged listlessly about the house with red eyes and a short temper—still the youngest, the child.

Grace would deal with the paperwork and settle the unpaid bills. She would make the difficult discovery that her father had far less money than any of them might have expected. She would look for a job that paid much more than the factory. She would find one at Pearson & Pearson.

Two

Nancy and George were married at 11:30 A.M. on December 22, 1917. They'd had to postpone twice because of canceled leave, and this opportunity had arisen because George had been sent home wounded. He'd been back at his parents' house for a good few weeks, recovering from an operation on his right leg at Queen Alexandra's Hospital in Highgate. A number of small scraps and shards of what appeared to be granite were removed from the leg, and George kept them as souvenirs, saying they were pieces of someone's grave. He'd been holed up in a churchyard during a heavy shelling bombardment at Ypres, and a tombstone very near him had taken a direct hit.

It wasn't the fairy-tale wedding Nancy had dreamed of—taking place, as it did, at the local Register Office, with just a smattering of friends in attendance. But there was nonetheless a romance to the occasion. Nancy was dashing in her squirrel-edged winter coat on that clear, frosty morning, her eyes sparkling. George, now a captain, cut a romantic figure in his uniform, propped up on crutches. He had about him a new remoteness and seriousness, but this was romantic in itself. He had been at the Loos Battle, where his brother was killed (now more than two years ago). He'd survived the Somme and the third battle of Ypres, and had come home to give his fiancée the nicest possible Christmas present: himself.

The day was a difficult one for Grace. Throughout the ceremony the brave-faced Catherine gripped her hand so hard that she could all but hear the cracking of bones. Although neither was clad in black, Grace felt they were a heavy, tragic presence, the pair of them. Widows in the corner. Certainly it was clear that the sympathy in the faces of their guests was directed not just at her mother, but also at her. The wedding had reminded them all of something they'd long forgotten— perhaps something that many of them had not even realized until today: If Nancy and George were one half of an equation, then she and Steven were the other. If Nancy was marrying George, then Grace must have lost Steven. But much as she didn't like herself for it, it wasn't Steven who was uppermost in Grace's mind today. Beneath her cheerful exterior she was struggling to quench something that kept surging up: the growing conviction that George should be marrying her, not her sister. His changed persona merely intensified her certainty that she understood him far better than Nancy ever would. What a mess she and George had made of their lives on that one, stupidly passionate and impulsive day in the summer of 1915. And how arbitrary everything had been since then. Really, you couldn't allow yourself to think about it all for too long—it was all so unbearably, horribly, and in Steven's case tragically, arbitrary.

After the ceremony there was a drab lunch at the nearby Woolton Hotel. Gray chicken soup followed by foul-tasting beef in aspic served with carrots and floury potatoes, and then spotted dick with congealed custard. You had to go heavy on the drink just to be able to get it all down. As the afternoon wore on, Grace began to benefit from the numbing effects of the alcohol, and her fixed smile grew brighter and glossier.

I shall get through this, she told herself, as she narrowly but deliberately evaded Nancy's hurled bouquet. Tomorrow morning will be dreadful but I don't have to think about that now. And, after today, it can only get easier.

But it didn't. The newlyweds stayed on with the Rutherfords over Christmas. It was George who stood carving the goose, and who took Mr. Rutherford's old seat at the table. George was the new, resonant tenor when it came to carol singing around the piano. He fixed the wireless. He set the fires every evening. He fought his way, on those crutches, through the neglected, bramble-infested garden with clippers and shears, restoring all to rights. Nancy watched him with adoration in her eyes, then turned those eyes on her sister and mother. See? they clearly said. See what a prize he is? See how lucky we are to have him?

Grace searched for signs of resentment in her mother, as, little by little, George moved further into her father's old territory. But Mrs. Rutherford was relentlessly cheerful, and Grace was unable to catch her eye. Increasingly, her unexpressed anger was directed at the stoic widow. She wanted to grab her mother by the shoulders and shout: They have turned us into guests in our own home! She's flaunting her happiness like a new dress! Doesn't it bother you that they've made your first-born into an untouchable spinster at twenty?

Worst of all were the nights. Mrs. Rutherford had surrendered the master bedroom, herself taking her younger daughter's tiny room. This meant there was only a thin, interior wall between Grace and the frisky newlyweds.

By Boxing Day, Grace's nerves were in tatters, and when George and Nancy had left the breakfast table to go for a walk, she felt compelled to say something.

"I've been thinking, Mummy. You must be terribly cramped in Nancy's room."

"I'm absolutely fine. The youngsters need the space much more than I do. More tea, dear?" Mrs. Rutherford was busying herself with the pot, and, as usual, Grace couldn't catch her eye.

"Why don't you swap with me?" she tried. "You'd be so much more comfortable in my room."

"As I said, I'm fine. Please don't trouble yourself about this, Grace."

"But it isn't right that you should be so inconvenienced. Not with Daddy . . . Not after the difficult time you've had. Nancy ought to be ashamed of herself, putting you out of your own bedroom."

A steely glare. "She has done no such thing. It was my idea entirely. And as I've already said, I'm fine. Now do let it alone."

"Of course. Whatever you say." Grace sat gripping the edge of the table, trying to calm herself. Focusing all her energy on not saying what she wanted to say.

Late in the evening, on George's last night, Grace found herself alone with him before the fire. Mother had turned in at her usual ten o'clock. Nancy had then become overwrought about his imminent departure and had gone up for a calming bath. The two were left in an uneasy silence, staring into the still-lively flames, drinking brandy.

"There's something I wanted to ask you, Grace." George swirled the golden liquid around his glass.

"Yes, of course I'll look after Nancy while you're away." Grace had finished her drink and was fighting the urge for another. "She's my sister."

"Thanks . . . but that wasn't it." His voice was uncharacteristically hesitant. Grace darted a look at him.

"What, then?"

"I just . . ." He raked a hand through the auburn hair. "Are you angry?"

"Why on *earth* should I be *angry* with you?" This was spoken in a kind of snarl.

"Yes, I thought as much." He looked up at her and smiled nervously. "You're not much good at hiding it."

"Light me a cigarette, would you?" She tried to calm herself. An opportunity had arisen unexpectedly, and she had to work out how to grasp it. If they were ever to talk openly with each other about what had happened between them—about what it all meant—then it had to be now. This might be the last time they would ever be alone together, after all. Oh, *God*. She mustn't allow herself to believe this could be the last time!

He had gotten up—no need for those crutches now—and was reaching for the packet that was tucked behind the clock on the mantelpiece. He was saying something about the difficulty of their all being here under one roof. He was mumbling halfheartedly, and she found she wasn't listening. Instead, she was working out what she wanted to say to him. She was looking at his long back. His neck.

"You've changed," she said, cutting across his vagaries.

"Of course I have." He handed the lit cigarette over and she set it in her holder. He'd lit one for himself, too. "How could it be otherwise?"

"You're not the old George anymore. All polite and proper and nice. Funnily enough, there's more of Steven in you now. It's as if the two of you have become one person—all rolled up in your body."

"What rot." It was spoken lightly but there was a visible tensing around his mouth and in his neck. He was sitting on the very edge of the chair.

Grace realized something. "*You're* angry with *me.*"

"No, I'm not. But would you blame me if I was? That was a pretty offensive thing you just said." He dragged hard on his cigarette.

"You saw us, didn't you? Steven and me."

"What?" But he was clearly playing for time.

The heat from the fire was oppressive and the room airless. She was dizzy with it all.

"You saw me with your brother that night. And it made you so angry that you went back into the house and proposed to my sister. You did it just to spite me! Of all the stupid things . . ."

A forced-sounding chuckle. "You have incredible vanity, Grace."

"Oh, really?"

"I love Nancy."

She blew out a smoke ring. "I hope that's true." This was turning into a battle of sorts, albeit a subtle kind. "You've certainly been very honorable. To her, I mean. You've done the right thing."

The fire made a strange, slow, squeaking noise. It was as if there was something alive in there—something that was having the life squeezed out of it.

"Nancy wants Mother to have one of those smart little gas fires installed in here," said Grace absently. "The new sort, like the one in her bedroom. Sorry—*your* bedroom. She says it'll be nice and clean and easy."

"I married your sister because that was what we both wanted. *Both* of us."

A loud pop from the fire. A fizz. She tried not to notice the way George flinched at the noise.

"Over my dead body, I told Mother. A real fire is something alive. I love all the smuts and the dirt. I don't like things to be too nice and clean and easy."

"Things never are, are they?" He got to his feet and threw his cigarette into the fire.

"Poor Nancy."

"Save your sympathy. We're perfectly happy."

"You're finding this as difficult as I am. Aren't you?" Her voice was softer now.

He took up the poker and prodded the logs to encourage the flames to die down. Carefully put the fire guard in place. "It was a world ago, Grace. That day on the Heath. Everything has changed since then. *Everything.* You have no idea what *difficult* is."

"I'm sorry." She was embarrassed. Humbled in the face of his grandly unknowable experiences. "You're right, of course. What could I possibly know?"

He closed his eyes.

"I wish I *did* know, George. I wish you'd talk to me about it all."

George sighed and opened his eyes. "When Steven and I first arrived in France, we were sent to Harfleur for technical instruction before going up the line. It was something they did with the new fellows. We were supposed to be there for a couple of weeks or so. It was all drilling, musketry, lectures about gas and bombs . . . One day, when we were waiting for an instructor to come and talk to us about bombs, a sergeant decided to give a little unofficial talk, sort of a pre-liminary session. Well, this sergeant was giving us a caution on what *not* to do with a percussion grenade, and he went and knocked the thing against the table to demonstrate his point. Damn thing went off, killing him and two others and wound-ing a further ten."

"Oh, my God."

"Grace . . ."

She knew what he was about to say even before he said it.

"Steven was one of the two. He never even made it to the trenches."

She heard herself protesting. "I saw the letter from the colonel. It said Steven died a gallant death—that he was hit by a shell during an offensive and died on the way back to base. Died of wounds, that's what it said."

"That was a form letter. The colonel sent out hundreds of those things."

She looked at his eyes—they had a dullness to them, a dead quality. And she knew it was true. "That's monstrous."

"It's all monstrous. Keep it to yourself, will you? I don't want my parents knowing just how pointless and arbitrary my brother's death was. Or Nancy—she'd worry about me even more than she already does." He got up and headed for the door. "Good night."

"I still want to know more. I still want you to talk to me about it all. If you should ever want to." The offer sounded pathetic, even to her.

"Good night, Grace." And then, a seeming afterthought, his hand on the doorknob: "You might send me a letter now and again. If you'd like to, that is. I don't suppose Nancy would mind."

His feet on the stairs. The creak of the floorboards. The sound of their voices somewhere above—his and Nancy's.

𝔓𝔦𝔠𝔠𝔞𝔡𝔦𝔩𝔩𝔶 ℌ𝔢𝔯𝔞𝔩𝔡

The West-Ender
May 2, 1927

I am not a Good Girl. This is patently clear to all regular readers of this column. I stay out late. I like the company of men. I'm vain. I wear too much makeup. I'm economical with the truth when it suits me. I never refuse a cocktail. I'm not demure . . . . Well, until recently, that is.

Standing in the rain at the end of a long night, I was asked a question by a splendidly handsome man of my acquaintance, and I said no when I wanted to say yes. I did it because I believed it to be the correct tactic. You say no and it drives the gentleman mad and he comes running after you like a boy chasing a kite when the wind has yanked the string from his hand. At least, that's what he's supposed to do. Not this time, readers. This gentleman appears not to understand the rules of the game. Perhaps he's mistaken me for a Good Girl, the sort of girl who says no because she really *means* no. Perhaps he's playing a different game entirely. This has not been a good week.

You'll perhaps want to know about some restaurants and dance clubs. Well, what can I tell you in my present mood? If you're forced by circumstances beyond your control to go to Morelli on Brewer Street, do not, I beg you, order the fish. Or the pork. Or the spaghetti. Or any of the puddings. Or the starters. If your pigheaded companion of the evening strong-arms you to drop in at Little Venice on Lower Regent Street, take a table as far away from the dance floor as you possibly can, as the place is more crowded than a football match and anyone within half a mile of the capering couples will be trodden on, kicked about the shins or worse. (If your week is as bad as mine, a large bald gentleman might actually fall right across your table as you sit with your drink and your *pommes frites,* and then have the audacity to complain that *you* had got yourself in *his* way.) Finally, if extraordinary circumstances beyond your control contrive that you should arrive, one night, at Marchesa's nightclub on Charing Cross Road . . . But no—surely *nothing* would drag any sane person into that ear-splittingly awful shoe box of sweat, watered-down cocktails and the Badly Dressed.

Also this week's letters are laden with complaint. Miss Gertrude Summerhouse of Peckham berates me for declaring Dexter O'Connell to be untrustworthy and has instructed me to publicize that, "Analysis of Mr. O'Connell's handwriting, astrological chart and fingerprints reveal him to be a true and honorable person, someone who can be absolutely relied upon." Miss Elizabeth Jones of Hammersmith is yet more emphatic: "How dare you talk that way about Dexter O'Connell? Call yourself a writer? You're not fit to lick his boots." Methinks these ladies and their fair companions in my postbag may be dancing a Charleston with the green-eyed monster.

So what do I do about my unruly gentleman? Answers

to the usual address, please. Obviously the correct tactic is to do nothing and wait, but I fear I'll wait forever. I could go and find that Devil and make sure he understands what a rare and precious thing a Diamond is. But that's what Bad Girls do, isn't it? And it never ends well for Bad Girls. I share my dilemma with you, dear readers, in a spirit of camaraderie. You might not understand or agree with me, but if you simply disapprove, then you are not a part of the modern world I'm writing for, and you shouldn't bother reading my columns.

Oh yes, a correction: I'm assured by a reliable source that "The good proprietress of the Morning Glory patisserie on Baker Street does not have a mustache. It must have been a shadow."

Five o'clock shadow, possibly.

Diamond Sharp

Three

It started as a whisper that grew louder. Grace heard it late one night at the Salamander, and then again the following night at the Lido. On the third morning she had a telephone call from Dickie. The rumor ran that Dexter O'Connell was to give a reading at nine o'clock that evening, at Ciro's of all places. Dickie's call to the manager of Ciro's had produced an odd response: He would neither confirm nor deny the rumor. This of course added fuel to the fire.

Dickie said, "You'd better get along there, Grace."

Grace said, "I'd rather not, if it's all the same to you."

"He's reading from the new novel. You should be the one to cover it."

"Dickie, there *is* no new novel."

"That's not what you said in the interview. Now just stop complaining and make sure you're there."

After replacing the receiver, Grace called Margaret into her office, closed the door and, without quite looking her in the eye, told her about the rumor, ending with, "I can't go so you'll have to go in my place and take notes. That is, if there's anything worth taking note of. Then I'll write it up."

Margaret's face wore an odd, fixed grimace.

"Well?" Grace tapped her desk agitatedly with the end of a pencil.

"I'd love to go, of course. I'd give my teeth to be there, if I'm honest—the whole lot of them."

"There won't be any need for that."

"But . . ." She frowned and pushed her glasses up her nose.

"But what?"

Another adjustment of the glasses. "I think it's wrong for you to let personal reasons get in the way of your going along this evening and writing a good piece about it."

"I *beg* your pardon? There are no 'personal' reasons. I simply have another engagement."

"You've been told to cover Dexter O'Connell's first public reading in five years, and you've got 'another engagement'? I'd be delighted and honored to go to the reading, and thank you for the invitation. But the fact is you should be there, too. If you're serious about your writing, you won't let anything get in the way of that—least of all some trivial slight."

The pencil broke in Grace's hands.

Piccadilly Circus on a sunny Thursday evening. Frisky dresses in bright colors, short enough to show calves and, in some cases, knees. Cloche hats, headbands, sporty spectator shoes. White scarves, starched shirts, enough hair oil to grease the length of Regent Street. Bobs of varying quality. Giggles. Gossip:

"He did."

"He never."

"He *did.*"

"He *never.*"

A drunk lurches off the pavement, a Bentley swerves to avoid him and a Citroën plows into its side. Honking horns.

"You bloody idiot!"

The drunk staggers on.

Over by the Piccadilly Restaurant, a hot-tempered spat is coming close to fists.

"He's not worth it, William."

"He *is* worth it."

Two red-faced boys dragged apart by their girls.

"I could've killed him, Agnes, if you'd only let me."

"You kill my brother and I'll kill *you.*"

A girl with long ginger hair and a hat with an unfashionably wide brim walks practically under the feet of the ranting boy, so that he turns and shouts, "You ought to look where you're going, miss."

The girl and her friend slip off around the corner to Orange Street. To Ciro's nightclub, which has opened its doors two hours earlier than normal.

Inside Ciro's, a crowd was gathering. A very untypical crowd for this venue. Mismatched and out of context, like a box of odd shoes at a jumble sale. As they milled about, buying drinks at the bar and peering at the fixtures and fittings, waiters were setting up rows of folding chairs on the glass dance floor. A lectern had been placed on the little stage.

"It's true, then." Margaret was hugging her copy of *The Vision.*

"We'll see." Grace was fussing with the long ginger wig and

hat she was wearing. The brim was pulled so low over her eyes that she could barely see.

Half past eight. Many had taken seats, though some lingered at the bar, where business was brisk. Nobody looked confident. Everyone seemed to be eavesdropping on each other:

"Jones had it on good authority. He's reliable, Jones is."

"Cynthia told me about it. She's a librarian. She knows about these things. Literature and all that."

Margaret pointed at a couple of empty chairs. "Let's sit down before the seats are all taken."

Grace kept catching sight of her reflection in the shining glass and metal around them. The wig was ludicrous. She swore under her breath.

Nine o'clock. The conversation had died down into nothing. The crowd was restless.

"Do you think he's going to turn up?" Margaret's face was a mess of hope and dismay.

"Don't ask me. My instincts about O'Connell have been worse than useless so far."

Margaret gazed agitatedly about. "*Surely* he must be coming. Why would they have opened up the club if he wasn't? Why would they have put all these chairs out, and the lectern?"

"Maybe they simply heard the rumor, like the rest of us, and thought it was worth a punt on the off chance. They're selling plenty of drinks, after all. Sisley, the manager, is conspicuously absent. Oh!"

"What?"

"Nothing." Grace tugged at her hat brim and slid down farther on her seat. She'd spotted someone she'd rather not have to speak to. What was *he* doing *here* of all places . . . ?

As the minutes passed, the tension in the room spooled out into a taut, thin thread. At half past nine, the thread broke. Muttered complaints grew louder. People shrugged and shook their heads and got up to leave. Waiters began stacking chairs and moving them out.

Grace felt quietly satisfied. In the faces all around her, she saw reflected the disappointment and anger she'd been feeling with O'Connell for over a week. It was a sort of vindication. Positively cheery, she turned to Margaret. "I'm heading off to the Tutankhamun on the Strand. Do you want to come?"

Margaret shook her head. "I'll stay on here a bit longer. Just in case."

The Tutankhamun Club was styled as a grand Egyptian palace: all marble columns and murals showing pyramids and slaves and nobles with huge eyes standing side-on. There were masks, statues and jeweled scarabs which Grace knew to be genuine ancient artifacts shipped over from Egypt. Waiters, clad in gold loincloths, carried drink trays high above their heads. Women in white robes fanned the guests with purple plumes and palm fronds. The dance orchestra wore black wigs and makeup.

Grace (having discarded the wig and hat) was greeted by Monique, the manageress, a great precipice of a woman wearing a lot of lace. They'd barely begun speaking when there was a whoop of "Darling! How marvelous!"—and she was being kissed on both cheeks and guided off to the best table by the effusive owner, Sheridan Hamilton-Shapcott, a man so stick thin that even the most expensive of Savile Row suits hung off him like a sack. (Really, he and Monique looked most peculiar side by side. Barely the same species.)

"Dwinks, dwinks." Sheridan clapped his hands at a waiter.

"Gwace, you're to twy my new cocktail, the Luxor Lizard. I concocted it myself so I can assure you of its deliciosity, and bla bla."

"What's in it?"

"Twy and you will know." This was Sheridan's motto. It was hung above the bar, inscribed in characters reminiscent of hieroglyphics. Grace had heard a rumor that he had it hanging over his bed, too.

The golden drink had a honeyed, golden taste. "It's yummy. Is it dreadfully potent?"

"Don't be so suspicious." He crossed his legs and frowned at her, a frown exaggerated by the Egyptian-style kohl all around his doe eyes. "Wemember to be nice, Gwace. I'm still cwoss with you for not coming here sooner. You—my oldest fwiend, and I've been open over a month!"

"I thought perhaps I should let you get properly started before I came in to distract you. Let you get your feet under the table, so to speak." This was almost the truth. She knew Sheridan too well to have wanted to be there on those first nights. Indeed, stories quickly reached her of his foolishness in letting the staff help themselves to free drinks—encouraging them even, for fun. The result was mayhem. On the third night someone had called the police in, and it was all Sheridan could do to keep the place open. The chaos ended only with Monique's arrival. She'd run bars and clubs for years and quickly knocked the Tutankhamun into shape, tolerating no nonsense from her supposed boss, a self-confessed nightclub virgin.

Sheridan had inherited the Shapcott Brewery and Distillery from his late father, Edward, but had failed to acquire the great man's drive and work ethic. His fluttering-butterfly attention span (hailing, along with his doe-eyed foppery, from his late mother, Amelia) did not mix well with the world of business, and he quickly passed all onerous responsibility over to his father's long-term deputy, the better to devote his time and energy to his evolving hobbies. And "evolving" really was the right term: It had all begun, before his father's death, with a brief stint studying ancient history at Cambridge. While there, he had fallen in with a group of archaeologists, who had persuaded him to drop out, join up with their forthcoming Egyptian venture and provide all funding. Shapcott Senior, keeper of the purse, had fallen in with the plan on being promised by his son that archaeology, and not ancient history, was "the thing." The Shapcotts' old friends Catherine and Harold Rutherford backed up Amelia's view that "the boy will settle back to his studies once he's got it out of his system." In fact, Edward wasn't at all bothered about the university degree. He could understand why a man might want to go digging about in foreign countries unearthing treasures. The desire to sit about in libraries reading dusty volumes, on the other hand, was a far less tangible one—and it was good to think of his son finally getting his hands dirty.

In the event, Sheridan fell in love with Egypt but not with archaeology. The pyramids were truly magnificent, and it was heavenly to float down the Nile on a lovely boat. Why would one want to spend all one's time grubbing about in the hot sun? One had simply to grease the right palms to get hold of the most fabulous treasures and ship them home, where one kept them as trophies or sold them.

It was around this time—as the family home began to fill with amulets and sarcophagi—that the disgruntled and tubercular Edward departed the corporeal plain while gazing confusedly at the mask of Anubis, the jackal-headed god of cemeteries and embalming, which had mysteriously appeared on his bedroom wall.

Not long after his father's death, Sheridan was contacted by Cecile Joubet, a Parisian costumier, who wrote to request permission to view the famed Egyptian collection, and to make free use of its motifs, colors and "spirit" in the creation of a fashion line for the House of Myrbor. Watching this tiny, passionate French girl running her hands over his bronzes, staring intently at his hieroglyphic slabs and holding his jewels up so that the light shone through them, Sheridan was reminded strongly of Cleopatra herself. One month later, he was married to Miss Joubet and utterly in thrall to her world of Egyptian-influenced fashion and interior design.

The present phase of Sheridan's existence, as the new owner of the Tutankhamun, came about after the untimely and abrupt end of his marriage. Cecile, when finished with Egypt, moved on to Orientalism and a passion for a French university professor with an expansive collection of Chinese objets d'art.

"The girl had no staying power," Sheridan moaned as he slumped on the zinc bar at the Coyote Club in Paris. "Changes her men along with her hemlines."

"Courage, *mon ami*." Monique, manageress of the Coyote, patted him on the back and handed him another drink. "All you need is a project—something to help you forget the girl. What you lack is a dream to follow. Now me—I have the dream but no means of making it real. We can help each other. *Vous comprenez?*"

"She's tewwibly cwoss with me." Sheridan jerked a thumb in the direction of Monique, who was back at the door, greeting newcomers. "Would you help me talk her wound?"

"What's she cross about?"

"Oh, she's always cwoss." Sheridan rolled his eyes. "You know who she weminds me of? That old nanny of mine. The cwotchety Iwish one. You wemember? She beat me with a poker, you know."

"Monique?"

"The Iwish nanny. Oh, you wemember her, Gwace. Big warty nose and bla bla."

"Yes." She could see them all as children, playing together: Sheridan, Nancy and herself, while their parents ate dinner and talked about grown-up things downstairs. Sheridan had always preferred it at the Rutherfords' because of their more amenable nanny and also the dolls' tea set. He'd not been allowed one of his own, being a boy. She and Nancy had liked having him about. Being a few years younger than them, he'd been quite easy to order around. That was the only real change in him: the fact that these days he didn't allow anybody to order him around. Except Monique, perhaps. In all other respects, he was just the same as when he was a little boy. "Funny," said Grace after a moment. "I remember your nanny pretty well but I don't remember the warty nose."

He flapped a hand. "Well, perhaps that was poetic license. She jolly well *should* have had a warty nose. Anyway, I think it's the snakes."

"Snakes?"

"The weason Monique's cwoss with me. I met this old snake charmer chappy, used to twavel with one of the big circuses. Gave me a vewwy good pwice on a couple of pythons. Big ones, you know. I thought they could lounge about the place, dwape themselves awound the artifacts. Exotic atmosphere and bla bla."

"*Sheridan!* No wonder Monique's cross with you! I tell you something, if you start draping snakes about this club, you won't catch me in here again."

"Spoilsport. You're as bad as Monique. They don't bite— pythons. They can't even squeeze much if you dwug them. That's what the chappy said. You just dwug the blighters."

Grace had spotted someone. "Margaret! Over here!"

Sheridan tutted. "Darling, what are you about, dwagging such a dwab personage into my club? She has the look of a secwetawy. Vamoose her, if you please, and I'll see you later."

With that he was off, leaving Grace slightly indignant on Margaret's behalf.

"Dwink? I mean, drink?" she asked as Margaret, rather breathless, took Sheridan's place.

Margaret shook her head. "I'm not staying. It's getting late. Work tomorrow and all that. Just had to come and tell you what happened."

"Well?"

A sly smile. "He was there among the crowd. I spotted him. He was wearing a fake beard and mustache, but it didn't fool *me*."

"*Really?*"

"I went up and tapped him on the shoulder. 'Mr. O'Connell,' I said. 'Would you kindly sign my book?'"

"And? What did he do?"

"Well, he pretty much jumped out of his skin. Then he steered me to the side of the room and told me he'd sign if I kept quiet about who he was."

"What was he doing, skulking about at his own reading in a stupid disguise?"

"He said he'd heard the rumor about the reading, and couldn't quite resist coming along incognito for a look."

Grace snorted. "What was he expecting? To sit in the audience and watch himself up onstage?"

Margaret shrugged. "I suppose he thought it was something of a novelty. I think he likes novelty."

"Quite."

"Anyway, you're one to talk. You were hiding under a *ginger wig* earlier."

A sniff. The girl was getting beyond herself again.

"Look at this." Margaret pulled out her copy of *The Vision* and opened it at the flyleaf.

To Margaret,
The smartest cookie in the barrel.
With admiration,
Dexter O'Connell

"He admires me, do you see that?" She was preening now. "Out of all those people who'd come to hear him read, *I* was the only one to recognize him. So now there's one person in this world who understands how smart I really am!"

"Well, that's very nice for you, I'm sure." Grace felt her face twitching.

"You're jealous! Look, there's no need for that. He gave me a message for you." Now she fell irritatingly silent. Drawing out her moment of power, perhaps.

"Well? What did he say?"

My, how she loved being the holder of secret knowledge.

"He said, 'Tell your friend it doesn't suit her to play demure.' And he handed me this." She produced from her bag a sealed envelope, which she slid across the table.

Grace took up the envelope. It felt heavy and contained a familiar shape.

"It's a key, isn't it?" said Margaret. "Must be to his hotel room. What will you *do*?"

"He's the most arrogant, presumptuous man I've ever met." She still hadn't opened the envelope. "And I'm tired of his games."

"But what will you *do*?"

"I shall post this back to him." And she put the envelope away in her bag. "Now, you'd better get going, hadn't you? Work tomorrow and all that?"

"I suppose so." She looked as though she was hankering to change her mind and have a drink after all. "Am I leaving you on your own though?"

"Not at all. She has company." It was John Cramer, standing beside their table. Cramer, with a broad smile on his face, the expression in the brown eyes barely discernible in the dim light of the club.

"What are you doing here?" It came out almost panicky. She tried to calm herself. Margaret was glancing from one to the other, but then her gaze slowed and lingered on Cramer's face.

She's attracted to him, Grace realized. And then, looking about her at the women at nearby tables, most of whom were staring: They're pretty much *all* attracted to him.

"Thought I'd better bring you these." From behind his back he brought out her ginger wig and hat. "I believe you dropped them on your way here."

"Were you *following* me?"

"Not really. Well—actually, I suppose I was." Cramer was blushing a little. "I was intrigued by the disguise. And I thought, I bet she's going somewhere worth going to. Let's find out."

Now it was Cramer who blushed and seemed lost for

words. Margaret waved awkwardly, mouthing something, and slipped off.

"Is this fellow bothewing you, Gwace?" Sheridan was back— and now the two men were all grins and handshakes and exclamations of, "Haven't seen you in years, old chap." Sheridan made a weak joke about the wig and hat and had them removed. Cramer started asking him about the Tutankhamun, and a waiter set down three more Luxor Lizards on the table.

"I met this old dog in Caiwo a few years back. What larks! I'd been on a dig. He was . . . What *were* you doing in Caiwo, John?"

Cramer shrugged. "Just taking a holiday."

"Have you wead any of his witing, Gwace? He's tewwibly good, you know, when he interviews people. Puts them wight at their ease and gets them to tell him all sorts of secwets."

"Enough of that, Sheridan." Cramer lit a cigarette.

"He made his big splash with an interview with Pwesident Harding a few years back. Did you know? The man was up to his neck in it—the mistwesses, the Teapot Dome scandal—you name it. You'd think the last thing he'd want to do would be to talk to someone like John. All so wevealing. What was that thing he said, John? 'I can deal with my enemies. It's my goddamn fwiends that have me walking the floor at night.'"

"Something like that."

"Gwace is a bit of a journalist too, did you know that, John?"

"Sheridan—"

"She wites that Diamond Sharp column in the *Hewald*. It's tewwibly popular. She's wather naughty, our Gwace." And then—seeing her face—"Oh dear. I've committed a faux pas. See how she's looking at me? As if she wants to thwottle me or something. I sort of forgot it's a secwet that Gwace wites that column."

The dance orchestra were playing a good, fast Charleston. Grace fixed a smile on her face. "Care to dance, John?"

They whirled and kicked around the dance floor, she and Cramer, and she sensed people staring. Grace had always found it impossible not to feel attracted to men who danced this well, just as she'd never been able to sustain an attraction for hopeless dancers. They moved close together and her arms went around his neck, and she knew that they looked like lovers. There was only one other man in London who could dance her about this well.

She had to find a way to calm herself down.

"You seem to be spending a lot of time with my sister," she said as they walked back to their empty table.

"Nancy's a lovely woman. But you know that. We've become friends."

Grace took out her cigarettes and passed one over. "She's had a hard time. I know that you have, too."

"She told you, then? About my wife?" She noticed, now, that he appeared still to be cold sober, while she was like something spilling over. Those damn cocktails! And he hadn't even touched his. The glass was still full. She reached for it herself.

"It's been five years since my wife died," he said. "But it doesn't make any difference. Time, I mean. That whole thing about time being a great healer—it's just something people say. An easy line."

"There are too many easy lines," said Grace. "The war caused so much loss and grief that we gave up wearing mourning clothes. Otherwise we'd *all* have been in black all the time. London would have become a city of crows. But when we put away the clothes, we lost the knack of how to mourn. We shoved it in a drawer, so to speak, and mislaid the key. It's all stiff upper lip and soldiering on these days. We don't understand how to talk about grief anymore."

"You're so right," said Cramer. "I've been lost, really, in my own secret world of mourning. After the first few months it becomes something unspeakable. Untouchable. You're supposed to get over it. Pick up the pieces and stick them back together in a new shape. But they don't tell you *how*." He shook his head. "God, it's good to speak to you about this, Grace. You and Nancy—you don't just turn away from it. You're the first people I've been able to talk to properly in such a long time."

"It's been less than two years since Nancy lost George."

"I know."

"She might seem robust and content but it's all on the surface. Underneath she's still very frail."

"I know that, too." He was looking at her oddly.

"The Rutherfords are a tight-knit family. Since we lost George we've been closer than ever."

"Grace, I have the utmost respect for your sister. I'm not playing any kind of game with her. We're friends."

Something twisted and tightened in Grace's belly and she looked away, down into the golden cocktail in front of her. "Good. Because if you hurt her, I'd have to kill you. Another dance?"

It was an old-fashioned waltz this time. Couples drifted slowly about as though floating over the floor. Held close to Cramer, Grace breathed in the inky scent of his skin. She supposed her sister must have held him this way. She couldn't imagine it somehow. He wasn't Nancy's type, not judging from the past. But then he wasn't hers either.

"Nancy doesn't like mustaches," she whispered into his ear.

"How about you?"

"Can't say I'm particularly fussed."

"You like Americans, though. At least it seems that way in your writing. But perhaps I'm not 'impossibly handsome' enough?"

Silently she cursed Sheridan. "What is it between you and O'Connell? You say you can't stand him but you seem to be following him around like a dog."

She felt him tense up at that name. "What about you? Why were you wearing that ridiculous wig and hat tonight?"

"Clearly I didn't want him to know I was there. Seems it was the other way around with you. You wanted him to see you."

He let go of her now, while the band played on, and headed back to the table. After a moment she followed.

Seated again, he asked the waiter for a tonic water with lemon. She knew she shouldn't drink any more but ordered a gin fizz anyway and placed a cigarette in her long ebony holder.

"So?" she said. "Are you going to tell me anything about you and O'Connell?"

A sigh. "We were friends at Yale, he and I. Roommates. Closer than close. Along came a girl—a very special girl—and that was the end of our friendship."

Grace blew a smoke ring. "You're seriously saying it's all about a girl?"

"Isn't it always? She was a very special girl."

"There has to be more to it than a squabble over a girl, no matter how special she was. This was years ago. Life has moved on for both of you. Or it should have."

A shrug. An expression of wry helplessness that infuriated her.

"So what happened?"

"I married her. He wrote a book and put her in it. She died."

"You were married to *Veronique?*"

"My wife's name was Eva."

The band struck up a new number. A jazz piece that seemed to turn in faster and faster circles. Over on the floor, the dancers were spinning and capering. Grace struggled for clarity as her thoughts went spiraling.

"Look, I could tell you that O'Connell's a bad lot, that he feeds off people, that he did it to Eva and that he'll do it to you if you give him the chance. But there's no point saying it, is there? You simply will not be warned because you're the kind of girl who's obsessed with intrigue. The more bad stuff I'd tell you about him, the more fascinated you'd become."

She tried to force a laugh. "Don't fraternize with my feminine mystique. I need it intact."

He shook his head. "Mystique? You're certainly trying very hard with your anonymity and your silly disguises. But Grace, anyone would have seen it was you under that wig and hat tonight. You're transparent. Now, let me be frank: You won't be able to resist getting his side of the story. And when he tells you a load of lies about me, it'll make you even more fascinated and you'll be back to me for the next installment. Before we know it you'll be all over us both like a rash."

The smoke came hissing out of her nostrils in an angry stream. "I *beg* your pardon?"

"Dwinks, darlings?" Sheridan was back, laying one hand on Cramer's shoulder and one on Grace's.

"No, thank you, Sheridan." Grace got to her feet. "I should be getting along, actually."

"Aw, don't leave yet. I promise I'll shut up and behave myself." But there was still mischief in Cramer's eyes.

Sheridan wagged a finger at Cramer. "You're a wogue and a scoundwel. Gwacie, dear, don't go home. This man is a wepwobate and I shall have him fed to the pythons as soon as I take delivewwy of them. Listen, there's something I need to talk to you about, just you and me. Something important. Cover your ears, Cwamer, this is none of your business."

"Sorry, Sheridan. Must dash. Another time?" She shot a smile at one man and then at the other. "I'm on my way to see someone."

Four

The moon was disdainfully slender in a violet, pinpricked sky. The West End was falling quiet, and Grace's heels were loud on the pavement as she walked along the Strand. Held tightly in her left hand was a hotel key.

She wasn't going because she was in love, she told herself. She didn't want to please O'Connell or to spite Cramer. And she certainly wasn't "fascinated" by either of those arrogant, slippery, self-obsessed so-and-sos.

What she wanted was to look into that impossibly handsome face, watch its expression become knowing and self-satisfied and then fling the key at it, hard enough to bruise. She would announce that she was certainly not the demure type of girl, and she would turn and walk calmly away, accompanied by her intact dignity and feminine mystique.

In spite of her resolve, the set of her jaw, the jut of her

chin, she wobbled a little as she passed the Hotel Cecil, once considered Europe's finest hotel, but now utterly outshone by its grander, glitzier next-door neighbor. The Savoy was even more imposing by night than by day. All lit up and full of promise. Even at this unsociable hour there were still a couple of Daimlers and a Bentley outside the entrance, a taxi was making a tight turn in Savoy Court, and a few well-dressed but tipsy stragglers were still trickling out through the revolving doors, chattering loudly.

She did her best to assume the air of confidence of one who belongs, dangling the key conspicuously so that the blue- and gold-clad doormen would see it and assume she was a guest. She avoided the eyes of the woman polishing the brass and the clerk at the desk as she strolled fake nonchalantly past Reception. The grand front hall was suitably mellow—not too much lighting for this late hour, with most of the revelers long gone and the morning papers not yet arrived. And yet a light still glowed from the Grill Room. She asked the lift boy for the fourth floor and pressed a coin into his hand. It would be a commonplace occurrence, of course—a well-dressed, purposeful young woman wandering into the hotel by night, knowing precisely where she was headed. Discreetly conspicuous. Respectably unrespectable. She hated it though—the very thought of what might be going through the mind of the lift boy. Her hand, the one that held the key, was coldly sweaty.

Standing before his door, she wished she hadn't drunk that last gin fizz. The key was in her hand, but the very idea of walking in unannounced was so bold and brazen that it made her cringe. She should knock. That was the thing to do. She raised her hand and then stopped, lowered it again. Knocking was the demure way. The key—her possession of it—was itself a challenge.

He was lying on his side in the bed, facing away from her, and his deep, even breathing told her he was asleep. It was too dark to make out more than the vague shape of him. Slipping her shoes off, she approached the bedside table and flicked on the lamp. Still he didn't stir. His shoulders and back were bare, exposed. One arm was curled around his head, the other stretched out over the covers. She looked around her at the huge bedroom, taking in its opulence. Plenty of drapery and tassels. A lot of gilt-edged ornamentation. An Oriental screen. Through a half-open door she glimpsed another room, made out the dim shapes of desk, chair, chaise longue. Through a second door was the marble bathroom.

A sound from the bed, making her jump. A murmur, nothing more. He'd rolled over onto his back. His sleeping face had a gentleness to it that she hadn't seen before. He'd lost the guile and swagger that attracted and repelled her in equal measure. So *now* what was she going to do? She could hardly hurl the key into his sleeping face. Was she going to wake him up simply in order to do so? Really, the very notion of throwing the key at him seemed ridiculous now that she was standing here beside his bed.

The smartest and most stylish course of action would be to place the key beside his face on the pillow and simply leave. That would be the way to regain control of this situation. He'd surely come chasing after her in no time. The idea lit a flame inside her, warmed her . . . Yes, she had to admit it to herself: She still wanted him. She wanted him more than ever.

But what if he *didn't* come chasing after her? What if he read her stylish maneuver as plain old rejection? Was she really the sort of man to go running after a disinterested woman?

Another sound. A sigh. There was a smile on his mouth. His eyes moved beneath the lids. He was dreaming, it seemed.

She wanted to get inside his dream. The idea gripped her, held her. Before she knew what she was at, she was unbuttoning her dress, stepping out of it, unclipping her brassiere . . .

There was more than one way to take control of this situation.

When she pulled back the covers and slid into the bed, he still didn't stir. Lying there beside him, her naked body only inches from his, she experienced an intense sense of anticipation. A delicious mingling of lust and nervousness that made her want to laugh out loud. At last she reached out and touched him. Tentatively, and then more definitely, placing her hands on his chest, warm and firm, lightly sprinkled with hair—feeling, as she did so, a kind of ownership—yet aware, nonetheless, that so many other hands had been placed here, like this.

"Hello, Grace." His voice was still laden with sleep, his eyes still shut. "I didn't know if you'd come. I thought perhaps I'd have to dance the dance a little more."

"I'm tired of the dance." She kissed one eyelid, and then the other. Tracing the edge of his face, stroking his neck.

His eyes opened. He reached up to touch her face, and brought his own to meet it. "You want to be known," he said. "Really *known* by someone. Don't you?"

She was aware that she didn't care, now, which of them was in control. In fact, the truth went further than that. She wanted to abandon control, to surrender it to him utterly.

"You want to fit with someone," he said. "Don't you?" And then he moved her, moved with her, manipulating her, fitting her body to his. There was no awkwardness in their movements. No clashing of limbs, no misunderstandings. She marveled at the ease of it all. She'd never been so unself-conscious with a man. When she looked down at their bodies moving on and against each other, the very sight made her want him more. And then, at last, he was inside her and it was the most incredibly animal experience, the most purely physical sex she'd ever had. She got up on top of him. He rolled back on top of her.

It had been over a year since she was last in bed with a man, and that had been a one-off with Dickie. It had finished between them long before, without nastiness or recriminations. After an initial period of difficulty and distance, they'd settled back to friendship, and both had seemed comfortable with that. But on this particular evening, out at the Mitre together, they'd both been lonely. He'd come back to the house for a nightcap and they'd sat by the dead leavings of the fire with their brandies, talking about inconsequential things. As they'd sat there, she'd weighed it up. Bed with Dickie would feel friendly and familiar, she'd thought. Safe. She could enjoy it without having to think too much about it. Their story was already at an end and this would be a kind of brief epilogue. A welcome interruption in the expanse of nothingness that was her love life at that time. A pleasant reminder that she might still be desirable.

She'd gotten up and taken hold of his hand and he'd looked up at her with surprise and confusion. They'd climbed the stairs in silence and gone quietly to her bedroom, where their lovemaking was gentle and melancholy. Afterward, huddled with him in the single bed, finishing up her brandy, Grace had found she was reeling with the sadness of it—the futility of the attempt they'd each made to escape their loneliness through the sex act, or at least to share the loneliness.

"We shouldn't do this again." It was Dickie who'd spoken. The words were in her head too and she'd been preparing herself to speak them aloud. It was such a relief to know he felt the same way as she did. It made her want to hug him. She'd been about to agree, vigorously, when he added: "There's still something special between us, Grace. We shouldn't squander it this way."

They were eating chocolate cake in the bed, Grace and O'Connell, and drinking champagne. Scattering crumbs over and between the crisp linen sheets. He had announced he was peckish and pushed the bell push marked "waiter." The waiter then appeared so rapidly that Grace couldn't help but wonder if he'd been standing behind the door the entire time, watching them through the keyhole.

"So it's true. You can get absolutely whatever you want just whenever you want it at the Savoy," she said.

He took a bite and passed the remains back to her, leaning against the cushioned headboard and grinning. "Sweetheart, I've always been able to get whatever I want whenever I want it."

"You like things carefully orchestrated, don't you?" She licked her fingers. "I wouldn't be surprised if it was you who started the rumor about tonight's supposed reading. You'd have done it just to see who'd turn up. Just to have a secret little laugh at them all under your fake beard."

He raised an eyebrow. "Do you really think that of me? Did you have that thought racing around in your head while you sat on a folding chair in your ginger wig and hat, waiting?"

"You have no idea how much I regret the wig and hat, Dexter."

"I told you not to call me Dexter."

"Then what do I call you?"

"Come here. Let's get down among the chocolate crumbs."

She was so aware of his strength when he took hold of her again. He could throw you bodily across the room with barely an effort and you'd lie there all broken and crumpled, and how glorious it would be to be broken by him.

"Happy?" he asked her afterward, as they lay side by side.

"I don't know." Now that the heat had ebbed away out of her, she felt ashamed of her weakness. She'd believed herself to be taking strong and decisive action, as she walked along the Strand earlier. But it was weakness, not strength, that had brought her here to him. He hadn't had to so much as lift a finger to get her into his bed. That key had been enough to make her deliver herself up to him like a birthday present. "I don't know where I am with you."

"You want me to tell you I love you or something? Sex isn't love. I wouldn't have thought I'd need to explain that to a woman of the world such as yourself."

She sat up against the headboard, drew her legs up under the blankets to hug her knees. "You once told me you're perpetually in love. That love makes us feel alive."

"Trouble is, you're too used to men falling in love with you. There's enough *bewitchery* in you to make it happen pretty reliably. You decide you want a man and you click your fingers, and down he goes—prostrate on the floor. But think about it. Did you really expect that from me? Is that really who you want me to be?"

She held her knees even tighter. Scrunching herself into a ball. "I wanted you to telephone me or send me a note."

"Sure you did. But don't you see it's better this way?" He reached for the cigarettes on the bedside table.

"For you."

"For both of us." He passed the cigarette across. "Grace, you're not in love with me any more than I am with you. If I'd done all the right things, the predictable things, you'd already have tired of me. I'd have been firmly dispatched with a one-liner in your column: 'Girls, you'd have a more exciting evening with one of his books than with him'—am I right?"

"Maybe." She blew a smoke ring and then stubbed out the cigarette.

Their third time was dreamy and slow. Perhaps it was the effect of the alcohol, but their bodies seemed not to be in the bed or the hotel room at all. It was as if they were in midair. Her eyes locked on to his and she couldn't allow herself to look away, feeling that if she did so, she would fall, and it would be a long way down.

At some point it must have ended. They must have dozed off, for Grace was dreaming about Margaret the typist, her coiled black hair transformed into a snake. John Cramer was in the dream too, playing a wooden flute, and the hair snake uncoiled and reared up to its hypnotic tune.

Five

"*Sit* down, Miss Rutherford."

Mr. Henry Pearson didn't look up from his paperwork.

"Thank you, sir." She sat on the visitor's chair, gazing around at the many miniature oil paintings of horses on the brownish-green, baize-covered walls. Walking into this office was like stepping back into a bygone era. Stale air, floating dust particles, creaking chairs, a very specific sort of silence rather like the silence of a library.

Her focus shifted from the room in which she now sat to a brighter, sunnier vista. After a rather sheepish breakfast at the Savoy, she and O'Connell had taken a walk along Victoria Embankment in the bright blue morning. Heavily laden boats were plowing busily by, churning up the water, making it froth and sparkle. There was as much traffic on the river as on the roads and bridges. London was pulsing with life, and Grace found herself thinking of the blood pumping through her own arteries. Walking beside O'Connell, her hand held in his, she'd been happier than happiness . . .

"Idle person. One who squanders money or opportunity." This was spoken loudly, so that Grace jumped. Mr. Henry's head was still down.

"I'm sorry, sir?"

"Seven letters." At last he looked up over his glasses, thick eyebrows raised. In front of him, she saw, was a newspaper crossword.

Grace swallowed. "Wastrel, sir?"

"Indeed." His smile was too large for the occasion, and vanished after only a second or two. "Obvious, when you come to think of it." Then his head was down again, presumably to write the word into his crossword—and yet she didn't think he did so. Instead, he seemed lost in some invisible detail, leaving her to stare at his bushy Victorian whiskers. His silver-topped cane was resting in a porcelain stand in the far corner of the office, along with an umbrella and an odd-looking object that might have been a suction plunger (though what would he want with one of those?).

How odd it had been to be out with O'Connell in the brightest daylight, beside the silvery, enticing river. A man like him should surely exist only in bars, restaurants and hotel rooms, softly lit and shrouded in smoke, husky laughter and erudite evening quippery. Yet there he was. There *they were*, a couple of night creatures out on the loose in the early morning. It had felt almost normal, almost natural.

Mr. Henry laid down his pencil and sat scrutinizing her. If only she wasn't still in yesterday's dress. She kept a spare outfit at the office for just this sort of eventuality, but had forgotten, today, that it was at the cleaner's. She'd been about to nip out to fetch it when Mr. Henry's secretary had knocked on her door. Still, she hadn't seen Mr. Henry yesterday—perhaps he wouldn't realize. There was such a reek of smoke about her, though, and she was sure there must be a kind of abandon in her appearance. A wild look in her eyes . . .

"My dear, I thought perhaps you might be tired of your occasional—or, really, not so occasional 'chats' with my brother on the subject of your ongoing performance and general demeanor. It occurred to me that you might have something to say to me about it all? Something redemptive, possibly? And since Aubrey is now sufficiently vexed that he's about to wash his hands of you altogether, I thought I should, as it were, step into the breach." While he was speaking, he made a steeple of his fingers; collapsed it; made another steeple.

"Well, Mr. Pearson, I . . ."

She and O'Connell, hand in hand by the river. As their walk had continued, she'd felt their togetherness, their "coupleness," becoming more real. Her confidence had grown, along with her curiosity. Under the shadow of Blackfriars Bridge, where the air was rank with rotting wood, sewage, dead things moldering on the silt bed, all mingling with industrial fumes and the distant whiff of tallow rendering, she'd started asking about Cramer, probing for O'Connell's side of the story just as Cramer himself had predicted.

"Eva was unique," O'Connell had said. "More alive than anyone I've ever known. Lived only in the present—to hell with the consequences. You never knew where you were with her because she didn't know *who* she was from one moment to the next. She was my first love. Perhaps she was my only real love."

Even hearing him talk about a *past* love in this way was difficult. "That's the way children are," Grace had said. "She sounds like a child."

He'd blown a trail of smoke into the wind and passed the cigarette across to her. "Maybe. She was crazy, that's for sure. She wasn't cut out for marriage."

"And yet she married Cramer."

"It was a huge mistake, that's what she wrote me. She wrote me lots of letters all those times he put her in the hospital. *Asylum*, I should say. That's what he did to her, Grace. Shut her away. In the end she killed herself."

"*What?*"

"It was tragic, of course, but entirely in character. Eva wasn't someone who would ever have settled down the way Cramer wanted. It's impossible to imagine her growing old."

"Miss Sharp?"

SNAP.

Mr. Henry had reached across the desk and clicked his fingers right in her face. This room was terribly hot. *What* had he just called her?

"Yes, you did hear right. I know about your other persona. Your other little job."

Grace touched her hand to her forehead, just gently. "How . . . ?"

"You're rather more naïve than I'd have expected, young lady. A secret of that sort doesn't stay secret for long. Not in the world of newspapers."

The sun had grown stronger over the river. Reflecting and refracting off the water in dazzling darts of light. Someone on one of the boats had been singing in a deep baritone. The voice was operatic and resonant, but Grace couldn't spot the singer, no matter how hard she looked.

"Cramer blames me for Eva's death," O'Connell had said. "I'm a convenient scapegoat for him so that he doesn't have to look closer to home."

"But how can he think it's *your* fault?"

"He'd have you believe I pillaged our shared experiences when I wrote *The Vision*, that I actually stole a part of his and Eva's lives and made it public property in a horribly distorted form. He believes she couldn't cope with that, and that it broke her down. Now he's taking revenge by writing his own novel."

"Are you sure? I thought he was a journalist."

O'Connell made a face. "He told me so himself. Made it a kind of threat."

"So what's it about? Is it his version of what happened between the three of you? Does he have a publisher?"

"I don't know." He threw his cigarette butt into the river. "All I know is that I've just spent five years out in the wilderness trying to get away from all this. And John Cramer is determined not to let it go."

"Remarkable bit of work, that column of yours." Pearson's fingers made a steeple. Then another.

"Really, sir? Thank you." She knew it wasn't a real compliment though. O'Connell and the river walk were evaporating now. The solid stuff of her life—Mr. Henry and his office, the dull and the everyday—was becoming vivid and worrying.

"Oh yes. But if you don't mind me saying so, you have a problem. It's rather like the occasions when I ask Miss Hanson out there to make me a little snack. Perhaps a sandwich or two filled with Potter's meat spread. Miss Hanson's sandwiches are always spread just a little too thin."

Grace swallowed and felt herself tense. Beneath the desk her feet were wrapped tightly around the legs of her chair.

"It isn't a good idea to spread yourself too thin, Miss Rutherford. It's not for me to tell you which path you should choose to follow in your life. But you *do* need to choose a path and stick to it. It isn't enough just to be talented."

"I understand, sir. I *am* serious about this job, sir." And she was now. She was.

"Right then." He rustled the newspaper in front of him.

"Thank you, sir." Realizing this was her dismissal, she got to her feet.

"Oh, Miss Rutherford . . ." He was writing something into his crossword. "The Potter's account is back with us. I thought you might like to know."

The horses in those paintings on the walls: All of them were caught midjump. Not one had a single hoof on the ground.

The West-Ender
May 2, 1927

Thank you, darling readers, for the veritable cacophony of agreement that Good Girls are Dull. Truly you are my sisters in high-spiritedness. Together we'll make our own Charleston-dancing, bob-cutting, cigarette-smoking contribution to Darwinian evolution, while the dissenters (there were a few in my postbag, I must admit) sit at home embroidering moral sentiments in cross-stitch and going to bed early. For those who have shown an interest, all is progressing very nicely now with that Handsome Devil, and this hasn't come about through sitting and waiting and being demure.

Life is so much better this week. Wouldn't you agree? This newly gorgeous weather has me all frisky and full of ideas and innovations. First, may I request that someone design and put in our shops a range of fully reversible skirts? On those awkward occasions when one is forced by circumstances beyond one's control to turn up to work in yesterday's clothes, one could simply turn the skirt inside out and—hey, presto, another outfit would be born and nobody would be any the wiser. Come on, couturiers. We have entered an age of mass production and this is an idea for the masses. Just think of the sales potential!

To my second seasonal notion: We're now at that delicate moment of the year when you want to start the evening with cocktails alfresco in that rarest of West End spaces, the hidden-away garden (my current favorites being a sweet, ivy-lined courtyard at the Bombardier on Drury Lane, and the newly opened terrace at the Lido Club, complete with Greek statuary)—but you then need to retreat inside around eight or nine o'clock when your arms and legs have broken out in attractive goose pimples and your teeth are chattering. Come on, publicans and nightclub owners: It's time to put your heads together to devise some form of gas-fired or

electrical outdoor heater so we can have our cocktails and drink them, too!

Innovation three: One of you nightclub owners should have a complete revamp in the Oriental style. Anyone who has ventured out on the wild side to Limehouse (I'll try anything once, as you know—even an intimidating stew of octopus, though that was not quite deliberate) would understand the appeal of eating Peking duck pancakes or sweet and sour pork whilst playing mah-jongg for money and watching people in kimonos try to dance a Charleston 'neath an array of gaudy Chinese lanterns. Go on, Sheridan Hamilton-Shapcott—you're a man who likes a bit of novelty, and I promise you this would be better than snakes. Yes, readers, you did read it right. My favorite fop is bringing live pythons to his new Tutankhamun nightclub, but apparently we shouldn't be nervous because, "They don't bite and they can't squeeze much if you dwug them." Enough to give you the cold shudders? Reptiles aside, though, I have to report that the Tutankhamun is now London's most remarkable nightclub, laden with treasures from Ancient Egypt and staffed by splendidly pretty boys and girls in black wigs, Egyptian makeup and, in some cases, loincloths. Hie thee along for a Luxor Lizard cocktail, and get there quickly before the serpents arrive!

A witty, disreputable friend whispered into my ear the other night, which struck such a chord with me that I've decided to adopt it as my personal motto.

"An opportunist is a girl who can meet the wolf at the door at night and appear the next morning in a new fur coat."

I think I might embroider this in cross-stitch and hang it above my bed.

Diamond Sharp

Six

Hedonism. That's what it was. Sheer, dizzying, magnificent hedonism. So delicious you wanted it to last forever. So wildly out of control that you knew it couldn't possibly do so.

Life at Pearson's had been just tickety-boo since Grace's little chat with Mr. Henry. She'd finally hit on a Baker's Lights campaign which directly addressed women. "Fancy a cake? Reach for your Baker's. Lose those unwanted pounds with Baker's Lights." She'd come up with the idea without even trying, and even though her head was miles away.

She'd be scribbling—head down—focused, the way Mr. Henry had suggested she should be, on the latest half-double for Potter's Wonderlunch or Baker's Lights—devising catchy phrases, thinking about what might make a striking image, congratulating herself on the sparkle of her original thoughts, the breezy efficiency with which she strung words together,

the intensity with which she applied herself to this, her role—
when suddenly she'd find herself on the telephone, asking to
be connected to the Savoy. And she'd have absolutely no idea
how it had happened, how she'd come to lay down her tools
in this way without even having made a conscious decision to
do so.

His voice down the receiver. Rich and resonant over that
thin, crackling line. "So, what's on tonight's menu?"

She'd loll back in her chair, kick her door closed and
allow her face to relax into a luxurious cat-that-got-the-cream
smile. She'd tell him their destination: the latest West End
play followed by Ben Bernie at the Kit-Cat Club, drinks at the
Café Royal followed by wine and cheese with a bunch of artists
and a gramophone in a Bloomsbury studio, a party on a river
barge, a duchess's birthday bash, a circus on Blackheath. Diamond and the Devil out to play, night after night, taxiing back
and forth across town in search of brighter lights, stronger
martinis, faster jazz, racier cabaret. Ending each night in his
room at the Savoy.

Bed with O'Connell was like dinner at the most fabulous
of restaurants. Rich, sumptuous, exotic. And nothing—but
nothing—was off the menu. It seemed to her, now, that the
men she'd slept with previously had been rather straitlaced.
She'd always known, instinctively, when to rein herself in,
how to avoid the dreaded *I thought you were a Good Girl.* She
had learned how to be desirably demure, how to deploy a sort
of covert suggestion. You couldn't actually say what you most
wanted in bed but you could use a form of subtle insinuation
to make the man think it was he who'd wanted it and initiated
it. She hadn't thought it could ever be any other way. But with
O'Connell there were no boundaries, nothing you couldn't
say or do.

THE JEWEL BOX   153

It was a full ten days before she took a "night off." She'd been running on adrenaline. Burning her way through her days at the office and fueling up her nights with alcohol and pure whirling excitement. During those ten days she'd gone back to Hampstead only occasionally, to bathe and change her clothes and shout hello to the family as she headed out the door again. Finally, she needed respite. A cuddle with Tilly and Felix. A decent night's sleep before she drove herself into the ground.

It was Edna's day off. The table was laid with the best crockery and Nancy, all flustered, was running in and out of the kitchen. Under her apron was a chiffon dress in dusky green, one of her best. The children were already in their nightdresses, but had been allowed downstairs again. Mummy was marshaling them needlessly from room to room, perhaps thinking that if they stayed in one place for too long, they'd make a mess either of the room or of themselves.

Cramer's coming for dinner, Grace realized. And with the realization came a weird little tightening of some muscle or other, somewhere in her stomach.

She put her head in at the kitchen. "What are you cooking?"

"Wiener schnitzel." Nancy was bashing at some thin, pink pieces of veal with the tenderizing hammer.

"John's favorite?"

"Not so far as I know." Nancy carried on hammering. Her cheeks were very red. "I believe he's spent time in Vienna though."

There was no "believe" about it. She probably had full details of his trip there, complete with the address of his hotel and a list of all the museums, theaters and restaurants he'd visited.

Her stomach tightened further and she had to take deep breaths to relax it.

It's all right, she told herself. *O'Connell is yours and Cramer is Nancy's. It's all settled and you don't have to worry. Just sit back and enjoy the evening.*

He arrived at seven-thirty on the dot. Grace, who was hiding behind a book in the living room, heard Catherine exclaiming with delight at a bunch of flowers he'd brought— then rushing off to find a vase. And now here he was, standing in the living room doorway. His shirtsleeves were rolled up and his jacket was slung casually over his shoulder. He was too real, somehow. His hair was too shiny, his eyes too dark, his laugh too loud. The fact of him being here at all—of his physical presence in her house—it produced in her a kind of shock. And Cramer's own manner, when he caught sight of Grace, was far from casual. There was a tensing of the shoulders, an unconscious touching at his mustache as though he were afraid something may be stuck in it.

He feels the same, Grace realized. *He's no more comfortable around me than I am around him.*

"Nancy's making Wiener schnitzel especially for you. With sauerkraut." She laid the book down but remained in her seat. Wasn't sure she quite trusted herself to stand with confidence. "Thought I should let you know in case you have difficulty identifying it."

"It's all right." He touched at his mustache again. "I know what Wiener schnitzel and sauerkraut are."

"Yes, but does Nancy? Her cooking doesn't, as a rule, stretch to much more than cooked ham and boiled potatoes."

"Grace . . ." He looked distinctly awkward. "The other night at the Tutankhamun . . . I offended you, and—"

"Though even *Nancy* is a better cook than me. *Tilly* is probably a better cook than me."

"Uncle John! Uncle John!" Tilly came skipping in, her blond hair loose over her shoulders, her bear dangling from one hand. "I know all the words of 'All Things Bright and Beautiful.' Listen."

She placed herself centrally, in front of the fireplace, straight and tall with her hands locked behind her back, and began to sing in her shrill, little-girl voice. She was pretty much word perfect, though substituting "growing collars" for "glowing colors." While she sang, Felix came crawling after her, getting his knees caught up in his nightie and squeaking with frustration—an articulately wordless command for Grace to scoop him up and cuddle him. She did just that, finding comfort in his warmth, as one might with a cat. Until he started wriggling madly, at which point she set him down and watched, with irritation, as he crawled straight across to Cramer and tugged at his trouser leg to be picked up again.

The hymn ended in applause and Grace was across the room in an instant, dragging Felix off Cramer with an expression that pretended to be an apology.

"Bedtime, children."

Tilly stamped a foot. "Oh, Auntie Grace! I was going to sing 'There Is a Green Hill Far Away.'"

"It's May, Tilly. Christ rose from the dead weeks ago."

"But I like the bits about dying and blood."

"Typical woman." Cramer caught Grace's eye, all jovial.

"You're lucky my mother's not in the room. She'd sling you out for less than that. Come on, Tilly. Bed."

"Auntie Grace, is Uncle John going to be my new father?"

This came out of the blue, at that moment when Tilly was

fond of asking her most difficult questions: after her stories, as she wriggled down in the bed, and just as Grace was about to turn off the light.

"Oh, darling." She looked into Tilly's wide-open eyes, and saw George. George's seriousness. George's intensity. "Nobody can ever replace your daddy. He'll always be with us."

"Will he come back from the dead, like Jesus?"

"Not exactly, no. He's alive in you, Tilly. In you and Felix."

But Tilly was cross now. She thumped her arms down on the counterpane. "That's a lie. He's gone. I can't even remember him."

Grace tried to hug her, but Tilly was too angry for hugs.

"It's not fair. Elizabeth has a new father. He got lots of medals in the war and now he's a bank manager and counts up all the money. I want Uncle John to marry Mummy so I can have a new father, too."

It was hard not to laugh. "Fathers aren't like library books, Tilly. We don't keep getting new ones. And anyway, perhaps Mummy and Uncle John don't want to marry each other. Did you think of that?"

Tilly scowled. "Why not? They like each other. And he's always here. He might as well just give up his house and live with us."

"Tilly . . ." Just how often *was* he here? She had to curb the urge to start asking detailed questions about when he came over and how long he stayed. He wasn't sleeping over, she was pretty sure. Nancy wouldn't give her all without a ring on her finger at the very least.

"Well, if he's not going to marry Mummy, he should marry you."

"*Tilly.*"

"Or me. He could marry me! I could be a bride in a white

dress. He'd be my bridebroom." And now she was smiling again and settling herself down for the night. Grace bent to kiss her on the forehead.

"This cabbage is quite peculiar." Catherine Rutherford prodded it with her fork. "Is it pickled or something?"

"It's in the Austrian style," said Nancy. "And frankly, Mummy, I think *you're* more pickled than the cabbage."

"Stuff and nonsense." But Catherine's accent was slightly more horsy than usual—a sure sign that she was tipsy. She rarely drank and tonight she'd taken a sherry before they'd even begun on the bottle of Hock. "Anyway, what if I am? Is there a written rule that only the young may get tight? Is the more mature lady to confine her evening activities to knitting, tea drinking and gazing into the fire, longing for her lost youth?"

"Well, you *do* have your bridge night . . ." Grace caught Nancy's eye and they both giggled. It was all much easier now they were sat around the family dinner table. The sisters had slipped into their traditional roles as accomplices, finishing each other's sentences and exchanging glances above their wineglasses.

"You flibbertigibbets don't know you're born! Let me tell you—" Catherine gestured with her knife and a fleck of sauerkraut flew at Cramer.

"Oh, here we go." Nancy rolled her eyes.

"I was thrown in a cell for the good of you whippersnappers . . ." Grace mimicked her mother's voice.

"Were you really, Mrs. Rutherford?" Cramer looked genuinely interested. "What was the charge?"

"I committed the most heinous crime of campaigning for a woman's right to vote." Catherine pushed her glasses up her nose and sat proud and erect.

Nancy leaned over and whispered loudly to Cramer: "She threw some eggs and flour at a couple of Members of Parliament at a Liberal Party meeting."

"I landed one of the blighters right on his bald head!" She was positively triumphant now. "I'll have you know, young man, that I was a member of the WSPU. I was arrested with Emmeline Pankhurst."

"That's the Women's Social and Political Union," Grace explained. "Mummy, you're forgetting that John's American. He won't have the first clue about the Pankhursts or the WSPU."

Behind the merriment, Grace was studying Cramer. His wineglass was filled with water and he hadn't had a single drop of the Hock. He'd been sober the other night, too—it had struck her at the time. Was he a teetotaller? A former drinker, perhaps?

"Did you refuse food, Mrs. Rutherford? Did they force-feed you?"

"Do call me Catherine." She was enjoying the male attention.

"Daddy got her out too quickly for all that," said Grace. "She didn't have time to refuse so much as one single meal."

"She was absolutely livid," added Nancy.

"They did put her in a cold bath, though," Grace added. "And they were jolly unpleasant." Again, the sisters looked at each other and giggled.

"You ungrateful wretches!" But Catherine appeared cheerful. Glad to have the conversation focused on her. Every minute or two, she glanced across at the flowers Cramer had brought, now in a vase on the mantelpiece. Cream roses and big daisies, cut from his garden.

"You know we're just teasing, don't you, Mummy?" Grace turned back to Cramer. "We can't quite help ourselves.

Underneath it all we actually think she was frightfully heroic. They all were, those women."

"*'Are,'* not *'were,'* if you please," said Catherine. "Anyway, enough of all this. Tell me some more about your work, John. What are you writing about at the moment?"

"Oh, you know. This and that."

Nancy leaned toward Grace conspiratorially. "There he goes again. All bashful. He won't say so but I think he's writing a novel."

Grace looked from one to the other. Nancy was at her most playful and attractive this evening—her eyes bright, her face aglow with something that might be happiness. Cramer was toying sheepishly with his cutlery.

"*Are* you, John?"

"Frankly I wouldn't have the time. There's too much going on in the real world. Who has the time for making things up?" When he glanced up, specifically at Grace, his eyes had resentment in them. *Only he,* they seemed to say. *Only he has time for all that.* Then the moment was over, and he was moving on. "I'm working on a big article about transatlantic flight at the moment. You'll know about the Orteig Prize?" Noticing Catherine's blank look, he explained: "Raymond Orteig has offered a twenty-five-thousand-dollar prize for the first nonstop flight from New York to Paris or vice versa."

"Is there any news on those Frenchmen? Nungesser or whatever his name is?" asked Nancy.

Cramer shook his head. "They were last heard of somewhere over Ireland. I'm afraid it's been too long now. They must have come down in the ocean."

"Those poor men." Catherine's hand was on her chest in a theatrical gesture. "Daredevil pioneers, the pair of them. What a terrible shame."

"There's another fellow about to try it though," said Cramer. "A mail pilot, would you believe? He plans to take off from Long Island on the twentieth. And he's going solo."

"You think he stands a chance?" asked Grace. "On his own, like that?"

"Well, they're calling him the Flying Fool back home. But I think they're wrong. He's going to be the first man to fly across the Atlantic, and I'm going to be the first man on the scene. I'm going over to Paris and taking a photographer with me. I'll write it up for the *New York Times,* of course, but you just wait and see—it'll be *my* name you'll see in your newspapers, too. And his of course—his name is Lindbergh." He gave her a look. "Sometimes you're better off on your own."

Afterward, Catherine served up her bread pudding with custard.

"This is very much like something Mama used to make." Cramer was already through his and scraping every last morsel from the dish. "We'd have had it with a caramel sauce." And then, a hasty afterthought—"Yours is superior, though, Mrs. Rutherford."

"Do call me Catherine."

"How about your wife?" asked Grace.

"Eva didn't cook." He laid down his spoon.

"She was very beautiful." This came, surprisingly, from Nancy. "That is, if the photographs in your house are anything to go by."

"Photographs don't tell the whole truth." Cramer was snappish. "They can't capture a whole person."

Grace glanced from one to the other. Nancy's eyes were cast down. Cramer looked as if he wished he hadn't been so abrupt.

Catherine got up and began to pile up the dishes.

"I have lots of photographs of George." Nancy's voice

was calm, measured. "Sometimes they comfort me. I look at him—at the way he was—and I remember how happy we were together. But sometimes it rips me apart to see him in his uniform with that stupid, unknowing smile on his face. It makes me so angry with him. How unreasonable is that, eh? Poor George is the one who's dead, after all. And there's something even worse. It's becoming more and more difficult to really *see* George—you know, in my mind. Increasingly, I have to look at the photographs to remember his face properly. I suppose it's inevitable that this should happen. But it makes me so very sad to realize that he's disappearing even from my memory. Really, there's no way of keeping him alive."

Looking at Cramer—at a new darkness in his face—Grace suspected this was the very last thing he'd wanted to hear. Cramer and his secret, incommunicable world of grief that lay behind and beneath and beyond everything in his life. When he spoke, it was directed more to Grace than to Nancy.

"Eva disappeared a long time ago. She was disappearing years before she died. Right from when O'Connell published that book. It was as if he'd used her up to create Veronique. Robbed her of her energy, her character, so that there was nothing left of her. Do you understand what I'm saying? For a long time she was ill and in the hospital, refusing to see anyone, hardly talking. Just scribbling letters and reading books day after day. Dreaming about how it would all be when she got better. Every now and then I'd get a glimpse of the old Eva—and then it would be gone again. I can't describe to you how awful it was to watch her disappear."

Later—much later—when Cramer had left, Grace attacked the washing up and Nancy grabbed a tea towel while they chewed over the evening.

"All that stuff about his wife," Grace said. "You don't lose your personality because someone's put you in a book. That's like the American Indians thinking that you could steal someone's soul by taking a photograph. What it comes down to is that Eva lost her marbles, and Cramer's decided to put the blame on O'Connell and his book."

"You seem to know a lot about it all." Nancy rubbed at a plate. "Or, at least, you think you do."

"Am I wrong?" Grace eyed her. "What's he said to you?"

"Bits and pieces." Nancy put the plate away and took up another. "Enough for me to know there are two sides to the story. Three, actually. I don't think you realize how biased you are."

Grace looked up at the kitchen window, at their two reflections. The glass was misted over, and their faces were blurred and vague. "What do you mean?"

"You're in love with Dexter O'Connell so you simply take on face value everything he tells you."

"I am not!" She clattered a plate in the sink.

"Are you quite sure? You were ridiculously happy, then hellishly miserable and then this last week or two you've barely been here at all. What's more, you have that look on your face."

"What look?"

"Your secretive look. You can't honestly have thought I wouldn't notice?"

"You don't always notice things. Not all the time."

"I've noticed."

"I'm not in love with him." She thumped the plate into the drying rack.

"Well, whether you're in love with him or not, you're obviously having a pretty torrid affair with him."

"Is that so wrong?" She drew a soapy hand across her brow. "I can look after myself perfectly well."

"But *can* you, Grace? After everything John's told me—"

"There you go again. What *has* he told you?"

"Oh, not much." She busied herself with the tea towel. "But you know as well as I do that O'Connell's as famous for being a cad as he is for writing novels."

"But he's fun. And clever. *And* good-looking. *And* rich. *And* exciting. *And* he likes me. Who else is around and available that would tick all those boxes, eh?"

"Well . . ." She seemed as if she was about to say something, but then changed her mind.

She's thinking of Dickie again, thought Grace. Will she *ever* get the message about me and Dickie?

"Look, just promise me you'll be careful. You have good instincts and I hope you'll listen to them. I love you so much, Grace. I can't bear the thought of that man hurting you."

"Oh, darling!" Grace put her arms around Nancy and for a time they simply stood there, holding each other, each sister aware of the other's gentle breathing, the other's heartbeat. "Of course I'll be careful." She could see their reflections in the window, merged into one.

When they'd released each other and returned to the washing up, there was an awkwardness to their silence.

"I read in your column that you've been to Sheridan's new nightclub," Nancy said eventually, perhaps just to break that silence.

"That's right."

"I didn't know you saw much of him these days. I've barely seen him since we were children. Since that nasty business with our parents. How old would we have been?"

"Not sure. Thirteen or fourteen. Let's not talk about all that."

"No." She polished busily at a plate. "No, of course not. But what's he like these days? Sheridan?"

"Quite like he was when he was a child. Odd. Delicate. Lovable, in my opinion, though not in everyone's. Inheriting all that money has made him more sure of himself. And being more sure of himself has made him more and more eccentric. It's as if he's consciously decided to heighten every aspect of his personality. Even his speech impediment."

"Crikey." Nancy raised her eyebrows. "I'd like to see him some time."

"John's an old friend of his," said Grace. "Perhaps you should get him to take you along to the Tutankhamun one evening?"

A frown. "I don't go about with John in that sort of way."

"Don't you?" Grace eyed her as she took up a cast-iron frying pan and began scrubbing. "You know, Nancy, you look happy this evening. Properly happy. I've not seen you this way since before George died."

Nancy shrugged. "Perhaps I am. It's been a lovely evening, after all."

"But?"

"But nothing. It's been a lovely evening. There's nothing more to it than that, Grace. So you may as well stop your prying."

"If you say so." Grace sighed and set the frying pan down on the draining rack. But she wasn't yet finished with the subject of Cramer. "You mentioned over dinner that you think John's writing a novel. What gave you that idea?"

"Oh, just something he said the other day. I can't even remember quite what it was now. And it seems I was wrong anyway. But there's something else, too . . ."

"What?"

"Well, I've been rereading *The Vision*. I was rather interested to look back at it given the current circumstances. I finished it last night in bed."

"And?"

"It's very strange reading a book once you know a little of the real-life people and events that lay behind it."

Grace waited for her to say something further. Grabbed a blackened saucepan and went at it with the brush.

"Now that I know John . . . Well, I have to say that I could hear his voice in it."

"What do you mean, *hear his voice*?"

"I'm not entirely sure. It was rather odd. It made me think about ghosts. Haunted houses, all that. Invisible presences. Not that I believe in any of that."

"What on earth are you on about?"

"Just that John was so patently present, in that book. It was as if he'd had a hand in writing it or something. I do know that sounds bonkers."

"Yes, it does." Grace laid down the saucepan. "Particularly having heard his opinion of it." She was quiet for a moment, mulling this over. "They were very close when O'Connell was writing it. Perhaps that closeness has somehow made its way into the novel."

"Perhaps so."

The window was entirely misted over now. The girls' reflections had vanished in the condensation.

Seven

The Past

On the afternoon of October 17, 1922, the Rutherford sisters, laden down with splendid purchases, stopped off for tea and cake at the Lyons Corner House on Piccadilly. Nancy, on the eve of her twenty-fourth birthday, was positively oozing happiness and vivacity. Grace was quietly cheerful and much occupied in ensuring Nancy had the delightful shopping day she truly deserved.

"I can hardly believe how lucky I am." Nancy's mouth was full of cream cake, and crumbs shot across the table. "Oops, sorry." She dabbed at her mouth with the napkin. "Everything was so horrible for so long. Do you remember my hideous twenty-first?"

"Of course." Grace sipped her tea and turned to look at the string quartet playing bravely on behind the hubbub of conversation, the clattering of teacups, the rumbling of cake trolleys pushed back and forth. "How could I forget? But that's all in the past now."

"You were such a trouper." Nancy took another big mouthful of cake. "Smoothing everything over with the guests and holding the fort. Helping me put George to bed when he finally came staggering back from the pub. Cleaning up the sick."

Grace rolled her eyes. "*Please,* Nancy, must you mention that? Anyway, birthday girl, it's about time you put all that nastiness behind you. George is fine now."

"Yes." Nancy's eyes were bright. "Thank goodness. You know, Grace, I really believed he was doing it to spite me. That he hated me, and I couldn't work out why. You remember how he used to speak to me, don't you? I couldn't look Mummy in the eye. Couldn't bear the fact that she witnessed so much. I mean, you did too, of course, but that's different."

"Let's have some wine," said Grace, brightly. "We should drink a birthday toast."

Oh, rather." Nancy bent to delve in one of the bags at their feet. "I *do* love the blue dress *so* much. You're a peach. I'm going to wear it for the party tomorrow night. Do you think George will like it?"

"He'll love it. You look divine in it."

The waitress came over and Grace ordered two glasses of white wine. The quartet was playing something familiar and cloying.

"Who wrote this music?" Grace asked.

"It was all anger about the war," said Nancy. "George, I mean. Pent-up rage. Boiling blood. Those nightmares . . . I couldn't wake him out of them. I just had to cling tightly to the bed and wait for them to end. I suppose that was what

I was doing more generally. Clinging on and hoping it would all come right again. And then it did."

The waitress brought the wine over. They clinked glasses.

"To you. Happy birthday for tomorrow. Is this Vivaldi, do you think?"

"And to you, too." Nancy clinked again. "For being such a brick. Really, I think it was you who held us together."

"Rubbish." Grace took a mouthful of wine. "Let's look to the future. Speaking of which, what time are you meeting Mummy?"

"Five o'clock. Grace, there's something I want to tell you."

"You'd better drink up then. It's almost half past four. Which film are you going to see?"

The lying had been going on for a very long time. One could argue it started that night in the summer of 1915 when George proposed to Nancy at the farewell dance. Or perhaps it wasn't so much lying as keeping silent. George and Grace had kept silent about what had taken place between them on the Heath earlier that day.

The "keeping silent" continued when he told her about how Steven had really died, and asked her not to speak about it. And then came the letters. He'd asked her to write to him while he was away. How could she have refused him and why should she? They weren't love letters, after all. They were impersonal and newsy—reassuring him that Nancy was well and content, but that she talked about him constantly and missed him. She passed on the Hampstead gossip: Philippa Green's pregnancy; Tabitha Ferrier's roving eye; Frederick Perry-Johnson's return home after losing an arm. She bemoaned the state the house was getting into: the blocked drains, the broken door handle, the damp patch in the kitchen, the drafts.

She told him that he'd better come home soon or the house would fall down around them. She said little about herself.

It seemed right to keep silent about the letters. It wasn't that she had anything to hide. It was just that she didn't know how to explain why she had suddenly taken to writing frequently to her sister's husband. It seemed such an odd thing to be doing. And the longer it went on, the less easy it was to speak of, particularly as George was keeping quiet, too.

The spring of 1918 arrived, and George continued to write only to Nancy, making no mention of the letters he received from Grace. His letters talked mostly of how he missed them all at home, but also of train journeys through lovely scenery, of long days spent marching, of trench foot, boredom and singing. His were letters unaltered by the censors. He kept off subjects that would frighten his wife. But the Rutherford sisters were reading about the big German offensive in the newspapers and listening to the reports. They knew George must be in the thick of it all, and that he couldn't possibly be telling them the whole story. Nancy showed the letters to Grace, who began to think she could discern secret messages through the trivia—messages intended for her only.

When he talks about the heavy rain, she decided, he is speaking about the experience of being shelled. Stories of kicking a football around with the boys back at the billets are really telling a much darker tale. He knows she won't see that. He knows that I will.

Over time, Grace felt increasingly entitled to read George's letters, and if Nancy didn't show her one, she would go digging about in her sister's bureau on the quiet, searching for it. She had begun to see herself as George's secret confidante. Her own letters became less self-conscious and more personal. The fact that George didn't write back to her directly made it easier for her to unburden herself. His silence was a warm one, a welcoming one. By the end of the summer, with all the news reports declaring the German army to be on its knees and the war all but over, Grace's letters had evolved into a kind of episodic diary from which there was little that she held back.

The much-heralded return was destined to prove difficult for all concerned. George's smiles seemed forced. He was overly polite, awkward and twitchy. He appeared to want to hide as much as possible: in bed, behind newspapers, at his job in the City, at the pub with old friends. Late at night, Grace would hear Nancy crying and railing at him. His replies were curt and quiet.

For herself, Grace was only too glad of George's reclusiveness. It was one thing to tell an absent and silent George all her greatest secrets and desires, and quite another to find herself sharing a home with him again. Just to be in a room with him was squirmingly embarrassing. The things he knew about her . . . There was no way to take them back. But she was already going out to work by this time, and took to leaving the house early and coming home late. Quietly she began to save money for a deposit on a flat of her own.

As 1919 wore on, it all got worse. George absented himself more often and drank more heavily. His moody silences were interspersed with episodes of anger. Nancy's disastrous twenty-first birthday party was the last straw. But when Grace announced her plan to move out imminently to a little flat in Bayswater, Nancy grabbed both her hands and begged her not to go.

"I can't cope with him alone . . . He *listens* to you. Yes, he does. He reins himself in when you're here because he doesn't want you to think badly of him. When it's just me, he doesn't care what he says or does."

"You have Mummy," Grace reasoned.

"Gracie, *please* stay for a bit longer. I need you to help me get him back on track. If you could spend a bit of time with him . . . Talk to him . . ."

They began taking walks together on the Heath every few days, Grace and George, at her suggestion. They'd talk a little but often they'd just walk silently. It was an easy silence between them. He seemed to relax in her company, her arm linked through his. Sometimes they'd sit for a while on the bench, near the top of Parliament Hill, where he'd once declared his feelings for her. Grace thought about it whenever they sat there, and she knew he was thinking about it, too. On the return to Tofts Walk, he'd begin to tense up. The silence would have turned stony by the time they reached the house.

Nancy seemed grateful out of all proportion.

"We just walk," Grace would tell her. "And sometimes we sit. He hasn't told me anything. Nothing about the war. Nothing about you. I can't see that it can be helping very much."

"But it *is* helping."

And evidently it was. He was softening, gradually but tangibly. Thawing. He stayed at home more. He eased up on the drinking.

The walks continued. One day, as they sat on their bench, George reached out for her hand, and she let him hold it. There was nothing more—just her hand held in his as they sat there. When they got back to the house, he was positively chipper for the rest of the day. On the next walk he did it again, and this time they sat much longer together. She was aware of his breathing, the sound of it, the subtle movements in his body. The warmth of their joined hands. But she didn't allow herself to turn and look at him. Kept her gaze fixed on the view: London, reduced to the size of a toy town below them.

On the next occasion, when it happened again, she did turn and look at him, at the golden strands running through his coppery hair, at his pale, hollow face—hollowed out by unhappiness and perhaps by memories he couldn't speak about. His hazel eyes were not tranquil as they had been before the war. But they weren't empty anymore either, as they had been when he'd first arrived home.

"Would you let me hold you, Grace?" he said. "Just hold you?"

She moved closer and his arms came around her. Leaning in to him, she tucked her head under his chin, and listened to the beating of his heart while all around them leaves were falling.

There was comfort in the way they'd sit holding each other—and it happened every time after that, of course. They'd sit longer and longer, even when winter arrived and the Heath was cold and wet and windswept. Where they touched, a sort of current ran between them and gave them both sustenance. Each time it happened she sensed how obvious and natural it would be to simply lift her head and bring her mouth to his, but knew this was the boundary she must not cross. It wasn't exactly innocent, what they were doing together, but there was still an ambiguity to it. They simply had to stay the right side of the boundary.

Then, one snowy January day, as they huddled together on the bench, it all became too much.

The trouble is, she said to herself, I'm dwelling on this more and more, and I think he is, too. The longer we resist it, the more obsessed we both become. Maybe if we give in, we can get past it, leave it behind.

She was going to do it, any moment now. She was going to lift her head and kiss him. It simply had to happen.

The Heath was muffled by a layer of snow. Flakes were falling silently, wetly, into their hair, onto their shoulders. Somewhere in the distance, some children were squealing as they hurled snowballs at each other. But it was all very distant. Grace took a steadying breath . . . And George, still holding her, began to speak.

He talked about a time in October of 1915, the La Bassée offensive in the Loos Battle, when his company was waiting in a trench for the order to go over. They'd thought they'd be waiting a few hours, but almost a week later they were still there in the rain and the mud, drinking copious amounts of whisky to keep their heads together, and failing to sleep when their turn came about. All around them were the corpses of their fellow men, growing more and more awful each day, their stomachs swelling and bloating and collapsing, their skin changing color. They watched rats feeding on the bodies of the dead. The stench, he said, was indescribable.

He talked about a soldier from the East Surrey regiment dying in No-Man's-Land.

"We could hear him—his agony—it went on and on and it was terrible to listen to but we couldn't go to help him. The shelling was too heavy. He kept apologizing for the racket he was making. When the stretcher-bearers finally found him, dead, he'd stuffed his entire fist into his mouth—so as to spare us, you see. And so as to be sure none of us would try some foolhardy rescue attempt.

"We never did go over, not that time. Word came eventually that the show had ended and we were to go back."

Grace looked up at him, expecting to see tears, but his face was all white anger.

"Do you know something? Hardest of all were my brief spells at home. All that bogus 'home service' that was all about, while life went on as normal. Women like your mother strutting about in their uniforms, absurd poems about the crimson cornfields and the spilled blood of the brave. We had *no idea* why we were there, Grace. Frankly we had more hatred for our damned colonel than we had for the Germans. You know, he complained, immediately after La Bassée, about the sloppy informality of officers who allowed soldiers to address them by their first names. I don't think any of us who were there could go on believing in God or England or anything much. But I tell you, Grace, it was easier being out there than it was being here, where everyone was so bloody ridiculous about it all. And now, too, with all those empty patriots with their grand words who saw not a moment of the war as it really was, having simply forgotten all about it, resuming the peacetime complacency and ignorance that we went out there to fight for."

Without any discussion, Grace and George stopped their walks. She felt they both knew how close they'd come to crossing that invisible line of theirs. Ironically, his decision to talk to her about his war experiences had prevented anything happening between them. How could the desire for an illicit kiss survive such talk? And yet their shared understanding had deepened as a result of his decision to speak to her. On the walk home he'd held so tightly to her hand that she thought he'd break her fingers.

"I'm going to crack on with my move," she told Nancy. "George is so much more himself again. You don't need me around anymore."

"You're right about George being better," said Nancy. "Life is really quite pleasant at home now, isn't it? In which case, why leave?"

A few days later she was up in her room, packing, the case open on her bed. Everyone was out and the house was quiet. She'd told Nancy she couldn't be dissuaded. It was time for her to get out from under their feet. They needed some privacy, and frankly, so did she.

When the front door banged and heavy feet came running up the stairs, she knew it had to be George. A moment later he came crashing in without knocking. He was red in the face and disheveled.

"You can't go."

"Why not? Because Nancy said so? Has she been crying on your shoulder in some café or other? Asking you to come straight here and try talking me out of it?"

"This has nothing to do with Nancy." He was still breathless from all the running. Just how far had he run?

She sighed. "You know why I have to go."

He appeared to be struggling for the right retort. She was reminded, as she looked into his eyes—all pent-up passion and words unspoken—of what she'd said to him on the Heath years before. *Say it. Make it real.* But then the struggle was over and he was sweeping aside the packing case and her carefully folded clothing so that it all crashed and tumbled down onto the floor. And then he was pushing her down on the bed and she was pulling open his clothes, and finally—finally—they were giving in to the thing that had gripped them both for such a long time, and the relief was immense.

Grace had pondered, in those days when she and George had clutched each other on the Heath, the possibility that if they gave in they could get past it—whatever "it" was. Predictably, this proved not to be the case.

They'd scraped themselves off the bed and dressed in the half-light, awkwardly and shamefacedly. He'd slipped away downstairs without either of them speaking a word about what had happened between them. But once she was alone again, the first thing she did was to push her case back under the bed and put her clothes back in the wardrobe.

From that day on, whenever Grace and George found themselves alone in the house, they were at each other. It was a compulsion. Both quietly encouraged special little outings for Nancy and Mother. Both would absent themselves from gatherings and events if they knew the other was at home on their own. Increasingly, they took risks—creeping about the house at night, sometimes even stealing into the garden shed together. Occasionally, they'd meet at a small hotel near Russell Square, signing the register as Mr. and Mrs. Sharp.

Grace wondered, sometimes, how she'd feel about George if it wasn't for all the subterfuge. Was she in love with the man for himself or simply because he was Forbidden Fruit? She hoped that it was the latter because that meant it would fizzle out over time. The novelty would wear off and they'd withdraw from each other. This, really, was the best way it could end. The least painful way. And it had to end one way or another—there was too much at stake for it to be otherwise.

But it was their sense of guilt, rather than their desire for each other, that wore itself out. The lying became second nature. They stopped worrying that they'd be found out. They even began to believe it was in everyone's best interests that their affair continued. They were all happier this way, after all, including Nancy.

This was the reasoning that gradually shaped itself in

Grace's mind during the two years and ten months of her affair with George. This was the way she saw the situation up until the eve of Nancy's twenty-fourth birthday, when she dispatched her sister and mother to the pictures and went home to sleep with her brother in-law as she'd done so many times before.

But something about October 17, 1922, was different. Grace sensed it, knew it when she heard keys rattling in the front door a good hour or so early, and before she heard her mother's voice saying, "That's it, dear. You go and lie down on the couch and I'll get you a nice cup of camomile tea."

George was deeply asleep, his head on her chest. She had to prod him in the shoulder three or four times before he stirred and coughed and half sat up.

"Shh." She held a finger to his lips. "They're back. Nancy's ill or something. I'll dress and go down. Wait a few minutes before you follow on."

As she slipped out of the room and down the stairs, there was a foreboding that sat, heavy and toadlike, in Grace's stomach. It wasn't so much about the possibility of having been caught, they'd had near-misses before—nearer than this—and somehow they'd always gotten away with it. If a person is trusting and unsuspicious, they simply don't see what's right in front of them. They don't see it because they're not looking for it. No, this was about something else.

"Nancy, darling!" Grace entered the lounge to find Nancy on the sofa looking pale, and Mother holding a hand to her forehead to feel her temperature. "What on earth has happened?"

"She fainted at the cinema," said Catherine. "Came over all weak and wan. Five minutes later she was claiming to be tickety-boo, but I thought it best we came straight home. Right. I'll go and make that camomile tea."

"Must you?" pleaded the patient.

Grace peered at her sister as their mother left the room. Yes, she was pale. But she looked . . . Well, she looked extremely happy. "Nancy, what's going on? Are you ill or not?"

"Not." And now Nancy smiled her biggest ever smile. "It's what I wanted to tell you earlier, Gracie, but I couldn't get a word in edgeways and then the moment sort of passed, and anyway I thought I really ought to tell George first."

"Oh, my darling!" Grace rushed forward, arms open, and in that moment her world shifted utterly. Holding Nancy tight, she glanced up and saw George standing hesitant in the doorway, his face in shadow.

"Well, look who's here," she said, as warmly as she could. "Nancy has something important to tell you." And then, in a slightly quieter voice, "I think I'd better leave you two alone."

𝔓𝔦𝔠𝔠𝔞𝔡𝔦𝔩𝔩𝔶 𝔥𝔢𝔯𝔞𝔩𝔡

The West-Ender
May 16, 1927

I've never been much of a one for cards. I don't have the patience for bridge, canasta confuses me and rummy reminds me of those wet Sunday afternoons in childhood which made me want to scream about the unbearable dreariness of life and rip my hair out at the roots (this was in my pre-bob era, when my hair was long and such a gesture would have been highly dramatic). So you can imagine how thrilled I was at the prospect of the Silvestra Club's new innovation, Wednesday Whist. Frankly, even the thought of a whole evening of card play accompanied by the Silvestra's sluggish jazz was almost enough to send me to sleep. But reader, how wrong I was!

First, I discovered that since my last sojourn, Dan Craven's orchestra has gone decidedly uptempo. Well done, Mr. Craven, for heeding my advice! Then came the revelation that whist is simple, quick and easy (rather like one or two acquaintances of mine, but we'll say no more about that). I swiftly mastered the rules and discovered—oh shock—that I was actually enjoying the game. I attempted an attitude of great seriousness—it seemed the thing to do, what with the tables being specially dressed for the night in green baize and topped with smart little lamps, and the packs of cards all being so new and pristine. But it was hard to keep a straight face when it turned out my gentleman partner was the most outrageous cheat! Really, this should have come as no surprise to me. It stands to reason that any bachelor as handsome and clever as he simply has to be a filthy rotten scoundrel or he'd have been snapped up and married off years ago. In fact, I suggest a trip to Wednesday Whist as an effective way of vetting the character of your new beau. My devilish friend's audacity was staggering, though he remained insistent that it was all down to skill and that no foul play was involved.

But the really fun feature of Wednesday Whist is what happens in between games. After each hand, and before you and your partner move on to the next table, the winning girl chooses to dance either with her own partner or with the opposition fellow. It was so delightful, deliberating between my chap and the other (we won quite a bit, due to the Devil's aforementioned dubious tactics), while the losing lady sat fuming and waiting for her fate to be decided. The resulting Charleston is all the more fun for the mild cruelty involved in these shenanigans, and what's more, there's no tiresome cutting-in.

Also, girls, you should get along to Selfridges to survey the new season's swimwear. It's what they're all wearing in Deauville and down on the Riviera, so I'm reliably told. Plenty of bold horizontal stripes, so probably not for the larger lady. And don't forget your bathing cap. Your bob needs thorough protection from all that sand and salt.

Finally, we should all be thinking, later this week, of Charles A. Lindbergh, a daring

American mail pilot (yes, they fly their post from place to place over there!) who, weather permitting, is to embark on what could be the first nonstop solo flight across the Atlantic, in his airplane, *The Spirit of St. Louis*. Cross your fingers for this fine hero as he takes off from Long Island on the twentieth. Cross your toes, too. Cross every-thing you have. They'll throw the party of the century for him when he lands in Paris.

I bet he doesn't cheat at cards either.

Diamond Sharp

Eight

Marylebone Library was packed. People were seated on folding chairs arranged in rows, but the standing space at the back was crammed, too. The room was usually cavernous and cold, but tonight it was sweltering. The heat came primarily from bodies. Heavy suits and hats had been donned on this warm May evening by people who wanted to look smart, and the effect was to swaddle and insulate the entire room. Much of the formal clothing was black, so the audience had a somewhat funereal persona. The library's habitual dusty aroma was intensified by a strong scent of mothballs and the backs of wardrobes.

The only noises in the crowd were the occasional cough or sniff, the rasp and drag of breath, and a muted something that might have been the sounds of people fanning themselves with hands and pieces of paper, or could even have been the sound of generalized anticipation and anxiety. But now a low hum was added to the subtle soundscape—a hum that vibrated unpleasantly in the ears, the teeth, the stomach. A hum that seemed to Grace to be an explicit escalation of the ever-present background hum that lies behind life; the hum that you sometimes hear when you sit alone in an empty house, or when you lie down in bed at night trying to sleep. Perhaps the sound of the blood in your head.

This hum—the vibrating hum running through the crowded library—was being emitted by the seated woman at the front of the room who was the focus of this gathering, and who faced the audience with eyes closed and palms held out, slightly cupped. She'd been in this pose for over five minutes already when she began her humming.

Grace, who was sitting beside O'Connell in the ninth row (near the back of the room), was trying to guess Mrs. McKellar's age. Her face, devoid of makeup, was pallid, with a suggestion of numerous years, yet there were few lines around the closed eyes and mouth and on the brow. She was dressed in a shapeless yellow robe, and her colorless hair was mostly concealed by a knotted yellow headscarf. She could be a sixty-year-old who'd somehow escaped the effects of age using her own psychic powers, a forty-year-old who had no idea how to dress and present herself, or anything in between. Whatever her age, she was strange, slightly frightening and almost certainly on the make.

The humming had lasted three or four minutes now. The audience as a whole was still and rapt, but Grace shifted on her seat and tried to stifle a yawn. When her stomach gurgled, O'Connell turned and raised an eyebrow.

"I can't help it," Grace whispered. "I haven't eaten since breakfast."

"What happened to lunch? Are you on some crazy diet that doesn't allow you to eat during daylight hours?"

"I had a deadline. But you wouldn't understand the prosaic necessities of my working life, would you? The meat and vegetables of it all." Heads were turning. They were like naughty children at the back of a classroom with their whispers and their giggles. "Where shall we go when this pantomime is over?"

"I think we'd better go someplace that'll give me a better understanding of the meat and vegetables of your working life. Since I obviously want to understand you completely and utterly, my darling." This was delivered with a squeeze of the hand.

"What are you up to?"

"Shh." O'Connell placed a finger on his lips. "You're disturbing the 'ether.'"

"Well, we certainly don't want that." Grace peered again at the humming woman, and then at the crowd around her. "There'll need to be a lot of spirits in that ether if everyone here's to get their money's worth!"

The humming grew louder and climbed a note or two up the octave. The woman sitting to Grace's right clutched at the jet beads around her neck with gnarled hands.

"Imagine how many shillings have changed hands here tonight," whispered Grace. "What sort of person makes a living out of other people's deaths?"

"An undertaker? A florist, a stonemason, a grave digger, a doctor, a lawyer . . . I imagine Mrs. McKellar would say she has a God-given gift and a vocation to help the needy, but that she also has costs to cover and mouths to feed."

"Yes, I expect she would."

"Quiet at the back!" The woman's green eyes were open

and directing a ferocious glare at Grace. "Keep your trap shut or sling your hook."

"Very spiritual," Grace muttered as Mrs McKellar's eyes slid closed again and the humming was resumed. From all around the room, people were staring at Grace. They should by rights have been a bunch of elderly people, this audience. This ought not to have been an appealing evening excursion for men and women in their thirties and twenties; for boys and girls barely over the age of consent.

Everyone in this room has been floored by grief, thought Grace. None of them is free of it yet.

"Ah, Edwin, there you are. And about time, too." Mrs. McKellar rose to her feet, the yellow gown hanging in voluminous folds as she swayed gently, one hand clutched to her forehead. She had already explained to the audience that her "spirit guide" was a boy by the name of Edwin who'd died in the influenza epidemic after the war. It was Edwin who would communicate with the spirits on her behalf. "Who is he, Edwin? Tell us his name." She paused then, cupped her hand to her ear. "Did you say Archie?" Her eyes were open again now. "Or Alfie?" At this last name there was a sharp intake of breath from a woman near the front. "Alfie," Mrs McKellar confirmed. "What do you have to say, Alfie? Something about the children?"

Grace could just about see the woman who'd gasped, between heads. She had to be forty or so. At the word "children," her shoulders slumped. Grace wondered what her facial expression showed.

"Alfie is very sorry," said Mrs. McKellar to the woman, "that he didn't give you any children"—and then, after a searching pause during which the woman tilted her head slightly to one side—"who survived."

There was a choking sound. The woman had started to cry.

"Anything you'd like to say to him, dear?"

"Only that I'll always love him." The woman's voice was cracking.

"He says he loves you, too. He's watching over you from the other side."

"This is obscene," Grace whispered.

"He says you should look after the box," added Mrs. Mc-Kellar.

"The box?" The woman appeared to sit up straighter at this. Her voice became sharp. "*Where* is the box?"

But Mrs. McKellar was done with Alfie. There was a little girl trying to get through now. A girl in a white nightie with a rag doll. This physical detail alerted two sets of grieving parents among the audience, who delivered up their dead daughters' names. A moment later Mrs. McKellar was able to confirm the child was Edith, not Mary, and offered up the usual vague reassurances of eternal love from the other side.

"There's not even any skill in this," whispered Grace. "It might as well be me up there. She's a vulture, and they're too desperate to see it."

"What about Alfie's box?" said O'Connell. "Where did she get that from?"

"Oh, everyone keeps something valuable in a box. It was a racing certainty."

"There's a soldier here," announced Mrs. McKellar. And Grace saw that awful hope on the faces of almost everyone around her. "An officer. Can't quite spot the rank or regiment. He's tall, with reddish hair."

O'Connell elbowed her in the ribs. "Listen up, Gracie. This could be your moment." His face wore that devilish gleam. Was this why they were here? So he could watch her reaction when this charlatan started spouting about dead soldiers? Not for the first time, she felt like a specimen being taken up between his thumb and forefinger and placed under a microscope.

"What's your name, sonny?" said the woman.

A deep breath and another glance at O'Connell. He was just joking with her, that was all. He'd touched a sore point, probably without even knowing he'd done it. They'd spotted the poster together, a couple of days ago, and had come here for a giggle. They hadn't guessed that it would be like this. They hadn't thought it through properly.

"What was that, Edwin?" Mrs. McKellar had her hand on her forehead, and was making as though she was struggling to hear something. "A 'W,' did you say?"

Wilkins.

The word was there in her head, and her heart gave a thud, even as she tried to get a hold of herself.

"There are two soldiers here," said Mrs. McKellar. "Brothers. They look so much alike."

O'Connell gripped her arm, hard. She kept her eyes on Mrs. McKellar, not wanting to look at him. Not wanting to look at anyone around her either—to see her own tension and excitement reflected in their faces. She was not one of them.

"Is it a 'W,' Edwin?" The clairvoyant's voice grew louder. "Edwin, I need names."

Grace closed her eyes, longing for this hideous, suspenseful moment to be over. Behind her eyelids, George and Steven were sitting at the Rutherfords' kitchen table, playing cards.

"Oh, so it's an 'M' now?" Mrs. McKellar sounded irritated. "Edwin, you really need to learn your letters better."

No "W" then. No Wilkins.

"Grace." O'Connell's hand was still on her arm. "Are you all right?"

"Pardon, Edwin? Did you say Michael? Matthew?"

The woman beside Grace sniffed loudly and clawed at the jet beads.

"Do you want to leave, darling?" His voice was full of concern. And perhaps something that was more than just concern. Grace allowed herself to turn and look at him.

"She's falling!" The psychic staggered and grabbed at her chair. "It's such a long way down! Poor girl, lying there on the ground with her necklace broken and her neck, too. Pearls scattered all around her."

"Let's get out of here." O'Connell got to his feet, reaching for Grace's hand. "I've had just about enough of this."

It was late—about 3.00 A.M. From outside the office window, the streetlights had joined forces with the moon to cast a silvery glow across the entirely empty surface of the long, oak desk. The floor was scattered with pencils, a pen, an ink blotter, a framed photograph of a woman with elaborate hair, two foolscap files, some loose sheets of paper and a telephone; the receiver of which lay as far distant as the cord would allow, in wild telephonic abandon.

Grace and O'Connell were sitting side by side on the dusty carpet, their backs against the wall, sharing a cigarette, tapping their ash into a china teacup. Her hair was tousled and her legs were bare. Her clothes were strewn somewhere among the desk debris. His tie was undone and his shirt open. He'd already retrieved his trousers from the mess and put them on again. Grace rather liked the fact that the bold, blasé O'Connell was too nervous to be here without his pants for more than a few minutes.

"What's his name, the guy who sits in this office?" O'Connell tugged on the bottle of white wine he'd smuggled out from Ciro's under his jacket, and passed it across to her.

"Aubrey Pearson. He's one of the two brothers who own the company. He's repellent."

"What does he think of you?"

"He thinks I'm a disruptive influence. He'd like to give me my marching orders."

O'Connell leaned over to kiss her lightly on the lips. "I guess we've just given him good reason to do it. If he ever finds out."

Grace shivered and took a long swig from the wine. Sobriety and common sense were returning swiftly and she didn't want them to. She wanted to stay in that deliciously perilous moment.

"So, have you gained a better understanding of the meat and vegetables of my working life, then?"

O'Connell took back the wine bottle. "No, but I do know how good it feels to have you on your boss's desk. What's next? I wonder."

What indeed? It was something that was starting to nag at her, just a little, at the back of it all. How long could this go on—this pushing at the limits, this breaking of boundaries? Every act seemed more sensational, more outrageous than the last. Surely the day would come soon when they'd run out of unfulfilled fantasies and unspoken desires. There'd be nothing left for them to discover but the sorts of utterly ludicrous or horrible acts that you simply wouldn't want to engage in. What then?

"Devil . . ." She still called him by that nickname sometimes—usually at times like this, these more intimate moments. "What happens when the party's over? I wonder if we can ever just be our plain and simple selves with each other. I wonder if that would be enough."

O'Connell dragged on the cigarette. A long column of ash was balanced precariously on its end. "Why worry about it? The party's still on, isn't it? Stay in the present, Grace. Enjoy what we have now. That's what I'm doing."

He passed the cigarette across and the ash dropped off onto the carpet. She found she was thinking of Eva. He'd once said Eva lived only in the present. She wasn't destined to settle down, that's what he'd said. It was impossible to imagine her growing old . . .

They'd eaten, that evening, at a shoddy little restaurant around the corner from Marylebone Library. The tablecloths were stained and sticky. The rabbit stew was an awful mistake. The wine they'd washed it all down with was vinegary but they drank it anyway, and giggled together about the séance.

"What on earth made that woman think she could wear yellow?"

"The only spirit she communes with is straight out of a gin bottle. I swear I could smell her breath from the back of the room."

After dinner, it was on to Ciro's for more drinks and dancing and yet more drinks—and now here they were. And here, in their aftermath, and in the quiet of Aubrey Pearson's office, as Grace blew her perfect smoke rings and O'Connell tried to copy her ("No, not like that. You need to put your lips just like this—like *this*, Devil"), she thought of Mrs. McKellar, earlier that evening, shouting about a falling girl, and about the expression on O'Connell's face as he got up to leave.

"I can't live only in the present," said Grace. "I'm not like Eva. I want a long, happy life and I care about the future. Meat and vegetables and all. I don't see that there's anything wrong in that. If you do, then I don't think *we* have one. A future, that is."

"Wow." O'Connell dabbed at his brow with a handker-chief. "I don't know about the future, but right now I love you, Grace."

"Do you?" She was so surprised that it came out as a sort of squeak.

"Why else would I want to see you night after night? I don't know how it's going to end up between us, but I can say this much for certain: You make me thirsty."

"I make you *thirsty*?"

"You quench my thirst but it comes back stronger and I need you to quench it all over again."

This, of course, was her worry. That what they had was a kind of compulsion. Driven by restless energy which would surely exhaust itself sooner or later. She blew another smoke ring to give herself a chance to work out what to say.

"You once said to me that you thought what I want is to be known. Really *known*. Remember?"

"Sounds plausible."

"Well, you were right. That's what I want. That's what love is, to me. A deep-down understanding between two people."

"Do you think we have that? You and me?"

"I know that I *want* us to have it. I'm going to tell you something I've never told anyone about. Something you need to know about if you're ever going to really *know* me. And then I want you to tell me something back."

"I'll show you mine if you show me yours?"

"I don't want us to have secrets from each other."

He nodded and took a gulp of wine.

"I had an affair with my sister's husband. It was more than an affair, actually. It went on for years. I ended it when she fell pregnant with her first child. I suppose the pregnancy brought home to me the seriousness of the situation; of what I was interfering with; of the fact that he was hers, not mine. And that unless I wanted to risk losing her forever, he always would be."

She turned to look at him. The playfulness was gone from his face. He was listening seriously to her.

"Nancy has no idea," she continued. "And now I can't tell her, even if I wanted to. He's dead and I'm responsible for her and the children. I can't do or say anything that might damage the family. It's in the past, and there's nothing to do but put it all behind me. But it's hard not to let the past blight the present."

Nothing but the ticktock of Mr. Aubrey's wall clock. The zheeesh of a passing motorcar and the office lit up momentarily by its headlights.

"That explains a lot," O'Connell said.

"Like what?"

But he didn't comment further. Just sat gazing at the wooden legs of Aubrey Pearson's "visitor's chair." Legs carved into strange spindly spirals that looked as though they wouldn't support anyone's weight.

"So now you know the darkest part of me. I've laid myself open to you and I want you to do the same."

She'd sparked his desire. That sly smile of his was creeping across his face and he was setting the bottle down. Reaching out for her.

"No," she said. "Tell me something. Tell me what happened in the past with you and Cramer and Eva. Tell me what was going on when you wrote _The Vision_."

Dawn found Grace sitting in Felix's room, watching him sleep. He was lying on his back with his arms flung above his head.

She'd disturbed him when she came in. His eyes had opened wide and frightened, and he'd begun to whimper. But she had only to lay her hand on his chest and tell him to go back to sleep, and those delicate eyelids had slid gently closed again; his breathing had deepened.

How marvelous to be able to trust in that way; to feel entirely safe and secure in the presence of another.

Grace's mind was racing and she knew it would be hopeless to go to bed. It was selfish to risk disturbing Felix, but she didn't want to be alone. Perhaps, after all, she was also at her most safe and secure in the presence of this particular little person.

What had she said to O'Connell after he'd told her his story? She couldn't remember anymore. Had she said anything at all?

"You want to know why I'm still here in England?" He'd said this just before they left the office. "It's for you, Grace. Just to be near you. There's nothing else for me here."

He'd reached out for her hand but she'd moved away from him, started searching about in the debris for her jewelry, her stockings.

"I didn't have to tell you," he'd said. "You asked. You said we shouldn't have secrets."

"I know." She buttoned her dress at the back of the neck. He'd undone that button, earlier, so he could kiss her—right there, in the place where the button sat. "It's just that I'm tired."

"So let's go get some sleep."

"I want to go home to sleep."

"I love you, Grace."

The "L" word again. How he flung it about. Did he really think the word itself was enough to make everything all right?

Felix sighed in his sleep. A sigh that was endearing in its world-weariness. She wanted to reach out and stroke the lovely downy skin at the side of his face, just below his ear, but resisted the impulse, nervous of waking him again. What did *he* have to sigh about?

There was a clatter in the corridor as they came out of Pearson's office, fully dressed but disheveled. The sound of broom bashing against bucket.

"Shhh," she'd hissed at him, seeing that he was about to speak, and dragged him through the fire exit into the stairwell.

Out on the street he put his hand against her face. "I know what you're thinking, Grace. But try to understand. For us. Because you don't want it to be over between us any more than I do. Try just the tiniest bit."

The early-morning sun was pushing through the curtains, making the room glow orange.

All right then, Devil, Grace thought, as Felix began to snore. I will think my way through it all, and I will try to understand what you did. Just the tiniest bit.

Two charismatic young men. One fair, one dark. The Devil and the Deep Blue Sea. College students. Roommates. The best of buddies but with a rivalry that intensifies their friendship. They're closer than close. They sit side by side on that thin line which separates love and hate.

These boys know each other's moods, the punchlines to each other's jokes, the insides of each other's heads. Each fears that he would be only half a man without the other. But each is also desperate to be free of the other, and longs secretly for the day when he will watch his rival sink.

The rivalry runs all through their college lives. They

compete over sports and examination results. Most of all they vie with each other over the girl they're both in love with. Of course they love the same girl—each has long since assimilated the other's values and tastes—artistic, personal, aesthetic. And of course this girl is the one whom everyone wants. She's beautiful and clever and warm and icy and trouble, and she dances like a dream and she kisses like no other girl. They've both kissed her so they both know.

Often they take the girl out together. They go to the movies and sit in the back row with the girl in between them. They go to dances and are so busy cutting in on each other that nobody else can get anywhere near her or them. Much of the time they revel in their exclusivity—the tight-knit trio that nobody else can penetrate. Sometimes they walk down the street together, the three of them, hand in hand, enjoying the stares. If they have one another, they don't need anybody else.

The girl enjoys the attentions of the two men but doesn't want the threesome to get too cozy and comfy. She likes a bit of edge in her life. Likes the idea of men fighting over her. Likes it when things hurt a bit—her own hurt as well as that of others. Out one day on a summer picnic with the two boys, she takes the Devil by the hand, leads him off to a spot where the trees grow thick and close together and the ground between is filled with shadows, and lets him get a lot further with her than ever before—holding back just a little. He's half crazy with lust when she gets up and dusts herself down. When they arrive back, Deep Blue Sea is a seething ball of jealousy and resentment, sitting alone with the half-eaten picnic. Cheer up, the girl tells him brightly. It's your turn now. Devil's expression, as she leads Deep Blue Sea off into the trees, is incredulous. She loves it more than she's ever loved anything. Perhaps she understands that their powerful emotions are as much

about each other as they are about her. In any case, she wants
to do it again.

The girl cares nothing for conventionality. She is driven
by forces that other girls would shun and shy away from.
Maybe she's already halfway down the path that leads to
madness (a path she will explore more fully as the years go
on). Soon the boys are smuggling her up to their room on a
regular basis. Each takes a turn at waiting outside while the
other is in the room with her. But this still isn't enough for
the girl, who wants to push the boundaries further—taking
bigger risks, seeking greater thrills. One day she keeps them
both in the room with her. One boy watches, then they swap
over . . .

Rumors have been circulating, and the boys' former
friends are starting to avoid them. The same is true of the
girl's friends; but while she doesn't much care, the boys are
not happy. They're both in love with the girl, but they're starting to hate her, too. Ironically, it is at this moment, when one
might expect them to bust up their friendship forever, that
they begin to overcome their rivalries and draw closer to each
other. They are both her victims. If they stick together and
support each other, then maybe they can survive this.

The boys have literary aspirations. They decide to write a
novel about the girl (what a great character she'd make) and
start scribbling notes for a book. Their collaboration is ab-
sorbing and fulfilling; they're spending so much time on the
book that they're not seeing much of the girl anymore. Their
fictional heroine is the only female around who can compete
with her.

The girl doesn't know what they're up to but she knows
they're slipping away from her and doesn't like it. She hasn't
given herself to them so that they might use her up and tire of

her. That wasn't the way it was supposed to be. She has to take control again—to set them against each other once more.

One day she summons both the boys and tells them they can't go on being a threesome. Real life is about coupling up and it's time for all three of them to join reality. She announces that she is going to choose between them, and that her decision will be final and lasting. She will take a week or so to think it over and will then summon them again to let them know her decision. The boys are far from happy about this. If she chooses between them now, it's inevitably going to tear their friendship apart and ruin the novel, too.

The boys vent their spleen together over a bottle of bourbon in their room. How can they let this witch be the one to decide their destiny? If she thinks she's in charge, she couldn't be more wrong. Their first impulse is that they should both give her up. But this is quickly squashed—they're still in love with her, the pair of them, and they couldn't stand to see her floating about the place with some undeserving schmuck. The way forward is to make the decision themselves and to impose it on her. Only one of them can have the girl. The other will get to write the novel in his sole name, spurred on by his broken heart and his jealousy. But how to make the decision?

In the end, they toss a coin. It's the fairest way, after all. Devil is to flip and Deep Blue Sea to call. If he guesses right, he gets the girl.

The nickel is flipped, spinning, into the air, and caught deftly on the back of Devil's hand. Deep Blue Sea calls heads. The coin shows tails.

Best of three? Deep Blue Sea requests.

All right, then.

This time Deep Blue Sea calls tails. The coin lands heads-up. Devil has won the girl.

In awkward, heavy silence, the boys return to the bourbon. Each tells himself he should be happy. All is now decided. It's over. They simply have to apply themselves to their newfound roles: Devil is the lover, Deep Blue Sea the writer. Why can't they be a bit more cheerful about it? For a while, they keep drinking the bourbon, barely speaking, barely looking at each other. Then, eventually they do look up. Each sees what's happening behind the eyes of the other. And finally they begin to smile.

It was past seven o'clock. Felix's sleep was getting lighter. He was fidgeting about in his cot and making little murmuring noises. Outside the room someone was walking across the landing, moving creakily down the stairs. Nancy or Mother?

O'Connell had given Eva over to Cramer and walked away with the beginnings of *The Vision*. He'd traded the girl he loved as though she were nothing more than a cow being taken to market. And he'd taken all the glory and the money for a novel that wasn't entirely his.

"Grace?" It was Nancy's voice out on the landing. Funny, how Nancy had been so perceptive about the book. She'd love to talk all this through with her sister—but how could she break O'Connell's confidence on something so important?

"Grace?"

And what about Cramer? One could argue that he came out of the story more favorably. After all, he chose love. And he was essentially the loser, which made him the more sympathetic figure. He'd been rewarded for his role in the unseemly trade-off by having to watch his friend become rich and famous while he spent years looking after a mentally ill wife who then went on to kill herself, leaving him widowed with a daughter to care for. He'd been punished enough, hadn't he?

But looked at from another angle, he was just as embroiled as O'Connell. He'd simply been less lucky over the years. If fate had unfurled differently, O'Connell might have ended up drinking away his sorrow for his lost love while his unpublished novel sat forever in the bottom drawer.

What a mess. A worse mess, even, than the whole sorry story of the Rutherford sisters and the Wilkins brothers.

And then Grace remembered something from a long time ago. Two jacks—diamonds and spades. Were she and Nancy really any better than O'Connell and Cramer? Frankly, who was she to judge anyone?

No, that was a silly thought. It wasn't the same at all. They'd just been a couple of schoolgirls playing a game. They'd never have settled their lives that way.

The door opened. Nancy stood there in her blue dressing gown, her hand resting on the handle. "I should have guessed you'd be in here."

Felix's eyelids fluttered open. He looked, startled, from his aunt to his mother, and then his face broke into a huge smile.

Nine

"*Put* out your tongues, boys."

Out came the tongues of Topping and Humphries, two young whippersnappers from the *Herald*.

Grace blew a smoke ring and watched as Dodo Lawrence, the *Herald*'s main writer on subjects Dickie had been known to refer to as "female frippery," inspected the two specimens. Topping's tongue was long and pink and doglike, while Humphries's was gray and unhealthy-looking.

"Definite win for Dum." Dodo had been referring to the boys as Tweedledee and Tweedledum, and then more succinctly as Dee and Dum, all evening. They were both too infatuated with Dodo, or perhaps too afraid of her, to object to this. "What's the score, Grace?"

"Three–two to Dum. What next?"

Dodo simulated deep thought for a moment—then,

apparently tiring of that, turned around on her chair and cast about for inspiration.

The Salamander Club was jolly tonight. Cocktails long past cocktail hour. Lots of giggling girls with floaty silk scarves (de rigueur, it appeared—both the scarves and the giggles). A good number of attractive men—many of that quiet, contemplative variety who met one's gaze with a gentle smile through the cigarette smoke but didn't press for any further attention. Even better, quite a few men who danced a good Charleston! She'd done the right thing in coming here with Dodo this evening. Dodo belonged to a category of women that Grace thought of as "professional blonde." There were lots of them about on London's newspapers and magazines, and not a few of them running art galleries, too. Platinum-haired, fine-sculpted flappers-grown-up, with loud voices and oodles of confidence and low-cut dresses in bold patterns. As with many of her ilk, you could rely on Dodo to be amusing and impersonal. There must be a serious side to her personality somewhere deep down—she was too clever for that not to be the case. But she didn't expose that potential inner seriousness too readily. This suited Grace just fine in her present mood.

It had been almost forty-eight hours since O'Connell had told her about the trade-off. She'd stayed away from him since then, mulling it all over. She knew it was wrong to judge him for what he'd done. After all, he hadn't judged her. But, having persuaded him to tell her his secret, she couldn't ignore what it revealed about him. He'd remained silent over the last couple of days. No pleading phone calls, flowers or torrid letters. That wasn't his style. He wasn't the sort to beg. He might have realized, of course, that she wouldn't want to hear from him yet. Though perhaps he simply didn't care enough to come running after her . . . She found herself thinking about all those newspaper stories about O'Connell the Cad, O'Connell the Playboy. She thought too about Nancy's warning to her. In a very fundamental way, he wasn't the man she'd thought he was. And she wasn't at all sure what she wanted to do now.

In the meantime, it was good to distract herself with cocktails.

"Shoes," Dodo announced. She and Grace ducked down to peer under their table. Humphries's were black, shiny and new-looking. Topping's were brown and slightly scuffed. What's more . . .

"Dum, you appear not to be wearing socks! Can this be true?" Grace straightened again to confront Topping's blushing face above the table.

"Some sort of holdup at the laundry," Topping muttered.

"A win for Dee," said Dodo. "That's three–all. I do like a close competition."

Grace bent for another look at Topping's bare ankles. So vulnerable in their knobbly nakedness twixt shoe and trouser. Strangely endearing. When she sat up again, who should be standing beside their table but the Deep Blue Sea.

"Where did you spring from?"

"Nice to see you too, Grace." He was looking tall. Had he always been that tall? He was smiling warmly at her. Then he turned to Grace's companion. "Dodo! How lovely. How long has it been?"

"John, darling. How marvelous!" Dodo was on her feet and they were embracing—the sort of ambiguous embrace that could be platonic or then again might not be. "Far too long."

The outpouring continued when they'd sat down.

"Do you remember that marvelous evening at the Ritz?"

"Oh, of course. Simply marvelous."

It all put Grace in mind of that evening at the Tutankhamun when Cramer had turned out to be an old acquaintance of Sheridan's. Did *everyone* have a past that featured him? He was inescapable, or so it seemed. He popped up everywhere and was connected to everybody. She looked across at the disgruntled Dee and Dum. "Want to dance with me, boys? There are points to be won."

Out on the floor, the orchestra was playing fast. She attempted to dance with the two of them simultaneously, while they barged about, each trying continually to cut in across the other. They weren't bad dancers, either of them, but they were foiled, to an extent, by their own determination to outdo each other. By the time Grace stepped down, her feet were distinctly trampled on.

Back across the room, Dodo and Cramer were laughing, their heads close together. She was continually touching his shoulder as she spoke. Then his arm. Her hands had a restlessness, as though they just had to be on him somewhere.

"Who won?" asked Humphries.

"Neither of you. You each lose a point. Now go and find someone your own age to dance with. This is becoming tedious."

As she arrived back at the table, there was a lull in conversation.

"Talking about me?" Grace tried to make her voice light. "I suppose I'm the only truly interesting conversational subject in this place?"

"Now, now, Grace." Dodo was brittle. As brittle, perhaps, as those carefully arranged curls in her hair. "Don't let your vanity run away with you. John was talking about that young man who's about to try to fly across the Atlantic. He's convinced the fellow's going to pull it off, and he's going over for the landing."

"I know." Grace turned to Cramer. "But what if he fails? You said they're calling him the Flying Fool."

"He'll get there. I just know it. You have to have faith sometimes, Grace. You have to believe."

"That all sounds a little bit religious, John. I didn't know you were the godly sort."

That smile was still there. "Just wait and see."

Cramer had ordered more cocktails. A gin fizz for Grace, a Singapore sling for Dodo, and monkey glands for Dee and Dum. Cramer himself was drinking something clear with ice and lemon. A surreptitious sniff confirmed that it was plain water. She'd forgotten about this business of his not drinking, and now it was too late for her to be wary of her own state. When she looked across at the raucous Dodo, she saw herself reflected back. The excessive delight in one's own shrill cleverness. The expansive, clumsy gestures. The loud laughter.

Cramer had come here this evening with a couple of friends who were over from New York. "I don't know what's going on with them," he was saying, shaking his head. "One moment we're having a fine old time and he's telling a story about a trip to Coney Island and suddenly I notice she's gathered herself up tall and there's this look in her eye like she wants to kill him. And he still hasn't seen the look—he's going on with the story, and it's all about shooting rabbits in that fairground game—and by now she's sort of reared up in her seat. She looks like a cobra just before it strikes. You know? Those snakes with the hoods like the ones in the Kipling story about the mongoose? And I swear—*swear*—that she makes a kind of hiss and shows her teeth—and he still hasn't noticed, and he's *still* talking about Coney Island and how they'd all gotten the boat home at the end of the night, and then she says *'Cecil!'*—just his name, that one word—and he finally looks at her, and in one split second, all the happiness is sucked out of him, just *sucked* out. And there I am, sitting at the table with this venomous snake and a kind of dry husk that, until one second earlier, was my old friend." He shook his head and took a mouthful of water.

"So what happened next?" asked Grace.

"Well, that's when I spotted you two," said Cramer. And then he turned back to Dodo and they were off again. "Really, Dodo, it's just so great to have run into you again!"—and Dodo was preening, and Grace was thinking, *please*, not *more* of this. Dodo had always been one to sit back and coolly survey the men present—blow a little smoke at them, allow them a flicker of her attention. But look at her tonight around Cramer! She was treating him like something rare and exotic that she simply had to take possession of.

"What do you miss most about New York?" Dodo was asking him now. "The food, perhaps? London is so woefully behind the times. Perhaps the coffee?"

"The roof gardens." Cramer looked wistful. "Now that we're in May, all the best dinner-dance joints will be opening up their roofs till all hours. I love those long summer nights. Trouble is, you're liable to turn up to meet your friends and find a padlock on the door and the usual pinned-up notice about closure. The padlocking is just the pits."

"We have some lovely gardens in London." Grace was folding the little paper coaster on the table in front of her into tinier and tinier triangles. Each fold was more decisive than the last. "Though they're not so often on the roof. I'll have to take you out to one or two." She smiled across at him, realizing a moment too late that she was flirting. An automatic compulsion to compete with Dodo, a refusal to be outdone by her. She should *not* flirt with Cramer.

"And I miss Betsy," said Cramer. Then added, "My daughter."

"Of course." Grace eradicated the flirtatious smile. "How old is she?"

"Fifteen. She's at school at the moment. Then she'll go to my mother for the summer."

"She must be lovely," Dodo gushed. "I'd love to have a daughter. It must be awful for you to be so far away from her."

"Yes." Cramer was staring mournfully into his glass of water.

If he missed Betsy so much, why did he choose to work abroad and leave other people to take care of her? Why wasn't he with her? But then a thought struck Grace: Maybe he couldn't cope with her now that Eva was gone. Perhaps she reminded him too strongly of her mother. Perhaps she even blamed him for her mother's death.

Cramer glanced up, as she was reflecting on this, then looked away.

He knows that I know, thought Grace. She caught his eye again, and this time he held her gaze, and everything around them slid. The smoke and the music and the laughter. Dodo's voice was chuntering away behind it all (she had Humphries and Topping speaking words backward). And still Grace could not look away from Cramer. Something was fluttering in her chest, catching at her throat.

It was Cramer who finally broke the long moment. "What do you want to do with your writing, Grace?"

"Do?" Grace was startled at the question and still unsettled.

"Your column's good. I'm really enjoying it. But surely it's only the start for you?"

"Oh, I see." She thought of her recent conversation with Dickie. The way she'd pushed for more work on the paper and been put firmly in her place. "I'm not sure I'm really a writer. It's a hobby that got out of hand. That's all."

"That doesn't have to be all. Not if you want more. On the surface your column is just reveling in and poking fun at a certain way of life, but there's always something else bubbling away underneath. There's skill in that."

"You think so?"

"Your strength, as a writer, is the comedic approach. It's a clever way of delivering a message. Essentially, you do some beautiful gift wrapping. The question for you, in the long term, is what you want to put in the parcel."

All that damn drink—she couldn't think straight. "I'd like to believe there's something more out there for me." She ran a finger around the top of her glass, tried to steady herself. "What do *you* want in the future, John? What else is out there for you?"

Dee and Dum were tripping over their own tongues just as they'd tripped over their feet on the dance floor.

"Now say 'platypus' backward," said Dodo's red lips. "Quickly! Now try 'inconsequential.'"

Something was passing between Grace and Cramer. A sort of recognition.

"Now say 'betrayal.'"

In the ladies', Grace stood before the washbasins and contemplated splashing cold water on her face. No—better not. Not with all this makeup on. She'd end up all stripes and smears like one of Tilly's paintings and it would take forever to put her face straight again.

Gripping the edge of the porcelain basin, she examined herself in the mirror. The crow's feet at the corners of her eyes. The lines on her forehead—were they new? She must remember not to frown in future. Frowning was fraught with danger.

Lips too thin, she told herself, as she had done countless times before. *But don't go thinking you can fix that with lipstick.* And then: *Is that mouth a mean mouth?*

Sometimes, when they were girls, she and Nancy had compared their faces in the mirror and tried to decide whose was best. Grace had sharper bones, distinct features. Nancy's face had a broad, appealing softness. Nancy would say she envied Grace her aquiline quality, her look of intelligence. Grace, on the other hand, envied Nancy's full, pouting lips. Her generous smile.

Had Cramer compared the two sisters? He wouldn't have been the first to do so. Had he kissed her sister's beautiful mouth? Nancy had denied that anything was going on between them, of course, but Grace knew to look beyond the words that were spoken. What, other than love, could have lit Nancy up so brightly after her years in the dark?

She closed her eyes and immediately opened them again. It was all spinning about in there: O'Connell saying he loved her and then telling her all that awful stuff . . . Cramer looking at her as though he knew her from the inside out and telling her things about who she might become if she had the will to do it. She was too drunk to fathom it, any of it. She should go straight home and get some sleep.

"Layarteb," she said, to her reflection.

"I beg your pardon?" said the woman standing at the basin next to her. Another blonde. Tiny nose, high-arched eyebrows, and wearing a dress that was a cascade of delicate pink petals (had to be a Madeleine Vionnet).

"Layarteb. That's 'betrayal' backward."

"Oh, sweetie, that's a word I know *all* about." The woman patted at her unruly hair. "I've been at both ends of that particular word, and let me tell you, neither end is especially comfortable. Take my advice: Stay at home with a book."

As she came out of the ladies', Cramer was just coming out of the men's.

"There's something I want to know," she said.

"What?"

"Come with me. I need to talk to you away from Dodo."

With that, she grabbed him by the hand and led him quickly around a corner and around farther corners until the corridor ended in double doors and kitchen smells.

"So, ask away." And then, when she failed to speak, "What next, Grace?"

He lifted her chin and kissed her. The kiss was like the look they'd shared—it was a continuation of that look. They kissed like they were trying to break out of themselves and into each other. Her back against the wall steadied her; anchored her to the solid, physical world while everything else was adrift on the Deep Blue Sea.

"Stop." She pushed him away.

"Why?" He was still bending over her, perhaps about to kiss her again. "I don't want to stop."

"But what about Nancy?"

"There's nothing going on between Nancy and me."

He kissed her again and, despite her screaming conscience, she grabbed him, reaching around his neck to pull him closer, tighter. She shut her eyes as they kissed, and Nancy was there. Nancy in the dusky green dress she'd worn on the night of the Wiener schnitzel dinner, her face all floury and happy. Again she broke away.

"She's my sister. I can't do this to her."

He shook his head, a look of bafflement on his face. "Nancy and I are friends. Nothing more."

"My sister's in love with you. She's in love with you, John!"

He took a step back. Rubbed at his forehead. Acrid smells from the kitchen. Something was burning.

"But I've never done anything. I had no idea that she—"

"Oh, God! You're either ridiculously naïve or utterly callous, and I'm not sure which is worse!" She tried to shove past him but he grabbed her by the arm.

"Grace, wait!"

"All that time you've been spending with her, just the two of you and the children. The walks, the café visits, the dinners . . ."

"We were both lonely. I've grown fond of the children. And of her. But that's all there is to it."

He was taller and thinner than O'Connell, but they were somehow alike. It was in the eyes, she realized. Cramer's were darkest brown, but their expression made them remarkably like the pale eyes of her lover.

"I think you know how I feel about you, Grace. I haven't felt this way in a long time. I think you feel the same."

"You have no idea about my feelings. If anything, I'm confused. *So* confused."

"Why? What about?"

"O'Connell told me about the bargain."

Cramer just stood there, looking perplexed.

"Don't pretend you don't know what I'm talking about. He's told me all about it."

"O'Connell says a lot of things, Grace. Very few of them are true."

She stamped a foot in impatience. "He says you were working on *The Vision* together. He says you made a deal—you got the girl and he got the novel. Why would he make something like that up?"

"I don't know and I don't want to know."

"It doesn't make sense, John."

Cramer raked a hand through his hair. "That book is his and his alone. There was no "deal." I genuinely don't know why he said what he said, but with O'Connell, it's all about what he *doesn't* say."

"What do you mean?"

"All right." When he spoke again, a nerve was twitching in his face. "You want to know about the poison between him and me? Well, I'll tell you." He leaned back against the wall. Lit a cigarette and passed it across to Grace. Lit another for himself. "There was no 'deal.' Eva chose between us and she chose me. We got married and lost touch with O'Connell, and we were happy together until that book came out. When Eva read it, she believed it held messages for her. She started accusing me of sucking all the color out of her, just like the numskull Stanley tries to do to Veronique. She read it over and over."

He inhaled deeply from the cigarette. Blew out smoke.

"She started writing love letters to O'Connell. I found the carbons. I never found any replies, but he *must* have been writing back."

"Did you confront her?"

"Oh yes." He swallowed hard, as though he were trying to force something down. "We had huge screaming rows. Then afterward she'd beg for forgiveness, tell me it all meant nothing. That it was a kind of madness in her. And then the madness got bigger and I couldn't go on ignoring it. She'd go running off on some two-minute errand, leaving Betsy alone in the house, and not come back for days. Then when she arrived home, she might go to bed for a week and cry and refuse to talk to anyone. I never knew where she went."

"Was she with him?"

"I don't know, even now. It tortured me. I decided to have it out with him. Wrote to him care of his publisher. When we finally met up, it was about as bad as it could be. We sat in a fancy New York restaurant and I watched him eating oysters. Sucking them up in front of me. There was something about him . . . His air of condescension, his shiny gray suit with the big shoulders, the way he ate those goddamn oysters . . . I couldn't speak to him about Eva. I couldn't bring myself to mention her name to him. He was waiting for me to do it. He was ready to put a look of pity on his face and be nice to me, and I couldn't stand that. Do you see?"

"I think so."

"By this time Eva was in and out of the clinic. You know, I never had her locked away. She always went in of her own free will. And it was a nice place. Cost an absolute fortune. We tended to get on better when she was in the clinic—those tight visiting hours and hospital rules suited us just fine. I was as much to blame as she was for the fights we had. I was drinking heavily. Poor little Betsy would come wandering downstairs in the middle of the night to find her father staggering about and her mother talking to the Virgin Mary. Eventually, we moved her out to my parents'."

"Children always get the worst of it." Grace wasn't just thinking about Betsy here. "Stuck in the middle of situations they can't possibly understand."

"You're right about that. Betsy was better off away from

it all. Frankly she still is . . . So anyway, it all got worse and worse. Eva was in the clinic more than she was out of it. I was very . . . absent. Then, on May 13, 1922, when we'd been married just over ten years, I came home from, let's be frank, a three-day drinking binge, to find messages from my parents, the police and the clinic. Eva had left the clinic without permission, made her way halfway across the state and died in a fall from a hotel balcony. They started out by talking about her 'fall,' but by the time I got to the mortuary they'd switched to 'jump.'"

A girl lying on the ground. A broken necklace and a broken neck . . .

"It was O'Connell's hotel balcony, Grace."

"*What?*"

He stubbed out his cigarette on the floor. "It seems she'd sought him out. He was giving a well-publicized lecture and she went looking for him at the fanciest hotel in town. She'd broken into his room, so the police told me, while he was out at his event. He claimed he'd had no idea she was in town and hadn't seen her. His cronies were at the police station—the publisher and the literary agent. They'd arrived before me. While I was still struggling for the vaguest understanding of what had taken place, I had the two of them on at me about the importance of keeping O'Connell's name out of the papers. I didn't find it difficult to comply with their wishes. I had no desire to run around shouting about what had happened."

"Oh God." She leaned against the wall and looked over at Cramer. His face was all darkness.

"I don't believe it's the whole story, Grace. I know O'Connell—and somehow it just doesn't add up. Over the years I've tracked him down and I've run into him, and each time I see him, I try to get the truth out of him. But five years on I still don't understand what happened, and he still hasn't given me an explanation that makes any kind of sense to me."

"You're not saying . . . He's not a murderer, John. Whatever he is, he's not that."

A shrug. "Like I said before, with O'Connell it's all about what he *doesn't* say." He reached out and put a hand against her face. "Come to Paris with me, Grace."

"What?"

"Come to Paris with me. Let's go see Lindbergh together. Share in his moment."

"Oh, John . . ." She pulled away from him and started back down the corridor. That hand against her face—that was a gesture she knew all too well. O'Connell would have done just the same thing at such a moment—laid his hand gently against her face.

"You wanted to know so I told you. I'm not leaving you to *him*." They were back outside the ladies' toilets and he was right behind her.

"I can't think straight. It's too much."

"John, sweetie!" It was the blonde from the washbasins. The one who knew about betrayal.

"Oh. Barbara."

"Where did you *get* to? We've been looking everywhere for you. Cecil thought you must have gone home but I told him, don't be silly. John wouldn't leave without saying good-bye."

Cramer was looking helplessly past the blonde at Grace, as she seized her opportunity to get away. Out of the corridor and back to the dancing and the jazz and the cocktails. Back to Dodo, who had gathered a stack of lemon slices from the bar and was feeding them one by one to Humphries and Topping, holding each slice carefully in her pointed red nails and slotting it into a willing mouth.

* * *

When Grace stepped out of the club, she was half expecting
to find Cramer waiting for her in the street. But there was no
sign of him. Unsure whether she was relieved or disappointed
or both, she stuck out her arm for a taxi and clambered in,
alone.

The taxi drove north. The driver kept trying to make conversation with her and she wished he'd stop. He was banging
on, for some reason, about the new greyhound racing stadi-
ums they were building at White City and Harringay. She had
no interest in dog racing and would have had nothing to say
about this even at the best of times. His talk floated all about
her while, in her lap, her hands clenched and unclenched.

Something big and frightening was happening to her. She
felt it in every cell of her body. It was throbbing in her head,
flying in her stomach. When she looked out of the window, it
was even echoed in the sky—in the sheer energy of day pushing its way up through thinning night the color explosion that
is dawn.

Somewhere in the background the cabby was chuntering
on. "I'll be heading back to Cricklewood after I drop you off.
Back home to the missus. Snuggle down under the candlewick
and have a good long kip. Lovely . . ."

"Layarteb," Grace whispered under her breath.

III.
Flight

The West-Ender
May 23, 1927

Two new lunch restaurants have just hung up their menus next door to each other on Beak Street, each being so much more interesting for the existence and proximity of the other. Let me explain:

Low Fat Feast is a place that does what it says on the tin. Most faithfully. The portions are tiny, the food devoid of fat (and hence, of flavor). The (floury) bread is spread with something thin and almost yellow that bears no resemblance to butter. The mayonnaise . . . Well, suffice to say it simply *isn't*. And yet the place is jammed with people of a lunchtime and there's a queue for tables that stretches out onto the street. My, but we're very bothered about our figures these days! I predict the current fervor will last until the end of August when Selfridges will have sold every last thread of its splendid swimwear collection, and then we'll all go back to stuffing our faces.

Next door to the dietary

establishment is Restaurant La Ronde. This place has a newspaper article stuck up in its window, warning of the dangers of dieting. Its food offers plentiful aid to any diner at risk from such perils. I went in yesterday for a splendid finnan haddock, which came with one of the richest cream sauces I've ever tasted. It should be noted, however, that the finnan haddock served at Low Fat Feast, though bone dry and half the size, is oddly similar. Indeed, if you compare the two menus, you begin to discern a pattern. Methinks I must get backstage to investigate the kitchen arrangements of these two easily uneasy neighbors. Lastly, would it surprise you to hear that the clientele of Low Fat Feast are, for the most part, on the large side, while those who dine at Restaurant La Ronde are a distinctly slender bunch?

Enough of lunch. I entreat you, on the next possible Friday or Saturday night, to visit the Tivoli Club on Coventry Street and saunter about for a while on the roof. Yes, they've gone alfresco for the season. There's some very good jazz being played up there and the dancing's not at all bad. Really, I must applaud the Tivoli for taking the risk. There'll be some nasty wet nights ahead, I'm certain, but they've made preparations for this. There is a sort of canopy, and I couldn't help but notice a great many umbrellas on hooks at the foot of the staircase. So now I have somewhere proper to take a certain American gentleman of my acquaintance next time he talks wistfully of the summer roofs of New York. A word of warning, however: Don't bring your boyfriend along if he is a proponent of one of the more flailing and unruly forms of Charleston, or he might just dance himself off the edge and take you down with him!

A Mr. Runcett of Camberwell has written to kindly offer his services as my escort for all "gadding about" purposes. He professes himself "moved and saddened" by my column of April 18th, bemoaning the plight of the intelligent woman as regards the attentions of gentlemen, and also by my mentions of Good Girls, Bad Girls and the Devilish fellow I've been out and about with lately. He assures me he has all his own teeth and most of his hair, and offers a very reasonable rate. Grateful though I am for this most dashing of propositions, I'm glad to say I don't require Mr. Runcett's services at present. Girls, I'm sure you'll know for yourselves that it tends to be feast or famine out there. And just at the moment I appear to be dining, as it were, at La Ronde rather than Low Fat Feast. (Though as I said before, I do need to look behind the scenes . . .)

Now readers, I'm off on a little jaunt and won't be writing next week. Miss me but don't cry for me or you'll smudge your makeup. If you're good I'll drop you a postcard.

Diamond Sharp

From the Editor: Miss Sharp, currently away on the aforementioned jaunt, has asked me to deliver the following personal message to Charles A. Lindbergh on her behalf:

"Attaboy, Lindy. Knew you could do it."

One

"A change? You?" Marcus Rino stroked his mustache and contemplated Grace.

"I've had this hairstyle for years. I thought perhaps . . ." Grace, in the chair, studied herself in the long mirror. Her bob was still one of the sharpest in London. She knew this. She knew Marcus knew this, too.

"So, what do you want, eh?" The hairdresser pumped furiously with his foot and the chair rose higher.

"I don't know. Something different. A permanent, perhaps? There are some nice waves about."

Marcus took a large white handkerchief from his waistcoat pocket and mopped his brow. "Your hair, oh sweet one, is fantastically straight. You have no cowlicks, not a single kink. If I cut it right, it makes the beautiful lines, the angles . . . Why do you want me to fry it into a frizz, eh? You want to destroy all your natural advantages?" He nodded meaningfully down the long, heavily mirrored room, where his brother Pietro had just finished putting rollers into the dull brown hair of a bejeweled woman, and was mixing something in a pot. Something that gave off a strongly chemical smell.

"I'd like to think my straight hair isn't my *only* natural advantage, Marcus. What say I keep it straight but change the color? How about blond?"

The hairdresser bit his little finger. "You want me to put peroxide all over that lovely, dark head and drain all the color out of you?"

"I know you do Dodo Lawrence's hair. Apparently it's all right for *her* to be blond, but when it's me—"

"Dodo Lawrence is a natural blonde. You, oh sweet one, are not. If I could wave a magic wand to show you how you'd look with a permanent or blond hair, I would. We'd both have a good giggle and then I'd magic you back again. I'm a pretty good magician, but this is one trick I can't perform. Uncle Marcus knows best. And I can't have you running about town with ghastly hair telling all and sundry who did it to you."

Grace had her sulky-child face on now. She spotted it in the mirror and disappeared it quickly. "All right, then. But cut it shorter than usual. Shorter than short. Bobs are two a penny these days and I need to stay ahead of the pack."

"That's my girl." Marcus's smile was slightly sinister, especially when he was brandishing his scissors. Grace could only imagine how chilling it must be to watch him smiling as he performed the saw-the-lady-in-half trick. He was looking about for the girl and calling out, "Shampoo for Miss Rutherford, Penelope." Turning back, he put a hand on her shoulder. "Sweet one, he'll like you best just the way you are."

"Who will?"

Marcus shrugged. "It's obvious that you're doing this for a man. There's no point denying it."

"I'm going on a trip." Grace's hands were working around each other in her lap. "Just a little jaunt, but I want to look my best. I'm leaving this afternoon."

A pat on the shoulder. "You don't need to change yourself for anyone, sweet one. Uncle Marcus knows best."

Two letters in Grace's handbag, down on the floor by her feet as her hair was washed. One, the white letter, was addressed to Miss Grace Rutherford in blue ink, in a slanting italic hand. Neat and attractive, though oddly difficult to decipher. The other, on pale blue paper, written in black ink, was all over spiky and spidery. Messy and angry-looking, yet easier to make sense of than its italicized companion in paper.

"So, who is he, then? Your friend?" Marcus lifted her thick hair, section by section, with a comb. Scissoring deftly. She marveled, every time she came here, at the speed with which he did this. At his dazzling precision.

"What makes you so sure I'm going away with a man?"

"Oh, Grace. Uncle Marcus is not a man to judge you for such a thing." A knowing smile. Head to one side. His hairdressing implements lay in a neat row on the dressing table in front of her. Scissors, combs, razors, odd little knives. Highly polished, with matching tortoiseshell-inlaid handles. When he finished work at the end of the day—or even simply to go out for lunch or a coffee—he'd put them away in a purpose-made calfskin wallet. He'd tuck the wallet into the inside pocket of his jacket, next to his heart. She'd seen him do it. His precious tools of the trade.

"Maybe I judge myself."

May 19, 1927

Dear Grace,

I've been meaning to write a note to say sorry. Sorry for ruffling your feathers and stirring things up. I'm not sorry for kissing you though. I'd do it again if you'd let me.

Don't let that last bit put you off. I'm quite the gentleman. Or, at least, I can be if that's what you want from me. That's a promise, actually.

Come to Paris with me. I'm leaving tomorrow, whether or not Lindbergh takes off on schedule. You won't regret it and nor will I.

I'll be at home all day, waiting for your answer.

Yours, as ever,

John

"I'm a Catholic." Marcus sliced the bob shorter and shorter. "We like to step inside a little booth every now and then, to deliver up our wrongdoings. Usually the confessor is a gnarled old man peppered with liver spots and with alcohol on his breath. Someone you would never want to have lunch with. But for some reason we go back to this old man over and over again, telling him everything we have to tell. It's marvelous, really. Makes one feel quite liberated."

Grace smiled. "I'm not a Catholic."

"All the more reason to tell your secrets to Uncle Marcus. Who else do you have to confess to?"

May 19, 1927

Darling Gracie,

What we need, you and I, is to get away from it all for a few days.

Somewhere far from Aubrey Pearson's desk, my rumpled bed at the Savoy, the sticky dance floor at the Salamander, the sleight-of-hand slipperiness of Wednesday Whist at Silvestra's, the all-over autographed Tour Eiffel, the rotting air of the Marylebone Library, the daily harassment from my publisher (who has paid me many dollars on the promise of the Great Novel, and reminds me of this each day in an ulcer-making lunchtime telephone call), the ongoing silent reproach and sinister presence (I almost struck "sinister," but it really IS the right word) of my one-time friend John Cramer, and the not inconsiderable burden (a lovely one, naturally, but a burden, nonetheless) of your family. Oh, and let's for God's sake get away from the rubber steaks they serve up in those dreadful West End grills. Somewhere far away from this cracklingly, pulsatingly, wind-rushingly, stomach-churningly, earsplittingly, head-shatteringly, breath-catchingly, jaw-droppingly, heartbreakingly (enough now?) electrifying city they call London, which I can't quite abide and can't quite tear myself away from and love and hate and hate some more and love some more.

Just a short vacation, my darling, from Diamond and the Devil and their amusing little parlor games.

Let's find out what it's like when it's just you and me. Our plain and simple selves and nobody and nothing else getting in the way.

What do you say, Gracie? Shall we give the wheel a spin?

Send me your answer today at the Savoy.

With love,

Your

D. O'C

"Maybe I'm someone who likes to leave things unsaid," said Grace. "Maybe I like to hug my secrets to myself."

"How very tedious of you, sweet one. I was relying on you to enliven an otherwise dull day of snipping and combing and curling. You're usually such a good gossip." He held up a tortoiseshell-framed mirror to show her the absolutely straight line that was the back of her hair.

"Yes, but my gossip's always about other people. And things that don't matter." Grace turned her head this way and that, examining the effect of the shorter-than-short hair.

"So, is this something that matters, then?" Marcus began to pack away his tools in the calfskin wallet. "Is *he* someone who matters?"

"That's what I need to work out." The new style made her neck look longer, her eyes larger. She appeared younger with her hair like this. There was an almost childlike quality to her face. "That's why I'm going away with him."

Two

Twilight. A fat moon looms over the airfield, holding its own against the thick banks of purple cloud which threaten it. Down on the ground, the fences have been reinforced against the crowd, and the police have created a further, human barrier. Ever since Lindbergh flew past Newfoundland and out over the Atlantic, cable reports have been buzzing in from ships. He's sighted at Goleen, Ireland, and then again over Cornwall. When the low-flying plane is glimpsed again over Cherbourg, vast numbers of people get into their cars and clog up the Route de Flandre, heading north out of Paris to le Bourget. "Lindy" fever has officially set in.

Grace is right at the front. As the crowd has swelled around and behind her, she has been shoved this way and that. Now, pushed and pressed from all angles, rammed against the fat belly of a gendarme, she waits, along with everyone else, gazing up at the sky. Sometimes darting a look at the control tower, where the American ambassador Myron T. Herrick is hobnobbing with French officials.

She is just beginning to fixate on the inevitable conundrum: "I need to pee. Where and how can I pee?" when there's a shout from nearby. Someone has spotted the plane.

Frantic peering. The clouds are thick now and there's no sign of Lindbergh. But . . . wait . . . yes: a sound. A buzz, growing steadily louder.

"C'est lui! C'est Lindy!"

The monoplane appears for a few brief seconds, lit by silver moonlight. Then it's behind the clouds again.

The people at the front have been waiting here all day. The anticipation is almost unbearable. They're pushing harder, scrambling over one another for a glimpse. A woman near Grace faints clean away. The gendarmes have to break their line to carry her to safety.

Here it is—the plane! It's out from the clouds, circling low overhead. The crowd is whooping and cheering.

The airfield is lit with klieg lights, and flares are being set off all along the runway. This pilot hasn't slept for forty hours but he's bringing his plane down right on target.

The crowd is chanting, *"Lin-dee. Lin-dee."* The police line has already been weakened and it can't hold out against the surge. Grace is carried forward in a human waterfall. She couldn't stand back if she wanted to. Down go the fences, trampled underfoot, and they're pouring into the airfield itself. Rushing forward with incredible momentum, beyond control. Grace can feel the laughter in her chest and her throat, though she can't hear herself over the hubbub. She's no longer being carried—she's carrying herself, running for all she's worth to get ahead of the pack. And suddenly she's up against immovable metal and she's reaching out to place her hands against it, throwing her head back to look at the wooden wing stretching out above her. There are words inscribed on the metal in front of her. *The Spirit of St. Louis.* She traces the letters. The man up in the cockpit is pulling off his hat and goggles to reveal a shock of red hair and a splendidly handsome face. He's looking down at her, and he's smiling and saying, "Why, hello, Grace. I knew you'd come."

Three

"*How* can you *still* be asleep?"

The abrasive shuttle of curtains being swept back.

Grace dragged open her eyes with an effort, blinking at the glare, and stretched. O'Connell was standing at the window, fully dressed.

"Look. I brought you tea." He pointed at the cup and saucer on the bedside table. "I even fixed it the way you like it, though the very *thought* of that sickly, milky concoction makes me shudder. You really ought to start taking it with lemon. That's how cultured people take their tea, donchaknow." He was silhouetted against the window, but she knew he was smiling. She could hear the smile in his voice.

"I was dreaming. Gosh, such a vivid dream. What time is it?"

"Time to walk on the beach in the sunlight. I can't tell you how long it's been since I last visited the seaside. We should build sandcastles, go swimming. You should bury me up to my neck in the sand and leave me there."

"Don't tempt me."

"Hey, maybe we should sneak back down tonight and swim naked. I haven't been skinny-dipping in the longest time." He came across and perched on the edge of the bed. Reached forward to kiss her on the mouth. His breath warm and mellow. Buttery.

"I dreamed I was in Paris to see Lindbergh land." Grace sat up against her pillows. "Has he landed, do you think?"

"I don't know. There might be a newspaper downstairs. I'll go and have a look."

She was about to point out to him that there would only be a paper downstairs if he'd been out to buy one, but he'd already disappeared, leaving her to drink her tea and reflect on her dream. Its vivid detail and intensity. The euphoria she'd felt.

Grace and O'Connell had come down to Dorset by train, arriving at Weymouth the previous evening. A man in a peaked cap had collected them at the station and driven them out of town and along winding roads to the cliff-top house which was being lent to them by O'Connell's English publisher.

"It's apparently a rather stark old place," O'Connell had said. "But the views over the bay are supposed to be superb."

Not that they'd been able to see the views. It was already dark when they drove up. A stormy wind was blowing in, and the crashing of the waves was hostile, vaguely threatening. Horace, the man in the cap, showed them around the house; and in the kitchen he indicated, with overstated flourishes, a meat pie covered over with a tea towel, which his wife had cooked for their dinner, with some graying boiled potatoes.

She'd also left a loaf of bread in the pantry, along with some butter, eggs and a jug of milk.

"I'll bring more supplies midday tomorrow."

"Is there any wine?" asked Grace.

"The cellar's full of the stuff." Horace wrinkled his nose. "He drinks it by the gallon, but if you ask me, those bottles have been there too long. Covered in dust, they are. I wouldn't touch them if I were you."

He took an age showing them how to make the water heater work, before finally heading off, leaving them to vent their suppressed laughter and go straight down to the cellar to search out a good bottle. Or two, as it turned out. And a half.

There was a gramophone in the front lounge, and some jazz records. They pushed the chairs out of their way, kicked off their shoes and danced together on the carpet, whirling about and smooching close. Stopping only to slurp more wine, and then dancing on. Finally, hunger drove them to investigate the pie, prizing open the pastry crust to reveal some lumps of gray meat of an indeterminate variety, mixed up with peas and carrots in a kind of fatty sludge. They ate it cold, standing at the kitchen dresser in their bare feet, and found it surprisingly good. Not so the potatoes, which they hurled at each other like snowballs, giggling all the while and chasing each other up the stairs.

Their lovemaking was of the drunken, fun sort. Plenty of rolling about and more laughter, followed by an aftermath which was, for them, unusually quiet and tender. As they lay together, her head on his chest, it came back to her that she wanted to find a way to talk to him about what she now knew about Eva's death. Cramer had assumed she would share his suspicions about O'Connell. In fact, the more she reflected on it, the more sympathy she felt for her lover. He'd been dragged into the heart of someone else's madness, someone else's tragedy. And ever since, that tragedy had stalked him, in the form of the grieving Cramer. She couldn't even be angry with him anymore for telling her the bizarre lie about the trade-off when she'd shared her secret about the affair with George. He'd probably have said anything rather than talk about whatever had taken place in that hotel room. In fact, it now seemed likely to Grace that Eva's suicide was the trigger for O'Connell's five years as a recluse.

How she wanted to reach out for his hand right now and tell him what she knew—soft and close, as whispers in the dark. Tell him there should be no boundaries between them, that he could trust her with even the most sensitive and private of truths. But then she'd also have to tell him how she'd found out about it all—through an intimate talk with Cramer, his enemy.

Eventually, tiredness overcame her. They were still entwined with each other as they drifted toward sleep; Grace's last conscious thought being, I did the right thing, coming here with him. This is right.

Grace was singing to herself as she came downstairs in her dressing gown. Cheerfully anticipating a beach stroll of the sort that involves poking about in rock pools and collecting precious pebbles and shells which one immediately forgets the existence of, and then rediscovers at a wildly inopportune moment some weeks later—perhaps in the foyer of a good restaurant, sprinkling sand over the carpet as one produces them from a pocket.

We need a dog, thought Grace as she headed for the dining room. It could run about and swim and shake water all over us, and we could throw pieces of driftwood for it to fetch. I wonder if they can be hired?

But then—

"Oh!"—and—"Well!"

Seated around the table with O'Connell were four extra people, eating boiled eggs and triangles of buttered toast, and sipping tea.

"This is Grace," said O'Connell. "Honey, I think you already know Sam?" He indicated their host, Samuel Woolton, who was stroking his goatee and looking on, quizzically.

"Not properly. Delighted, of course." This was too hideous. And if only she'd dressed before coming down.

Next to Woolton was a frail-looking woman with translucently pale skin and bulbous eyes. Opposite were a squat, bald man in spectacles and a woman with curly blond hair, arched eyebrows and a tiny nose.

"Oh, I'm sure we have. Weren't you at our rather try-hard Ciro's party, Miss Rutherford?" Woolton couldn't leave his goatee alone.

"Indeed, I was." Grace felt her face color up as she turned to O'Connell. "Try-hard" was the expression she'd used when she mentioned the party in her column. Now, what else had she said in that column? "That was the night we first met, wasn't it, darling?"

"What a splendid Cupid you make, Sammy." This from the translucent woman. "I'm Verity. And here we have my sister Babs and her husband, Cecil. Oh, and it's mea culpa and all that. When Sam mentioned who he'd lent the house to, I told him we had to come straight down to join you! We've all been simply *dying* to meet you. Pat's been such a bore, holding out on us. Should I call you Grace? Or do you prefer Diamond?"

"Verity!" The sister raised the arched eyebrows so high they all but retreated into her hairline. "You're embarrassing her dreadfully. Do excuse us, Grace. We're quite uncouth, and we're all awfully jealous of you for landing Pat. He's such a terrible cad but so handsome and we do love him so."

"Don't listen to them." O'Connell was basking in the attention. "My cad days are well and truly over."

"Are they, 'Pat'?" Grace wanted to kill O'Connell. Slowly. "Are you sure about that?"

"My darling! How can you doubt my sincerity?" O'Connell put his hands over his heart.

"We'll vouch for Pat, won't we, Sam?" Verity nudged her husband. "He's a reformed character. He's not been so smitten in all the years we've known him."

Woolton stroked the goatee. "That's right. Well, not since . . ." But then he seemed to think better of it. "Welcome to our little circle, Grace. We're a friendly bunch, as you'll see. What we lack in glamour, we make up for in warmth and wit."

Oh. That was the other thing she'd said in the column: that the world of books had no glamour . . .

"You know, I'm certain we've met somewhere before," said Babs, the eyebrows darting together in a frown. "Quite recently, too."

After breakfast, Grace returned to the bedroom to dress. Glancing out of the window at the Wooltons' two spaniels yapping away in the garden, she told herself: At least we have dogs.

O'Connell came into the room, chuckling. "Gracie, you should have seen your face!"

"How did it look, then? Horror-struck? Furious? Embarrassed?"

"All of the above." He winked at her in a way that made her want to punch him in the mouth. Instead, she did her best to regain her composure.

"This was supposed to be our weekend alone, just our plain and simple selves. Remember?"

"I'm sorry, darling." Finally, his expression became slightly more contrite. "They're good fun though. I promise you'll like them."

She sat on the bed to pull on a stocking.

"It *is* his house. I could hardly forbid him to come here." He was looking at her legs as she reached for the other stocking.

"Well, perhaps we should have gone somewhere else."

He sat down beside her. "You're right, of course. Next time I'll make sure we're on our own. But for now, I'd love you to get to know some very old and dear friends of mine. Will you forgive me, darling?

"How long have you known they were coming? Why didn't you tell me earlier instead of waiting for me to walk in on them? You let me go into that room in my dressing gown, clueless."

"Oh honey, it was just a little joke." Another infuriating wink. "I'll make it up to you."

She clipped the stocking into her garter belt. "Anyway, why are they all calling you Pat?"

"What? It's my middle name. Patrick."

"Strange. You think you know someone really well, but then you're reminded just how little you *do* know."

"You know everything that's important." He put his arm around her shoulders.

She shrugged it off, switched her attention back to the garter belt. "I could have been in Paris this weekend, you know. With John Cramer. Did I mention that?"

"What?"

It had the desired effect. Finishing with the stockings, she stood up and straightened her skirt. "That's right. And I bet *he* wouldn't have let a whole bunch of people turn up uninvited."

"Grace—"

"Don't worry. It's you I want." Then, tossing the words back at him as she was halfway out the door, "For now."

Down on the beach, in the early afternoon, the sun was hot. It felt more like August than May. People were dotted about, sitting in deck chairs or stretched out on the gravelly sand, but there weren't too many of them. The three men, in swimming costumes, were at the water's edge, skimming stones out across the waves, competing with one another over whose would go farthest. The dogs scampered and splashed, barking and frolicking, chasing the skimming stones.

Farther up the beach, the three women—all clad in the much-vaunted Selfridges summer swimwear range, and looking like an advertisement—were sitting under the shade of a huge parasol, watching them. Babs and Grace were both smoking cigarettes in long holders. Bug-eyed Verity was nibbling shortbread, squirrelish.

"I've just remembered where I've seen you before," Babs announced. "It was at the Salamander, only a few days ago. I'd have probably realized earlier but I was so fearfully tight that night. It's a wonder that I can recall anything at all. We spoke in the ladies', do you remember? And then I found you talking to John Cramer. It's surprising, actually, that you should be a friend of his."

"Is it?"

"Rather. You do know about him and Pat, don't you?"

"Yes. Well, yes."

"Cecil was at Yale with them. He's always prided himself

on being the only person who *did* manage to stay friends with them both."

They were watching the men, down by the water. Hairy Woolton, still stroking the goatee; Cecil, all shiny and pink and pot-bellied, a knotted handkerchief on his bald head to stop it getting sunburned; O'Connell, tall and broad and muscular, hurling a stick out to sea for the dogs to go fetch. Turning to salute the women, aware they were all watching him. All three waving back.

"The girl was to blame," said Verity. "They'd both have been fine if it wasn't for that girl."

Grace looked from one to the other. Barbara striking an elegant pose with her cigarette. Verity restless and fidgety, munching compulsively on the shortbread.

O'Connell was wading into the water, diving down with a splash and swimming out to sea. They watched the scything motions of his arms and the occasional bobbing up and down of his head as he swam farther and farther away.

The other two were coming back up the beach with the wet dogs.

"Don't know how he can do that," said Cecil. "It's devilish cold in that water."

"Oh, you know Pat," said Woolton. "He'd do anything if it made him look good in front of the girls."

Verity sighed and took another piece of shortbread from her tin.

A short distance away, a man lay on his back with a newspaper over his face. On the front page was a photograph of a small plane in a cloudy, moonlit sky.

The evening kicked off with cocktails on the veranda, followed by halibut with green beans and then rice pudding, courtesy

of Horace and Mrs. Horace, and then party games. First they
played a literary game in which they took it in turns to pluck a
book from Woolton's shelves. They all had to write fake opening lines and try to guess which was the real one. Protests that
O'Connell had an unfair advantage proved ill-founded when
it transpired he was completely unable to conceal his distinctive style.

Next was a taste-and-identify competition, in which Woolton had them all sampling a wide array of liqueurs and trying
to label them correctly. Nobody was any good at this, and all
were thoroughly drunk by the end.

An attempt at charades dissolved rapidly in laughter when
Cecil acted out the entire plot of *Wuthering Heights* with an energy and seriousness which simply couldn't be bettered or even
tolerated. The game was swiftly abandoned in favor of hide-and-
seek outside, with the sea hissing and shushing behind it all.

The garden was wild and sprawling. It sloped sharply away,
all long grass, bindweed, dog roses and briars, and sprawled
down to an old wooden fence, ten yards or so from the cliff
edge. Ragged trees, strung with faded and torn Chinese lanterns from some long-ago party, leaned at impossible angles.
Up nearer the house the ground was flatter, and the grass
shorn back. A stone fountain, long since defunct, sat centrally.
Beside it, a burned, ash-ridden space where someone had recently played at campfires.

Back and forth through the garden they ran squealingly,
hiding in trees, down among the grass and behind bushes.
Stopping only to drink more, and perhaps to tilt their heads
back and gaze up at the clear, limitless, starry sky. Darting behind an old potting shed, Grace collided with O'Connell, who
grabbed her and kissed her hard. Whispered, "I've been waiting all day to be alone with you."

"Have you?" Grace was giddy.

"You know I have. This bunch—they're such children. They're driving me crazy."

"Really? I thought they were your old and dear friends . . ."

"You were right, Grace. We should have gone away on our own. All I want now is to be alone with you."

"Do you?"

He kissed her again, more softly this time.

When they came apart, she smiled. "You needn't worry. I'm having a fine old time. I admit I found Woolton and company rather tricky at first. But now I've worked it all out, I've decided I like them."

"Worked it all out?"

"They're in love with you. Not just the women. Sam and Cecil, too. They're all besotted."

O'Connell laughed. Shook his head.

"They're suspicious of me because I'm the outsider," she continued. "The interloper. They resent letting me into their little club, but they know they have to if they don't want to risk losing you. It's all perfectly reasonable and understandable when you think it through."

He kissed her neck. "Is it true that Cramer asked you to go away with him? I mean really, honestly true?"

She took a moment before replying. She'd spoken on impulse this morning, and in anger. She'd regretted mentioning Cramer almost as soon as she'd spoken. And yet it might be just as well if O'Connell wasn't entirely sure of her. It wouldn't hurt him to find out what it felt like to dangle just a little.

"What do you think?" she said.

For a time they stood there silently, holding each other, leaning against the shed wall, which was covered in thick ivy.

Listening to each other's breathing, feeling the beating of each other's heart. She imagined them staying there, forever, like statues, as the ivy grew over them, wrapped them in its tendrils, took possession of them.

It was Grace who eventually broke the dream. "It's all gone rather quiet, wouldn't you say?"

"I suppose so." He stroked her hair. "Why don't we take a walk together? We could go down to the beach like we planned to this morning."

"Oh yes, let's. I'll just fetch my wrap."

She knew she'd left the wrap—a silk one, all pink and gold, Oriental, with a long fringe—slung over the back of her chair after dinner. But when she looked, it wasn't there. Neither was it up in the bedroom. Returning to the lounge to check for it, she found Babs at the drinks table, pouring gin into a highball glass. Reaching for a second.

"Have a gin fizz with me, Grace?"

"Actually I was just going off for a walk with O'Connell."

"Funny how you call him that." Babs squeezed lemon juice into both glasses and added sugar. "I thought he was Pat to everyone. Go on. He can wait a few minutes. Anyway, I've poured it now." She added a squirt from the soda siphon to each glass.

"Well . . ." But she'd already taken a glass. Hadn't she decided it was a good thing for O'Connell to dangle a little, after all?

"Chin-chin." Babs raised hers and they clinked. Then she sat down on the sofa and patted the seat beside her. "I absolutely *adore* your column, Grace. Oh, something's wrong. Was that a faux pas?"

Grace winced. "It's just that you shouldn't know it's me who writes it. I don't tell people."

"Oh, that naughty Pat!" Babs shook her head. "He wanted

us to be impressed with you. Don't worry, though, darling. Your secret's safe with me. And Cecil, of course."

"And Verity and Sam . . ." She was thinking too about all those other people who'd found out about Diamond Sharp lately. Sheridan, Cramer, Margaret, Henry Pearson . . .

They both sipped. The drinks were very strong.

"So, you've known Pat a long time, then?" prompted Grace.

"Oh, I should say. Years and years. Practically as long as I've known Cecil. We have a sort of . . . enduring understanding, he and I."

The implication—that Barbara and "Pat" had at one time been lovers or had at least considered the possibility—was clear. Just how recently would this have taken place? She imagined O'Connell still hanging about the garden, waiting impatiently for her. Dangling . . . "And John Cramer?"

"It's as I told you earlier. They were both at Yale with Cecil. I knew them all when they were merely young slips of lads." She frowned. "Can one talk about someone being a 'slip of a lad'? Or is the expression just for a 'slip of a girl'?"

"Perhaps you could call them striplings?" said Grace. "I can imagine them as 'striplings.'"

A light smile. "How exactly do you know John?"

Grace took a big gulp of the gin. "He's a friend of my sister's."

"They're quite something, those two boys. Both of them special. *She* couldn't choose between them, certainly. You know who I mean. I don't like to say her name. And then, even after it was all decided and she was married to John, she couldn't leave Pat alone."

They both looked at Barbara's reflection in the French windows. She was one of those women who never simply "sit." They're aware, all the time, of their own dramatic effect, continually striking a pose.

"Did you know her well?" asked Grace.

"Not really. She wasn't my type at all. Mad as a hatter, always was. Men are so stupid, aren't they, to fall for that sort of girl? She was beautiful, of course. And often very entertaining. It was that unpredictable streak that got the boys hooked. She was a bit dangerous." She eyed Grace over her highball glass. "No common sense or caution and she didn't really care what happened to her or anyone else. Always going too far. That was why she ended up being locked away so much. That and the black moods and the potty fantasies." Babs emptied her glass. "Another?"

Grace nodded. Passed her glass over.

Babs poured. "Really, Grace, if you knew the half of it. Her plan, in my view, was to use her suicide to cause the biggest amount of trouble that she could. For *both* of them. When I think of her sitting there in that clinic of hers plotting and scheming—well, it makes my blood boil."

It was on the tip of Grace's tongue to remark that Eva must have had other things on her mind, but what would be the point in saying that? She hadn't known Eva, after all. Why should she go jumping to her defense? Better to draw Barbara out further on other matters. She was clearly in the mood for gossip after all . . .

"So, being around Pat and John for all these years, you must have seen a lot of women come and go . . ."

A chuckle. "I should say. Probably enough to fill Wembley Stadium." But then she eyed Grace thoughtfully. "Pat's women have been purely recreational. There's been nobody serious since *her*. Not until you, that is . . ."

Grace felt herself blushing and gazed down into her glass. Somewhere in the distance, a strange unworldly melody was unfurling itself.

". . . As for John's women—well, with him it was a more desperate sort of escapism. Went hand in hand with the drink."

"Bit of a womanizer, is he?"

A smile. The kind that comes from toying with a treasured
memory. "'Womanizer' is such an unpleasant word. What's
your interest, anyway? Does your sister have her eye on him?"

"Possibly. Should I be warning her off?"

"Oh, I shouldn't think there's any need for that. Our John
may have strayed rather close to the edge but he's drawn right
back, I can tell you. These days he's sober and well behaved to
the point of being, frankly, rather dull."

"I see." Grace felt herself scrutinized closely. Too closely.

Babs put a hand on her shoulder and turned to check her
reflection in the French windows. Pose: elegant woman giving
confidential advice to young, inexperienced friend. "At least
there's two of them and two of you this time."

"I'm sorry?"

"No need to get all tangled up again, eh?"

The peculiar tune in Grace's ears was growing louder. It
was as if someone was wandering about the garden playing
on pipes. She imagined, briefly, that O'Connell was doing just
that. Striding cockily around in the moonlight, piping away
like an overgrown Pan . . .

Barbara's face wore an expression which hovered at
some indeterminate position between concerned and wryly
amused.

"What has Pat told you about my sister and me?"

But Babs had risen quickly to her feet and crossed to the
French windows. "Oh God!" She was peering out into the
garden. "Do you hear it? Sam's at it again. And after all those
promises. Come on, we'd better go out."

In the next instant, Grace's hand was grabbed and she was half led, half dragged out to the garden, where the most curious spectacle was taking place.

Samuel Woolton was reclining, entirely naked, in the bough of a horse chestnut tree, playing on a set of panpipes. His pointed goatee, the dark hair on his body, the paleness of his skin in the moonlight and the proudly erect phallus (from which both women quickly averted their gaze) made him resemble some mythical god or creature. Priapus, perhaps, crossed with a faun.

Around the disused fountain danced Verity Woolton. She was wearing only her underwear, and was draped about with Grace's Oriental wrap. Her pirouettes were almost balletic, but for the wobbles and the odd capering. Even in the darkness of the garden, one could discern her bulbous ever-startled gaze.

"I wouldn't mind so much if he could actually play a half-decent tune." Barbara's tone was withering. "Or if she could dance remotely well. Perhaps, if I tried some of the stuff they're so fond of, he really *would* seem tuneful and she graceful." She raised her voice to a dry, ash-ridden shout: "Sam, do come down, there's a pet! Verity, *please* . . ." Then something seemed to occur to her and she began to turn this way and that, looking all about her. "Cecil? Where the devil . . . Cecil!"

She was interrupted by a resonant, "Tally-ho!" and a glimpse of pink flesh and fast-moving little legs as Cecil went darting back and forth between the trees, as naked as Sam Woolton, the bald head glinting.

"Heavens!" Babs was flushed. "Cecil, for goodness' sake, stop it and put some clothes on. We've seen it all before, darling, and we don't want to see it again."

But the shout came back: "Bugger off, you old hag!" For a few seconds he was freeze-framed, standing still in the moonlight, between two trees. A squat Bacchus with pink hairless chest and overhanging belly. Letting out a huge whoop, he ran, full pelt, down the hill, vaulting clean over the back fence and disappearing entirely from view.

"Oh, God," said Grace. "The cliff . . ."

The piping came to an abrupt halt. Babs hitched up her dress and ran after Cecil, almost colliding with her sister as she went. Grace followed in her wake, as a flaccid Sam climbed down from the tree, and as Verity pulled Grace's wrap more closely about her and assumed a forlorn look.

Climbing over the fence, Grace found Babs standing alone, gazing over the edge. "Oh no . . . Is he . . ."

Babs, ignoring her, put her hands on her hips and bellowed, "You fool! What did you think you were *doing*?"

Arriving beside her, Grace looked down. The view wasn't quite so dramatic as she'd feared. The sea was black and foamy where it lapped over the sharp rocks on its bed, but the initial drop was only about ten feet, down to a grassy ledge. Cecil was sitting on this ledge, clutching his ankle.

"Sorry, darling." His face, as he gazed up, was abject. "Beautiful night, wouldn't you say? Bit cold now though . . ."

Babs turned to Grace. "This is so embarrassing."

"Don't be silly. He's all right. That's the main thing."

"Not when I've finished with him, he won't be. Cecil, you'd better get yourself back up here right away."

The face below twisted into a grimace. "Not sure I can, my sweet. Think I might have broken my ankle."

"You blithering idiot!" Babs turned back to Grace, and her eyes softened with worry. "Now what do we do?"

Woolton, clad in a tartan dressing gown, climbed over the fence. He was carrying an identical dressing gown, which he flung down to Cecil. "Here you are, old chap. Cover up the . . . old chap, there's a good fellow." Then, turning back to the group, he announced, "I shall climb down and bring him up!"

"You most certainly will not." Verity had appeared beside them. She had Grace's wrap over her head and was clutching it tightly about her, a sort of pink-and-gold widow in mourning. "Or there'll be two of you to be rescued."

"Perhaps we should ring for the fire brigade?" Grace suggested. "Or the police?"

"The police? Here?" Woolton's voice rose to a squeak. "Over my dead body!"

"For goodness' sakes!" Verity appeared to have sobered up rapidly. "Go and get the ladder, Sam. Just go and get the ladder."

Woolton scrambled off. After a few minutes, and just as Grace was wondering what on earth had happened to O'Connell, a cheerful whistling rang out. It was O'Connell, a ladder balanced on his shoulder, calling merrily, "Anyone want their windows cleaned?" Sam trotted along beside him.

Together, and with a certain amount of drunken fumbling, they extended the ladder down the cliffside. Sam and Grace knelt down and gripped the top as firmly as they could to keep it steady, while O'Connell climbed down to Cecil.

"It's not broken," O'Connell announced, feeling the ankle. "A sprain at worst."

"It hurts a lot though." Cecil seemed annoyed at the demotion of his injury. "I don't think it'll take my weight."

With difficulty, O'Connell hoisted Cecil over his shoulder in a fireman's lift, and, grunting, began slowly to ascend the ladder while Grace and Woolton struggled to keep it in position. Eventually, a groaning Cecil was deposited on safe ground, and O'Connell stood brushing himself down.

"It's like carrying a very heavy bride over a very steep threshold."

"Oh, Pat, you're our hero." Verity clasped her hands together.

O'Connell was looking oddly at Grace. "Just how much do you weigh, Miss Rutherford? Let's try, shall we? Be sure I can manage when the time comes to carry *you* over the threshold." Ignoring her protests, he grabbed her around the legs and threw her over his shoulder, proclaiming, "Oh, she's a mere feather after that lump!"

The blood rushed to Grace's head and she beat with her fists against his back. "Put me—"

"Down? Why, certainly." Seconds later she was back on terra firma, and he was helping Woolton carry Cecil over the fence and up to the house, followed by Verity.

"Are you all right?" Grace addressed Babs, who was dusting herself down.

"Fine. Glad this ludicrous episode hasn't been entirely pointless."

"What do you mean?"

Babs frowned. "I wouldn't have thought you'd be so obtuse. Pat just proposed to you, Grace."

Four

"*What* a night." O'Connell was sitting on the edge of the bed, pulling off his shoes. "Think I'd better tell my agent to get me a new English publisher. I'm not sure I'll be able to look Sam Woolton in the eye again!"

"Yes, it has been quite a night." Grace sat down at the dressing table and began to cleanse her face, keeping an eye on O'Connell in the mirror as she did so.

"We never did get our walk." He was taking his socks off now.

"I was waylaid by Babs. We had a couple of drinks together."

"Oh yes?"

"She enjoys a bit of a gossip, doesn't she?"

A chuckle from O'Connell. "Good old Babs. We go back a ways, she and I."

"So she said." She wiped an eyelid with cotton wool. "She obviously knows you very well. She actually seemed to know me rather better than I'd have expected, too."

"Oh yes?" He began unbuttoning his shirt.

"She thinks you're serious about me."

"And so I am." Was that a hint of tension in his voice?

"She even thought you were *proposing* to me back there in the garden."

"Really?" He chuckled. Dropped a cuff link with a clatter on the bedside table. "My, but that woman's imagination does fill in some pretty big gaps!"

"So you weren't, then? Proposing to me, I mean?" She wheeled about on her stool to face him. "I didn't think you were, but then I do keep getting things wrong when it comes to you. Everyone else seems to know you so much better than I do, *Pat*."

He came across to where she was sitting. Crouched down in front of her and took her by both hands. "Darling, I was just having a bit of fun back there in the garden. Babs is an incorrigible troublemaker, really she is. I'd like to think that when I get around to proposing to you, I'll manage it with a little more style and finesse." He reached up to ruffle her hair as though she were a child. Then, straightening up, he slipped off his shirt and threw it on the floor.

"So you might propose to me one day?" She tried to make her voice light and playful like his.

"That depends. Are *you* planning to go waltzing off with John Cramer?"

"I'm not planning to go waltzing off with John Cramer."

He smiled broadly. "Then we'll have to see what we can do, my darling. You know that I'll never be worthy of you, of course? I've quite a past, I'm afraid: I've had affairs with more women than I can remember. I've dived naked into city fountains. I've been at parties where everyone takes each other to bed and steals each other's jewelry. I've had women who have destroyed hotel rooms, food fights that have destroyed hotel restaurants. I once lost a racehorse in a game of poker. I once drove a white Bentley smack into the foyer of a hotel in Alabama. Shall I go on?"

"No need."

His shoulders relaxed visibly. "Do you think you might look kindly on a proposal from a slippery, caddish sort such as myself?"

"Your past doesn't bother me, Devil. And neither does your caddish reputation. But behind all my bravado, I'm a very ordinary girl who wants very ordinary things. I want to love someone who loves me back. I want to marry a man I can trust with my life."

"Grace, you're such a sweet thing."

"Not really." She could hear the dead note in her voice. Turning back to the mirror, she looked again at his reflection and at her own. And for a moment, both appeared as strangers to her.

The night was long and restless. The curtains were open a chink, letting the moonlight smear its way in to the bedroom, illuminating O'Connell's face on the pillow, accentuating his large features, the hollows in his cheeks, making him appear entirely different from his daytime self. His profile was more severe by moonlight, his skin waxy gray.

It's a glimpse of how he'll look when he's old, thought Grace. He'll look like this in his coffin.

Sleepless, she lay propped on an elbow, watching him. She'd been watching him for a long time. Her tired eyes would start to swim every so often, and his face would distort further—becoming skull-like, the flesh melting away. Then she'd try, once more, to close her eyes and slip away into blissful unconsciousness, only for it to continue to evade her.

Why had he gone and told Barbara? *Why?* Had he chosen her as his confidante? Poured out all his worries and doubts about his new relationship? Or did it simply make an amusing anecdote? And was it only Barbara or had he told others, too? Did he toss it casually into conversation with the boys over cigars and brandies? God, she could just imagine how it would go. *"That new girl of mine—well, she might appear to be just a nice English girl, but beneath that impeccable bob and behind that shiny smile, there's something of a Pandora's box. Doesn't bother me of course—I'm rather enjoying opening it up. A little dirt piques my interest."*

When sleep did make fleeting appearances, it was only to tease her with its elusiveness. She'd be sliding beautifully off, when suddenly she'd find herself cast back into the bedroom, with its thick brown curtains, faded carpet and cracked ceiling (the cracks seemed to be growing); with the heavy, even sleep breathing of the stranger lying beside her (for he *was* still a stranger to her, she could see that now); with the ticking of her alarm clock evolving into a constrained but relentless taunt. The spaces between the ticks seemed to extend themselves over the hours; to stretch out and grow, until on came the next sickeningly inevitable tick.

How could he sleep so deeply while she fretted and whirred beside him? How could he be so utterly oblivious to her fury? His sleep was an affront. The more she thought about it, the more she burned inside.

Why had he brought her here to this monkey house and lied to her about it? This was supposed to be a weekend for the two them to get to know each other better. How ironic that she perhaps *was* getting to know him, finally.

Eventually—the clock showed five o'clock—she got out of bed, dressed in the previous day's clothes, and threw her belongings into the little case she'd brought with her. Throughout her hurried and not particularly quiet packing process, he slept on. His sleep was obscene.

She took a brief look back at him from the doorway. The sun was coming up now, and his face was softening again, his skin honeying. For a moment she almost dropped the case, took off her clothes and got back into bed with him. Perhaps she should wait for him to wake up, give him a chance to explain . . . Her grip tightened on the handle of the suitcase. Just then, he stirred in his sleep and made a tiny sound in his throat, which had something of his laugh in it. His laugh. She turned and headed out the door.

Walking down the lane, Grace was soothed by birdsong and the sparkle of morning sunlight on the sea. She'd thought it would take a good hour to reach Horace and Mrs. Horace's cottage and feared it might be longer still, but in fact it was only a twenty-minute walk. Cars distorted distances so.

It took a while before the upstairs curtains twitched. Shortly afterward, Horace appeared in a beige dressing gown.

"What the devil's up, miss? Is someone taken ill or something?"

"I'm sorry to disturb you so early. Nothing's wrong. But I'd be most obliged if you'd drive me to the station." Grace couldn't quite look him in the eye as she shoved some coins at him.

"Righto, then. Back in a jiffy. Would you like to step in a moment, miss . . . ? Very well, then, as you please. You just wait here and I'll be down directly."

A cockerel was crowing somewhere nearby. A dog was barking. Grace sat down on the doorstep, her case beside her, and waited to start out on the drive back to the station. Once there, she'd catch the grindingly slow milk train to London. Alone in her carriage, she'd come upon a folded copy of yesterday's *Telegraph*, its front page emblazoned with a photograph of a monoplane coming down over a floodlit airfield, and she'd settle back for the journey with the story of Charles A. Lindbergh's epic flight. And long after she'd finished reading the article, she'd be sitting thinking about the man who wrote it. Turning things over in her mind. The things he'd said. The way he'd kissed her. John Cramer.

Five

"*Nancy?*"

Grace's heels were loud on the tiled floor of the hallway, the emptiness of the house ringing out at her. It seemed bigger than when she'd left. "Nancy?" she called again, though she knew by this time that her sister wasn't at home, and wasn't quite sure why she had shouted her name a second time. As if she could summon her up like a genie.

There was a faint smell of baking. In the kitchen, the two halves of a sponge cake were laid out on a wire rack, waiting to be pasted together with jam and cream and put away in a tin. Grace wanted this to mean that Nancy was, after all, somewhere about the place. She needed so badly to sit down with her sister and find out, absolutely and definitively, how Nancy felt about John Cramer. This was crucial now. She had to know for certain whether or not her sister was in love with him.

She stepped forward and touched the cake. It was still warm.

There was a noise from the living room. A creaking floorboard.

"Nancy?" Grace felt slight trepidation as she approached.

"Just me, dear." It was Mummy, sitting on the couch and bundling something swiftly into a wooden box. Looking flustered. "Did you have a nice time?"

"What have you got there?"

"Nothing of interest. Anyway, I thought you weren't coming back until tomorrow. Is everything all right?"

"Fine. I just decided it was time to come home."

"Shall I make us some tea? I've baked a cake." Without waiting for the answer, Catherine got up, deposited the box in the bottom cupboard of the sideboard next to the drinks bottles and trotted off to the kitchen.

Sitting on the couch, waiting and listening to the distant clatters from the kitchen, Grace wondered what was going on. She was tempted to go and look in the box, but knew this would be a transgression.

"What were you doing?" she asked when Catherine finally came in.

"Nothing much." She set the tray down on the low table and perched on the edge of a chair. Grace's slice of cake was far too big. "I'm glad you're back, though. We've a chance for a little talk." She busied herself with strainers and tongs.

"What about?" Grace tipped the spilled tea back into her cup. In fact, she knew what this was going to be about. Nancy had warned her some time ago.

"Well, it's your column, dear. It's such a splendid opportunity. So many people reading you every week. What I'd have done to be in your position, at your age . . ."

"But?"

"All those words, week after week, devoted entirely to the latest hairstyles and dance steps . . . Why you should never order fish at such and such a place; how you stop your silver-fox coat from molting all over your dress. Frankly, I'd have thought you'd have something more *substantial* to say."

Grace stared at her cake. Its daunting size. Here they were again, at their perennial difficulty: Catherine's disappointment in her. It had been the same when she'd dropped out of university and then again when she'd first joined Pearson & Pearson—back in the days when Catherine pretty much lived for the WPS, patrolling self-importantly about Hampstead in that ridiculous uniform, shouting at drunks and chasing the couples off the Heath. Whatever Grace did, it would never be enough.

"It's a column about going out in the West End. What would you have me write about?" But why had she even said it when the answer was so obvious?

Catherine set her cup and saucer down on the tray. "There are thousands and thousands of women across the country whose voices are simply not heard when it counts most. Your own sister is still one of them."

"Mummy, it's not my fault that you didn't win your battle. I have my life to live. Must I live yours as well?"

"The battle is not lost! We won a partial victory and we're still fighting."

"Sorry," said Grace. "I didn't mean to belittle what you've done. I know we joke about it all, Nancy and I, but we both think you're absolutely marvelous." She glanced at her mother. Frowned. There was something not quite right about all this. She'd been expecting this talking-to, but oddly Catherine looked as though she wasn't even paying attention to her own tirade. "Mummy, what are you up to? I know you're bothered about my column, but there's something else going on."

Catherine shook her head. "I've no idea what you're talking about."

"What's in the box, Mummy?"

"Just some photographs."

"Mind if I take a look?" Before Catherine could answer, Grace was across the room and fetching the box out. Opening it up.

"See?" said Catherine. "It's just photographs."

There were only three photographs in the box. Formal groups, taken at a studio, each in a cardboard frame. One showed Grace and Nancy, aged about six and five respectively, wearing identical pinafore dresses, their arms around the shoulders of a tiny boy who stood between them—skinny with overlong blond hair, an absurd lace collar and knicker-bockers.

"Sheridan," said Grace.

The second picture showed the children's parents. The women were seated on chairs: Catherine's round, young face had a fresh, intelligent look to it, while Amelia, with her luxurious black hair and catlike eyes, was altogether more exotic. Behind them stood Daddy, with his shock of untamable hair, prematurely white, and his round glasses, every inch the mad professor; and Edward Shapcott, a good six inches taller with enormous shoulders and fierce eyes.

The third photograph had the whole group together. It was obvious, on examination, that this shot was taken at the end of what had been a rather prolonged session. The children's expressions displayed an obvious boredom and impatience, as though they couldn't wait to get away and play. The adults were somewhat fixed and rigid in their posture.

"I've never seen these before," said Grace.

"Dreadful, aren't they? The photographer was quite hopeless."

"I wouldn't have said they were *that* bad. They're not part of our collection though, are they? Where did they come from?"

But Catherine appeared thoroughly absorbed in cleaning her glasses.

"Are they Sheridan's?" She knew, as soon as she'd spoken, that she was right. "Did he bring them round?"

"Yes, he did." Mummy put the glasses back on for a moment. Then, dissatisfied, took them off again, blew on the lenses and continued with her polishing. "You only just missed him, actually. Nice boy. He tells me the two of you are quite friendly these days?"

"That's right. Mummy . . . ?"

"He wanted to talk to me about his parents. His mother in particular. Go trawling through the memories, sort of thing. He's rather lonely, you know."

Grace was staring at her mother. The words were making sense, the voice was light and normal-sounding, but Catherine was far from being her normal self. Her eyes were full of anguish and there was a tangible tension in her—as though it was taking all the effort she had to keep her emotions from bubbling over.

"Mummy . . ."

"I hadn't seen him since he was a boy. There's so much of his father in him! Rather took the wind out of my sails."

"Yes, it must have." Poor Catherine! There was a tear sliding down her face now. Grace reached out for her hand, touched it gently. They'd sworn they'd never tell, she and Nancy. They'd made a pact. "Mummy—" She was still hesitating, but if ever there was a right moment to speak out, it was surely now.

"Mummy, I know. I mean, I *know*."

Catherine looked up at her with startled, watery eyes. "What?"

"About you and Edward Shapcott."

"I see." She got up. Moved to the mantelpiece, ostensibly to put her glasses away in their case. "How . . ."

"We've known for a long time, Nancy and me. We saw you together up on Parliament Hill. You were kissing. We weren't so very young. I was thirteen. We'd guessed already. It was just a confirmation of what we both knew, each of us privately. It went on for years, didn't it?"

It was out there now, taking shape between them. There was no going back.

"Oh, gosh." Catherine was leaning heavily on the mantelpiece, her back turned to Grace. "I don't know what to say to you."

"It must have been very hard for you." Grace wanted to go over and put a hand on her shoulder, but somehow she couldn't. "I do understand, Mummy."

"Don't be ridiculous!" The passion flared up in Catherine's eyes as she looked around. "How could you possibly understand?"

The temptation to tell her mother about George was

strong. But no. No. "Mummy, you wandered off the path, but you did the right thing in the end. You both did. You ended the affair and you stood by your families."

"Yes. We did." She drew the back of her hand across her wet eyes. "And it was the hardest thing I've ever done. You know, I did love your father very much. You do realize that, don't you, Grace?"

"Of course you did."

"But Edward . . . Edward Shapcott was the love of my life and I had to give him up." Catherine was a sturdy woman, but in that moment she looked so frail, so fragile.

Grace swallowed. "Did Daddy ever know?"

The tiniest of nods. "I don't want to speak about this again. Not ever. I don't want Nancy to know about this conversation." And then, after a moment, "Or Sheridan. Sheridan doesn't know about any of this, Grace."

"Whatever you want, Mummy."

A cavernous silence opened up between the two women. Catherine returned the cups to the tray, rattling about. Grace simply watched her, feeling a sadness, a sense that she had irrevocably lost something. There are times when the sharing of a secret brings people closer. The secret strengthens the invisible bonds of time, experience, friendship. It tightens those bonds. Not so here.

"Where's Nancy?" Grace asked, at length, unable to bear the silence any longer.

"She's gone to Paris with John."

"*What?*"

"She telephoned yesterday, full of news about Lindbergh's landing. They had seats with the American ambassador. She's been having the time of her life, meeting all sorts of people."

"I see. Yes, I expect she has." Nausea soured her insides. Everything was dark clouds. The distant buzz of a plane.

Mummy's voice had lightened. Her relief at the change of subject was audible. "Edna's taken the children out. They'll be back in an hour or so."

"Right. I think I'll go and unpack my case." Grace got shakily to her feet.

"Grace." Catherine put a hand on Grace's arm. "John is your sister's beau."

"Of course he is." Grace tried to toss the words out casually. "And a jolly nice pair they make."

"My dear." That hand was still on her arm. "She's too young to stay alone forever."

"Has he proposed to her, then?" She shouldn't have asked it. Should just have headed straight up with the case. But she had to know.

"I rather think he might, if you let them alone."

"If I . . . What are you saying?"

"You chose the other chap. That was the right thing to do."

"No, it wasn't. I don't want O'Connell."

The grip on her arm tightened. "She's too young to spend the rest of her life alone. And she has those children to bring up. It's your turn to do the right thing, Grace. Your turn to stand by the family."

"All I ever *do* is stand by the family! It's always about Nancy, isn't it? *I'm* your daughter as well. *I'm* too young to stay alone forever!"

"It's different for you." Catherine relinquished Grace's arm. "My dear, you're just like your mother. You'll always be the one to look after others. That's just how it is with us."

Something was stirring in Grace. Something dark. It was

like staring down into the Thames at the objects that lay on the riverbed among all the mud and silt. The things that lay buried, and had done for a very long time. Mysterious shapes. Shadows.

"You needn't worry. John Cramer's the last man on earth I'd want to be with. Nancy's welcome to him."

Two overlarge slices of cake untouched on their plates.

Summer's arrived to send us all gaga. That old card, that party jester. At the first glimmer of even the tiniest ray of sun, we all go running about the West End in our sandals, exposing our unpalatable toes, displaying our lily-white legs and our flabby arms. My, what an unwieldy sack of potatoes we Londoners are. All through the winter we are so chic in our silver-fox coats and our plumed hats and our nicely cut tweeds. It's as though we've all signed a pact, agreeing not to look or not to care for the next three months.

All this gay abandon simply doesn't bring out the best in me. I am not of the type that is all ruddy complexion and flaxen hair and overflowing wholesomeness. My red-lipped, jet-haired white-skinned visage is offset nicely by ice and darkness and the contrasting roaring fires. Today, while dashing about Dickens & Jones (there are pleasing summer dresses about that place in pastel colors for those who are the pastel type), I beheld my reflection in a long changing room mirror and was, frankly, aghast at my own ghoulishness. I resembled nothing so much as a vampire caught out in the daylight, and don't know what I can do about this beyond a fastidious avoidance of mirrors for the rest of the season.

The hideous truth is that no matter how well dressed one might be or how sharp the angles of one's bob, one can't forever escape the ravages of the years. Summer is kinder to the young, with their golden flesh and their pure souls, than to the likes of me. I suppose I still think of myself as a flapper; indeed, as one of the original flappers: the pioneers who first danced the dances now performed so lithely and casually by the two-a-penny whippersnappers clogging up the floors at Ciro's and Kit-Cat and Salamander. But it's time to face facts: I'm a was-flapper, a former-flapper, a flapper-grown-up or even grown-old. When young gentlemen in tall hats and tails glance in my direction, they're not, as I'd thought, admiring my décolletage or my shapely calves. They're wondering why I'm not at home in a housecoat with the children and the knitting, or tucked up in a twin-bedded room with hubby. I should say, dear readers, that this is not an attempt to garner sympathy. I'm simply stating the facts of this week's shock realization.

But surely it isn't just the unflattering mirror in Dickens & Jones that has brought this home to me? No, girls. I have been in Dorset, parading about in my swimming costume with a collection of people even older than my good self, who really Should Know Better. Fashionable dissolute types who look terrible in their swimwear; who like to indulge in children's party games and who run about their gardens naked, play panpipes and jump off cliffs. These are people who are becoming increasingly desperate in their refusal to grow old. I suppose what I'm saying is that I don't wish to become one of *those* people any more than I wish to join the children-having, churchgoing, flower-arranging set. There must be another way, mustn't there? Please tell me I'm not the only modern girl in this predicament?

And so it is good to cheer oneself up with ice cream! What a heavenly substance this is. The Yanks have been on to it for years, of course, and sell it by the quart in every corner store. Now it is finally here, too. I suggest you go this very day to your nearest Lyons Corner House (it's certainly being served in their larger establishments, at any rate); crossing town by bus, tram or train if necessary (it's worth it, I promise), and order yourself a dish of their wondrously refreshing and luxurious vanilla, chocolate, strawberry or lemon flavors. (It can't *really* be fattening, can it? This meltingly unreal dessert of the gods?). Around and about the West End today, I noticed that plenty of cafés are putting their tables and chairs out on the pavements, French-style; so where possible, eat your ice cream outside in the sunshine.

As I was passing through Trafalgar Square yesterday, a man stopped me and tried to sell me some half crowns at a shilling each. Being the suspicious sort, I gave him a skewiff smile and shook my head, whereupon the chap leaped in the air, whooping with glee, and then ran off to try someone else. Too late did I realize that rather than evading his trap, I had stepped neatly into it! Now, it irks me to think that this fellow may win his bet or prove his theory so easily. So, if you come across him, readers, you know what to do, and together we'll have the last laugh.

Only in London . . .

Diamond Sharp

Six

"*Tell* the driver to get a move on, will you?" Grace was resting her head against the leather upholstery, her eyes closed. "I'm absolutely parched."

Dickie, sitting beside her in the back of the taxi, patted her hand. "Settle back, old girl. There's some sort of holdup. An accident or something. We'll just have to wait."

Opening her eyes, Grace gazed out on Oxford Street, all shuttered shops and stragglers. Selfridges had a melancholy quality about it when closed, like a beautiful girl dolled up for a dance but left a wallflower. "Oh, Dickie, this is no good. I happen to know there's a nice little place tucked around that corner. Why don't we stop off for a cocktail and stroll over to the party in half an hour or so?"

"Won't work. I need to be there to greet the guests." He was twitching at his tuxedo, smoothing his hair again and again, though it was uncharacteristically well oiled, not a strand out of place.

"Darling, you're a bag of nerves. Trust me, a nice cocktail would steady you up. That place I mentioned—"

"No." Dickie's voice was sharp enough to attract the driver's attention. He continued more quietly, "You needn't worry, Grace. There'll be plenty to drink at the party—sufficient even for your needs, I should think."

"Dickie!" She'd been glad when he'd asked her to partner him to the *Herald*'s party. They threw a party every summer, but this year was also the paper's fifteenth anniversary. The *Herald*'s circulation had soared since Dickie had taken over as editor in 1925, and it was very much his night. She was touched that he wanted her center stage with him. It suited her, just at present, to be on the arm of someone so absolutely safe as him. Now though, with Dickie so unpleasant, she wondered if she'd made a mistake.

"Sorry." He patted her leg, his hand lingering for a moment on the red velvet of her dress. "Thing is, Nancy came to see me today . . ."

"I should have guessed you'd be ganging up with her."

"Don't be so daft. Nobody's ganging up. Nancy's concerned about you. She says you haven't been in to work at Pearson's for over a week."

"That's none of her business. Or yours."

"She says you're out every night with Dodo and her cronies. And then you hide in your room all day."

"A girl has to get her beauty sleep *some* time."

"She says you're barely speaking to her. She's blaming herself, thinks she must have done something wrong. What could Nancy have done to warrant that kind of treatment, Grace? *Nancy?* I mean, she's just the loveliest—"

"Oh, do shut up about Nancy." Grace fixed her gaze on the pillars of Selfridges. "When is this damn taxi going to *move*?"

"She says you've gone through pretty much every bottle in the drinks cabinet."

"I'm having a little off patch, Dickie. That's all. You surely have off patches? Nancy certainly does, though she's conveniently forgotten, it seems. I'd be fine if everyone would just leave me to get on with it and get over it."

Dickie. That oh-so-familiar face of his—pale and lively and edgy. He wasn't handsome, neither in the classical sense nor unconventionally. But he exuded intelligence and wit—practically sweated it out of every pore. And women adored him for it. This would never have been true in reverse, of course. The bright-but-plain sort of girl stood no chance with a high-caliber gentleman. Not unless she was also filthy rich. Perhaps, Grace realized, somewhat randomly, it was the very fear of finding that she herself was the bright-but-plain type that had always driven her to shun that kind of girl and to strive so hard with her appearance, her persona . . .

"Grace, this is more than an off patch. What's going on? This can't all be about Dexter O'Connell. Can it?"

She rolled her eyes. "Jealousy is not attractive, Dickie. Not in the least."

A sound that was almost a scoff. "Heavens, you think I'm still in love with you!"

Well, aren't you? The words were almost out. She had to fight them back. Then the embarrassment came flaring up in her face, hot in her cheeks. And the big yawning space that had been opening up inside her over the last week or so seemed to widen just that little bit further.

"I think I should go home." But as she said it, the traffic began to move and the taxi jolted into motion.

"Dead horse in the road," the driver called back over his shoulder. "Can you believe it, in this day and age?"

Grace peered out as they drove past. Three policemen and a couple of workmen were trying to move it out of the road, watched by a bunch of bystanders. Five men struggling to shift one dead horse.

"Come to the party with me, Grace." Dickie felt for her hand. "I'll stop prying, I promise. You're my best chum, in spite of everything—perhaps *because* of everything—and I want you there with me."

The cabaret was already in full swing up on top of the Tivoli Club, in the roof garden. The Chaz Rowney band were playing loud, while a bunch of black dancers from Harlem, in glittery costumes, danced something entirely new. It started out as a Charleston, but as Rowney launched into one of his crazy trombone solos, the dancers broke away from their partners to improvise elaborate solo moves. All around the dance floor, the bright young things were watching closely while the sun went slowly down beyond Trafalgar Square. Some of them were tapping out the steps, determined to be among the first to bring them to London's nightclubs.

"It's the Breakaway." Dodo was wearing a golden dress with a single gold-painted rose threaded into her hair. "Quite something, isn't it?" She was flanked on either side by Topping and Humphries. They'd become, so Grace had thought of late, her guard dogs. They were always with her, but you didn't have to bother speaking to them anymore. You might toss them a biscuit quite legitimately.

"Looks like a Charleston with a bit of extra showing off," said Grace. "Perhaps dances will always be variations on the Charleston from now on. It's the definitive dance, wouldn't you say?"

"Well, there's another column," said Dodo. "I wish *my* job was so easy."

Grace was looking about for Dickie, but he was still over by the top of the stairs, shaking hands. "I need a drink." As she said it, a waiter placed a glass of champagne in her hand.

"I bet you do." Dodo took one for herself. "That's *him*, isn't it?" She gestured across the roof.

Grace hadn't seen O'Connell since the morning she'd run from Sam Woolton's house. He looked unworldly tonight in a suit of purest white with a single red rose, the same red as her dress, in the buttonhole. The only man not to be wearing a black dinner jacket. He was standing talking to a girl in front of a white-painted fence entwined with plastic vines and lilies and fairy lights. As Grace looked over, he caught her eye and smiled distantly—the kind of smile you'd give to an acquaintance. His raven-haired companion, in a blue satin dress that glowed green under the lights, was familiar.

"Yes it's him all right. And that's not all. I know the girl, too."

It was Margaret the typist, her face all over an ecstatic kind of happiness until she belatedly spotted Grace and adjusted her expression. Her hair was newly bobbed, her glasses abandoned. Poor cow was wandering blindly about the place so as not to be seen in those thick-lensed specs of hers. The transformation was remarkable, though. The bob had the look of Marcus Rino about it. The dress showed a figure far better than Grace would have suspected. Margaret didn't look like Margaret, and in a good way. But how did she come to be here?

"Gwace!" Sheridan, appearing suddenly at her side, was all painted up in thick Egyptian makeup, prompting many a stare. "I'm not sure whether to thank you or curse you for that column of yours the other week. You have such a sweet-and-sour tongue that I simply can't tell if you're fwiend or foe."

"Barbed, that's what her tongue is," said Dodo, helpfully. "Barbed like the wire."

Grace was still glancing across at O'Connell and Margaret, and experiencing the oddest sensation—a kind of slow fall. Was she falling or was the roof garden around her rising? It was impossible to tell.

"*Did* you like the club?" There was a touch of anxiety in Sheridan's voice. "I have to know what you weally think, darling, just between ourselves."

It took an effort to focus her attention on him, what with those two standing just over there . . .

"It's as I said. Yours is the most remarkable club in London."

"Gwace, you're incowwigible." He looked, as he spoke, like the little boy he once was. She could see him in their garden, squealing in alarm while she and Nancy tortured worms in front of him. And the memory brought with it other memories . . . a veritable cascade of them.

"What were you up to, calling in on my mother the other day? It wasn't just about the photographs, was it? If I was paranoid, I'd say you waited for a time when Nancy and I were away so you could get her on her own . . ."

"Not at all. Don't be daft." He appeared to be waiting for Dodo to wander off before continuing. "I wanted to talk to Cathewine about my mother. That's all. I miss her *so* much and yet I feel I've never understood her. There weren't many people who were close to Amelia—she didn't let people in." While he spoke, he kept fiddling with his signet ring.

"But our mothers hadn't seen each other for years, you

know that. I can't imagine Catherine would have had anything very enlightening to say?"

"Well . . ." Still he twisted at that ring. His face looked just the way it did when he fibbed as a small boy.

"What's *really* going on, Sheridan?" A memory flickered up. "Last time I saw you, you wanted to talk to me confidentially about something. What was it?"

His kohl-rimmed gaze darted about, landing anywhere but on her. "It's not the time or the place, darling."

"Then I'll come to see you tomorrow. I could drop by your house."

"All wight."

Grace watched him slip off through the throng. Perhaps Catherine had been wrong when she said he didn't know what had happened all those years ago . . .

The glittering dancers sashayed off, to be replaced by a bunch of stilt-walkers dressed as cocktails. Then came a magician who did tricks with newspaper: pouring water into a copy of the *Herald* and shaking it out dry; ripping it into tiny pieces and transforming the shreds into paper dolls; placing the dolls in a dish, setting fire to them, quenching the flames and pulling forth a gigantic, intact copy of the *Herald* with a photograph of Dickie's face on its front page.

At this point the music stopped and the spotlight skidded across the crowd to fix on a jubilant Dickie.

"Good evening, everyone, and thank you." His voice carried well across the roof. "Welcome, one and all, to the *Herald*'s fifteenth anniversary party. Gosh, but I'm happy . . ." His speech was all exuberance and eloquent froth. Once or twice he caught her eye, and his look was so light and clear. He might just float away into the sky. Grace drained her champagne glass. She could no longer see O'Connell among the crowd.

"Is that your sister over there?" Dodo again. Did she have nothing better to do than continually claw open Grace's life with her gold-painted talons? "So divine in that pink dress. Look how she's threading back and forth through all those people over there. She's looking for someone. Perhaps for you?"

"I doubt it." Grace didn't bother looking.

Dickie had finished and the stage was taken by a Chinese contortionist, who twisted her rubbery body into such peculiar knotted shapes that it made one quite queasy. Heading over to the bar for a glass of water, Grace looked up at the mirror that stretched along the back wall and saw, reflected in it, John Cramer. He was perched on a high stool down at the far end of the bar, gazing at nothing in particular and toying with a highball glass. The suddenness of this—his nearness—was too much. She wanted to turn and slip away, but he'd already seen her in the mirror. They'd seen each other.

"Have a nice weekend with Nancy, did you?" She tried to keep her voice icy. Didn't want the emotion showing through.

He shook his head as if despairing of her. Swore under his breath. "Grace, you turned me down flat and went straight off on your little trip with O'Connell. Why the hell should I tell you anything about my weekend?"

At the sound of that slurred voice, Grace realized the obvious. The sullen, oddly malleable look about his face, the glassiness in the eyes . . . The teetotaller was drunk! Probably too drunk to do anything but prop himself up on that bar.

"What are you *doing*, John?"

"I wish I knew." He looked away, back down into his glass, and Grace felt herself sinking even further inside. Somewhere nearby, Nancy was searching for him, she was sure of it.

Threading back and forth through the crowd looking for her lover.

"Go home. Out of respect for my sister, if not for yourself."

"Grace . . ."

She turned her back on him and was instantly enveloped in a crowd of celebratory colleagues. A big pack of news writers, feature writers, reviewers, copy editors . . . A herd of jolly, smiling faces full of mirth and gossip, wanting to show her that she was one of them. That she belonged. Usually she would have been gratified but tonight her mind was on other things. She was there, among them, bathed in their niceness, for what felt like forever. When they finally moved on and away, Cramer was gone from his seat at the bar. She couldn't see him or O'Connell for that matter—and she found herself narrowly evading Sam Woolton and Verity, who were deliberating over a tray of vol-au-vents (that naked hairy body and that *thing* of his so vivid in her mind's eye . . . those bulbous eyes and her own whirling Oriental wrap . . .), and then someone trod heavily on her foot and—

"Sorry, Grace." Margaret, pink-faced from the drink or the awkwardness. "Didn't see you."

"I don't suppose you can see much at all without your glasses. What are you doing here?"

"Ah." The face went from pink to magenta. "You *don't* know. Thing is, they sent you an invitation at the office and—"

"I see. You decided to be me."

"Please don't be cross! I can't go on as I am. As I have been. My life is like something hollowed out. Like a . . . Is it true that French people eat snails? I'm like the shell that's left behind after the snail's been eaten. That's what it's like, being me."

"For goodness' sakes, Margaret, I'm not bothered about your using my invitation. Not when there's so much else to be bothered about."

"Oh. You know then?" A fierce intelligence was burning away in Margaret's myopic eyes. And a hunger. An insatiable hunger. "I'm sorry, Grace."

"Know what? What are you talking about?"

"Ah." A sheepish look. Slightly nervous. "I'm going to be Dexter O'Connell's secretary. I'll book his restaurant tables and take his suits to the cleaner's and type his letters, but *also* I'm going to type up his novels! I'll be the very first person to read the new book!"

There was a stiffness in Grace's face.

"I'm sailing to New York with him. I'll be going wherever he goes. Following him all over the world! Can you *imagine* it?"

"He's going back to New York?"

"I wrote to him at the Savoy. I know I should have told you but . . . Well, it all seemed a little delicate, what with you and him and . . . I met him, remember? And he thought I was clever. So I sat down and wrote to him about his books and I mentioned that if there was ever a chance to meet him again, or if there was anything I could do for him . . ."

"Unbelievable!"

A quick shake of the head. "It's not like that. I'm not trying to compete with *you*. But it's over between the two of you anyway, isn't it? And in any case, you surely knew it wouldn't last? He isn't the type to belong to anyone but himself."

"And how do you know all this? How do you know him so much better than I do?"

A shrug. "I've read all his books. Have you?"

It was like the most dreadful dream—Margaret standing there all pretty and knowing and full of herself. You couldn't wake out of this dream, no matter how hard you tried. And then things got even worse.

"Grace!" It was Nancy, in pink with daisies in her hair. Tugging at Grace's arm. Her eyes wild and panicky. "Come with me. Quickly. Please."

Even before Grace had grasped what was happening, there were sounds of shouting. You could hear it above the music. A doorman went running, cutting through the crowds, followed closely by Dickie. The sound of bone colliding with bone over by the staircase. A man's yell. Women squealing.

Nancy was shouting at people in an authoritative way as she pushed through. "Make way! Out of the way!" Grace, in her wake, was tongue-tied.

Two doormen had hold of Cramer. He was struggling, yelling about how he was going to kill "that bastard." His face was wild and full of hatred, his shirt ripped and bloody. It was only now—seeing Cramer so out of control, so *not* himself—that she realized just how gentle he normally was, how gentleness was one of his defining characteristics. His eyes were looking at her now, but without seeming to see her, seeing only his own rage. As Nancy hurried to his side, Grace felt the prickle of tears.

Over on the staircase, seated on the top step, was O'Connell. There was a lot of blood on his white suit. He appeared to be quietly watching Cramer, as the blood flowed freely from his nose and lip. When he spotted Grace, he gave a grimace that might have been a smile. He spoke, and his words were blurred but discernible.

"Some would say I had that coming. What do you think?"

"I don't know."

Nancy was speaking to Cramer. Grace couldn't hear what she was saying, but whatever it was, it was working some kind of magic. He seemed to go limp, the rage ebbing away. Then she turned angrily to O'Connell. "What have you done?"

"You must be the lovely Nancy."

Dickie was speaking to the two doormen, persuading them to let go of Cramer. Once they'd done so, Nancy took his arm, holding him up. Dickie, talking intently to Nancy, took the other arm. His hair was working free and was sticking up all over in greasy strands. Turning back to the room, he said loudly, "Righto. Sideshow's over. You hear me? Excuse us, please." And together, they half carried, half dragged Cramer past Grace and O'Connell, heading down the stairs and out of the club.

"You know, Grace, I've been to many places, seen many things, but this is my first time inside a ladies' bathroom. I only wish I had my notebook with me." O'Connell was perched up on the edge of the marble-topped counter beside the sinks. Next to him was a pile of bloody, sodden tissue. Grace had a wad in her hand and was dabbing at his lip and nose. Mostly he was stoic, but every so often he winced and groaned.

"I think this lip may need a stitch," she said. "We should go to a hospital."

"No need for that. I'll be fine." The lip was sufficiently swollen that his words were blurred. "Hey, lady." He was addressing the only other woman in the room, primping and preening into the mirror at a neighboring sink. "That lipstick is too pink for you. You want a darker tone to set off that red hair."

"You shouldn't even be in here," snapped the woman. "He shouldn't even be in here."

Grace silently mouthed the word "sorry" at the woman, who made her way past and back out to the party. "So you're an expert on makeup now?"

"Just trying to be helpful. It's always been my downfall."

"Right. That should do it." She gathered up the pile of tissue and threw it into the bin. Then she delved into a cupboard and produced a hand towel. "Hold this to your face."

"It's just as well your dress is red." He took the towel and did as he was told.

Grace caught her reflection in the mirror. There was a tired and vaguely distressed look about her. O'Connell, on the other hand, somewhere behind all that blood and swelling, was positively chipper.

"You're enjoying this, aren't you?" she asked.

"Well, it *is* a party. Isn't one supposed to enjoy parties?"

"What did you say to John?"

"Oh, it's *'John'* now? The man's a drunk. A one-man justification for Prohibition."

"So you're saying it was unprovoked? He hit you for no reason at all?"

A sigh. Beneath the swelling his face became serious. "It's between me and him and our shared past. Nothing to do with you."

"Why don't you just tell him what happened on the day that Eva died? For five years that man has been torturing himself over not knowing and thinking the worst possible thoughts about it all. Tell him the truth, whatever it is. Yes, she chose you over him, but hasn't he suffered enough for it?"

O'Connell lowered the bloody towel and gingerly put his hand to his face, touching his lip and nose lightly. Exploring. "My dear girl, do I have to remind you that you *left* me, the other day? That you hotfooted it back to London while I slept?

Without even paying me the simple courtesy of leaving a good-bye note? I'm . . . 'touched,' shall we say, by your interest in my private life, but frankly this was never any of your concern, and it's even *less* of your concern now."

Grace swallowed hard. "Did you wonder *why* I left? Did it remotely bother you to wake up and find me gone?"

A sound that might have been a laugh but which turned into a yelp of pain. "Say, want to know what's always fascinated me? On one day you can feel something really strong for a person—I mean, those big intense emotions that dominate your whole world and simply dwarf everything else—and then the next day you wake up and that incredible love you felt for a day or a year or whatever—it's vanished. Pff, like smoke. There's nothing you can do to bring it back." He set down the towel and began washing his hands.

"I know you said that to hurt me," said Grace. "But it actually makes me feel sorry for you. It must be awful to be so alone and empty as you are. Playing your stupid pointless games with people's heads and hearts."

O'Connell was still rubbing his hands together under a stream of water from which steam was now rising. "Are you in love with John Cramer, Grace?"

She sighed. "I hope you have a good journey back to New York. Be nice to Margaret. She'll do a good job for you and she deserves the best."

"Of course I'll be nice to her. Why would I be anything other than nice to my new secretary? You're getting carried away with your little theories about me." He was still washing his hands, though the steam was rising thickly and his skin was turning red. As the water reached what must have been a scaldingly hot temperature, he finally turned off the tap. "Say, it was so delightful to finally glimpse your sister this evening. I hadn't expected her to be so utterly beguiling. I should have guessed after everything you'd told me about the two of you with George and Steven. And now poor old Cramer. You're like a couple of gems in a jewel box, you two." He shook the water off his hands. Examined his swollen face in the mirror. "Nancy has a rare and beautiful dignity. You might even call it nobility. She's . . . fascinating."

"Shame on you, O'Connell." The room was too small or else he was too big. She had to get out.

"Running away again, are we?"

"Walking away. There's a difference. And you'd do well to learn that for yourself."

"What do you mean?"

"Well, look at you and Cramer. By refusing to talk to him about Eva's death, you've made damn sure that he'll never leave you alone. Cut him loose, for goodness' sakes." She made herself look at him one last time. "Good-bye, Devil. Good luck with the new novel."

Seven

Grace was woken by building noise. Hammering, drilling and great metallic clangs that reverberated through her head and in the roots of her teeth. The air smelled faintly of dust and cat. When she opened her eyes, she couldn't work out where she was. She was lying on her own in a narrow brass bed, wearing only her underwear. Nothing was familiar: the cluttered dressing table draped all about with silk scarves, the oversized and vaguely ominous wardrobe, the walls papered in what might once have been cream but was now beige. It took her a moment to remember. Having done so, she got up and wrapped herself in the unbecoming yellow dressing gown that lay on the bed.

Beyond the bedroom was a tiny lounge-kitchenette, where Margaret, smartly dressed and wearing her glasses, was filling a battered kettle and setting it on one of the two gas rings. Spooning tea leaves into a pot. "Morning, Grace. Headache?"

"I should say." Grace sank into the single tatty brown armchair, and then sank a little farther with the broken springs. "Thank you for letting me stay. It was very kind of you. I couldn't have faced my sister—not last night, not after all that drink. Not sure I want to face her today either, come to that."

"Well, I'm afraid you can't stay a second night. I'm not sleeping in that armchair again."

"Oh God. I'm so sorry." Grace covered her face with her hands. "I never intended to put you out of your bed."

"And yet last night you went striding straight into the only bedroom and lay down on the only bed without so much as a by-your-leave."

Grace winced. But actually Margaret sounded cheerful enough. She was humming brightly as she fetched two cups and saucers from a little cupboard.

"It's quite all right," she said eventually. "Gave me the chance to even things up a little."

"What do you mean?"

"Well." Margaret shrugged. "On one side of the equation I took advantage of your relationship with Dexter O'Connell to get myself out of a rut. And then, on the other side, you took advantage of my hospitality. So now we're equal."

Grace wasn't so sure about this particular piece of algebra but decided not to say so. "You're really going away with him, then?"

"Of course! You surely don't think I'm going to turn down the job of my dreams just because my future employer behaves badly to his lovers? He's a famous cad. I've always known that." She smiled. "I'm not trying to get him to fall in love with me. That's not what this is about."

"I suppose, when you put it like that . . ." The unspoken truth sat plainly between them. It was she who'd been naïve; she who'd chosen to ignore what everybody knew about O'Connell. You had only to have read the newspapers now and then to know he was a cad. Perhaps that was the crux of the matter, the reason she'd overlooked the obvious. She knew too much about newspapers to think you could believe what they said about anyone.

"I'm meant for bigger things," Margaret said. "It's not just about loving his books. I'm going to travel the world, meet extraordinary people. At the moment my world extends no farther than the bus ride from Battersea to work and back."

"Is that where we are, then? Battersea?"

In answer, Margaret crossed to the grimy window and yanked open the curtains that were still half closed. "It's not a bad bit of London. Except for all the building noise. So much noise! And that's only going to get worse. They're planning to build an enormous power station here—big enough to generate as much electricity as all the others in London put together. Can you imagine the fumes and the filth? It's a shame, really."

Grace peered out at squat terraced housing in yellow brick—and at the end of the road, a building site. Men in overalls, steel girders, ropes and pulleys and rubble.

"There are people in Battersea from all corners of the Empire. So many fascinating lives and experiences and religions. Lots of Communists, too. Our MP's a Communist, though he's sort of masquerading as a member of the Independent Labour Party. You might have heard of him—Shapurji Saklatvala? He's from India. Well, I say he's 'our' MP, but of course *I* haven't actually had the opportunity to vote for him or anyone else, being twenty-seven." The kettle began to whistle. "I'm a

Communist, too, actually." This was said sheepishly—something she was proud of but didn't want to brag about.

"*Are* you?"

"Have been for years." She poured hot water into the teapot and gave it a stir. "This country's held back by its class system—by the fact that upper-class twits like Oscar Cato-Ferguson go sailing their way into the best jobs while people like me are left to type their inarticulate letters. As for the monarchy—well it's simply absurd. How can we allow it to continue if we're to be a truly modern society?"

This was a whole new Margaret. Put Grace in mind of her mother. "Well, you're certainly fully of surprises."

A smile. "So. Bathroom's out on the landing. Should be free by now. There's a towel over there by the door, and my soap and my loo roll. Have you a spare outfit at the office? I can lend you a long coat to cover your party dress till you get changed."

"What? I wasn't planning on going in to the office today."

"Oh?" Margaret raised an eyebrow. "So when, precisely, were you thinking of going back? I've already told a pack of lies about visiting you with flasks of soup, how hideous your flu is and how deathly gray you're looking. I'm running out of things to say."

"But I didn't . . . ." She was about to protest that she hadn't asked Margaret to lie for her, but swallowed the words. "Thank you. You're a true friend, and I haven't appreciated you properly. Did you say we catch a bus?"

A nod, as the tea was poured and passed across. "Are you all right, Grace? I mean, about what happened with you and O'Connell?"

"Yes. It ran its course. I knew, from early on, that it would burn brightly and burn out. It was exciting while it lasted, but it was all surface, all sensation. No real substance." She sipped her tea and tried to order her thoughts. "For a while I wanted it to be otherwise. He told me he loved me, and it made my head spin so that I couldn't see what was what."

"Do you think he did love you?"

"I think he lives and loves only in the moment. He's the most handsome, charming, clever cad that I've ever met. But he *is* a cad, and he always will be. I'd rather not see him again. I'll be glad when he's left London."

"Well, you don't have long to wait." Margaret took off her glasses and polished them up on her tweed skirt. When she replaced them, her face was all ill-concealed excitement. "We set off for New York in a couple of weeks."

Eight

On arriving at work with Margaret, Grace succeeded in changing out of the party dress and into her spare clothes without anyone noticing what she was up to. She settled down quickly and by late morning was making good progress with some copy for Baker's. And nobody had spoken a word about her weeklong absence from the office. All of this lulled her into a false sense of security. It was then, of course, that the Pearsons sent for her.

It was Mr. Henry who issued the summons, but when Grace saw that Mr. Aubrey was with him in his office, she knew she was in trouble. It was Mr. Henry who did the talking. Soft-voiced, bushy-sideburned Mr. Henry, his habitually twinkly eyes devoid, today, of the slightest twink.

"I've been your champion, Miss Rutherford," he was saying. "Because you have potential—sparkle—whatever you

choose to call it. You're a clever young lady and you could
have gone far at Pearson's . . ."

Could have . . . He was already using the past tense about
her, even as she sat there in front of him. All the while Mr.
Henry spoke, his brother stood by the window, gazing out at
the street, perhaps too angry even to look at her.

"You did an excellent job with Baker's Lights," said Mr.
Henry. "Your ideas for Potter's Wonderlunch were positively
visionary."

It was as though she were listening to her own obituary.
There had to be *something* she could do . . .

"It doesn't have to end there, sir. I can come up with *more*
visionary ideas; I *know* I can."

"Not here, you can't. Not after what you've done." Mr.
Aubrey's back was firmly turned and the sun through the window reflected off his bald patch. As he stood, hands behind
his back, he rocked a little, heel to toe, heel to toe. Probably
didn't know he was doing it.

Mr. Henry's neck was red. "What would happen if everyone behaved as you do, Miss Rutherford? You seem barely to
understand that rules exist, let alone observe the need to follow them. You appear to have no sense of common decency."

"But *what* have I done?" She was cringing even as she
asked the question. The fact was, she'd committed so many
misdemeanors of late that she wasn't even sure which one had
tipped her over the edge.

"You were seen, miss!" Mr. Aubrey spun around to face
Grace and banged his fist down on the table. "You and your
gentleman friend. Though clearly the man is no gentleman."

"There was a cleaner working in the building that night,
Miss Rutherford." Mr. Henry fiddled with the papers in front
of him, avoiding meeting her gaze. "The poor girl was quite

distraught when she told Mr. Cato-Ferguson. I'd be grateful if
you'd clear your office and be out of here by lunchtime. We'll
make your wages up to the end of the week. In the circumstances, I consider this to be more than generous."

"If you were a man—" Mr. Aubrey was biting his knuckles
in anger.

"You were our first lady copywriter," said Mr. Henry. "I
can't see that we shall be hiring another in a hurry."

In the silence that followed, Grace realized they were waiting for her to say something. Eventually, she managed, "Thank
you, sir." She got to her feet and was about to go, but couldn't
quite stop herself from having the last word. "All women
aren't the same. Don't use me as an excuse not to give some of
the others a chance. If you fail to see what women copywriters
can contribute to this firm, you'll be forever stuck in the nine-
teenth century while your competitors go racing ahead into
the modern world."

"Enough!" Mr. Henry held up his hands as though to blot
her out.

On her way out of the building for the last time, carrying her
box of odds and ends, Grace saw that Cato's office door was
wide open—perhaps so that he'd have a good view of her
departure. Glancing up, she caught his eye and he waved
cheerily.

Setting down her box on the carpet, Grace wandered
over. Cato was lounging in his chair, feet on desk, talking on
the telephone, and he didn't break his conversation as she
stepped into his room. His smile wavered though, just a little.
It wavered again as she picked up the vase of fresh flowers
that sat on his desk. White, impersonal flowers with a vaguely
geometrical appearance. Raising them to her face, she took

a good whiff. Scentless. Lifting them out of the vase, she reached over and poured the water over his head.

The receiver dropped from his hand.

"You . . . You . . ." But that was as far as he got.

"You never could find the right words, could you?"And Grace turned and left the room.

Outside, a cheer went up from the typists. Grace casually distributed the flowers among them, before retrieving her box and strolling out of the building.

Out on the street, she didn't feel so casual. The big doors swung closed behind her in a very final way, and there she was, in the dazzle of the morning sunshine, clutching her box, a waif and stray. What should she do now?

She ought to go home, of course. But the thought of tea and sympathy with Nancy was not an appealing prospect in her current mood. And anyway, Nancy would be busy looking after Cramer, fretting and fussing over him, helping him to get back on the proverbial wagon. As for Mummy—well, Grace didn't feel strong enough to face all that maternal disappointment and disapproval, not this morning.

For want of a better plan, she decided to take her own advice, and made her way to the Lyons Corner House on Piccadilly to cheer herself up with ice cream—one scoop of vanilla and one of lemon, served in a glass dish. She ate like a child who wants to savor a treat and draw it out as long as possible, taking the tiniest mouthfuls. Then she ordered a pot of tea and sat so long with the full cup in front of her that it turned cold and acquired an oily gray sheen.

Nancy and I sat here on her twenty-fourth birthday, she thought to herself. Here at this table. That was the day I ended it with George.

The realization didn't upset her. Why should it? It was just a table in a café. In fact, she and Nancy had had a rather nice afternoon on that day, but for the invisible wall between them. No, it simply made her reflect on the way we revisit moments of our own history. Here she was again at that table—and here once again, in her head, trying to work out how to draw a line under recent events and move on. Last time, she'd broken with George but had remained at home with the family, deciding that they must come first—that they would *always* come first. This time, she wondered whether perhaps it would be better for all concerned if she did the opposite—she could move out, go somewhere far away and start afresh.

Tempted to order another pot of tea, Grace found she couldn't meet the eyes of her waitress. She knew, if she did, she'd find there that look of irritation bestowed by waiting staff on those who sit too long. Instead, she asked for the bill. And it was as she groped about in her purse for some change to tip the waitress (she intended to leave a large tip, perhaps to prove she *wasn't* one of those "sit too long" people) that she remembered something. She *did* have somewhere to go this morning.

It was one of those large, white, clean-looking Georgian houses in a smart square just along from the Victoria and Albert Museum. Grace generally considered South Kensington to be a place of flat bright sunshine and cheerful prosperity. Hampstead, on the other hand, was a steep, mossy green patch of London, a place for brooding melancholy and deep thought.

She'd been to the Hamilton-Shapcotts' family home many times when she, Nancy and Sheridan were children, but hadn't been back since they'd grown up. Both of Sheridan's parents had died since her last visit, and under his ownership the house had acquired some distinctive Egyptian additions. His gateposts were topped with black and gold sphinxes with languid, sensual eyes. His knocker was a brass jackal head. The very number on his door—8—was a curled snake with its tail in its mouth, seemingly attempting to eat itself.

A squat man in butler's livery answered the door, relieved her of her box, and led her through a hallway with walls decorated in gold-painted hieroglyphics (rather like those on the business card) into a room that was more museum space than lounge. Glass cases contained ancient chipped ceramics, evil-looking daggers, jewels so opulent that it was hard to believe they could be real. The walls were book lined and hung with scrolls and tapestries, the ceiling painted with a mural showing the building of the pyramids.

"Mr. Hamilton-Shapcott will be with you directly." The butler gestured to one of two crimson chaise longues. "Do please recline. Would you take tea and biscuits?"

"Gwace, my darling! Sheridan was sporting a white cotton shirt of a billowy romantic sort, and gray flannel trousers. Without his usual makeup he looked refreshingly unremarkable. "I'm so glad you've come." He stood to one side to let the butler past. "And, I confess, a twifle surpwised. I thought you'd forget all about our little awangement."

"Not a bit of it. My, but this room has changed. I seem to remember passementerie and big English oil paintings. Gainsborough—that sort of stuff."

"That's wight. And bla bla." He rolled his eyes, kicked off his slippers and flopped down on one of the chaise longues.

She took the other, removing her shoes and setting them on the rug in front of her.

"I thought that if I twansformed the house utterly, it would become twuly mine and stop being my father's."

"And you've succeeded."

He shook his head. "It may not be his style anymore, but it's more his house than ever. He's there under all the gold paint and objets d'art, cwiticizing my foolish ways and fwippewy. I have a big Egyptian coffin upstairs—I'll have to show you later. Sometimes I dweam of Father jumping out of it, all wapped in bandages like a mummy."

Grace had to laugh.

"The other pwoblem is Cecile." He turned onto his back, gazing up at the ceiling, his hands knotted behind his head. "Did you ever meet my wife, Cecile? Ex-wife, I should say. I wanted tewwibly to impwess her. So much of what I've done here was for her. Now she's gone, it all seems wather pointless."

"I'm sorry."

"Don't be. It's my own stupid fault." The butler arrived with a tray of tea and biscuits. "Jenkins, you're splendid. Do the honors, would you? There's a good chap."

Jenkins, white-gloved and silent, poured, nodded and retreated.

"How *are* you, Gwace? You look a little peaky this morning. Too many of the old whatsits at the party? Jenkins has a marvelous wemedy, if you're intewested. Something he learned fwom his mother, appawently."

"No, thank you. I shall be fine directly."

The eyebrows were raised, disbelievingly.

"Look, if you really want to know, I've gotten myself in a pickle over a man. Two men."

"*My,* but you've been busy!"

"What's more, I've just lost my job. I've behaved rather badly. I'd rather not get into it, if you don't mind, but frankly I could do with getting away from the family for a bit. Mother's disapproval and Nancy's . . . Well, it's all a bit much at the moment."

"How intwiguing. Well, you can always come and stay with me. I'd be glad of the company." And as she opened her mouth to protest. "I mean it, Gwacie. We're family, you and me."

"Thank you." The emotion welled up in her throat so that she couldn't say anything further. Just sat with her tea staring at the artifacts in the glass case.

Sheridan followed her gaze. "You must think my Egyptian collection is widiculous—an expensive hobby for a spoiled wich boy."

"Not at all."

"Well, I wouldn't blame you if you did." He got up, crossed the room to a tall bookcase and took down a heavy-looking photograph album. "Take a look at this." He opened the album, flipped over a couple of pages and handed it across.

One photograph showed a line of men leaning on spades, picks and other tools. They were all in short trousers with heavy boots and wide-brimmed hats. They all looked happy. It was difficult to make sense of the other photographs. They showed a dark space with various indiscernible objects scattered about.

"It's the tomb of a nobleman—we think it was possibly a mayor of Luxor. I was there when they opened it up. I was the vewwy first person to step inside. Look at this one."

He turned the page for her. Another photograph showed some black, charred-looking objects.

"Those are the internal organs of a queen. They would have wemoved them fwom the body after death. I bwought them back here and donated them to the Bwitish Museum. At the moment they're just sitting in a vault there. I think the museum people are afwaid that if they poke them about too much, they'll simply disintegwate. It's a miwacle, weally, that they still exist. But my hope is that one day we'll have machines or devices that will help us to analyze them more conclusively—to find out exactly what the queen ate, how she died, how old she was. I long to weally *know* her and I think one day we will. She's waited a long time for us to decipher her—I expect she'll wait a little longer. I only hope I'm still here by then."

Grace looked again at the smiling lineup of men before the nobleman's tomb.

"The Egyptian nobility take all their favowite things with them for their journey to the afterlife," said Sheridan. "The tomb of this mayor was more intimate, somehow, more we-vealing than many of the more gwand tombs. The walls were all painted with pictures of parties: people making music and chasing each other about. There was a large portwait of a beautiful woman—his wife, no doubt—in a long, white dwess. Lots of gwapes, too, all over the place, and wine."

"I think I know one or two people who'd want to take those sort of memories with them to the Great Hereafter," said Grace.

He put the photo album away. "My mother has vanished fwom the world as completely as those Egyptians. Perhaps more completely, in some ways. The things she told me when she was dying—just fwagments, weally, but they gave me a glimpse of a totally diffewent woman than the one I'd thought she was. And actually, a new perspective on myself, too."

"How so?" Grace drained her teacup.

"Well, this is going to sound ludicwous, but I've never understood myself—not when considered in context. If an archaeologist dug up my family, he'd immediately think some-thing was wong. Consider: my mother all gentle and wefined and my father a wough northern industwialist. A man who bwewed bad beer for people who don't know any better than to dwink it. Yes, it's pwetty bad, the family tipple, but don't tell! You do see the discwepancy, don't you? How did two such people ever fit together? And what about me, their fweakish son?"

"But surely no family would make sense if you considered it in that way," said Grace. "People fall in love for the oddest reasons. And when it comes to the children—well, nobody can ever guess how they're going to turn out."

"Perhaps you're wight." He poured more tea. "Maybe I developed my whole personality as a weaction against Daddy."

"Well, I wouldn't go that far . . ."

"I don't suppose you would, but then your father was a perfectly lovely man, so far as I wemember him. A man of culture and intellect—a Darwinist. Must have been stwange for our mothers—two close school chums getting together with two men who were pwactically polar opposites. How surpwised they must have been when the husbands hit it off. And how lovely for the two families to be so tight-knit for so long."

"It *was* lovely," said Grace. Then, testing the water, "What do you suppose happened to make them suddenly sever all contact? It must have been quite a falling-out, wouldn't you say?"

"Do you wemember that Iwish nanny of mine making us all eat twipe?" asked Sheridan, somewhat randomly. "What about the day when you and Nancy made me wear that Bo Peep bonnet?" He looked up with sad doe eyes. She could see him now, in that bonnet, his face framed with lace. "I was always vewy jealous of you and Nancy."

"Were you? Why?"

"You had each other. There was only one of me. It was

worse after the falling-out, of course. It was awful to lose you both."

Grace steeled herself. "Sheridan, why did you visit my mother the other day? You didn't just sit about reminiscing over those photographs, did you? You had something in particular that you wanted to talk to her about."

A shake of the head. "Oh, Gwace. This is vewy difficult. I wanted so much to speak to you, but Cathewine made me *pwomise* not to say anything."

"Funny, that. She did the same with me." Grace bit her lip.

Sheridan eyed her. "Thing is, my mother—well, as you know, she wasn't the most diwect and forthcoming of people, but she got wather a lot off her chest on that deathbed of hers."

"Oh yes?"

"She talked about the past, and bla bla. Something happened, Gwace. Between our pawents . . ."

"Sheridan . . . I know about it. Nancy too. It's all right—we've always known."

His face lit up. "Thank goodness for that! How marvelous to be able to talk fweely about it. Cathewine was utterly convinced that neither of you knew a thing." He sprang to his feet and seized her by the hands. "*Do* come and stay with me for a while. We shall have such fun. Blood wuns deep, doesn't it?"

"Steady on." The extent of his elation was puzzling. "I mean, thank you, and it's extremely kind of you but—"

"What my mother told me—you know, when she was dying—well, I think I'd always known it in my heart. I was never able to welate to my father, you see. I always felt that I was a wholly diffewent species, wight fwom when I was a small boy. There was nothing—*nothing*—that we had in common. And of course, it turns out there was a *weason* for that. I am not some sort of abewwation, and it wasn't all in my mind." He released her hands and straightened up, smiling at her. "I've always felt so alone . . . And now it turns out I'm not. Of *course* you must come and stay here, my dear sister."

Sister? Was this a faux-Egyptian endearment? "Sheridan, I have fond memories of our childhoods, too, of course I do. But all this talk of blood and not being alone . . . I simply don't understand what you're trying to say."

"Oh, I'm sowwy! I must have misunderstood. I thought you said you knew. I'm your bwother, Gwace. Well, half bwother, anyway. But half is good enough, isn't it?"

She couldn't stop the laugh. "Are you bonkers? I think I'd have known if my mother had had another baby!"

But now it was Sheridan with the confused frown, Sheridan who seemed to be struggling for the right words. "My dear," he said eventually, "we appear to have been at cwoss-purposes. If I understand your implication cowwectly, you are suggesting there was an affair between your mother and my father. I don't know anything about that. What *I've* been talking about is the long affair that took place between *my* mother and *your* father. *Our* father, that is."

IV.
Journeys

One

The Past

November 5, 1925. Grace and Dickie stood with two-year-old Tilly on the Heath, watching some men build a bonfire, heaping up a great stack of branches, bits of old furniture and broken-up crates. It was a clear, fine day, but the air had a touch of winter in it. A touch of death.

"Where's the fire?" asked Tilly.

"They light the fire tonight, darling." Grace's voice was weary. She'd already explained this a number of times. "And there'll be a firework display and baked potatoes and—"

"I want the fire now!" Tilly folded her arms and put out her sulky lip.

"Don't worry, sweetie." Dickie patted her on the shoulder. "We'll all come up here tonight to join in and watch them burn Guy Fawkes." When Tilly abruptly burst into tears and ran away across the grass, he appeared stunned. "What did I say? Should I run after her?"

"Don't worry." Grace put her arm through his. "She won't go far. Thing is, I'm not sure she's properly understood the Guy Fawkes story. She might have thought you were saying they were going to burn a real person."

"Sorry, Gracie. I suppose I'm just not used to children. What a clot."

"Rubbish. You're lovely with her. Poor little thing's not herself at the moment."

Tilly had darted closer to the men now, drawn to the great pile of wood. She'd stopped crying, had picked up a small branch and was trailing it along the ground behind her.

The wood stack was already nine feet high. Tonight's fire would be a huge, roaring, leaping one. The thought of it—the very notion of something that was all energy, all hunger, all heat—made Grace shudder and cling closer to Dickie. Thank God she had Dickie. Her rock.

"When the time comes, George wants to be cremated," she said quietly.

"Really? How peculiar. I thought you said there was a family mausoleum in Highgate Cemetery?"

"Yes." She was still staring at that huge wood stack and at the child who was now circling it. Running round and round with her arms outstretched, pretending to be an airplane. "But he doesn't want to be put in it. He has nightmares about being shut inside coffins and trapped under cold stone. He's asked me to help Nancy explain it all to his parents."

"Poor chap. Poor parents, come to that."

"Dickie." Grace was fighting tears. "Could we go away somewhere? Afterward, I mean? I couldn't leave Nancy for longer than a few days. But I do think I'm going to want a few days away from it all. I'd like some breathing space so that I can rally myself a bit. Come back stronger and be more of a help to her. Would that be all right?"

"Of course, my darling. Whatever you want." He took her in his arms and she let her head rest against his shoulder.

"The doctor says it might only be a matter of days." The wind sent the dead leaves scattering all around and about them. And then, "Nancy's pregnant again. Almost three months. She's sick as a dog."

"I know," he said quietly. "You've already told me."

"What will we do without him?" She stood there in Dickie's arms, knowing that he was holding her together. Holding her up. If he let go of her right now, she might just fall.

Later that afternoon, Grace took a seat beside George's bed as she always did at this time. Nancy was downstairs with Tilly. The day nurse had gone home and the night nurse hadn't yet arrived.

George, rake-thin and hollow in the face, was propped up on his pillows. He couldn't get out of bed on his own now.

"Mind if I open a window?" Grace got up without waiting for a reply and fumbled with the catch. The room smelled very bad. As if the cancer was rotting him from the inside. Perhaps it was.

The doctors didn't seem to know where the cancer had started or when. It had crept its way through him, spreading fast while he remained oblivious. He likened it to a silent, stealthy and utterly deadly army. By the time he'd been diagnosed, it had conquered his lymphatic system and invaded his lungs.

Inevitably, George blamed the war. Claimed he'd been poisoned by gas in the trenches. They'd been sent gas mask after gas mask, all different designs, but none of them had proved effective against the foul stuff the Germans wafted at them. They'd even succeeded in gassing themselves a few times, when the wind happened to be blowing the wrong way.

"You look awful." George's voice was thin and breathless, transparent in quality. "When did you last see your hairdresser?"

"Cheeky!" She came back over and patted his knees through the blankets. He looked so small. As if he'd shrunk in length as well as breadth. "Haven't exactly had a lot of time for that kind of thing lately."

"Now, now." He wagged a finger. "Don't you let yourself go, young lady. You'll never catch a husband that way." As he said this, he reached for her hand. His hand was surprisingly warm and firm.

"Who says I want one?" She wanted to sit there forever, her hand in his. They hadn't held hands like this in more than three years. "There's only one man I've ever wanted to marry. I was waiting for him to ask me but he went and married someone else."

"Rubbish. You'd never have said yes. You're one of those infuriating women who's only interested in the things they can't have."

"Think that if you like. You didn't ask so you'll never know."

His eyes seemed to roam across her face. "I know all there is to know about you, Grace."

For three years they'd been courteous and considerate to each other. She had stuck to her decision that their relationship had to end, and he had respected that. Neither had made any reference to their affair in all that time. But just lately, this last week or so, they'd become playful and sentimental around each other. Now that he'd been robbed of a future, George was choosing to live in the past. And Grace was allowing herself to go there with him, just a little.

"What about Dickie?" His words broke the magic.

"I don't want to talk about Dickie."

"Has he proposed to you?"

She pulled her hand from his.

"He *has,* hasn't he? What was your answer?"

"George, please. I said I don't want to talk about him."

"Ha!" His eyes glittered. "I knew it! Same old Grace. Like I said, you're only interested in what you can't have."

"If you must know, I told him it was the wrong time to ask me. I can't think about getting married at the moment. Surely you of all people should understand that. I don't think I'll ever get married, actually."

"I see," he said, flatly. "Perhaps that's just as well."

"What exactly do you mean by that?" She was looking at his hair. Still thick and coppery, streaked through with gold. She was looking at his sad, hazel eyes.

"I'm going to ask something of you, Grace."

"No." She knew what was coming. "Don't say it. Please. The answer is yes, but please don't speak it. I can't bear to hear it."

"You irritating baggage! How could you possibly know what I'm going to say?"

"I know all there is to know about you too, George." The smallest of smiles which slipped quickly away. A sigh. "Of course I'll look after Nancy and Tilly. And the baby when it comes. You know I will."

His face became serious. "Promise me they'll always come first, Grace. You're the only person who can do that for me. You're the only one I can ask. I want you there with her when she has the baby. I want you always to be there because I can't be."

"Oh George, *please* stop." Tears clouded her eyes.

"It's been the three of us for a long time, hasn't it? Since Steven died. I wonder what would have happened if he'd lived?"

"Everything would have been different. Four is such a different number."

"So is two," he said. "Two is what you'll be soon, you and Nancy. Two is a good number."

"There's Mummy too, don't forget."

He waved a dismissive hand. Catherine didn't count. Not in this calculation. And nor did Dickie, apparently.

"Promise me, Grace."

"Yes, yes. I've already said it, haven't I?" She batted his hand away. Her best impression of bright and breezy. "Now do shut up about it. How about I give you a shave? Get you all smartened up for Nancy when she comes up to see you. Would you like that?"

"Oh, not now." He sank back against his pillows. "I'm too tired." His face, with the eyes shut, was barely more than a skull.

She took his hand again and held it and they sat silently for a while. Eventually, he seemed to have fallen asleep and she laid his hand gently down and got up to leave.

"What a lovely dream." His eyes were still closed but a smile played around the corners of his mouth.

She patted his knee. "See you later, petal."

It would be the last time they'd speak to each other.

The West-Ender
June 20, 1927

Dexter O'Connell Heads for Home

The following is a farewell message from a toiling scribe to his Muse, a message which the scribe has, for reasons unknown to himself (but perhaps to do with his ingrained tendency to live his private life in public), decided to put in a newspaper. Indulge me if you will. My darling lady, on our first encounter I thought you couldn't be more exhilarating, varied, elegant or unpredictable. I was wrong. With each day that passes you become more exciting. I see you before me all decked out in vivid red. Red, the color of blood and of danger, is your true color. It becomes you. You're so changeable. I have only to blink, and everything is different. You're more hectic than you used to be, my love. You pulse with a nervous, restless energy that approaches madness. Indeed, you're famous for it. Yet there is an order underlying your chaotic surface. And your best features have about them a permanence and grandeur. You will endure, my love. You will live forever.

In the mornings you're fresh and sparkling. Enlivened by the new day. In the ripe golden afternoons you're languid and relaxed. You're at your most exotic at night, glittering through those long summer evenings, dazzling in the dark. Your music is stirring, your dance divine. It has to be said, though: you can be a little dirty.

In a few days I am due to return to my wife. Yes, it's true. I belong somewhere else. My wife is more straitlaced than you, more bogged down in rules and regulations, more religious. Perhaps that's why I stay away from her for long stretches of time. She's younger than you, yet she's obsessed with history and traditions and is all caught up in the most snobbish of social codes. Maybe that's *because* she's young. Still, there's more fun to be had behind her closed doors than is at first apparent. And after all, she belongs to me and I to her. I'll always return.

I have other lovers dotted around the globe. This won't make anyone like me better, but I'm just not the kind to hang around too long. At least I'm honest about it. People may tut and wag their fingers, but would they be able to resist the lure of that little French thing any better than I? She's so chic, bohemian, artistic and—well—frisky. Yes, all right, she's snotty too, but nobody's perfect.

But forget Paris. Forget my own New York. You, lovely London, are the biggest and the best city in the world. This has been my first visit in seven years, and boy, did you have some surprises up your sleeve. The shock of Piccadilly Circus without Eros, a face without a nose, while somewhere under the ground, an enormous subterranean station is being birthed from rock. Perhaps it will be the biggest in the bewildering network that is tunneling its way beneath you. Up above there's so much more traffic than there used to be, but you're taming it with all your rules and regulations, your spangly new traffic lights. This is what characterizes London, to me: the conflict between crackling craziness and tightly ordered control. The buildings have been growing year on year, like children. Look at all those big department stores and banks that have sprung up with their Greco-Egyptian pillars and classical Italianate statues; their modern black granite, geometrical lines and smooth curves. If I didn't know better, I'd say you're trying to thumb your noses at us upstart Yanks. Well, we'll see who laughs last.

What a pleasure it's been to relax in your pubs with a pint of beer or sip champagne in your swanky nightspots. "Greetings, Constable. Fancy a tipple?" No padlocks here, no drinking dens, no flask in the jacket pocket, no climbing out the back window when the cops come in through the front door. Other things make less sense, such as your worship of the game of "football" (though, yes, the new Wembley Stadium is something to behold). Also cricket, clearly an ancient forebear of baseball struggling against the imperative of Darwinian evolution. Do yourselves a favor and give it up.

Then there's the way you cook a steak—is this in fact a side product of your leather-tanning process? Then there's the rain . . .

Enough quibbling. One can always find fault if that's the lens through which one chooses to view the world. This is my leave-taking declaration. My darling, you have been my inspiration. You're a wonderfully crazy set of contradictions. You took a cold, dead heart and made it beat again. Perhaps I have been afraid of my own throbbing heart. Perhaps I am simply not a good man. Whatever the reason, I have wronged you and I apologize. You're not the only one I've wronged, but you're the only one I love. There's another good heart out there, and it's beating the same natty jazz rhythm as yours. I hope you'll find each other. And now, with the blood running hot through his arteries, this Devil is heading home to write his Great Novel. I'm ready to do it, at long last. It will be dedicated to you.

(*Diamond Sharp returns next week.*)

Two

Grace had been staying at Sheridan's for almost a week when her mother turned up. It was a hot morning, and she was alone in the pocket-handkerchief back garden, sipping lemonade under a parasol. She heard Catherine before she saw her. A scuffling of shoes on the tiled floor inside and sounds of muffled protest, before the French windows were flung open, revealing Mother, flushed in the face, a carpet bag over one arm and the latest issue of *Time and Tide* under the other—with a tight-mouthed Jenkins following.

"Ah, there you are, Grace. This fellow is determined to take my things!"

"I beg your pardon, madam, I was only—"

Catherine dropped the carpet bag. "I know what you were doing. Indeed, I'm well aware of what you're *for*. But it doesn't interest me and I'm quite capable of carrying my own bag. Let me make the most of my remaining years as an able-bodied woman, if you please."

Seeing his opportunity, Jenkins swooped on the carpet bag. Catherine's hands were on her hips. "Well, of all the—"

"Mummy, do leave off." Grace grabbed her mother by the shoulders and planted a kiss on a cheek. "It's *so* good to see you. Such a lovely surprise. Come and sit down in the shade. Jenkins, could you bring us a jug of the lemonade, please? You must try this lemonade, Mummy. It's really *too* delicious. I'm simply fanatical about it."

"Yes. Well . . ." Catherine sat down stiffly, looking distracted. "The bag has some clothes in it. Yours. You'd barely brought a thing with you, so far as I could see. I thought to myself, she must be rinsing her smalls out each day by hand or making the maid do it, and neither seemed to me to be appropriate."

"Thank you." Grace reached over and squeezed her hand. "That was very thoughtful. If you'd only telephoned, I'd have—"

"You'd have what? Made some sort of excuse to stop me coming?" She dashed her hand quickly across her face, but wasn't quite fast enough.

"Oh, Mummy. Don't get upset."

"Well." Her face grew redder. "What am I supposed to think? We've heard nothing from you since that first abrupt telephone call. We've no idea when you're coming home. Tilly keeps asking, and I keep worrying, and Nancy's convinced she's offended you horribly in some way she can't understand, poor girl."

"I'm sorry, Mummy."

"So you should be. What is going *on,* young lady?" A large bee buzzed close to Catherine's face, marvelously oblivious to her frenzy.

"Look, I don't want anyone to worry about me. That's the *last* thing I want. I simply need some time to myself. Time to think. That's not exactly easy at home."

"It's not easy for any of us. Life is very rarely easy." Catherine crossed her arms and stuck her chin out. "We just have to get on with it. But you—running away, losing your job . . ." She looked about her at the Egyptian statuary and the tiny model pyramids positioned here and there in the flower beds: "And Grace, why did you come *here*?"

Jenkins appeared with a tray. The lemonade was a cloudy yellow. Ice cubes jangling bell-like against the glass jug. They appeared to have a hypnotic effect on Catherine, who sat gazing at them.

Grace waited for Jenkins to go back into the house. "We've always been close, Sheridan and I. He said I could stay for a while."

"Close?" This was delivered with an expression of extreme discomfort. It was rather as if the bee had crawled inside Catherine's clothing, and she knew that at any moment it could be about to sting her.

"He's been the kindest of friends. He's looked after me. He's like a brother, actually . . ." Her eyes met her mother's— and yes, there it was: a sort of panicked recognition. She poured the lemonade, the ice cubes jostling and splashing their way into the glasses. She waited.

"So he told you." Catherine's voice was quieter now. "He promised me he wouldn't. *You* promised—"

"Oh, Mummy. It's out of the box now. There's nothing to be done about that."

"No. I suppose not."

"He didn't want to break your confidence. I knew something was going on and I made him tell me. But why didn't *you* tell me, the other day? Why did you let me go on believing all the wrong was yours?"

"Not my secret to tell." A sniff that was somehow dignified. "Your father isn't here to speak for himself. What business would I have blackening his name with his daughter? What good would that have done? Anyway, his bad behavior doesn't excuse mine."

"It sheds an entirely different light on the situation, can't you see that? All four of you were caught up in an utter mess. They had a *baby*, for goodness' sakes!"

Catherine stared at the honeysuckle. "Look at those bees. All so busy doing what they're supposed to do. What they were born to do. Where is Sheridan this morning?"

"Over at the Tutankhamun with his bookkeeper. Mummy, you should tell Nancy, too. Now that I know, she's going to have to know, too. It would be so much better coming from you."

"I suppose you're right. Oh dear." She sucked the air in sharply through her teeth and made a visible effort to rally herself. "He's a nice boy, isn't he? Odd, of course, but bright and entertaining. I'd say he's really quite a dear chap." And now a frown. "Frittering his life away though. Rather like someone else I could mention . . . He really ought to go back to university. Perhaps I should speak to him about it. After all, if I don't, who will?"

Grace rolled her eyes. "So anyway . . . Did you all know about each other? About the two affairs? I mean, did you all know while it was going on?"

A sip of the lemonade, a jiggling of the ice. "Yes, we did. I say, this really *is* nice."

"Did you enter into some sort of arrangement? Was it all a frightfully modern social experiment?"

"Well, I wouldn't put it quite like that."

Once again Catherine had that look about her as though the bee was crawling down her back or up her leg.

"And both couples ended their affairs when Amelia became pregnant?" A pause while she waited for the nod. "What happened? Did you sit down in a room together and just talk about it, as friends? How do four people decide something like that ?"

"We voted."

The laughter came before she could stop it. "Oh, Mummy!"

The lightest of titters. "Yes, I suppose it is rather absurd, when you think of it that way. We were trying to do the right thing about a situation that had got well out of hand. It was all very sensible and democratic. In case you're wondering, the vote was unanimous."

"Good." Grace's thoughts were coming thick and fast. A kind of waterfall. She struggled to slow it all down.

"Your father was a good man. Never think otherwise. I doubt he'd have strayed off the path at all, but Amelia enticed him. Snared him like a rabbit. I don't know if she really loved him or not. She was very deep, you see. One of those irritatingly fathomless women one comes across from time to time. One is forever trying to plumb the depths with that sort of woman. They were both drawn to that, Edward and Daddy. Me too, in a way, when Amelia and I first became friends at school . . . Often there's nothing really *there*, you know, with that sort of woman. Just a vacuum." She looked down at her lap. Cleared her throat. "Daddy and Edward were opposites. I think so much of it was about the difference between them, and between me and Amelia of course. Daddy was smitten with her for a while." She was twisting her hands around each other in her lap. "We *did* do the right thing in the end. For you children, but for ourselves, too. For each other."

"You can't always love the people you're supposed to love. Love just happens. You can't will it away."

"But you can walk away." Catherine moved her chair closer to Grace's. "Sometimes you have to, no matter how painful it is."

"I know."

The bush nearby was covered in ladybirds. Smothered in them, really. And all those cabbage-white butterflies. This tiny garden was teeming with life.

"What are you going to do, Grace?"

A breath. "I'm going to leave London."

"You can't do that!" Catherine smacked her lemonade glass down, the ice cubes clinking loudly together.

"Why not? We're both agreed that I should walk away. Well, I just happen to think the farther I walk, the better."

"But what about us? What about Nancy?"

"I thought you'd understand, Mummy. It really *is* for the best. I'll start afresh. I'll send money."

"This isn't about money. Tilly and Felix are missing you so much. You're so important to them!"

Something caught in her chest at the mention of those two little names. The sharpest of pangs. "I miss them, too. But I have to leave."

Catherine shook her head slowly. "I wish things didn't have to change. I love *both* my daughters. Won't you *please* just come home?"

It was tempting—so tempting—to say: All right, I'll come home. She could go and put her few things into the carpet bag while Catherine relaxed in the sunshine with the lemonade. They'd talk, on the bus, about the trouble at

Pearson's—perhaps Mummy would be cross, perhaps not—and then, as they walked through the front door, Felix would come crawling from the living room. He could crawl so fast now—and grab her leg with both arms till she swung him up into the air and held him close. Tilly would be cross and stand-offish, but after a while she might deign to glance up from her drawing, and then she'd say, "Have you brought me a present, Auntie Grace?" She'd have to say no but the ice would be broken anyway. They'd be friends again. And then she'd be writing words for Tilly to try to copy, and hugging Felix, and all would be like it used to be—until Nancy came in, that is.

"Tell me one thing," said Grace. "Do you think Nancy is in love?"

"Yes."

A curt nod. They were quiet for a moment with the buzz of the bees and the bright pinks and golds of the honeysuckle and fuchsia.

"Don't worry. I shan't be going anywhere in a hurry. I have no idea where I'm going, after all." She tried to force her mood to lighten, and her voice with it. "So, what have you been up to, Mummy? Did you go to that Women's Freedom League rally?"

"I'll tell you about that when you've told me what happened at Pearson's. What's been going on, my girl?"

And they sat on together in the sunshine, talking, as the ice in their glasses melted away.

Three

It was a few days after her mother's visit that Sheridan announced he'd had a telephone call from a newly enlightened Nancy, and had invited her to come and spend that afternoon at the house. A chance for them to begin their new relationship.

"Join us for a cweam tea, darling," he said. "Thwee siblings together, and bla bla. What larks."

Grace was aware that she'd have to encounter Nancy at some point soon. She could hardly leave town without saying good-bye. She knew too that her dread of the occasion was illogical. Lovely Nancy was still Lovely Nancy, no matter whom she was in love with. Nonetheless, John and George were both looming large in her head at the moment, and she *was* dreading the encounter. And really, she said to herself, it didn't have to be *today*, did it? Their reunion didn't have to be *quite* so soon?

"Oh, what a shame that I already have an engagement," she said lightly to Sheridan, and spun around on her heel so that he wouldn't see her face.

This did, of course, provide the perfect opportunity for Grace to call by at Tofts Walk and bring out a further suitcase or two of her belongings. Her sister would definitely not be at home. So as the younger Rutherford sister traveled by bus and tram from Hampstead to Kensington later that day to embrace her newly discovered brother, the elder sister was traveling in the opposite direction, reading and rereading Dexter O'Connell's one-off West-Ender column, which had appeared in that day's *Herald*.

She'd been warned about the piece by Dickie ahead of time. "You don't mind, do you, Gracie? Thing is, nobody in my position could refuse a column from Dexter O'Connell. He hasn't written for a newspaper in years. And you did say you could do with a break . . ."

She knew she should be glad that O'Connell had said sorry to her in his piece, flattered that he had made a half-open statement of his onetime heartfelt love for her. But the manner of his apology and declaration rankled. He had barged in on her column in order to say his bit. He was asserting his power even as he confessed that she had made him vulnerable. Then of course, the piece itself was a typical piece of O'Connell game playing. An apparent gesture of simple honesty buried in so many layers of fakery and vanity that she couldn't unpick it. Frankly, it made her think of O'Connell as being like some high-pitched, whining mosquito that you just have to swat. She'd had absolutely enough of him and would be all the happier once Margaret had packed his case and marched him off to that damn boat.

She was so distracted by her own rage at the column that

she was barely aware of getting off the bus, barely aware of the ten-minute walk to her house, of the familiar clink of the front gate, of the rooting about for her keys. So distracted was she that she didn't notice the second clink of the gate, or the whistled tune: "Five Foot Two, Eyes of Blue," so that when her name was called out cheerily and a hand touched her arm, her heart thudded and she squeaked aloud. And when she turned around to see John Cramer standing right behind her, her heart thudded yet again.

"Sorry." Cramer's shirtsleeves were rolled up to the elbow, showing brown, sinewy arms. "I didn't mean to startle you. I spotted you from the window and I just had to come over. How are you?"

"Fine, thank you," she said in her frostiest voice. And then she frowned. There was something different about him. "Your mustache—you've shaved it off."

He winced and stroked his upper lip. "Penance for bad behavior at the *Herald* party. It's a rule I have for myself. My face is too big without it, don't you think?"

"Mustaches are like dead mice stuck under the nose."

"That's harsh! I was attached to mine. Or perhaps it was attached to me . . ." He smiled. She could feel an answering smile of her own trying to break out. It was all she could do to hold it back.

"It's good to see you, Grace. Would you come across to the house with me for a cup of tea?"

A tight little shake of the head.

He rubbed at his forehead. "I said something to you at the party, didn't I? I'm sorry. I must have been boorish, perhaps downright offensive."

"Not at all. I simply have lots to do." There were sounds behind the door. Feet coming down the stairs. Catherine, or possibly Edna. Grace looked up into Cramer's mustache-less face. You could see his mouth better now. He had a nice mouth—wide and generous . . . "Though perhaps I could spare the time for a walk. Just a quick walk."

To begin with, they walked in silence, side by side, over the cobbles of Flask Walk. She had no idea what he was thinking. For herself, she was absurdly choked with emotion—couldn't trust herself to speak a word. He finally began to talk as they wandered up Well Walk toward the Heath.

"About the party . . . I want to explain . . ."

"No need."

"The drinking—that night was the first time I've drunk alcohol in years."

"I don't doubt it."

"I won't be doing it again, Grace. Really, you have to believe me about that."

"It's none of my business, John."

They were entering the East Heath now, where the grass grew in long tufty clumps on the uneven ground. The trees arched thickly overhead, their roots pushing up the sandy paths as though struggling to get to the surface.

"Back in my drinking days, I used to have a recurring dream about driftwood. Old bits of worn-out wood washing up on anonymous gray beaches, and just being left high up on the sand with all the weed and debris. It was a very weird dream. Slow-paced. The repeated sound of the waves against the shingle—that endless slow shushing noise . . . It terrified me." But now he shrugged. "God, this sounds so lame, even to me."

"Not at all." It was dark in this part of the Heath in spite of the weather, with the trees' thick foliage blocking out the sun. "I know exactly what you're talking about. I dream sometimes about a half-open door. There's a strong draft in my dream and the door is shifting very gently back and forth in that draft. Tiny movements. As it moves, it creaks. A subtle creaking noise—nothing more, but it keeps on coming, over and over. There's nothing I can do about it. I have dreamed about monsters and war and disease—all the usual nightmares. But this dream about the door—it's much more frightening."

"Then you *do* understand," he said. "When I stopped drinking, I stopped having the dream. But since the night of my little relapse, it's come back. Quite a few times. I can't have that nightmare back in my life, Grace. I won't let it happen."

They were walking beside the Mixed Bathing Pond, the water a deep green and the humid air filled with gnats. Nobody swimming about today but the ducks.

"I'm glad you hit O'Connell."

"*Are* you?" He took her arm and linked it through his. Decisively.

"I'd have liked to have done it myself. I'm immensely glad he's leaving. I had him all wrong."

"So did I, actually." His arm tightened around hers.

"What do you mean by that?"

"Well, he came to see me the day after the party. Dropped by at my house, just like that."

"*Really?*" She remembered what O'Connell had once told her about Cramer—how he'd followed him all over the world. He'd joked that Cramer would somehow manage to be there at his deathbed, like the Grim Reaper . . . Cramer had been at the Savoy, of course, on the day of her first date with O'Connell. "*He* came to see *you?*"

"It was so strange. His manner was polite and formal, as if we were a couple of distant acquaintances. I asked him in and we drank tea together, holding our cups correctly, talking about the *weather*—we've obviously both been in England too long! And all this 'niceness,' in spite of his swollen nose and split lip. In spite of my hungover red-rimmed eyes . . ."

"What did he want?"

"Once we'd gotten through all that politeness, he told me he was sorry he hadn't been straight with me all these years. He said that while he was alone, writing *The Vision*, he went through a kind of crisis. Eva had chosen me but, really, he'd already withdrawn from her. Effectively, he chose Veronique. But the process of writing the story rekindled his love for Eva. He said he relived the whole relationship alone in his study—the good and the bad. He was eaten up with jealousy at me for having it all for real while his life was just a dusty room with a typewriter. He said the nights were the worst. It was during that time that he began to hate me."

"And he just decided to go to your house and tell you this after all that time? Do you believe him?"

"Actually, I do. I know when he's lying and when he's not. He told me he'd gotten over it all once the book was published and he was out of the wilderness. But it's remained his big regret that he chose art over love. By the time he reached the end of *The Vision* he was all dried up inside. He tried to make himself fall in love with other women over the years, but it was all fakery."

"But then Eva started writing to him?"

"By then it was too late. Veronique had wrung him out and hung him up to dry. There was no love left in O'Connell, not even for Eva. He said her letters made him sad and regretful. Sometimes they made him angry with me—he blamed me for the state she was in. He said he only replied to about half of them. Some of his replies were nostalgic, dwelling on the past. Others detailed his life and how far removed it was from hers. Then it all became too much for him and he wrote her a three-liner telling her to leave him alone."

"How did she respond?"

A sigh. "She ran away from the clinic to go search for him on the day of a lecture. He told me she knocked on the door of his room when he was dressing. Black tie, tux, dinner jacket—and there's this wreck of a woman crying and pleading with him to love her like he used to. It was all too real for O'Connell. He was brutally dismissive. Told her he didn't love her and he never would again. Had to physically prize her off him to get out the door. As he was leaving, he suggested that she stay on to take a bath and pull herself together. He said he'd thought at the time that he was being generous. His parting words were to tell her to leave the key at the desk."

"How daft that he refused to talk to you about this for all these years."

"He hated me. And I followed him around, asking the same questions over and over again because I hated him. It was all about Eva, but it also stopped being about her. It became simply about us. Me and him and our hate for each other."

"But now he's told you. What now?"

As they arrived at Parliament Hill the world seemed to open out. The overarching trees gave way all of a sudden to a bright blue sky that had never seemed so huge and so full of promise. They climbed together, up the steep path. Above them, a small boy was trying and failing to launch a purple kite into the air. Two girls threw sticks for their dog to chase.

"I love this place." Grace could feel the blood pumping through her. "I belong here."

"And yet you've decided to leave."

"That's right."

They reached the top of the hill, and Grace's bench. London was spread out below them in a shimmering heat haze. He sat down. Patted the seat to ask her to join him. After a brief hesitation, she did.

"I've never felt I really belong anywhere," he said. "Perhaps I've belonged to people rather than places. Yes, I'm sure that's right."

She thought of herself and George sitting together on this bench. The holding of hands, and eventually of each other.

"I've always longed to belong to someone. Entirely and completely. My whole self. My everything."

"Oh, Grace. Don't leave." He put his arms around her, here at this place that was the center of her world. And here, with her memories looming large all around and about them—*even* here in this place—she found that she'd stopped thinking about the past or the future, and for the longest moment it was just about him. His mouth. The warm, inky smell of his neck. But even as the moment stretched out, golden and green and sweet, it was suddenly over again and she was pulling away from him. Getting up, smoothing her hair, turning away.

"You know why I hit O'Connell at the party?" came his voice. "Sure, I couldn't stand to see him acting like he was king of the place, swanning about in that ridiculous white suit, surrounded by admirers. But that wasn't it. Sure, he'd put my Eva in a book and made a load of money out of it and tried to poison my marriage, and refused to talk to me about my wife's death. But that wasn't it either. None of it."

"So, what was it then?"

"Do you *really* not know? It was about you, Grace. *You.* Because you were his, not mine. Because he came over to gloat about that. To tell me that he *had* you, body and soul, and that he'd go on *having* you until it became too dull to continue, and until he'd used you up like an old cloth, and that I would never, *ever* have you, even when having you was no longer worth anything—because you were his and because he'd make damn sure of it."

"How dare you!" She turned to look at him, and his eyes were dark and wet.

"I'm telling you the whole truth, Grace. That's what he said. He was taunting me because, actually, he sensed something between us and he couldn't stand it. I hit him because I love you."

"Oh. Oh dear." She'd come over all dizzy, and he was instantly on his feet, guiding her back to the bench. She tried ineffectually to bat him away as she sat down.

"What is the *matter* with me?" she snapped. "I'm not the fainting sort. I've never fainted."

"That night at the party," he said, more softly. "The *thing* between O'Connell and me—well, it stopped being about Eva and the past. And it became about you and about the present. Because, actually, he loves you, too."

"That's rubbish! Him and me—well, I don't really know what it was all about but it wasn't love."

"He loves you. Or loved you, I'm not sure which. As much as he's capable of loving anyone. And actually, enough to want you to find happiness."

Grace could feel her hands shaking. Her whole body felt quivery and strange. "What do you mean?"

"You've seen his column today, surely? He wrote, 'You're not the only one I've wronged.' And then he wanted to tell you there's another good heart out there. He said, 'I hope you find each other.'"

That feeling again—of a shared understanding between her and Cramer. Something fundamental in their bones and their blood.

"He came to see me at my house because of you. Because you told him he should tell me the truth about the past, and you made him feel ashamed of himself. Because he finally saw that he'd been clinging to the past as much as I. Because he realized, when you and he were standing there in that bathroom, that he'd lost you and that he was behaving like a child."

Gradually, the shaking abated. As Grace tried to assemble her thoughts, she kept her gaze fixed on the towers and roofs and spires of London.

"Let me tell you something," she said eventually. "Twelve years ago I sat on this bench, looking out at this view, and listened to a boy telling me he loved me. That same night he proposed to my sister. Four years later, I sat here again with a hollowed-out soldier who couldn't talk to his wife. He told me his secrets and we began to clutch at each other, and things happened between us which were utterly wrong and which should never have happened. It was George. Nancy's George. John, whatever there is between you and me—what*ever* there is—it isn't worth as much to me as my sister is. I will not get myself embroiled with another man who can't choose between Nancy and me."

"That's quite a story." The arm around her shoulders was withdrawn. He sat forward and appeared to be thinking this through. "But Grace, we're not all the same. It's you that I want."

"That was what he said, too."

"I am *not* George." An angry glare. "And I'm not O'Connell either. You're the only woman who's even *registered* with me in over five years. How many times do I have to tell you that Nancy and I are just friends?"

"But you took her to Paris!"

"God!" He bashed at his own temples. "I took Nancy to Paris because she's good company and I didn't feel like being on my own. We had separate rooms. Hell, your sister deserved a holiday, Grace!"

Two boys were kicking a football about a little way off. Back and forth it went between them.

"And anyway," he continued, "what exactly were *you* up to that weekend?"

"This isn't about what *I* did. I went away with O'Connell because I knew I had to leave you to Nancy."

"Oh, Grace, you're quite incredibly hypocritical and obtuse when you want to be. You're refusing to see the most obvious thing! It's *you* who couldn't choose. Not me."

"I don't want O'Connell."

"So what *do* you want?"

Back and forth went that football, just down the slope.

A sigh. "Nancy's in love with you. I can see it even if you can't or won't. God, even my *mother* can see it. I will not jeopardize my sister's happiness or her children's. Not again."

"Your sister and I will never be together. *Never.*"

The bash-bash of the football. A low hum that might have been the sound of the city below them. Of all the life surging through it.

"Good-bye, John." Grace stood up and dusted herself down.

"Grace, for five years my world has been nothing but hate and darkness and grief. You've changed all that. *You.* I'm living again. Really *living*. And I think you feel the same."

"You asked me what I want. What I want is to leave London. What I want is to be far away from you. Good-bye."

She turned for one last glance at him. He looked deflated, defeated. Nothing left to say. When she walked away, he didn't try to stop her.

The West-Ender
June 20, 1927

Once upon a time people believed that, before it dies, the swan sings a beautiful and mournful song. Hence the expression "swan song." But really, did any of the simple folk who propagated this notion ever bother to listen to a swan? She might have a slender neck and a nicer-than-average plumage but, in case you were in any doubt, let me assure you that as a chanteuse, Miss Swan is hardly on a par with Bessie Smith.

This, nevertheless, is Diamond Sharp's swan song. You, dear readers, will long ago have decided whether my dulcet tones are any prettier than those of my fair-feathered friends. Either way, this is the last time I shall ask for your indulgence.

Today I shan't be worshipping the choux pastry at Chez Noisette (though it is so light they must surely have to glue it to the plates to stop it floating away); bemoaning the boiled-to-pulp vegetables of Florence Finnegan's (may the proprietor drown in a vat of his own frothing cabbage water); accusing the manager of the Salamander nightclub of watering down the spirits (I josh, of course); or lauding the eye makeup of a certain Mr. Hamilton-Shapcott (Sheridan, where did you get that mascara? I must have some posthaste!).

By now you will all know where to go for a jolly evening out in the West End and I shan't waste any more ink on the subject. Instead, I want to talk about a subject of somewhat more substance than where to go for the perfect bob cut.

My mother, Catherine, was a suffragette. In her tender years she marched with the WSPU and was arrested for hurling eggs at members of the Liberal Party. Even now, in her dotage, she goes as often as she can to Women's Freedom League rallies and bangs on endlessly about their four demands. (For those woefully ignorant souls who know nothing about the demands, they are: (1) pensions for fatherless children; (2) equal guardianship; (3) equal franchise; and (4) the rectification of the Sex Disqualification [Removal] Act.) I must confess to having ignored, rolled my eyes at and even mocked my mother as she launches into her lengthy speeches on the plight of Twentieth-Century Woman. Frankly, I'd much rather spend my day off at home painting my toenails, sipping a gin fizz and listening to jazz on the gramophone than go out to Speaker's Corner or some such place to stand in the rain with a placard. In fact, let's be honest, I'd rather spend the day having my toenails yanked off one by one with a pair of pliers to the strains of Beethoven's Fifth than at one of those rallies.

And yet, dear readers—and yet, I rather believe that I've always promoted equality for women. My words are less weighty than those of my heroine Catherine (that's not sarcasm, Mother, you really are my heroine, in spite of everything), but emancipation has many faces. Some may seem trivial, but this trivia is the very fabric of our lives, yours and mine. Is a woman truly emancipated when she's tripping over her own petticoats? Is it fair and equitable that a young lady is forced to stay home with a book on a Saturday evening for fear of her parents' disapproval while her even younger brother is out dancing the night away at the Hammersmith Palais? Why should it be that the woman who dines alone by choice once in a while should have to tolerate being pointed at and whispered about by all those half-cut idiots propping up the bar? And while we're on the subject, what's wrong with a girl taking a cocktail or three of an evening? Drinking is fun for females too, and we're not "loose women" or "secondhand goods." Come to think of it, maybe some of us are. Maybe there's nothing wrong in that either.

That's the end of my rant. Now I'm off to dance my fin-

est Breakaway in pastures new (the Breakaway, for those who've been hiding under a rock lately, is a Charleston with extra frills). I'll be back in dear old London sometime when the moon is full and the band is playing fast. Look for me at cocktail hour and you'll know me by my splendidly geometrical bob (the name of that man, by the way, is Marcus Rino), by the lipstick smear on the side of my glass and the smoke rings I'll be blowing. If you see me, come over and we'll have a drink for old times' sake.

It's been a pleasure, my darlings, and I only hope the pleasure has not *all* been mine. May your nights be long and your dresses short. Always keep your head clear, your mind open and a spare pair of knickers in your handbag, and remember that Life Is the Spice of Variety.

Kisses.

Grace Rutherford
Alias Diamond Sharp

Four

Dickie had reluctantly agreed to Grace's only stipulation for her farewell lunch party: Keep it small. In addition to the two of them, there would simply be Sheridan, Dodo, Margaret and Nancy. Nancy, who was still out on a limb, being avoided by Grace as though she had done something terrible.

When it came to the choice of venue, Dickie took no notice of Grace's list of preferences and booked Tour Eiffel. Grace was vocal in her protests but secretly glad. It was soothing to know that whatever else might change, Dickie would always be Dickie.

She'd made an effort for this lunch, choosing a printed chiffon dress by La Samaritaine, all petals and softness and luxury. It had been a gift from O'Connell, but she was determined not to let that put her off. It was far too nice a frock to be left on its hanger for personal reasons and enjoyed only by moths.

When she entered the restaurant, there were only three people seated at the corner table.

"Here she is." Dodo's eyebrows were even more finely arched than usual, and she was wielding a cigarette holder longer than any Grace had ever seen. Margaret, sitting beside her, had her mouth stuffed full of bread and had to wave her greeting. (Could *anyone* eat like that girl?)

"Darling sis!" Sheridan was becoming a little overexuberant about their newly discovered bond. Just how many people had he told? "I've instwucted them to bwing their finest champagne and they've gone to delve in the cellar. Dickie's paying, so I think we should enjoy ourselves, don't you? Serves him wight for being so outwageously late. And what about our divine sister? Is she a habitual late awwival too?"

"How extremely annoying of the pair of them," snapped Grace, more from nerves than genuine irritation. "They know very well that I like to be the last to arrive, and I'm on the dot of my usual thirty minutes en retard!"

"Oh, weally, Gwacie. Lateness is so vewy last year."

"Dickie had urgent business at the *Herald,*" said Dodo. "He said he'll be here as soon as he can. Actually I think there's something afoot."

"What sort of something?" Intrigued, Grace took a seat at their window table.

"I don't know, but he had a very shifty expression on his face." And Dodo did something extraordinary with her eyebrows.

"Nobody's expwession could be as shifty as that!"

The champagne arrived, and some very good French onion soup.

"So, Grace, why Edinburgh?" asked Margaret.

Grace shrugged. "May as well be there as anywhere else. I'm off first thing in the morning. I'll stay with an old schoolfriend for a bit. Then we'll see."

"Awfully cold place," said Sheridan.

"Doesn't bother me. I look good in furs."

"There'll be some nice cashmere in the shops this autumn," added Dodo, in a making-the-best-of-it tone.

Grace looked from one to the other of them. Three skeptical faces.

"It's bonkers," said Sheridan.

"You're just running away," said Margaret. "And there's no need to. *He's* leaving anyway, after all."

"This is not about O'Connell," snapped Grace. "Frankly, you're welcome to him. Bon voyage!" Then, in a lighter voice, addressing them all: "People don't have to stay in one place all their lives, do they? Perhaps I want to go somewhere where nobody knows me. Perhaps I want a new adventure. Margaret should understand that perfectly well even if the rest of you don't."

"A toast." Dodo held up her champagne glass. "To new adventures!"

Grace clinked her glass with theirs, wishing she could feel more wholehearted about this new adventure of hers. She'd be all right when she got there, surely? Millicent was kindness itself—she'd said Grace could stay as long as she liked. Edinburgh seemed rather wonderfully foreign in prospect without being too far away. She'd considered Paris, but suspected she couldn't be properly witty there, hampered as she was by her schoolgirl French vocabulary. There was New York, of course, but . . . no . . . Edinburgh was the best plan, all things considered. She'd certainly manage to dazzle in Edinburgh. She'd conquer the place in weeks . . . wouldn't she?

Sheridan leaned over. "You can always come back."

But Grace hadn't properly heard him. Her eye had been caught by something down in the street. A figure in white on the far side of the road.

She started and blinked. A bus was blocking her view. Another blink and it had moved on, and he was still there.

O'Connell, in his white suit and hat. She couldn't make out his expression but she was certain he was smiling. That usual sly smile of his. He was gazing up at her. Right into her face.

The room around her continued as normal. Her friends talking, smoke wafting up from cigarettes, Joe the waiter coming to collect the empty soup dishes. But Grace was holding her breath.

He was here to see her, she was certain of it. He was about to cross the road and enter the building. Rudolph Stulik would be all over him at the door and he'd be ushered over to their table like the long-awaited guest of honor and he'd sit down in Dickie's place and Margaret would be all wide-eyed admiration and Dodo would flirt and Sheridan would stir things up and . . . Well, what *then*?

She hadn't expected to see him again.

But he wasn't crossing the road. He was still standing there. As she watched, he raised his hat with a flourish, then set it back on his head.

"He promised he wouldn't make a nuisance of himself." Margaret's eyes were cast down. "He wanted to say good-bye."

Grace looked back at the sun-drenched street. O'Connell wasn't there anymore. A cab was pulling out into the traffic.

"Hello, stranger!"

Grace twisted around to find Nancy standing beside their table in a turquoise dress and with a fetching new bob cut, softly waved.

"Nancy, darling." There was a tension in their hug. A distance. Each of them was trying to look happy to see the other. Each of them was sizing the other up, endeavoring to work out what was going on behind the smiles.

"Have I missed the soup?" Nancy glanced at the empty bowls. "Do you think they'd fetch me one if I smiled nicely enough?"

She looks radiant, thought Grace. I've never seen her looking so radiant.

Dodo was signaling to the waiter. Margaret was glancing edgily from one sister to the other.

"Wight!" Sheridan seized Nancy's left hand, Grace's right hand, and his moment. "If I don't say it now, I never shall. Gwace, you absolutely *mustn't* leave. We've only just discovered each other, my lovely sisters, after all these years. We should all be together and be nice to each other and look after each other like a pwoper family."

"It's utterly daft that you're leaving," added Nancy. "What's happened to you, Grace?"

Grace looked down at the table. At Nancy's hand, held in Sheridan's. There was a ring on her finger. A ring so big it would weigh your whole arm down. A huge ruby with tiny diamonds clustered around it.

"Nancy! You're engaged!"

"Wonderful, isn't it? You're the very first to know. Well— you were *supposed* to be. But then Mummy came across the ring in my underwear drawer this morning and jumped to *such* a wrong conclusion that I had to put her straight. Can you *believe* the nosiness of the woman?"

Grace managed the kiss and hug. She did her best to smile. But it was all she could do to keep from crying. The higgledy-piggledy drawings, etchings, paintings and cards all over the walls of the restaurant had never looked more like crazily chaotic gravestones. With Sheridan calling for more champagne, and Dodo and Margaret gasping and clutching at Nancy's hand, she hotfooted it out to the bathroom.

"So," she told her reflection in the mirror, "here we go again." She turned on the cold tap and then stood there, gripping the edges of the sink, peering into her own face without really seeing anything. Why had Cramer kissed her the way he had on that day? Why had he told her all that rubbish as they sat there on that damned bench? Were they downright lies or, like George, did he just not really know himself? Bloody man!

She hadn't allowed herself to believe him, even as he was making his declarations of love. Experience had taught her that she couldn't. She'd known that she should get right away from an engagement that she'd assumed was inevitable— but even *she* hadn't expected it to happen so quickly, before she'd even left town! Before her memories of their walk on the Heath and the things he'd said to her had begun to cool down. Well, at least she already had her suitcases packed and her ticket bought. She was certainly not going to hang around the happy couple and wait for it all to go wrong—not this time.

This time she would do the right thing.

But then again, was it really the right thing just to leave and say nothing to Nancy about what had happened between her and Cramer? Wasn't it her duty, after all, to warn her sister that her fiancé's newly declared love might not be quite so steadfast and enduring as he was presumably making out?

God, if only it didn't all hurt so damned much!

"What are you skulking about in here for?" Nancy came in and closed the door behind her. "And why have you been avoiding me so fastidiously? If I didn't know better, I'd think you were leaving town because of *me*."

Grace found she couldn't speak. She turned off the tap and stared down into the sink. There was a single dark hair lying in the basin, perhaps one of her own.

"Tell me you're *not* leaving town because of me?"

Still Grace couldn't speak.

Nancy moved closer, put a hand on her shoulder. "Darling Grace. I know it's been hard on you, having to look after all of us. It's become too much for you, I see that. Mummy was shocked when you lost your job, but I wasn't. It would be too much for anyone after a while, always having to put others first the way you have. It must have ground you down over time. I think perhaps that's what drove you into all the madness with O'Connell."

"It's not that—"

"I wish it was you getting married, Gracie, I really do. It's your turn. It should have been your turn years ago. But that isn't the way it's happened. And don't you see—it'll be more likely to happen for you too now. You won't be looking after me and the children anymore because there'll be someone else to do it. You'll be free to live your own life."

Grace took a couple of steps away from her, retreating from the hand on her shoulder—the hand with the ring. "I wish it was as simple as that," she said quietly.

Nancy looked confused and slightly crushed. "Sometimes life *can* be simple. I'm going to marry a lovely man and have a beautiful wedding. I want you there at my side, not off in Edinburgh or some other faraway place. Grace, you're not really going off to stay with Millicent, are you? Moon-face Millicent from school?"

Grace was back at the Register Office on that crisp winter day, years ago. Standing with her mother, widows together, watching her sister, the war bride, marrying George.

"I'm sorry, Nancy. I couldn't be happier for you, but I'm still going. It's as you say—I have to start putting myself first."

A frown appeared on that oh-so-clear brow. A look of suspicion. "Are you jealous? Is that what this is?"

"No."

"You *are*. You're jealous. I know that face! My God, Grace. You had your chance with him. Do you really begrudge me your leavings? Do you begrudge *him* happiness?"

A shake of the head. A great welling up.

"You didn't want him, Grace."

She couldn't hold it back any longer. "That's not true! I was confused at first—O'Connell made it all confusing—but then I realized it was *him* I was in love with, not O'Connell. He asked *me* to go to Paris, Nancy. He asked me *first*. I said no because of you. Because he's yours. And now . . . Well . . . I can't be around you both. Just can't!"

"Oh, *Grace!* This is so *silly*."

But Grace was rushing for the door, bolting back out into the restaurant, and colliding with Dickie, who'd just arrived at the top of the stairs.

"Hey." He grabbed her to steady her, and looked down at her quizzically. He was so much smarter than usual today. Debonair, even. His hair had been newly cut. His suit was crisply pressed, and he was altogether more handsome than he'd ever been. His very *eyes* were more handsome.

He let go of Grace now, and looked past her to address someone else. "Hello, my love. Did I miss our big moment?"

Grace glanced from Dickie to Nancy and back, and something dark that had sat inside her for a long time shifted out of its hiding place and scuttled away. It was the nastiest, blackest thing—something like a spider, but heavy, so heavy. It had squatted inside her for years. Perhaps since that night in 1915 when she'd kissed Steven Wilkins and Nancy had become engaged to George. And now, finally, this dark thing had upped and left, and Grace felt lighter than air.

Five

When they finally got on with lunch, Grace sat back with the almost inedible jugged hare that was brought from the kitchen, and let the whirlwind romance take center stage.

Nancy kept shaking her head and saying, "Grace, I thought you'd guessed about Dickie and me, I really did."

"I suppose I have Dexter O'Connell and John Cramer to thank." Dickie was ebullient. "You might say it was their little spat at the *Herald* party that finally brought us together. We took the inebriated Cramer home and put him to bed. And then we sat in his kitchen with cups of tea and some damn fine chocolate cake that we'd stumbled on, and we just talked and talked for the rest of the night. It was quite magical."

"I know it all seems rather rushed," said Nancy. "But it's so right. And we've known each other for years, after all. There's simply no point in wasting any more time."

With dessert came Dickie's farewell speech to Grace. The story of Diamond Sharp.

Just over a year ago, he told his audience, he'd telephoned Grace one morning to cancel a lunch. One of his writers had gone AWOL without delivering his copy, and Dickie explained to Grace that he would have to sit down and write the article himself, in addition to everything else he had to do that day, or there'd be an empty page in the *Herald* when they went to press.

"Don't you *dare* cancel our lunch!" Grace had replied. "Get on with your piffling bit of editing, and *I'll* write you something."

He'd laughed. "Just what would you write about then, Gracie?"

"The first damn thing that comes into my head, that's what. And I promise you'll like it."

Dickie smiled at the faces around the table. "If I'd had an ounce of common sense, I'd have told her not to be ridiculous. She'd never written anything for a newspaper before. Well, nothing but advertising copy. It was foolhardy, at best."

"But you took a risk," said Margaret. "Why did you take the risk?"

"Because I'm absolutely terrified of her!"

Amid the laughter that followed, Grace flapped a hand at him. "Dickie, for God's sake, call a halt to this obituary and get the bill."

Afterward, Grace and Nancy caught the bus up to Hampstead.

"The children will be so happy to see you," said Nancy.

"And I them. I was so sad not to catch them when I came by the other day. But there's someone else I have to see first."

"Of course. What chumps we've been. If only you'd listened to me when I said there was nothing between us."

Grace shook her head. "It's strange. I was so convinced. I thought I knew you well enough to be able to see past what you were saying."

"Well . . ." A shrug. "You weren't entirely wrong. I suppose I was attracted to him in the beginning, just a little. But that wore off pretty quickly. Whether he felt the same or not, I don't know. He certainly never said so, and nothing ever happened between us. We shared our grief and that was a good thing for both of us. It bound us together as friends. That's the whole story."

They were quiet for a moment, watching people getting on and off the bus. Then Nancy piped up again. "You know, John told me he'd met someone. He mentioned it in Paris—said he thought he was falling for a girl for the first time in years but that she was in love with someone else. If *only* he'd told me it was you! Believe it or not, I'd actually been hoping there was a chance the two of you would get together. That O'Connell was such a nuisance—I'm so glad that's all over. John is perfect for you."

"It's just as you and Dickie were saying," said Grace. "There's no point in wasting any more time."

Cramer's house was locked and lifeless. Grace, pounding the knocker, stamped a foot in frustration. Nancy had told her he was always in at this time, working. So why not today?

"Here." Nancy was coming across the road from the Rutherfords', a set of keys dangling from her hand. "He has me keep a spare set in case of being locked out. Shall we have a peep inside?"

The house was much like their own. Tall and thin; a little dark in the back rooms. Creakingly old. But it was different from theirs. Tidier, more formal. The furniture looked some- how too small for the rooms.

"It's not really a *home*, is it?" It was Nancy who spoke, but Grace had just been thinking the same.

"It's strange to imagine him rattling around this place," said Grace. "It's all wrong for him. Much too big for someone on their own."

They had wandered into the living room. The chairs were a grim, grayish green. The couch looked hard and unwelcom- ing. On the mantelpiece was a photograph of a girl with big, dark eyes and curly, bobbed hair. She was sitting cross-legged in a field of wildflowers, and wore a daisy chain on her head. She was laughing.

"This has to be Eva." Grace took the picture down to exam- ine it more closely. To Eva's left, at the very edge of the photo, lay something that might have been a picnic basket. Could this photograph have been taken on that very first day when Eva, O'Connell and John went for that picnic, the three of them together? Grace wondered which of them had taken it.

"Such a shame, what happened to that girl." Nancy was close behind her, peering over her shoulder at the picture. "When I last saw John, a few days ago, he told me he thought he'd finally let the past go." Then, with emphasis: "We should all do that, Grace."

Grace turned and gazed into the fireplace, worried about what her eyes might reveal. Something had suddenly crystal- lized in her mind. Nancy knew about her affair with George. Perhaps she had always known.

She said, quietly: "I do love you, Nancy."

"I know."

A loud knock on the front door that startled them both.

"Can't be him," whispered Nancy. "He'd have his key. Shall we ignore it?"

Grace was still staring into the grate, at the mess of ash and charred paper that was heaped up there. Great wads of the stuff.

"What's he doing, having fires in this weather?" said Nancy.

"I think he had something he wanted to burn."

Another knock on the door.

"What do you think it was?" asked Nancy.

Picking up the poker, Grace prodded at the ash. Fragments of soot-blackened paper broke into even smaller pieces. Typewritten words were visible here and there.

A third knock.

"The past," said Grace. And Nancy headed out to answer the door.

As they came into the room, all noise and color, they seemed to bring the sunlight in with them. Tilly had one of her grandmother's hats on her head and her mother's seed pearls wrapped several times around her neck. She was brandishing a feather duster and muttering, in a teacherly tone: "What are the consequences? The consequences of the consequences. Hello, Auntie Grace."

Catherine was carrying Felix, his face covered in jam, and complaining about her back. Once she'd set him down, he was straightaway across the room, crawling at speed to his aunt. Pulling himself up against her legs and bleating to be cuddled.

"You're bizarre, Felix," said Tilly, in her grandest manner. "You're so bizarre." And then ran for a cuddle herself.

"Spotted the two of you through the window," said Catherine. "Thought I'd wait for you to come across to the house but you were taking *such* an age." She held out an envelope to Nancy. "This came through the letter box earlier."

Nancy frowned as she took it. "Mummy! You've already opened it!"

Felix was wiping jam on Grace's shoulder. Tilly was announcing: "Felix is a bad boy and I'm cross of the consequences."

Catherine was saying, "I forgot to mention to you yesterday, dear, that final column of yours was not at all bad. Not at *all* bad."

"Grace." Nancy held out the letter she'd been reading. "Look at this."

Dear Nancy,

I'm sorry not to be saying good-bye in person, but I saw you going out earlier and I'm afraid I can't wait for your return. This has all come about rather suddenly. The fact is, I'm going back to New York.

You'll understand, from this, that it hasn't worked out between me and that girl I was telling you about. But no matter. Good things are happening to me all the same. I'm not running away. Not this time. This girl, she's been good for me even if it never really got off the ground. There's been a kind of sparkle inside me lately, a quickening of the pulse. Something I haven't felt in years and thought I might never feel again. It's helped me to exorcise certain ghosts. Funny how things turn out. Help can come from the most unexpected places and people.

I've been running around the globe for far too long, and Betsy needs her father. She's always needed me but I've been too preoccupied to see that. I've told myself she's better off living with my parents, but it just isn't true. We belong to each other.

This is all rather sudden, of course, but it's the right decision. What's the point in hanging around once you've made your mind up? I've got a berth on a boat that sails from Southampton tonight. It's time to go home to my little girl.

You've been a wonderful friend to me, Nancy. You've taught me a lot—you and your lovely family. I hope I haven't inadvertently misled you. I've always felt that we understood each other pretty well. I will continue to think fondly of you and I wish you every happiness in the future. I hope we'll meet again.

I've written to my landlord and Mrs. Collins and have paid them up to the end of next month. Would you mind looking in at the house every so often until then, just to check that everything's all right? I'd be most grateful. I'll wire you when I arrive.

Love to Tilly and Felix,

                                        As ever,
                                        Your friend,
                                        John

Six

As the taxi drove past the register office, Grace blew out a perfect smoke ring. The cigarette between her fingers was marked with the red imprint of her lips.

"Waterloo, eh?" said the cabbie. "You catching a train or meeting someone?"

"Both, I hope." She took another drag on the cigarette. "Catching a train, *then* meeting someone."

It had all happened so quickly. She'd been standing there, holding the note limply in her outstretched hand, when they'd started bustling about her, practically shoving her out of the door and across the road to the Rutherford house.

"Get a move on, Grace." Nancy went darting about, chucking things in a bag. "You've no time to waste."

"What are you talking about? He's gone."

"Not till tonight," Nancy said. "You can catch him at South-ampton. You can stop him from getting on that boat."

"Or else get on it with him," added Catherine.

"You're mad, the pair of you. It's too late." Her heart was thudding at the very thought of it.

"For goodness' sake," said Catherine. "What do you have to lose by trying?"

"It's not *losing* that frightens her," said Nancy. "My chump of a sister is scared that she might actually get what she's al-ways wanted."

"Please!" Grace dropped the letter and put her head in her hands.

"You're not *meant* to be a spinster," said Nancy. "That's not who you are. Oh, Mummy, *tell* her."

Catherine put her hands on her hips. "Grace Rutherford, I did not bring you up to be lily-livered. Cowardice is something we do not tolerate in this house. Now, pull yourself together and get a wriggle on."

Tilly wagged a finger. "The consequences of the conse-quences are the consequences."

"Is it your fella? Is that who you're meeting?"

"Perhaps." Another smoke ring.

"Hope he's a good'un," said the driver. "Hope he treats you like he should. There's a lot of bad'uns about."

"I know." Down into Bloomsbury they went, passing smart, leafy squares.

"Where are you going, then, on your train?"

Maybe they were right, Nancy and Mummy. Maybe she'd been afraid of finding happiness. She'd donned a hair shirt at some point over the last few years and then become ac-customed to it. It had been almost reassuring when the relationship with O'Connell had gone wrong. How could it have ended in any other way with a man like him? It was yet another demonstration that she wasn't destined to find happiness in that most ordinary and fundamental of ways—through loving someone and having them love you back.

"The traffic seems awfully slow. Is something going on, do you think?"

"Well, there's some sort of march on in the West End. Them peculiar wood-cut people. All camping and funny green cloaks and then a bit of nationalism thrown in. Know the ones?"

"Do you mean the Kibbo Kift?"

"Yeah, them's the buggers. John Hargrave or whoever he is. Funny bloke. Give themselves fancy names and all, don't they? White Dove, Golden Eagle, all that sort of rubbish."

The taxi had slowed to a halt now. Grace gazed out at a tall gray house with a red door. Three or four months back she'd been to a jazz party in the upper rooms of that house. She'd capered about with two Vorticist artists—one in a ridiculous beret, the other with a pointlessly pointy beard—and got giggly on gin cocktails, aware that somewhere on the other side of the room, Dickie was watching. She must have looked like she was having the time of her life. Actually, she was terribly lonely that night.

"Bunch of overgrown Boy Scouts with a bit of a nasty underside, if you ask me," said the taxi driver. "Haven't heard that Hargrave say anything that's worth getting the streets all clogged up."

They'd been still for almost two minutes now. She leaned forward and peered out at the choked-up street. Cars, buses, trams, all motionless. "When's the march due to finish? Do you think we'll be moving again soon?"

"No idea, love. What time's your train?"

Round and about them, drivers were changing their minds and directions, pulling out of the jam and peeling off east.

"Can't we go another way?"

"Not unless you want me to go all down through Clerkenwell. Don't fret, I'm sure we'll be moving again in a minute."

"But you just said you had no idea how long the march was due to go on for!"

The bus driver ahead of them was sticking his arm out the window to signal a change of direction. A bus bound for Waterloo, like them, about to swing out east through Clerkenwell.

"If you ask me that's downright irresponsible." The cabbie tutted. "He'll have people on that vehicle wanting the West End."

"Will you *please* make a detour," asked Grace through gritted teeth.

In her head, John was walking slowly up the gangplank onto a ship—not a modern ocean liner, but a Spanish galleon with sails and cannon and a skull and crossbones flying from its mast, all set to spirit him away.

"What time does your train go?"

The advertisement on the side of the bus read: "Let's go to Lyons." A small boy sitting inside was drawing with his finger in the muck on the window. A baby was crying, its face red, its mouth wide. There were several old women in hats.

"My life is slipping away from me while we sit here. I have to get to Waterloo!"

There was a dark-haired, dark-eyed man on that bus. He was gazing out at the street with a face entirely absent of expression. The look of one who has abandoned hope.

John!

No, it couldn't be. Could it? Surely he'd be at Southampton by now. He'd left hours ago. Though maybe, just possibly, he'd gone somewhere else first . . . Errands to run, people to say good-bye to . . .

She blinked. Strained for a clear view of him just as the bus swung out to join the stream of eastbound traffic.

It was him. It *was.*

"Stop!" Though, of course, they were stopped already. Shoving her cigarette into the ashtray, she groped for the door handle.

"Hey, what d'you think you're up to?" The driver was twisting around in his seat.

"Got to go." She delved in her purse and randomly shoved a handful of coins at him.

"You sure, love? Ta."

She had the door open, and was clambering out, holding her hand up to try to halt the moving cars, scissoring her way through to the bus.

"Your bag, miss. You forgot your bag."

The bus was lurching into motion, pulling away into the moving traffic.

"John!" she yelled, waving her arms. "Wait! John!"

She began to run. Running in high heels, her arms flailing, after that bus. Running in a stupid, girlie, chiffon-floaty sort of way. Desperation personified, her heart hammering. Some schoolboys were laughing and pointing. A woman with a pinched face tutted. A workman whistled. But all Grace knew was that she had been given another chance and she was damned if her chance was rumbling away with that bus.

The bus was picking up speed. Inside her head, she pleaded—not with God, in whom she didn't believe—but with herself. *Got to catch that bus. Got to catch that bus.* Hitched up her dress and pushed herself to run even faster.

A tightening of the traffic—just a momentary one, but enough to narrow the gap. The back platform of the bus was almost within her reach. She could jump for it. A flying leap of faith and a grab for the pole.

Scared to get what she wanted, eh? She'd show them. Oh yes, she'd show them now.

She wasn't close enough . . .

"Stop, you bastard driver!"

A pink-cheeked young conductor appeared, looking down at her. Dinged his bell.

"Now, now, miss, I won't have language like that on my bus." It was slowing up. He was reaching down for her. "No need for all that. Just ain't ladylike, is it? And running like your very life depended on it!"

She grabbed his arm, hard, and up she went, with a half jump, half step, onto the platform.

"But it does, you see." She was panting so hard that she could barely get the words out. "My life *does* depend on it."

The conductor pushed his cap back and scratched his head, as the crazy girl flashed a smile at him and went lurching past, along the bus, teetering on her heels, struggling to keep her balance as the bus hit a pothole. Cheeky sort of smile, she had. Not his type, of course. Hard as nails, you could see that at a glance. Good-looking, but she knew it a bit too well. One of those faces it's difficult to forget. He'd choose commonplace prettiness over her sort of looks every time. Would tire you out, waking up each morning to that face. None too young either. Probably one of those modern girls, would give you a verbal thick ear soon as look at you. Uppity madam. Still, she had something, there was no doubt about that. Plucky sort. That was quite a sprint she'd just made. And all to catch her man, by the look of things. He heard her shout the name "John!" and then, "It's me." He saw a man's head turn, startled eyes and then the widest grin.

The bus lumbered on.

Afterword

The Columnist

The first columnists appeared in the mid-nineteenth century, with the rise of mass market newspapers and magazines. The earliest columns were political essays, satirical sketches or caricatures, many of them one-off articles. But it wasn't long before the cleverest, funniest and most popular obtained regular spots, bylines, headings and avid readerships.

The column, as a form, established itself most rapidly in the United States, where its proponents could earn a good wage, thanks to the syndication system. In the United Kingdom, the columnist had to scratch about for income from other sources, whether through journalism or otherwise, and consequently it took longer for the column to take hold. Had Grace Rutherford really lived and written her column in 1920s London, she would have been something of a pioneer.

Not that Diamond Sharp would have been the first frivolous gossip writer in London, nor the first Englishwoman to try her hand at it. As early as 1846, Marguerite Gardiner, Countess of Blessington, was commissioned by Charles Dickens as a "purveyor of fashionable intelligence" for his *Daily News*. Her reign lasted only six months, however. When Dickens stepped down as editor, his successor swiftly ditched Lady Blessington.

Viscount Castlerosse, author of "Londoner's Log" in the *Sunday Express,* is often credited as the first English gossip columnist. For fifteen years from 1926, he wrote as an eligible, roving bachelor sharing intimate secrets. English readers enjoyed a blend of gossip, opinion and self-revelation, and the *Daily Express* emerged as its principal supplier. Notable columns included "Talk of the Town" by Dragoman, D. B. Wyndham-Lewis's "By the Way," J. B. Morton's "Beachcomber" columns and my personal favorite, Tom Driberg as "William Hickey."

Women columnists established themselves earlier and more conclusively in the United States than the United Kingdom. In 1879, Louisa Knapp Curtis began a monthly column on housekeeping in her husband's magazine. This was so successful that ultimately Cyrus Curtis sold his *Tribune and Farmer* in order to back his wife's new *Ladies' Home Journal.* In a rather more glamorous arena, Louella Parsons became the first Hollywood movie gossip columnist in 1914. By the 1930s she would be joined by Hedda Hopper, and the two would lock horns in a fierce rivalry. Dorothy Thompson, meanwhile, started out as a newspaper reporter, and from the mid-1930s became a significant anti-appeasement and anti-isolationist voice in "On the Record."

Diamond Sharp owes something to many of these, as well as to later columnists such as Jill Tweedie, who wrote for the *Guardian* from the 1960s to the 1980s; a campaigning feminist who exposed her own struggle with the difficulties of putting feminist principles into practice in life. Also Anna Quindlen's "Life in the 30s" column, written for the *New York Times* during Quindlen's three-year extended maternity leave, and finally abandoned when she began to tire of the self-exposure. Diamond's biggest influence, though, is the 1920s *New Yorker* columnist "Lipstick," alias Lois Long. This dashing flapper-about-town delivered spiky and highly opinionated verdicts on New York's restaurants, dinner-dance clubs and illicit drinking dens. In one column she even reviewed a police raid on an after-hours club.

As to my other characters—well, Dexter O'Connell, John Cramer and Eva owe something to (but are certainly not based on) F. Scott Fitzgerald and Zelda Sayre.

John Cramer's mustache actually belonged, however, to a youthful Ernest Hemingway.

Oh, and Ciro's nightclub really did have a glass dance floor.

Acknowledgments

Thanks are due to the following,
for their help:

My agent, Carole Blake at Blake Friedmann.
My editors, Katie Espiner at Transworld, Lauren McKenna
at Simon & Schuster, and Jeanne Ryckmans
and Larissa Edwards at Random House Australia.

My lovely colleagues at Curtis Brown.
Bronwyn Cosgrave, in her role as the
Savoy's Brand Ambassador.

Rhidian, my brother.
Simon, my husband—thanks always and most of all.
And Natalie and Leo, who were not helpful
but were extremely cute.

Introduction

The Jewel Box

Anna Davis

1927: *This year, London girls are wearing their hair and dresses shorter than ever, copying the Hollywood flapper look. They want the life that goes with it, too—dancing the Charleston all night, having romances with dashing young men. It's the dream. A life just a little bit wild.*

In her weekly newspaper column, Diamond Sharp gives her readers a taste of that little bit of wild. She dances at the newest clubs, throws back the best martinis, and flirts with London's most eligible bachelors . . . all in the name of research.

What her readers don't know is that Diamond, the woman with the sharpest bob in town, isn't all sparkle and shine. Her real name is Grace Rutherford; her real job is that of a lowly advertising copywriter; and her real life is spent supporting two widows, her mother and sister.

But when two handsome American writers begin to compete for her attention, Grace's reality becomes a drama that spins out of her control. As she seeks to understand the dark past that binds the two writers, Grace realizes she must deal with her own dark secrets—and those of the people closest to her.

QUESTIONS AND TOPICS FOR DISCUSSION

1. "And at the heart of this ever-changing city, there is a fundamental core of values which remain unchanged, and which must remain so" (page 7). What were the values of this time, and how were they changing? How was this change reflected in London's society?

2. "The bobbed hair . . . it's symbolic" (page 40). What does the bob symbolize in *The Jewel Box*? How do you think men viewed this hairstyle? Do you think the bob is still a powerful statement today?

3. Did you like the book-within-a-book plot? What is the significance of O'Connell's title, *The Vision*? What do you imagine the cover for this fictional book looked like?

4. Competition is a large theme in this novel. Who are the players, what are they competing for, and does anyone win?

5. Compare and contrast the two men who made these statements: "You're beautiful girls, and you're so alive and so different—and each of you is more special, more valuable, for the existence of the other one" (page 49). "You're like a couple of gems in a jewel

box, you two" (page 280). How does the title of this novel pertain to not just one woman but to all women of that time?

6. Do you believe O'Connell when he says: "I like the not knowing. I like life to be unpredictable" (page 91)? Does Grace share that sentiment? Do you think they are similar or complete opposites?

7. Analyze Grace's dream: "Grace was dreaming about Margaret the typist, her coiled black hair transformed into a snake. John Cramer was in the dream, too, playing a wooden flute, and the hair snake uncoiled and reared up to its hypnotic tune" (page 140). How is this dream meaningful? Where else do dreams appear in *The Jewel Box*? Why do you think the author used dreams in such a manner?

8. "You couldn't actually say what you most wanted in bed, but you could use a form of subtle insinuation to make the man think it was he who'd wanted it and initiated it" (page 151). Do you consider Grace to be a feminist? Why or why not? Are there other characters in *The Jewel Box* whom you would describe as feminists?

9. "She didn't know how to explain why she had suddenly taken to writing frequently to her sister's husband. It seemed such an odd thing to be doing. And the longer it went on, the less easy it was to speak of, particularly as George was keeping quiet, too" (page 168). What do you think of Grace's relationship with her brother-in-law? Do you think he is her true love? Or do you

think Grace is guilty of only wanting what she cannot have?

10. "They'd both have been fine if it wasn't for that girl" (page 237). How do you see Eva—as a predator, destroying the lives of everyone who loved her; as a confused, mentally ill woman; as a woman who was simply living, and loving, like a man might do; or some other way?

11. "There are thousands and thousands of women across the country whose voices are simply not heard when it counts most" (page 256). What does Catherine's history as a suffragette add to *The Jewel Box*? What other elements of Catherine's past are revealed? How do these secrets affect Grace?

12. What do you make of O'Connell's "message from a toiling scribe to his Muse" (page 306)? Did you think it was respectful or glib? What do you think the future holds for him? Will Diamond/Grace be a character in his next novel?

A CONVERSATION WITH ANNA DAVIS

Q. Your last novel, *The Shoe Queen*, was also set in the 1920s. Why did you stay with this time period for *The Jewel Box*?

A. It's a time period that I loved reading about and researching. I wrote *The Shoe Queen*, but I wasn't done with the twenties. It's often described as the first "truly modern" decade, and I was very interested in the idea of all that change and how it affects society. London (my home) was the world's biggest city in those days. It was a vibrant and buzzing place; the world's nerve center to a great extent. And yet London was and is a city steeped in history and long ingrained in tradition. I enjoyed reading about and thinking about that conflict between old and new values, and how the conflict is played out in individual lives. I also adore the fashion, the art, and the wild stories of the ultimate-party decade. The First World War was firmly behind them, but the Great Depression of the 1930s was just about to appear over the horizon; and beyond that, the Second World War. Those flappers were dancing the Charleston on the edge of the abyss, really. The Roaring Twenties is a decade with many parallels to our own.

Q. Why did you have Charles Lindbergh flying in the background of this novel instead of Amelia Earhart?

A. I think the story could have worked very well with Amelia Earhart's transatlantic flight appearing in place of Lindbergh's. But Earhart flew across the Atlantic in 1928, and I wanted to set my story in 1927. This may seem like an odd quibble, but in order to have the story working properly with its setting, I had to think very carefully about what was going on in the world I was writing about, and particularly the London I was writing about. I gave considerations to quite a few years in the 1920s and weighed up a number of issues. I wanted this story to take place in summer so I could feature those long balmy evenings and hot romantic summer days that we have in London at that time of year. So, for example, the summer of 1926 wouldn't have been good for my purposes because there was a General Strike in May that brought London to a standstill for ten days, and I didn't want this to take over my novel. I also couldn't use the summer of 1928 because the Equal Franchise Act was passed in May 1928, giving the vote to all women over twenty-one in Britain. If women under thirty had the vote in my novel, all the tension and energy of Grace's conflict with her mother, and to an extent her conflict within herself, would have just bled away.

Q. How did you come up with the scene with the psychic in the library? Have you been to séances before?

A. I've never been to a séance, but they were very popular at that time. Quite a few of the key characters in my story are dead, and I liked the idea of Grace and O'Connell going along to an event like this in search of a bit of fun, and actually coming away feeling rather troubled. It's not so much that either one is haunted by spirits from the "other side" but rather by their own dark memories and past actions. It also gave me the opportunity to give Grace and the reader an early hint about what might have happened to Eva.

Q. "Perhaps, Grace realized, somewhat randomly, it was the very fear of finding that she herself was the bright-but-plain type that had always driven her to shun that kind of girl and to strive so hard with her appearance, her persona . . ." (page 268). This is an interesting epiphany. Have you met many women who fit this description?

A. I think it fits many women—particularly young women and girls—and I suspect I'm not entirely innocent of it myself. We want to be glamorous and to appear to others to be glamorous. But we have a sneaking suspicion that we're actually not, and that we're about to be found out. We steer away from people who appear drab because we see ourselves reflected, and we fear exposure by association. Grace is rather insecure behind her Diamond persona, and this is exemplified in her attitude to Margaret. She can't see beyond the fact that Margaret is a "lowly" typist and wears thick glasses. Margaret appears to Grace as bright but ordinary, and this is how Grace sees herself (shown when she frets about O'Connell finding out her true identity). Ultimately, she comes to know Margaret and to value her, and I'd like to think she may have learned something about herself from this experience.

Q. Have you ever written under a pseudonym? If so, what was that experience like for you?

A. Yes, about five years ago, when I had a regular column in a British national newspaper. I was writing the story of a fictional teenager, in weekly installments, told in the first person voice of the teenager. The column was published under the character's name, Jane Lockett. It was comical, and a lot of fun to write. But I have to confess, I felt frustrated that people didn't know I was the author behind it. I like to see my real name on books and articles, even though the name itself is not a particularly striking one!

Q. Diamond Sharp could be the 1920s version of Carrie Bradshaw. Did shows/novels like *Sex and the City* spark your imagination to go back in time and find such independent women at a time when their independence was new?

A. I loved *Sex and the City* (the TV show, that is. I haven't read the novel), particularly the friendships between the main characters. I can't think of many shows/novels in which close female friendships are drawn so sharply. I wasn't consciously aware of it as an influence on this book, but I guess everything we read and watch and enjoy finds its place in our imaginations. And in my case that includes everything from *Sex and the City* to the novels of Edith Wharton and F. Scott Fitzgerald.

Q. "People don't have to stay in one place all their lives, do they?" (page 333). What role does travel play in your life as a writer?

A. At the moment, not much of a role at all. I have two small children and money is tight! We go on holiday once a year, usually to France. And once in a blue moon I grab a much-treasured weekend away with family or friends. One of the good things about living in Europe is that you can get to other countries very quickly. I used to travel more before I had kids, and hope I will again some day.

Q. Siblings play an important role in this book. How has your family influenced your fiction?

A. I've never written anything that is based directly on my family, but I suppose they're in there somewhere. I have a brother who's very important to me. Our parents died young and this brought us siblings closer together. We became a little family unit. But now I'm a mother and wife myself. I suppose, like Grace, I'm not a stranger to responsibility. I had to grow up and be independent of parental support younger than most of my friends.

Q. With two of your novels set in the 1920s, you obviously have a love of history. Is there a subject that would inspire you to write a nonfiction book?

A. At this time, I don't feel inspired to write nonfiction. But I'd like to think it's something I could move on to if ever the right subject does come along. I think the challenges would be very different. The skills required of a writer of nonfiction are quite different. When it comes down to it, I like making stuff up.

Q. Have you written anything contemporarily? If so, how is the experience of writing in a historical era different? Is it more freeing, more limiting, or both?

A. My first three novels were set in the here and now. There's a kind of exoticism about historical settings. As you do your research, you can feel as though you're discovering other worlds in which everything is more vivid, more romantic, more dangerous. And yet, so much is the same. People are essentially the same, with many of the same priorities, preoccupations, and problems. In some ways it's easier to set novels contemporarily. You can have a character get into a taxi without having to check whether it would be horse-drawn or motorized. You can have someone order a cocktail without needing to find out whether it had yet been invented. But you can get things wrong in a contemporary novel just as easily as in a historical one. And both historical and contemporary novels depend on convincing characters, good plotting, and strong writing. There's more to a novel than its historical setting.

ENHANCE YOUR BOOK CLUB

Sparkle like a Diamond: In the style of Diamond Sharp, write a one-page review of your favorite restaurant, bar, or club and share it with your book club members.

Wig out: Have everyone wear a bobbed wig. (Any male members? Have them wear a 1920s-inspired hat.)

Cheers!: Serve cocktails highlighted in the book (gin fizzes, Singapore slings, martinis, and champagne) and make a toast to women—those who fought for our right to vote, to work, and to play!

Made in the USA
Middletown, DE
21 December 2018

La mirada de una bruja

Antonia J. Corrales

La mirada de una bruja

Historia de una bruja contemporánea

amazon publishing

Publicado por:
Amazon Publishing, Amazon Media EU Sàrl
5 rue Plaetis, L-2338, Luxembourg
Diciembre, 2018

Diseño de cubierta por lookatcia.com
Imagen de cubierta © Paul Burley Photography © Benjamin Lee / EyeEm / Getty
Producción editorial: Wider Words

Impreso por: Ver última página
Primera edición digital 2018

ISBN: 9782919804047

www.apub.com

SOBRE LA AUTORA

Antonia J. Corrales es una escritora española nacida en Madrid en 1959. Después de varios años trabajando en el mundo de la administración y dirección de empresas, decidió dedicarse de lleno a la escritura. Comenzó a adentrarse en el mundo de la edición en 1989 como correctora, y desde entonces ha trabajado como lectora editorial, columnista, articulista, entrevistadora en publicaciones científicas, jurado en certámenes literarios y coordinadora radiofónica. Ha sido galardonada con una veintena de premios en certámenes internacionales. Es autora de las novelas *La décima clave*, *La levedad del ser*, *As de corazones*, *Epitafio de un asesino*, *En un rincón del alma* y su segunda parte: *Mujeres de agua*. Con *En un rincón del alma*, lleva más de cinco años en el top de ventas en España, EE.UU. y América Latina. Traducida al inglés, griego e italiano, su última novela publicada de forma independiente es *Y si fuera cierto*, y se estrenó en el sello Amazon Publishing con *Una bruja sin escoba*, la primera parte de la trilogía *Historia de una bruja contemporánea*. *La mirada de una bruja* es la segunda parte de dicha trilogía.

No sirve de nada volver al ayer,
porque entonces yo era una persona distinta.
LEWIS CARROLL, *Alicia en el País de las Maravillas*

A todos nos ocurren cosas extrañas a lo largo de nuestra vida sin
que durante cierto tiempo nos demos cuenta de que han ocurrido.
J. M. BARRIE, *Peter Pan*

EN LA PRIMERA ENTREGA DE LA TRILOGÍA...

Cuando Diana retoma la vida que había dejado tras, en apariencia, haber viajado al futuro y regresar de nuevo al presente, vuelve sabiendo lo que va a suceder y, aunque debe ocultar lo que ha descubierto, no consigue controlar sus impulsos ante Alán. Llevada por el dolor que le produce saber que él le miente, provoca una paradoja al insinuarle que es consciente de la atracción que él siente por Azucena.

Se reencuentra con Ecles, Elda y Desmond, pero nada se desarrolla tal y como ocurrió la primera vez que lo vivió junto a ellos. Su imprudencia al utilizar sus conocimientos desencadena una serie de sucesos imprevisibles que cambiarán el destino de ella y de quienes la rodean: Alán se muestra más cercano, parece más enamorado, incluso planifica su vida de otra forma tras instalarse en el ático de Antonio. Por otra parte, Ecles, Elda y Desmond no reconocen a Diana, que regresa sin escoba, sin su libro y sin su gaveta. Solo *Senatón* y Claudia parecen saber quién es.

Abandona la investigación sobre sus orígenes durante un tiempo y lucha por olvidar la magia que la rodea desde niña, pero no lo consigue y termina aceptando que es una bruja y que, haga

lo que haga, siempre lo será. Una bruja débil, demasiado humana, como afirma y le recrimina el nigromante. Tras el acoso y las amenazas de este, decide protegerse de él usando algunos de los hechizos que Antonio le revela.

Alán sigue ajeno a los sucesos extraños que vive Diana. Permanece asentado en la vida y el tiempo al que pertenecen los *muggles*, ese entorno en el que los ojos solo ven como real lo establecido. Sin embargo, Diana comienza a aceptar que es diferente al resto de los mortales y que puede ver más allá de lo convencional. Sabe que debe recuperar la gaveta, aquel cajón de madera de haya negra en cuyos laterales aparecen unos símbolos pictos grabados, el mismo en el que la dejaron junto a la puerta de un hospicio siendo un bebé. Y también ha de conseguir de nuevo el libro de cubiertas rojas confeccionadas en un material que parece tener vida propia y páginas en blanco, un objeto tan misterioso como todo lo que le sucede desde niña. Un libro en el que, tal vez, halle las claves que la conduzcan a saber quién es en realidad y de dónde procede.

Samanta, su mejor amiga y mayor apoyo, se encuentra lejos, participando en una excavación en Egipto. Diana no puede relatarle lo que le está sucediendo, y la añora. Así, sin nadie que pueda ayudarla ni con quien compartir lo que le ocurre, decide enfrentarse a ese presente tan distinto al que había vivido, a los seres extraños que van apareciendo en su vida con una frecuencia inusitada desde que se instaló en aquel edificio habitado por personas fuera de estereotipos, tan especiales como fascinantes. Casi irreales.

Mientras Alán duerme ajeno a todo, Diana, en la terraza del ático, rememora lo acaecido desde que regresó del futuro. Se arropa con la vela roja de su ala delta pensando en Desmond, en la atracción que siente por él y, sin saber cómo, se eleva sobre el cielo de

Madrid. Un cielo sin estrellas en donde las brujas, las auténticas brujas, jamás utilizaron escobas para volar, sino para otros menesteres que Diana aún desconoce. Un cielo y una ciudad que poco a poco terminarán conduciéndola a un mundo lejano y diferente. A una realidad que solo la mirada de una bruja puede ver, entender y habitar.

Capítulo 1

No volví a ver a Desmond hasta varios días después de aquel primer encuentro, cuando él y Alán se enzarzaron en una especie de disputa por atraer mi atención, cuando pareció cortejarme sin el más mínimo reparo delante de mi novio. Pensé que se había olvidado de mí, también de aquellos libros sobre hechizos que se ofreció a prestarme y del vuelo que me pidió realizar en mi ala delta. Durante unos días tuve la sensación de que había desaparecido, que por alguna extraña razón se había ido de aquel presente tan caprichoso como imprevisible. Tampoco me encontré con Ecles. Las ventanas que daban a su terraza permanecían cerradas durante el día, con las persianas bajadas y los toldos echados hasta el atardecer. Los recogían cuando los rayos del sol dejaban de incidir sobre los tejados y las losetas de barro cocido comenzaban a templarse, a perder el calor que habían acumulado durante el día. Cuando yo regresaba del trabajo, por lo general ellos ya no estaban en la casa y, aunque las persianas ya estaban subidas, los estores impedían ver el interior de la vivienda. Sin embargo, aun teniendo la certeza de que debido a sus trabajos a esas horas estarían durmiendo o ya se habrían marchado, no perdía la esperanza de que alguna tarde, antes de que Alán llegase a casa, vería a Ecles zascandileando en el chiringuito. Me consolaba la idea de encontrarlo reparando alguna radio vieja o lijando y barnizando uno de aquellos muebles despreciado

por su anterior dueño, abandonado sobre la acera de cualquier calle de la ciudad y rescatado por Desmond antes de que lo llevaran a su destino final, el punto de reciclaje. Allí, probablemente, lo destruirían para siempre y, al hacerlo, matarían aquellos recuerdos, aquella vida que, según Ecles, poseían todos los objetos y que le hacían sentir, ver y oír las voces del alma de sus antiguos propietarios. Sonreía al recordarle y me estremecía al rememorar sus abrazos, la calidez de su enormidad y aquellos enfados de niño pequeño encerrado en un cuerpo de más de dos metros, con la piel cubierta de cicatrices, como también lo estaban su corazón y su alma de gigantón vuelto a la vida. A una vida y un presente que le dolían y que no reconocía como suyos, igual que me sucedía a mí.

Poco a poco volví a la soledad que, como antes de mudarnos Alán y yo, me esperaba al regresar a casa. A los atardeceres cálidos de aquel verano que parecía no querer marcharse. A contemplar a los gorriones y los vencejos revoloteando en busca de insectos cuando el sol caía en Madrid. Al anochecer de brisa infrecuente y esquiva y a la serenidad que me producía que el ruido del tráfico se fuera atenuando, yéndose poco a poco de las calles. Me habitué a contemplar el brillo de aquella estrella tan solitaria como yo y que, a veces, pensaba era la segunda a la derecha, la misma a la que se refería Peter Pan. Esa que, tras girar, me llevaría directa hasta el amanecer. Pero mi vuelo no era el mismo que emprendía Peter Pan; no seguía la misma dirección. El mío parecía dirigido por un astrolabio defectuoso que, en vez de marcar el rumbo correcto para alcanzar la estrella, me alejaba de ella y del país de nunca jamás. Me conducía una y otra vez a un cuásar que, poco a poco, iba tragándose todo lo que había a su alrededor. Y yo, noche tras noche, sueño tras sueño, esperaba que, tarde o temprano, ese cuásar acabara de absorber toda la materia y crease para mí una nueva galaxia; una nueva vida, un nuevo futuro en el que no me faltaran ellos: mis amigos.

Me sentía como si me hubieran devuelto a un pasado que en parte ya había vivido. A los pocos días de mudarnos, comencé a recibir los mismos mensajes de WhatsApp que Alán me había mandado en la otra realidad para que no lo esperase despierta, mensajes que hablaban de reuniones de equipo inesperadas e inventarios sorpresa. Al leerlos, me sabían a cañas de cerveza, risas, besos y fandangos a pie de acera. Pensé que aquellas noches debían de oler como las que yo había compartido con él. Olerían a primavera, a aire de tormenta, a cielo anochecido, a piel desnuda y a planes de futuro. Pero en aquellos momentos, a diferencia de lo que me había sucedido entonces, no me importaba que fueran tan semejantes a las que había vivido conmigo. Las ausencias de Alán pasaron de ser soportables a resultarme necesarias. En cierto modo, precisaba de aquella soledad nocturna para que, de darse un encuentro con Desmond, este fuera más íntimo y yo no estuviera cohibida por la presencia de Alán.

Las palabras que componían los mensajes de disculpa o excusa que Alán me enviaba casi todas las tardes pasaban por mis retinas de refilón. No me detenía en ellas, ya no permitía que se quedaran a dormir, que ocupasen mis pensamientos más de lo necesario. Ansiaba recibir esos pretextos porque necesitaba aquella soledad, tan parecida a la que había vivido antes de regresar a su lado, y porque la soledad y el distanciamiento de Alán me permitirían volver a acercarme a Desmond; traerlo de nuevo a mi vida como yo quería y necesitaba. Y porque ahí, en ese futuro que tanto anhelaba, Alán ya no tenía cabida.

Todas las tardes, al regresar del trabajo, seguía la misma rutina. Me daba una ducha, ponía música y, con el pelo mojado, salía a la terraza. Me sentaba en el suelo y tomaba un refresco para atenuar el calor. Cerraba los ojos y, sin poder evitarlo, pensaba en Desmond. Lo imaginaba apoyado en el muro de ladrillo que separaba nuestras terrazas, con una copa de vino en la mano. Abstraído, con la mirada

perdida en la calle o puesta sobre aquella luna tan blanca como las sábanas que, prendidas en las cuerdas de los tendederos, ondeaban movidas por el viento en las azoteas de ese horizonte de tejas acanaladas y chimeneas que esperaban el cambio de estación para volver a la vida. Echaba en falta su voz, el encuentro de nuestras miradas y el azul añil de sus ojos tiñendo mis pensamientos. Deseaba volver a aquellos sentimientos anárquicos y esquivos que parecían jugar al escondite con los dos, a esas emociones que tanto nos costaba manifestar. Añoraba aquellas conversaciones que, aparentemente, solo yo recordaba haber mantenido con él; sus explicaciones sobre la situación de las galaxias, la composición de los planetas y lo inhóspito y bello que era el universo en el que permanecíamos zarandeados por el destino, hijo de un dios menor tan caprichoso e imprevisible como un niño malcriado.

Los echaba de menos. A los tres. Mi vida sin ellos no era más que un puzle al que le faltaban piezas. Me habría bastado con tocar el timbre de su puerta o esperar a que Desmond, de madrugada, saltase el muro de ladrillo y cruzara nuestra terraza para entrar en casa de Claudia, pero no quise propiciar el encuentro: estaba segura de que se produciría tarde o temprano. Debía esperar, dejar que el tiempo corriese, que el futuro se hiciese por sí mismo, sin mi intervención. Sin favorecer un cambio que podía apartarme de ellos para siempre. En aquellos momentos sabía demasiadas cosas, una de ellas transcendental: el futuro no existía porque cambiaba constantemente, segundo a segundo, minuto a minuto...

Por las mañanas, al abrir la ventana del salón, notaba el olor que desprendían las baldosas recién mojadas en la terraza de los vecinos y me imaginaba a Desmond o Ecles regando el suelo y las macetas. Captaba su presencia en el aroma a vida, a la tierra mojada de los tiestos, y aquello, su recuerdo, me impulsaba a tomar el primer café de la mañana a pleno sol. Un sol que aún no quemaba, que me acariciaba como lo habían hecho los labios de Desmond cuando, al

presentarse, dejó un beso en mi piel. El recuerdo de aquel roce aún seguía ahí, dominando mis pensamientos.

—Voy a pedir presupuesto para instalar unos toldos —me comentó Alán la mañana del quinto día de estancia en el ático—. El vampiro ha sido listo. No hay quien soporte este sol directo. El calor que desprende el suelo se cuela en la casa. Los toldos nos darán un respiro y son más baratos que el aire acondicionado —me explicó con la taza del café en las manos, mirando los toldos naranjas—. Me gusta cómo tienen la terraza. —Se apoyó en el muro de ladrillo que separaba las dos viviendas y dejó la taza de café sobre él—. Lo único que les sobra es ese chiringuito destartalado. —Lo señaló con el dedo índice—. Les quita espacio y rompe la estética que le dan las plantas. Parece una choza. Aunque tengo que reconocer que la terraza está muy decente para ser de quien es. No se puede pedir mucho más de un basurero y un vigilante nocturno. Al menos huele a limpio.

—No sé de qué vas —le dije, irritada—. Desmond no es basurero, y si lo fuese daría igual. ¿Qué tiene de malo? No los conoces de nada. ¿Acaso te crees mejor que ellos? —concluí cogiendo la taza y, molesta, me dirigí al salón. Él me siguió.

—Pues sí, me considero más que ellos. Tengo un doctorado y un trabajo infinitamente mejor. No me parece que sea un pecado decir lo que pienso. Todos nos consideramos por encima de alguien, es una condición de cualquier ser vivo. Y no es solo que lo creamos, Diana, es que lo estamos. Eso es lo que llamamos sociedad, la pirámide jerárquica sobre la que se sustenta nuestra forma de vida. El vampiro ese que tenemos por vecino está en la base, y no es culpa mía. Estoy por encima de él igual que otros están por encima de mí.

—¿En serio? ¿Estás hablando en serio? —solté, enarcando las cejas en un gesto de incredulidad. Él asintió, bajó la vista y dio un sorbo de café—. ¡No doy crédito! —exclamé sin dejar de mirarle.

—Es evidente que te cae muy bien, que te han hecho gracia sus tonterías de donjuán callejero, pero para mí no deja de ser un listillo oportunista, aunque te moleste que lo diga.

—A veces no te soporto —respondí mirándolo con aire desafiante.

—Lo sé —dijo sonriendo divertido, como si mis palabras no fueran con él o pensara que yo no hablaba en serio—. No me soportas pero me quieres —apostilló, seguro de sí mismo.

Lo dijo sin mirarme, con la cabeza gacha, mientras restregaba el polvo de ladrillo que se le había adherido a las suelas de las deportivas. Cuando Alán y yo visitamos la tienda de Claudia antes de alquilar el ático, pude comprobar la eficacia de esta sustancia para mantener a raya las presencias amenazadoras, de modo que durante los días que llevábamos viviendo allí había protegido mi nuevo hogar de esa forma.

—No podrás quitártelo mientras estés en casa —dije, señalando su calzado.

—Si tú lo dices... —respondió, pero siguió cepillando la suela sin levantar la cabeza.

Era terco como una mula. Sabía que yo tenía razón, que el polvo se desprendería de la suela en cuanto cruzase el umbral. Sin embargo, aunque aquello sucedía diariamente, él siempre intentaba quitarlo antes de salir. Se negaba a creer que se despegaría de las suelas por sí solo, sin necesidad de hacer nada, que bastaba con pasar por la puerta para que cayera. Alán renegaba de la magia porque le asustaba, y no solo eso: parecía querer combatirla con lo que fuese. En aquel momento, con un cepillo para el calzado; en otras ocasiones se había hecho el distraído, como hacían algunos *muggles*.

—Espero que, en algún momento, quites esta porquería de aquí. ¡No lo soporto! Me pone nervioso, no le encuentro ningún sentido —expuso, sin dejar de cepillar las suelas.

No le respondí. Aquel polvo seguiría allí por mucho tiempo, tanto como fuera necesario, pensé recordando al hombre que me había amenazado, aquel personaje que parecía un espectro venido de otra dimensión. El mismo al que Antonio y él habían calificado como un hombre perturbado pero indefenso. Dos adjetivos que, en mi opinión, se repelían entre sí.

—Me marcho —le dije ya en la puerta—. ¿Cenas en casa?

—No lo sé. Tenemos que preparar las rebajas y resolver todo el lío de los *destalles*, que se han multiplicado como las setas en otoño. Sé que te había prometido que me tomaría el fin de semana libre, pero después de ver el estado del almacén, creo que no va a ser posible.

—Si tuvierais personal suficiente, no se guardarían parejas de tallas diferentes en las cajas. No entiendo cómo la gente puede comprar unas deportivas de números distintos y no enterarse.

—No son de números distintos, suelen ser de medio número más o menos, por eso algunos no lo notan.

»Mejor no cuentes conmigo. Si veo que salgo antes, me pillo unos sándwiches y una ensalada. Si se hace tarde, cenaremos unas pizzas en la tienda. ¿Quieres que te acerque? Hoy me da tiempo a dejarte en la oficina —explicó mirando su carísimo reloj de pulsera.

—Prefiero ir en metro. Así durante el trayecto aprovecho para organizar el trabajo en el ordenador y caminar un rato antes de entrar. Necesito que me dé el aire —respondí.

Durante la mudanza y en toda aquella semana no había tenido tiempo de volver sobre mis investigaciones. Tenía demasiadas cosas que recomponer, demasiados legajos que organizar y revisar. Debía recuperar la escoba que me había regalado Claudia la primera vez que me instalé en el ático. La necesitaba para protegerme. También quería volver a ver a Virginia, la mujer de Duncan, y lo más importante: encontrar mi libro y buscar la forma de que Desmond me diese la gaveta sin suscitar demasiadas preguntas.

11

Senatón no dejaba de darme empellones con la cabecita en los tobillos. Me agaché y lo aparté con cuidado antes de salir al rellano. Alán se quedó en casa restregando el polvo rojo con ahínco al tiempo que mascullaba. Salí del ático pensando que, por la noche, de seguro Azucena se las apañaría para que Alán la acompañara de vuelta a su casa. Yo estaba convencida de que tarde o temprano acabarían liándose y que mi novio me dejaría por ella. Y, aunque ya lo había vivido y tenía la certeza de que aquello había de suceder, me molestaba saber que nuestra relación tenía los días contados y que no podía ni debía decírselo a él. De momento no me quedaba más remedio que mantener esa mentira.

—Sé que no me crees, pero... te quiero, escocesa. —Alán había salido de la casa y me contemplaba sonriente bajo el dintel.

Era tan guapo y tan atractivo como el típico galán de cine contemporáneo. Ese día vestía traje azul marino, camisa blanca de algodón, corbata roja y deportivas de marca americana y modelo exclusivo. Tan alto como seguro de sí mismo, pero... ¡tan diferente a mí! ¿Cómo no me había dado cuenta de lo poco que teníamos en común? ¿Cómo me había enamorado de él?, me pregunté.

—Y yo a ti —le respondí desganada, en tono apagado. Agaché la cabeza y escondí mi mirada en el interior del bolso, más que nada para evitar que él viese en mis ojos las dudas que me asaltaban—. Pensé que me había dejado las llaves en casa —le comenté al tiempo que levantaba el llavero y se lo enseñaba.

Capítulo 2

Desde que me instalé con Alán en el ático, todas las mañanas, cuando me marchaba a trabajar, esperaba unos segundos junto al descansillo de la casa de Elda. Olía el aroma del café recién hecho que escapaba por las ranuras de su puerta y escuchaba sus pasos apresurados. Siempre lo hacía simulando estar buscando algo en el bolso. También me paraba en los buzones y me quedaba un rato allí esperando a que ella saliese, pero luego se me hacía tarde y terminaba marchándome sin haber conseguido cruzarme con ella. Sabía que si me empeñaba en propiciar nuestro encuentro, este no se produciría, al menos como era debido. Pero no conseguía controlar mi necesidad de volver a verla, de modo que, durante cinco días, había repetido los mismos pasos, los mismos movimientos frente a su puerta. Lo mismo hacía frente a la tienda de Claudia: me detenía un rato allí y miraba el cartelón donde estaba escrito el nombre del local: EL DESVÁN DE ARADIA. La atracción que ese establecimiento ejercía sobre mí se había ido incrementando día a día. Era como si me llamara, como si aquel lugar tuviera vida propia y reclamara mi presencia. Me acercaba a la gran puerta de madera vieja y áspera, cubierta de aristas secas, y pasaba la mano por la superficie en una especie de caricia. Al hacerlo, sentía un murmullo que iba y venía, que se alejaba y volvía a resonar en mis oídos. Parecían voces ininteligibles y ruidos que me recordaban el tintineo de cristales al

entrechocar entre sí. Al oírlos pensaba que aquellos sonidos debían de provenir de los rosarios de cristal que había colgados en su interior. Seguramente dentro del local había alguna corriente de aire que los hacía oscilar lo suficiente para producir aquel eco maravilloso, pensaba abstraída. Me imaginaba deteniendo su movimiento con las manos, acariciando aquellos cristales de colores mágicos. Algún día regentaría ese local, me decía, porque aquel sueño seguía vivo en mí.

Esa mañana, después de dejar a Alán en casa, como de costumbre, me paré en el rellano e imaginé a Elda frente a la cafetera, esperando a que el agua subiese al filtro y la válvula comenzara a sonar. Aspiré el agradable olor del café recién hecho y salí a la calle. Me acerqué a la puerta de la tienda y apoyé la mano sobre la madera, vieja y resquebrajada. Cerré los ojos y deslicé la palma de arriba abajo. Quería volver a captar la vida que aquellas paredes encerraban. Aquellos sonidos que parecían darme energía para no perder la esperanza de que todo, tarde o temprano, volvería al punto en que lo había dejado, al momento en que aquel edificio y ellos, Elda, Ecles y Desmond, mis amigos, eran una parte importante de mi vida, de aquella existencia que había desaparecido de golpe y sin previo aviso. También ese día me imaginé detrás del mostrador. Pero aquella mañana nada sucedió como en las cinco anteriores.

Cuando apoyé la mano sobre la puerta no oí absolutamente nada. Contrariada, repetí el gesto, presionando la mano contra la madera. Al deslizarla hacia abajo, una de las aristas secas de la puerta se me clavó en la piel como si fuese una esquirla. Justo en el preciso instante en que la punta de madera entraba en la palma de mi mano, un estruendo similar a una explosión me aturdió. Apreté los párpados instintivamente, como si aquel gesto pudiera protegerme de la onda expansiva, y me apoyé unos segundos en la puerta, con la cara pegada a la hoja. Escuché los gritos de la gente, los frenazos de los coches y las carreras de algunos viandantes cerca de mí.

Tardé unos minutos en reponerme de la confusión. Me volví, aún aturdida, y dirigí la mirada hacia el tumulto que se arremolinaba en la acera de enfrente, junto a la floristería de Amaya. La gente murmuraba y señalaba confusa el suelo y la fachada del local. Las baldosas de la acera estaban cubiertas de gruesos cristales. El escaparate de la floristería y la puerta de entrada, que era también de cristal, se habían hecho añicos. Un hombre de rasgos asiáticos permanecía en la acera, frente a la tienda. Estaba inmóvil. Su expresión evidenciaba el pánico que había sentido. La cristalera del escaparate y de la puerta había estallado frente a él. Los pedazos de cristal habían formado un círculo a su alrededor, como si un escudo invisible lo hubiera protegido en el momento del estallido. En su mano izquierda sostenía un llavero, un cordón largo y grueso de color malva intenso, casi morado, que parecía hecho de algodón trenzado. De él pendían varias llaves y una pieza oval roja acabada en punta, semejante a un péndulo, que brillaba como si fuese de metal pulido. El cordón giraba entre sus dedos, trazando círculos cada vez más concéntricos y más rápidos. Ensimismada, seguí el movimiento, los giros que daba el cordón, sin percatarme siquiera de la esquirla de madera que aún tenía clavada en la palma de la mano ni de la sangre que me resbalaba por la muñeca. Las gotas fueron salpicando la acera y manchándome los zapatos. Retiré la vista del cordón cuando uno de los viandantes agarró las llaves y preguntó al hombre de rasgos asiáticos si se encontraba bien. Él no contestó, como si no le hubiese oído. Su falta de respuesta, su inmovilidad, me sobrecogió tanto que permanecí ensimismada esperando una reacción, cualquier movimiento que demostrase que no le había sucedido nada. Intenté retirar la vista de él, pero no pude. Fue como si los dos estuviéramos sometidos a una especie de hechizo que nos había inmovilizado. Solo conseguí apretar los párpados con fuerza. Entonces capté una voz hueca, ronca y amenazadora detrás de mí:

15

—¡Maldita bruja sin escoba! No deberías haber vuelto. Eres la única responsable de lo que ha sucedido. Tu ineptitud y debilidad humana solo acarrearán problemas. Deberías marcharte cuanto antes, y para siempre.

Sobresaltada, me di la vuelta, pero no había nadie.

—Pero... ¿cómo han podido reventar los cristales de esa forma? —dijo Elda.

Mi vecina había salido alarmada a la calle y pasó a mi lado sin detenerse. Cruzó la calzada y se acercó al hombre que momentos antes había sostenido el llavero que giraba entre sus dedos. Vi que ambos conversaban y me fijé en que él le entregaba el llavero. Elda se lo guardó en el bolsillo del pantalón vaquero y regresó.

Oí el ruido de algunas persianas al ser levantadas, las voces de los vecinos que se asomaban y, asustados, preguntaban qué había sucedido. Miré hacia las terrazas de los áticos y distinguí a Ecles. Desmond no estaba. Supuse que no habría salido porque el sol, en aquellos momentos, incidía de lleno sobre la terraza. Las sirenas de los servicios de emergencia se oían cada vez más cerca. En ese momento Alán apareció en la puerta del edificio, preocupado por el estruendo de la explosión.

—¿Te encuentras bien? ¡Estás herida! ¿Dónde te han dado los cristales? —me preguntó, mirando las gotas de sangre que había en el suelo.

—Se le ha clavado algo en la palma de la mano —explicó Elda, que justo en ese instante pasaba por nuestro lado—. Parece una astilla. Es eso, ¿verdad? —me preguntó. Pero yo no respondí.

—¡Una astilla! ¿Y de dónde ha salido una astilla? —cuestionó Alán.

Señalé la puerta de la tienda. Elda y él la miraron y después me miraron a mí.

—¿No nos hemos visto antes? —me preguntó ella. Me cogió la mano, pellizcó la astilla y tiró de ella con fuerza.

CAPÍTULO 3

Cuando Elda extrajo la esquirla de mi mano, tuve la sensación de que aquella astilla era la responsable de mi desorientación, porque en el mismo instante en que salió de mi piel la confusión que sentía hasta aquel momento desapareció.

Después de mostrarme el trozo de madera, Elda lo soltó. Una racha de viento arrastró la liviana esquirla hasta la puerta de la tienda, junto al sucio escalón de la entrada. Mientras Elda hablaba, yo miraba el escalón, incapaz de apartar la vista de la astilla que, llevada por el viento, se alzaba levemente para después volver a caer. Parecía que tuviera vida y que intentase alcanzar el lugar de donde se había desprendido.

—Si quieres, vamos a mi casa y te desinfectas la herida. Esa puerta está llena de porquería. Vivo ahí. —Señaló una de las ventanas de la fachada del edificio y me ofreció un pañuelo de papel para que me limpiase—. Me llamo Elda.

—Yo soy Diana. Y él es Alán —le respondí.

Se mantuvo en silencio y pensativa unos segundos.

—¡Ya sé de qué te conozco! —exclamó finalmente—. Del bloque del Manuel Becerra. Te cayó encima parte de la pintura del bote que mi compañero derramó. Tú estabas asomada en el balcón de tu casa, ¿recuerdas? ¡Qué casualidad que ahora estuvieras aquí!

—No es casualidad. Nos hemos mudado a uno de los áticos. Somos vecinos —le respondió Alán, señalando el edificio.

—Entonces ¡sois los nuevos! —exclamó Elda—. Yo pinté vuestro ático. ¿Y dices que no es casualidad? ¡Anda que no hay pisos en Madrid para que hayáis venido a parar a este edificio! Y lo más curioso es que las dos veces que nos hemos visto ha sido después de un incidente. Espero que la próxima sea más agradable —comentó con una sonrisa.

Fijó sus ojos en los míos como si intentase adivinar mis pensamientos o intuyera que se le había pasado por alto algún detalle importante, y volvió a insistir para que entrásemos en su apartamento a curarme la herida, que ya había dejado de sangrar, pero Alán se mostró reticente.

—Te lo agradecemos, pero no es necesario. Lo haremos en casa. —Señaló el ascensor—. Somos vecinos, ¿recuerdas? —le dijo en un tono que me pareció descortés e inoportuno.

Le di un pequeño puntapié.

—¿Qué? —dijo él.

Elda respondió con una sonrisa de complicidad dirigida a mí.

—Venga, os invito a un café o un té. Después de lo sucedido nos vendrá bien a todos, ¿verdad, Diana?

—A mí sí, desde luego. A ti no sé —dije mirando a Alán.

Apenas llevábamos unos minutos dentro de su casa cuando sonó el timbre de la puerta. Era Desmond. Mientras Alán me limpiaba la herida con las gasas y el alcohol que Elda nos había dado, oí que ella le invitaba a entrar, pero él rechazó la oferta.

Elda regresó rápidamente al interior.

—Es Desmond, un amigo mío que, por cierto, vive en vuestro mismo rellano —nos comentó al volver al salón—. Ha bajado para comprobar que estoy bien. Voy a darle su llavero, que se dejó ayer en la floristería —explicó al tiempo que cogía el llavero que le había entregado el hombre de facciones asiáticas y que ella había dejado

18

sobre la mesa del salón—. Precisamente el dueño de la floristería venía hacia aquí para devolvérselo cuando se produjo la explosión. —Levantó el llavero, mostrándolo—. Su hija, Amaya, es amiga de Desmond. Anoche él le prestó unos libros y se olvidó las llaves en la tienda —explicó. Por su tono de voz intuí que no acababa de aprobar aquella amistad—. Tal vez eso le salvó de que la explosión lo pillase de lleno.

—El vampiro no ha podido resistirse. Tenía que verte de nuevo —susurró Alán en mi oreja cuando Elda volvió a reunirse con Desmond—. Pero la jugada no le ha salido bien, porque no esperaba que yo estuviera aquí. —Chasqueó con la lengua al tiempo que me guiñaba el ojo derecho—. Ya veo que no podré separarme de ti. Tienes mucho peligro, escocesa. —Y me dio un beso en la frente.

—Pero mira que eres idiota —le recriminé y le mandé callar con un gesto. Quería oír la conversación entre Elda y Desmond.

—El padre de tu amiga está convencido de que tu llavero ha evitado que la onda expansiva le alcanzase —comentaba ella—. Dice que el cordón comenzó a girar cuando el cristal del escaparate y el de la puerta estallaron y que el círculo que se formó alrededor de él fue por las vueltas que daba tu péndulo. Según él, eso impidió que le cayeran los trozos encima. Cuando se produjo el estallido se dirigía hacia aquí para dártelo.

—No le hagas caso. Está desorientado. Y no es para menos. Ahora mismo iré a verle —le respondió Desmond.

—Yo qué sé, no voy a llevarte la contraria, pero te aseguro que al oír sus palabras he pensado en lo que nos dijo Ecles. Tiene razón: tu péndulo, el material del que está hecho, se parece mucho a las cubiertas del libro rojo. Hizo bien en deshacerse de él, porque desde que lo encontrasteis no dejan de suceder hechos extraños, tal como él nos advirtió que pasaría. Y, aunque te moleste, pienso que si tu péndulo es del mismo material que ese libro, deberías hacer lo mismo que ha hecho Ecles con el libro.

Oí la voz de Desmond respondiendo, pero no conseguí entender lo que decía, porque él bajó el tono y la conversación se convirtió en un susurro ininteligible.

Luego, mientras Elda nos hablaba del edificio, de Antonio y de las peculiaridades del barrio, yo no pude evitar seguir pensando en lo que había escuchado momentos antes. Tal vez ese libro rojo al que se había referido Elda era el mío, pensé. Si estaba en lo cierto, Ecles era el único que podía conducirme hasta él y devolvérmelo.

—Te debemos una. Cuando quieras te pasas a tomar un café —le dije a Elda, ya en el descansillo.

—Pues la verdad es que me encantaría ver cómo ha quedado el ático amueblado.

—Entonces, hablamos —respondí sonriente, ante la mirada incrédula de Alán, que se despidió de ella con un simple gesto de la mano.

En cuanto Elda hubo cerrado la puerta, Alán me miró.

—No sé por qué, pero no me gusta la pintora. Mira de una forma muy extraña y el color de sus ojos es igual de raro que ella.

—Son grises. No sé qué tienen de sospechoso los ojos grises, a mí me encantan. No son muy comunes, por eso son más bonitos, ¿no crees?

—No. El suyo es un gris turbio —dijo convencido—, y su amabilidad me ha parecido impostada. Creo que sabía quién eras desde el primer momento en que te vio. No me gusta —repitió—. Hay algo en ella que me intranquiliza.

Le sonreí. Lo hice porque al comentar que, a su entender, Elda me había reconocido desde el primer momento, eso me dio ánimos, me supo a esperanza de reencuentro, y deseé que Alán tuviese razón.

—¿Y ahora qué he dicho para que sonrías? —inquirió. Enarcó las cejas y me miró a los ojos a la espera de mi respuesta.

—Llego tarde, ¿me acercas a la oficina? —le pregunté, desviando la conversación.

—Estás rarísima. No sé lo que te sucede, pero algo te está pasando. ¿Me esperas abajo o subes conmigo a por las llaves del coche?

Preferí quedarme esperando en la calle. Me senté en el escalón de la entrada del portal y, con la vista puesta en la floristería, recordé la conversación que Desmond y Elda habían mantenido sobre el llavero y el libro. Volví sobre cada una de sus palabras. Quizás estuviera equivocada, pero todo indicaba que el libro del que hablaban era el mío y que Ecles se había deshecho de él. Aquella expresión me asustaba, podía significar cualquier cosa, como que lo hubiese destruido o tirado en cualquier contenedor. Si ese era el caso, aunque consiguiese que Ecles me dijera dónde estaba, no podría encontrarlo nunca, pensé. Pero si el material del péndulo de Desmond era el mismo que el de mi libro, ambos objetos siempre se atraerían, lo harían eternamente. ¿No sería ese el motivo por el que yo había vuelto al ático, al lugar donde estaba aquel péndulo que en un tiempo tal vez formó parte del libro?, me pregunté sin saber cómo había llegado a esa hipótesis. Y se me ocurrió también que aquella suposición quizás era parte de un recuerdo. Cabía la posibilidad de que hubiera vivido más de lo que recordaba y por ello supiera que ambos objetos se atraían, me dije.

De pronto sentí el impulso de buscar el trozo de madera que me había herido y que Elda había tirado. No tardé en encontrarlo junto a la puerta de El desván de Aradia. Lo recogí y lo guardé dentro del bolso, en mi cartera. No sabía bien por qué lo hacía, simplemente me dejaba llevar por el sexto sentido que parecía acompañarme desde que había vuelto al ático de Antonio.

Alán no tardó en llegar con las llaves del coche.

—Es muy extraño lo que ha sucedido porque, en apariencia, el local está intacto —dijo Alán mirando hacia la floristería, que aún seguía siendo el centro de atención de los viandantes.

»¿Te duele? —preguntó, sosteniéndome la mano—. Si quieres, nos acercamos a que te lo miren.

—No. Solo ha sido un pequeño corte. Ya sabes, las heridas en las manos sangran mucho aunque solo sean un rasguño.

—Ese es el loco que nos observaba fuera de la tienda el día que estuvimos con Antonio, ¿verdad? —me preguntó Alán, señalándolo. El hombre estaba en la acera de la floristería. Recogía los cristales que había sobre los adoquines y los iba introduciendo en una especie de saco de esparto. Me pareció que el cristal, al tomar contacto con sus manos, dejaba de ser transparente y se tornaba violeta.

—Sí, es él —respondí, y retiré la vista del hombre.

El individuo, como si hubiese captado mi voz, se irguió justo en el momento en que respondí a Alán. Me miró, me señaló con el dedo índice y gritó como un poseso:

—¡Ella es la culpable! —Hizo una pausa para tomar aire y alzó el tono de voz aún con más fuerza—: ¡Bruja! —exclamó con una expresión de asco que torció sus gestos.

La gente que caminaba por la acera lo miró y siguió la dirección que marcaba con el dedo. Se escucharon cuchicheos. Los viandantes se separaban de él. Lo evitaban. Alán me miró y se encogió de hombros.

Un ruido metálico y constante, como una melodía desacompasada e inexacta, sonó detrás de nosotros.

—Cuando nací, sabía quién era y de dónde venía. Recordaba mi vida anterior. Luego, poco a poco, fui olvidando. Olvidé todo y me convertí en quien soy ahora. Nos pasa a todos. Si no fuese así, sería muy difícil vivir. A él no le pasó lo mismo —le dijo a Alán una anciana con aspecto de indigente que se había colocado frente a él—. Él no olvidó. —Señaló al individuo—. No quiso hacerlo. Le pudo la ambición. Logró mantener todos los recuerdos de sus vidas anteriores. A los que lo consiguen los llamamos nigromantes, seres

que saben caminar entre la vida y la muerte. Hay que mantenerse alejados de su influencia, de sus artes oscuras. Son peligrosos.

—No entiendo —dijo Alán, desconcertado ante la perorata de la mujer.

—Me refiero a él. —Volvió a señalarlo—. ¿Es que no se ha dado cuenta de que no es una persona normal? —preguntó, esta vez mirándome a mí. Se dio la vuelta y comenzó a empujar por la acera el carro lleno de latas, propiedad de un supermercado cercano.

—Por un momento pensé que a ese loco le había dado por ti —comentó Alán—, pero ya veo que se refería a ella. Tiene todo el aspecto de una bruja. Solo le falta la escoba —dijo, señalándola—. Estaba detrás de nosotros. No sé quién de los dos está peor, ¡qué lástima! —concluyó, cogiéndome de la mano sin dar mayor importancia a lo sucedido.

Pero yo sí se la di. Cada una de las palabras que pronunció la mujer tenía sentido para mí. Lo tenía porque yo también sabía que aquel ser no era como nosotros y que la bruja a la que se refería el hombre de la gabardina y el sombrero era yo.

Capítulo 4

Seguía extrañando a Samanta tras aquel panel gris que separaba nuestras mesas de trabajo. Echaba en falta nuestra complicidad, aquel sabernos la una a la otra sin necesidad de hablar. Siempre nos había bastado una mirada para tener que reprimir la carcajada. La mayoría de las veces, muertas de risa, agachábamos la cabeza o fijábamos la vista en el montón de datos que desfilaban en la pantalla de nuestros ordenadores. Y, aunque el resto de los compañeros intentaron que su ausencia me fuese lo más llevadera posible, aunque quisieron atenuar la nostalgia que me abrumaba y que no ocultaba, nadie logró ocupar su lugar en aquel edificio frío e impersonal.

Nada más llegar a mi puesto de trabajo coloqué la astilla encima de la mesa y pensé que, de haber estado ella al otro lado, me habría preguntado qué era aquel trozo de madera seca afilada y vieja. «Una astilla que se ha desprendido de la puerta de El desván de Aradia, un local que espero poder regentar algún día», le habría dicho. Y ella, arqueando las cejas con expresión de desconcierto, se habría levantado con un folio en las manos para disimular. Lo habría puesto encima de mi mesa y lo señalaría con el dedo simulando que me preguntaba algo sobre el contenido de la plana. Después habría cogido la astilla y, bajito, con sus labios pegados a mi oído, me habría dicho: «En unos minutos nos tomamos un café y me cuentas. Mientras tanto, ten cuidado, no sea que vuelvas a pincharte con ella y esta vez te suceda

como a la Bella Durmiente con la aguja de la rueca». Fueron tan reales mis pensamientos que hasta me pareció oír su voz junto a mí y notar su aliento en mi oreja, aquel siseo en que se convertía su voz cuando no quería ser escuchada más allá de nuestras mesas de trabajo.

Seguí observando la esquirla con detenimiento. Esperaba ver en aquella superficie vieja y seca algún vestigio de magia. Los hechos habían sucedido de una forma muy extraña, sin nada que los entrelazase, como si formasen parte de una misma acción. De pronto pensé que el hecho de que la madera se hubiese clavado en la palma de mi mano podía haber sido la causa, el detonante de todo lo que aconteció después. Ese detalle absurdo, sin importancia, podía haber generado aquel embrollo. Un aleteo de mariposa que dio paso a una tormenta, como sucede en la teoría del caos. Tal vez el hombre de la gabardina, el nigromante, como lo llamó la anciana, tenía razón y yo era la culpable de lo sucedido, me dije.

—Es una aguja antigua, parece de las que se utilizaban en las ruecas. ¡Qué bonita! —exclamó Carmen, una de mis compañeras de trabajo.

Estaba detrás de mí, pero yo no me había percatado de su presencia. La miré desconcertada y, sin responder, miré la astilla que se había convertido, tal y como Carmen terminaba de decir, en una aguja de madera fina y puntiaguda.

—Sí, tienes razón —dije después de permanecer unos segundos en silencio, ocultando mi sorpresa y el desconcierto que me produjo la transformación de la astilla en un huso—. La encontré en la calle esta mañana y me llamó mucho la atención. —expliqué, guardándola de nuevo en mi cartera.

—Aparte de esto —dijo levantando la pila de hojas que traía—, tengo un cotilleo. —Dejó los folios sobre mi mesa. Bajó el tono de voz y dijo—: Se rumorea que habrá reducción de personal en breve, o sea que no te mates introduciendo toda esta mierda...

***

No esperaba que Alán estuviera en casa. Me había confirmado por WhatsApp que al final no vendría a cenar porque los *destalles* y la organización del almacén iban para largo y que cenarían todos allí. Abrí la puerta del ascensor pensando en que después de darme una ducha bajaría a casa de Elda y la invitaría a tomar un refresco antes de la cena. Al tiempo que cerraba la puerta metálica del ascensor, vi que se abría la de la casa de Claudia. Sonreí. Me volví con la esperanza de verla en el rellano. Deseaba tanto volver a hablar con ella que aquella posibilidad se me antojó un regalo.

—Queridísima Diana, no sabes cuantísimo te he extrañado —me dijo sin sacar los pies del felpudo, como si el pisar fuera de él le estuviera prohibido o algo se lo impidiese—. No he sido la única en notar tu ausencia en este edificio, Desmond también te echa de menos. Pasea su melancolía todas las noches por mi casa —dijo con una sonrisa...

—Diana —dijo una voz femenina a mi espalda.

Era Azucena.

—¿Qué haces tú aquí? —le pregunté desconcertada.

—¿Estás bien? —inquirió ella sin contestar a mi pregunta. Miraba la puerta de Claudia, que permanecía cerrada—. Me ha parecido que hablabas con alguien.

—No, solo estaba pensando en voz alta. Pero ¿qué haces tú aquí? —volví a preguntarle.

—Vengo a la fiesta que habéis organizado por la inauguración de vuestro nuevo piso. Me invitó Alán.

—¿Qué fiesta? No hemos organizado nada de eso —respondí con sequedad y sin mirarla, mientras buscaba las llaves de casa en el interior del bolso.

—¡Ostras! Debía ser una sorpresa, por eso Alán insistió tanto en la hora de llegada. ¡Lo siento! Creo que he metido la pata. —Miró su reloj de pulsera—. He llegado tarde. Tendría que haber estado antes y así no me habría encontrado contigo. Claro, ese debía de ser

el plan de Alán. Me va a matar, seguro —explicó en un tono apesadumbrado, aunque desmentido por su expresión facial y su mirada, que parecían reflejar cierta alegría al haber fastidiado la supuesta sorpresa que quería darme Alán.

—No me digas —repliqué, irónica.

—El metro se retrasó en Cuatro Caminos. Por lo visto alguien vio a un sujeto caminando por la vía con un maletín abierto del que iban cayendo folios. Dijeron que se internó en el túnel como si estuviera desorientado, sin atender a los gritos que le avisaban del peligro que corría. Pararon el servicio durante más de una hora, pero no encontraron a nadie. En fin..., lo que no pase en el metro de Madrid no pasa en ningún sitio. Me fascinan las historias que hay sobre esa línea, la 6 —puntualizó como si todo lo anterior no tuviera importancia—, y me quedé a ver qué sucedía. ¡Soy tan curiosa!

Aunque su relato me hizo pensar en Duncan y me habría gustado saber más detalles del suceso, estaba tan enfadada que ni siquiera le respondí. Introduje la tija en la cerradura y abrí la puerta de casa. Ella entró detrás de mí.

—¡Sorpresa! —exclamó Alán al verme entrar. El resto de los invitados, una veintena, repitieron su grito y destaparon los botes del maldito confeti que tenían en las manos. El salón se llenó de papelitos de todos los colores y tamaños. Algunos eran pedazos de periódicos con caracteres orientales, por lo que deduje que Alán los había comprado en uno de los establecimientos chinos del barrio. Ya había visto aquel timo otras veces.

Azucena también gritó aquel «¡Sorpresa!» estridente, que no sentí que fuera conmigo, y coloreado por los papeles del confeti que también cubrieron mi pelo y mi ropa. Lo hizo contoneándose como la serpiente de *El libro de la selva*. Incluso me pareció captar un pequeño silbido que escapó de sus labios, teñidos de rojo carmín, cuando pasó a mi lado. Me esquivó y se apresuró cuanto le permitía su falda de tubo, tan ceñida que parecía iba a reventar en cualquier momento,

27

para tomar su bote de confeti. Sin el más mínimo reparo lo abrió sobre los hombros de Alán. Él, cubierto de colorines y con cara de tonto, le rio la gracia. Los demás hicieron lo mismo, mientras yo, sin el más mínimo reparo, la miraba de arriba abajo y la imaginaba vendiendo deportivas con esa actitud, adoptando posturitas imposibles para medir el número de pie de los clientes. Creo que la apuñalé con la vista varias veces, pero ella, a pesar de que me observaba de soslayo, no se dio por aludida. Lo cierto es que ni yo misma me explicaba a qué se debía mi visceral aversión hacia aquella mujer. ¿Por qué me irritaba tanto, si sabía que mi relación con Alán estaba llegando a su fin? ¿A qué venía tanta rabia, si en ese momento solo me importaba recuperar a mis amigos y ese vínculo tan especial con Desmond? Desde luego, habría sido normal que no me cayera especialmente bien, pero ¿a qué se debía tanto encono? Todas estas preguntas se mantuvieron en un segundo plano, porque en ese momento en lo único que podía pensar era en mi descomunal enfado. La tensión en el ambiente aumentó de tal modo que los invitados notaron que algo raro estaba pasando.

Por unos segundos la música pareció que dejaba de sonar y todos enmudecieron al advertir mi mirada fría y asesina puesta en Azucena. Así fue hasta que Alán me dio un beso en la mejilla y me condujo al dormitorio.

—¡Qué mona es tu compi y qué inocente! ¿Verdad? —le espeté—. Pobre, ella no tiene la culpa. Qué le va a hacer si la dibujaron así, como a Jessica Rabbit. No puede evitarlo.

—No empieces con tus celos absurdos. ¿Crees que si escondiera alguna intención de tener algo conmigo lo manifestaría delante de todos, y más en tu presencia?

—¿«Quién engañó a Roger Rabbit»? —repliqué, guiñándole un ojo.

—¿En serio? ¿Serás capaz de estropear la fiesta que he organizado para ti? Creo que te estás pasando —expuso, visiblemente enfadado.

—Pues sí —le respondí—. No sé cómo has sido capaz de invitarla. Yo diría que eres el único de los presentes que no sabe que le gustas. Salta a la vista, porque desde luego ella no se molesta en disimularlo. ¡Es que no la soporto! —espeté.

—Pues ya me explicarás cómo iba a invitar a toda mi plantilla y dejarla a ella fuera.

Lo miré con un gesto reprobatorio.

—Deberías haberme consultado antes de organizar la fiesta. Habría sido lo más lógico. Has metido en casa, y sin avisarme, a un montón de gente con la que no tengo nada que ver.

—Pretendía que fuese una sorpresa, por eso no te consulté. Y sí los conoces. Has ido mil veces a la tienda. Estás harta de verlos.

—Pero no son mis amigos, y yo, a mi casa, solo invito a mis amigos —repliqué, indicándole que saliese del dormitorio porque quería cambiarme.

—Es que tú, Diana, no tienes amigos, y de un tiempo a esta parte, tampoco serenidad. Solo hace cinco días que nos hemos mudado, pero tengo la sensación de que algo ha cambiado entre nosotros. Creo que ya no eres feliz a mi lado —me soltó ya de espaldas, mientras salía del dormitorio.

Capítulo 5

Dejé que la fiesta siguiera sin mí, mientras intentaba buscar una excusa para no salir del dormitorio. En aquellos momentos solo me apetecía echar a correr, marcharme sin cruzar una palabra con nadie, caminar por las calles sin rumbo, sin un destino concreto. Sin embargo, me sentía presa, encadenada a una vida y unas circunstancias que no consideraba mías, que no había previsto, pero que, irónicamente, me ataban a aquel lugar.

Finalmente, después de permanecer unos minutos sentada en la cama, cuando recobré la calma que había perdido después de que Alán me recriminara que no tenía amigos, me uní a la fiesta. Le sonreí desganada cuando me rodeó la cintura con el brazo. Me dio un beso en la mejilla y me guiñó un ojo, como si la discusión que habíamos tenido hacía unos minutos no se hubiera producido. Dejé que llenara mi copa de vino e intenté disimular ante sus amigos. A fin de cuentas, no era asunto suyo, y menos de Azucena, que de seguro disfrutaría viéndonos distanciados, pensé mirándola de soslayo, indignada. No estaba dispuesta a darle ninguna alegría a Jessica Rabbit, no se merecía nada, me dije devolviéndole el beso a Alán, mientras ella nos miraba.

La noche fue cayendo sobre los toldos naranjas de Ecles y Desmond, sobre las losetas rojizas de nuestra terraza, y atenuó las voces de nuestros invitados. Los grupitos comenzaron a formarse.

Mientras los observaba pensé en lo fácil que era detectar los que congeniaban realmente y los que solo simulaban hacerlo, y recordé las palabras de Samanta sobre las reuniones laborales: «La gente, Diana, es igual en todas partes. Por distintas que sean nuestras facciones, el color de pelo o de piel, tenemos los mismos instintos, deseos, carencias y ambiciones. Créeme, en las fiestas de empresa es donde mejor se nos conoce. Perdemos la vergüenza y la noción de dónde y con quién estamos y nos convertimos en presa fácil. Por eso no me gustan nada esos eventos, ¡pero nada! Pierdo el control con demasiada facilidad...».

Al pensar en las palabras de mi amiga, decidí ser ambigua en mis comentarios, guardar la ropa mientras nadaba entre tanto desconocido. Hablé del calor sofocante de aquel verano. Sobre la altura de los techos del ático, la maravillosa terraza que teníamos y las vistas privilegiadas de las que disfrutábamos. Sonreí con frecuencia y de forma mecánica, casi impostada, y deambulé entre los invitados como a veces lo hacía por las calles de Madrid: ajena al tumulto, distante y solitaria. Así fue hasta que Ecles salió a su terraza y comenzó a recoger los toldos. En apenas unos segundos, el tiempo que tardó él en girar los ganchos de metal con los que recogió la tela, se hizo el silencio. Solo se oía la música que salía del salón y el chirrido que producía el hierro dando vueltas dentro del mecanismo. La gente dijo en voz baja: «Es enorme», «Fíjate, parece Frankenstein», «Qué feo es el pobre». Los susurros se difundían entre la inmovilidad y la expectación de todos los que allí estaban, incluido Alán, que le miraba estupefacto desde dentro del salón.

—¡Ecles! —grité. Levanté la mano para que pudiera localizarme y caminé hacia él.

Mi vecino se dio la vuelta sin soltar el gancho de los toldos y buscó la procedencia de la voz que lo llamaba. Me acerqué al murete de ladrillo que dividía nuestras terrazas con una copa de vino. Como si aquello fuese un espectáculo extraño e inesperado,

todos siguieron mis pasos, expectantes. Algunos se retiraron para dejarme pasar. Ecles sonrió tal y como yo recordaba, con aquella maravillosa expresión infantil. Sus ojos mostraban su habitual brillo lleno de inocencia, de una ingenuidad que la mayoría, cegados por su apariencia física, no percibían.

En el momento que puse la copa sobre la valla de ladrillo la fiesta retomó la normalidad perdida. Fue como un *Off-On*, como si todos ellos, incluido Alán, hubieran estado inmersos en una pausa y mi acercamiento a Ecles hubiese dado un sopapo a sus prejuicios y les hubiese mostrado su actitud ridícula e impresentable.

—Tú debes de ser Diana —me dijo Ecles, apoyado en el muro—. Desmond me habló de ti. Eres tan guapa, pelirroja y pecosa como dijo —explicó divertido, mirando mi pelo y señalándolo con el dedo.

—Y tú tan grande como él te describió el día que llegué. Se disculpó en tu nombre, nos dijo que no podías darnos la bienvenida —le respondí.

—Y feo, debió avisarte de que también era muy feo.

—¿Quieres tomar una copa? La fiesta es por la inauguración de la casa —le indiqué señalando a los invitados, que ya no nos prestaban atención.

—Tal vez en otro momento. Tus amigos se asustaron al verme —adujo—, mejor lo posponemos para cuando no estés tan bien acompañada —dijo en tono irónico.

—Como quieras, pero si te sirve de algo, ellos me dan igual —contesté, guiñándole un ojo.

Me miró y, sin responderme, se rascó la cabeza y entrecerró los ojos como si estuviera buscando un pensamiento perdido. Luego levantó la mano, señaló la puerta de su salón y dijo:

—Por favor, no te vayas, vuelvo enseguida.

Seguí con la mirada su caminar silencioso, aquella manera tan extraña de andar sin hacer ruido, a pesar de su gran tamaño y su

aparente torpedad. Parecía que fuese un fantasma, pensé sonriendo. Enseguida estuvo de vuelta junto a mí.

—Casi lo olvido. Desmond me dijo que, si te veía antes que él, te diese estos libros. Son de hechizos, de brujas y pócimas —explicó, poniendo la gaveta que contenía los libros sobre la valla de ladrillo.

—¿Este es el cajón que encontrasteis en el altillo de nuestro armario? —le pregunté, y él asintió con la cabeza—. Es una preciosidad —dije pasando los dedos sobre los símbolos pictos grabados en su superficie.

—Si te gusta, puedes quedártelo. Te lo regalo.

—Pero ¿no es de Desmond? —dije, apurada.

—No. Es mío. Yo fui quien lo encontró, por eso es mío. Quédatelo, te lo regalo —insistió.

Fui sacando los libros y poniéndolos sobre el murete.

—No veo el libro que encontrasteis junto a la gaveta; el de las cubiertas rojas. Me gustaría mucho leerlo. Me parece recordar que Desmond me dijo que me lo enseñaría —le comenté con la cabeza gacha, simulando leer los lomos de los libros para que no pudiera mirarme a los ojos. No quería que viera en ellos o en alguno de mis gestos que le estaba mintiendo.

—Es imposible que Desmond te hablase de ese libro. Además, no se puede leer —me respondió con voz profunda y observándome fijamente, como si quisiera entrar en mis pensamientos... o ya lo hubiera hecho. Levantó la mano y con el índice señaló mi terraza—. Te reclaman —dijo.

Volví la cabeza. Su dedo apuntaba a Alán, que en ese momento me pedía que fuese junto a él. Respondí con un gesto de la mano que esperase y me di la vuelta para continuar la conversación con Ecles, pero él ya se había marchado.

—Veo que el vampiro tiene bien enseñado a su amigo, el jovencito Frankenstein —dijo Alán, bajito, con sus labios pegados a mi oreja, mientras miraba la gaveta que yo llevaba—. Es una copia

exacta de tu cajón —comentó—. ¡Qué amable! Debe de haberla buscado con ahínco por toda la ciudad. Seguro que lo ha hecho porque le has contado tu historia —comentó y le dio un golpecito con los dedos a los ejemplares que había dentro—. Estarás contenta, ahora tienes dos cajones antiquísimos con los que volver a perder la noción de la realidad. Ay, cariño, me parece que tu amiguito te ha hecho un flaco favor.

—Eres idiota, pero muy idiota —le respondí, dolida y molesta por sus palabras y por el tono que había empleado—. Los celos te están secando las neuronas, las pocas que te quedan, vaya. Te digo lo mismo que me has dicho tú antes: algo te pasa desde que nos hemos mudado porque estás intranquilo e inseguro, demasiado inseguro y suspicaz. Has perdido la serenidad y pareces infeliz a mi lado. De lo contrario no me harías daño, porque te aseguro que me lo has hecho. Estarás orgulloso. ¡Qué muestra de madurez! —exclamé en tono irónico, y me encaminé hacia el dormitorio sin darle tiempo a una réplica.

Los sentimientos son silenciosos e incorpóreos, tan libres como el viento y, contrariamente a lo que pensamos, visibles. Todos ellos dejan un rastro inequívoco en cada uno de nuestros gestos, en nuestra mirada, en cada movimiento o ademán que hacemos, por pequeño que sea. Aunque intentemos camuflarlos, ocultarlos en lo más profundo de nosotros mismos, siempre toman cuerpo y se muestran ante los demás como niños malcriados, rebeldes y anárquicos, escapando a nuestro control. Y ese día, durante la fiesta, los sentimientos de Alán, al igual que los míos y los de Azucena, recorrieron la terraza, el salón y, como alcahuetas, se pasearon contando a los invitados lo que nos sucedía. Todos supieron que entre los dos había cierta crispación. Advirtieron la pequeña sacudida, apenas perceptible, que torció nuestros gestos, nos distanció y apagó el tono de nuestras conversaciones. También detectaron la alegría y la esperanza en los ojos de Azucena cuando percibió que Alán y yo

estábamos discutiendo. Observaron el deseo de ella cuando, como quien no quiere la cosa, recostaba por momentos la cabeza en el hombro de mi novio. Sonreía como si le fuera la vida en manifestar su felicidad. Intentaba mostrarse tan cándida y femenina ante él que en más de una ocasión pensé que, mientras le hablaba, iba a escupir margaritas de colores fluorescentes por la boca.

Se merecía que la mandase a barrer un desierto, pensé mirándola con descaro, el mismo que ella exhibía ante mí al mariposear alrededor de mi novio sin el menor reparo. Y lo habría hecho en aquel mismo momento, cuando vi que sujetaba el brazo de Alán y se lo llevaba a la terraza susurrándole alguna estupidez al oído. Pero no tenía escoba para enviarla a barrer con ella, y aunque la hubiese tenido, pensé, no se la habría dado. Ella era una arpía y yo una bruja, no teníamos nada que ver, a pesar de que el lenguaje se empeñase en convertir las dos palabras en sinónimos.

Apenas llevaba unos segundos en la alcoba cuando escuché la voz de Azucena:

—¡No me lo puedo creer! —exclamó—. ¿No lo veis? —Señaló a *Senatón* y miró al resto de los invitados, que no pudieron contener las carcajadas—. Me cambio de sitio y él me sigue. ¡Es increíble!

Senatón daba zarpazos dentro del arenero y echaba la tierra fuera de él, sobre los pies de Azucena. Cuando esta se apartaba, el gato seguía sus movimientos y se situaba en la misma posición que ella. Se colocaba dentro del cajón y volvía a escarbar y echar la tierra fuera. La arena parecía tener vida propia, porque caía siempre en los zapatos de Azucena, sobre sus pies y sus tobillos. Alán se apresuró a retirar el arenero, cogió a *Senatón* y lo metió en el salón.

—Lo siento muchísimo —se disculpó—. No sé qué le ha pasado. Tal vez esté nervioso por el ruido. No está acostumbrado, porque siempre está solo o con nosotros. Desde luego, habría sido mucho mejor dejar el arenero en la cocina. Voy a por la escoba —dijo mirando el montón de tierra que cubría los zapatos y los

tobillos de Azucena—. También te traeré unas toallitas húmedas para que te limpies el polvo blanco que suelta la arena.

Observé a la arpía mientras esta sacudía los pies y se retiraba del montón de arena. Cuando Alán llegó, ella se apresuró a quitarle la escoba y se puso a barrer como si, una vez más, le fuese la vida en demostrarle a mi novio lo perfecta y maravillosa que era... incluso barriendo.

Seguí los movimientos de sus brazos, el ir y venir del cepillo sobre las losetas, y una sonrisa asomó a mis labios. Bueno, aquello no era un desierto, pero se le acercaba, me dije aupando a *Senatón*, que había entrado en el dormitorio y me daba empellones en los tobillos.

—Eres listo, bichito, pero que muy listo —le dije, acariciándole una orejita.

Volví a mirar a Azucena, que seguía barriendo encaramada en sus zapatos de tacón de aguja, inapropiados y demasiado inestables para aquella tarea.

—No entiendo qué le habrá pasado —se excusó de nuevo Alán. Se agachó y le acercó el recogedor—. Es la primera vez que hace eso.

—Da igual, no te preocupes. Pero... para evitaros más incidentes, deberíais poner el arenero del gatito pelón en otro sitio más apropiado, al menos cuando tengáis visitas. Y de paso evitaréis que estropee el ala delta de tu chica, porque lo mismo le da por hacer un pis en la tela —le respondió Azucena.

—No le gusta —dije desde la ventana, mirando a Alán. Sonreí modosamente mientras contenía la carcajada que luchaba por escapar de mi garganta y que me provocó un golpe de tos.

—No le gusta..., ¿el qué no le gusta? —me preguntó ella con voz de pito, como si una de esas margaritas se le hubiese atragantado.

—Que le llamen «pelón». Su nombre es *Senatón*. Ah, y tampoco le gustas tú —le respondí, y entré en la habitación sin esperar réplica ni reacción alguna a mi comentario.

—¿Es en serio? —Oí que decía—. ¡Alucino!

—No le des importancia. Te aseguro que no es nada personal. Adora a *Senatón* y no le ha sentado bien que le llamases «pelón» —le explicó Alán.

Tras el encontronazo que provoqué con Azucena, el ambiente se enrareció y los invitados comenzaron a marcharse. Yo no salí del dormitorio. Alán fue despidiendo a todos y disculpó mi ausencia sirviéndose de la socorrida excusa de la jaqueca repentina. Jessica Rabbit anduvo remoloneando por ahí para ser la última en marcharse, igual que había sido la última en llegar. Finalmente la música dejó de sonar. Solo se oía el ruido de sus tacones de aguja y el de los vasos que debían de estar recogiendo mano a mano Alán y ella.

—Voy a llevar a Azucena a su casa. Después del feo que le has hecho delante de todos, es lo menos que puedo hacer. Casi me muero de la vergüenza. Espero que te disculpes con ella cuando vuelvas a verla —me dijo Alán, al tiempo que cogía las llaves del coche que estaban sobre la cómoda del dormitorio. Ni siquiera me miró al hablar—. No tardaré mucho.

No le respondí. Cuando sonó el ruido de la puerta al cerrarse salí a la terraza. Caminé entre los trocitos de confeti que alfombraban el suelo dándoles puntapiés. Aún me sentía rabiosa y molesta, y seguía sin entender el porqué. Debería haber asimilado la ruptura que se produciría entre Alán y yo porque ya sabía lo que iba a suceder, lo había vivido, aunque de otra forma. En aquel tiempo, en aquel futuro, cuando Alán me dejó por ella, Azucena era casi una desconocida para mí, de modo que aquello fue algo menos doloroso. Sin embargo, en el presente, debido a mi intervención, al haberme dejado llevar por la ira y provocar una paradoja, le había allanado el camino y ella había conseguido entrar en mi casa, acercarse más a mi novio. Todo lo ocurrido de resultas de ello —verla cerca de Alán, su flirteo, su descaro y el beneplácito de él a todo lo que Jessica Rabbit hacía— me ponía de los nervios. Me hacía sentir

aún más tonta y ridícula de lo que me sentí cuando Alán, en aquella cena, en aquel restaurante, me dijo que se habían enamorado y que habían decidido irse a vivir juntos. Los acontecimientos nos llevaban al mismo lugar y el resultado sería idéntico, pero el camino que estábamos recorriendo era diferente. Todo se desarrollaba de una forma más dolorosa para mí, porque aunque ya no amase a Alán como lo había amado entonces, aún quedaba un pequeño resquicio en mi alma de lo que hubo entre nosotros, de lo que ella, Azucena, me había arrebatado sin permiso.

Me apoyé en la barandilla y miré el cielo buscando las estrellas que Desmond me había propuesto contar en su DeLorean, pero no las encontré. Debían de estar en otro lugar, dejándose contar por él, pensé sonriendo. Vi el camión de la limpieza, el agua cayendo sobre el asfalto y cómo las escobillas arrastraban la suciedad que se acumulaba junto al bordillo. Las luces anaranjadas de las sirenas, sus destellos, rozaban las fachadas de refilón una y otra vez, como las de un carrusel. Apreté los párpados y deseé que, cuando abriera los ojos, el ático volviera a ser el que había dejado tiempo atrás.

—Diana, creo que necesitas una escoba —me dijo Claudia desde el murete de ladrillo que separaba nuestras terrazas—. Aunque esta escoba no es precisamente para barrer —comentó, señalando los papelitos del confeti que cubrían el suelo—, creo que no pasará nada si por esta vez la utilizas para eso, ya que las herramientas de una bruja se adecuan siempre a sus deseos. ¡Toma!

La sostenía en sus manos. El mango era de marfil y en él se apreciaban varios símbolos pictos grabados.

Capítulo 6

Volver a ver a Claudia me hizo olvidar el ambiente enrarecido y monótono que rodeaba mi vida. Su simple presencia me sacó del desánimo en el que había estado sumida durante toda la fiesta, de la tristeza que habitaba dentro de mí desde que regresé a aquel presente que no me pertenecía, que no sentía mío y repudiaba.

—¡Qué alegría volver a verte, Claudia! —exclamé sin poder reprimirme.

—A mí también me reconfortan y complacen nuestros encuentros. Me gustaría verte con más asiduidad, pero las cosas casi nunca suceden como deseamos.

»Toma —me dijo, ofreciéndome su escoba—. Cuélgala sobre el dintel, como hiciste cuando te la regalé la primera vez, en el otro tiempo. Lo recuerdas, ¿verdad? —me preguntó.

Yo asentí moviendo la cabeza.

—¿Cómo es que tú también recuerdas lo que pasó entonces?

—Pues porque también lo viví, ¿por qué iba a ser? ¿De qué te extrañas tanto?

—Porque eres la única que parece recordarme. Tampoco sé el motivo por el que puedo verte y hablar contigo, si nadie más lo hace.

—¡Ay, niña! No irás a creer que solo tú ves más allá de esta realidad, ¿verdad? —me preguntó con cierta condescendencia, como si

hablara con una alumna no especialmente inteligente—. Si es así, te equivocas. Hay muchos más, aunque no lo manifiesten. Ya deberías saberlo.

Sus palabras y el tono que empleó me recordaron a Koldo, el cantautor del metro al que conocí cuando viví esos días por primera vez, porque en esa ocasión me había dicho: «¿Acaso crees que eres la única que puede ver más allá de esta realidad? ¿De verdad crees que eres la única persona especial y diferente que camina por estas calles? ¿La única que cree en la magia?».

—Ninguno de los que me rodean, nadie de aquellos con los que comparto mi vida, te ve. Sé que Antonio, tu hijo, tampoco puede verte... ni oírte —puntualicé tras una pausa en la que la miré a los ojos—. A veces pienso que solo existes en mi imaginación.

—Mi hijo no me ve, pero me siente. A fin de cuentas es casi lo mismo, incluso más real y certero. La vista engaña; los sentimientos, no. Él sabe que estoy aquí, aunque no pueda verme como tú lo haces. A mi hijo no le hace falta tener ninguna prueba física para saber que sigo existiendo. Sin embargo tú —hizo una pausa y subió el tono—, siendo quien eres, tienes dudas y te pierdes buscando certidumbres absurdas sobre si existo o no.

—Tal vez Antonio te añore tanto que se niegue a pensar que te has ido —insistí.

—¿Tú crees? —me preguntó con un deje cargado de intención—. Los ojos engañan, querida. ¿Se te ha olvidado lo que te sucedió en ese tiempo paralelo que ya viviste, cuando el nigromante tomó la apariencia de Elda para engañarte e intentó convencerte para que escribieses sobre las páginas del libro? —expuso. Sentí un escalofrío al revivir la escena—. Lo tenías delante de ti, tanto era así que su aliento rozaba tu cara, y sin embargo veías a Elda. Tus ojos te engañaron. Algo te decía que esa persona no era Elda y te avisaba de que estabas en peligro. Tal vez fuera ese sexto sentido con el que

naciste y al que, incomprensiblemente, siempre has temido y del que muchas veces has renegado.

»Te llevará tiempo comprender, pero tarde o temprano lo harás. Ahora lo más importante es que utilices bien lo que sabes o perderás la cabeza. Vagarás de tiempo en tiempo, del pasado al presente y del presente al futuro, y así sucesivamente, regresando siempre al mismo lugar. Lo harás una y otra vez, como te ha sucedido ahora, pero el resultado terminará siendo siempre el mismo: volverás a perder el libro, la gaveta, a tus amigos, y regresarás con Alán de nuevo —expuso con expresión de preocupación. Después calló.

En su rostro se dibujó una expresión de desconcierto. Levantó el dedo índice y señaló a mi espalda. Di un respingo al oír la voz de Alán justo a mi lado, porque no le había oído llegar.

—Creo que tardarás toda la noche en recoger el confeti si lo haces con esa escoba, que parece más indicada para adornar una pared que para barrer —dijo él.

—¿Cuánto llevas aquí? —le pregunté, sobresaltada.

—Apenas unos segundos. Estabas preciosa ahí tan quieta, sumida en tus pensamientos, y no he querido decirte nada —comentó dándome un beso en el cuello al tiempo que me rodeaba la cintura con el brazo.

Me volví buscando a Claudia, pero como ya venía siendo habitual, ella ya no estaba.

—Pensaba en Rigel —le respondí, intentando darle una respuesta coherente y creíble—. Últimamente me acuerdo mucho de él, sobre todo cuando miro el cielo..., ya sabes. Recordaba la cita de *Los inmortales* que él siempre me daba como respuesta cuando yo no comprendía algo o mi vida se torcía. Como ahora. —Esto último lo dije bajito, tanto que Alán no lo escuchó.

—¡Qué película más buena! —exclamó. Me estrechó contra él y repitió la cita—: «Paciencia, escocés. Lo has hecho muy bien, aunque te llevará tiempo continuar. Generaciones enteras nacen y

mueren continuamente. Tú estarás con los que viven mientras quieras, los pensamientos y los sueños de cada hombre son tuyos ahora. Tienes más poder de lo que se pueda imaginar. Utilízalo bien, amigo mío, no pierdas la cabeza».

Después volvió a besarme en el cuello y apoyó la cabeza en mi hombro, pero yo no pude responder a su caricia ni al beso. Tampoco a sus palabras.

—¿Aún sigues enfadada? —preguntó al ver que yo no me mostraba receptiva a sus caricias y que ni tan siquiera me movía—. No te entiendo, debería ser yo quien estuviera molesto contigo, y no lo estoy. Comprendo que la mudanza, el cambio de casa, pueda haberte alterado, es algo bastante frecuente, pero no me explico que te muestres tan distante. Pareces otra persona desde que nos hemos mudado. Diría que incluso antes, desde el momento en que te hablé de Antonio y del ático —expuso, retirando sus brazos de mi cintura.

Se puso frente a mí y me miró con aire inquisitorio.

—No sé qué quieres que te diga. Solo es una crisis, nada más —le respondí, y agaché la cabeza para evitar su mirada.

—Este ático parece haberte embrujado. No fue una buena idea mudarnos. Tal vez sería mejor que buscáramos otra casa. Haría cualquier cosa con tal de recuperar a mi chica.

—¡No! —exclamé como un resorte, alzando el tono de voz involuntariamente—. Me gusta esta casa. Me siento cómoda en ella. Tú, el que no cree en la magia, ahora me hablas de embrujos, ¡no fastidies!

—Entonces, si no quieres mudarte, dime qué demonios te pasa.

—Creo que necesito tiempo.

—¿Tiempo? —me preguntó, desconcertado—. ¿Para qué?

—Para adaptarme a tu nueva forma de vida, a tus fiestas, a tu amiguita y vuestro estúpido flirteo, que tú disimulas mal y ella no se molesta en ocultar —le espeté.

—No sé qué habré de hacer para que entiendas que Azucena no significa nada para mí —replicó en tono impertinente—. Al final vas a conseguir que entre nosotros haya algo. Le estás poniendo tanto empeño que voy a terminar creyéndomelo. ¡Joder! —protestó dando una patada a los papelitos de colores que cubrían el suelo de la terraza. Se dio la vuelta y caminó hacia el interior de la casa.

No hice nada para retenerlo. Oí el ruido de sus pasos camino del dormitorio y un rayo de luz cruzó la ventana e iluminó parte del suelo de la terraza casi al mismo tiempo que Alán pulsó el interruptor al entrar en la habitación.

No tenía ánimos para hablar con él. Sabía que no me entendería y, aunque quisiera hacerlo, no podía compartir nada de lo que me sucedía con él. Si lo hacía, corría el riesgo de volver a embrollarlo todo. Debía seguir el consejo de Claudia y utilizar bien mis conocimientos.

Apoyé la escoba en la pared y me acerqué a la barandilla que daba al exterior. Contemplé las calles vacías, las luces de los semáforos cambiando intermitentemente de color, la apariencia de escenario cinematográfico vacío que tenía la ciudad a aquellas horas, cuando no era ni demasiado tarde ni demasiado pronto para nada, cuando todo parecía suspendido en una pausa. La hora bruja, como decía Samanta. Esbocé una sonrisa triste al recordarla y me pregunté qué estaría haciendo en ese momento, con quién se encontraría y si me echaría tanto de menos como yo a ella.

Miré la fachada de la floristería. El escaparate permanecía con la persiana de aluminio bajada, igual que la puerta de entrada del local. Ya no había rastros de los cristales rotos sobre la acera. En el contenedor de la basura sobresalían los extremos de las tiras adhesivas del cristal repuesto en el escaparate y la puerta del comercio, ondeando a merced del viento. Y allí, junto al contenedor, en la penumbra, descubrí su silueta, el contorno del sombrero y sus manos enguantadas. Instintivamente, sin retirar la vista de él, pasé las manos por

la barandilla buscando el polvo de ladrillo que debía protegerme. Seguidamente me agaché y recogí un puñado del confeti que había esparcido por el suelo. Con las manos llenas de papelitos de colores me incorporé y los lancé con determinación a la calle. Al hacerlo, imaginé que lo que arrojaba al vacío era arena y no papel. Deseé que cayera sobre los pies del nigromante y que, al rozarlos, la arena tomara la consistencia del cemento y convirtiese sus pies en parte de los adoquines que formaban la acera; que lo atrapase e inmovilizara para siempre. Cogí la escoba y cerré los ojos mientras los papelitos iban cayendo hacia abajo, despacio y sin control. Con los párpados apretados repetí los nombres que había grabados en el mango. Las llamé, convoqué a todas y cada una de las brujas cuyo nombre estaba tallado en el mango de la escoba y les pedí que me ayudaran. Si había funcionado con Azucena, si mi deseo de que barriese un desierto se había cumplido en cierto modo, ahora, con la ayuda de ellas, pensé, tal vez conseguiría alejar a aquel ser de mí para siempre. Cuando abrí los ojos vi que los papelitos iban convirtiéndose en pequeñas mariposas de colores que revoloteaban a su antojo, como si terminasen de abandonar el capullo y apenas hiciera un segundo que hubiesen tomado contacto con su nueva vida. El espectáculo era tan hermoso que, por unos momentos, me olvidé del nigromante y seguí su maravilloso, vital e irregular vuelo de arriba abajo. Así fue hasta que las mariposas comenzaron a descender. Una a una, fueron cayendo sobre los pies del nigromante y, al rozar los zapatos de este, perdían el vívido colorido de sus alas y se convertían en mariposas negras que morían en el mismo instante en que lo alcanzaban. Horrorizada por la imagen, aparté la vista.

—Creo que no es buena idea que tires el confeti a la calle —dijo Alán desde la ventana del dormitorio.

—Solo ha sido un puñado, me apetecía ver cómo volaban los papelitos de colores —le respondí, y me retiré de la barandilla.

—Digas lo que digas, estás rarísima. Hazme un favor: déjalo todo y acuéstate. Son las cuatro de la madrugada.

—Prefiero recoger ahora —le respondí mientras tomaba la escoba.

—Como quieras —dijo. Se retiró de la ventana y apagó la luz del dormitorio.

Cogí la escoba y la cimbreé en el aire, evitando así que las cerdas dieran en el suelo y pudieran quebrarse con el roce del piso. El confeti se elevó con el aire que la escoba levantaba. Miré hacia la terraza de Desmond y pensé que él sí entendería aquel baile de colores, tan lleno de vida. Cuánto te echo en falta, pensé. Incliné la cabeza al ver que uno de los papelitos caía sobre mis pies. No parecía pertenecer al confeti. Era blanco y estaba muy bien doblado. Me agaché. Lo recogí y lo desplegué. En su interior había un texto:

No digas tonterías, escocesa, tú no me echas de menos, no me extrañas. Ni siquiera me quieres un poco, al menos no como siempre te he querido y te querré yo a ti.

Las manos me temblaron al leer el contenido, y el papel, como si tuviese vida propia, vibró y se me escurrió entre los dedos. Al caer se convirtió en una mariposa blanca y brillante que voló hacia la calle. Volví a la barandilla para poder seguir su vuelo. Aleteó durante unos segundos frente a mí y, finalmente, descendió en picado. Cayó sobre los pies del nigromante como si fuese un avioncito de papel con una plomada incrustada en su morro. Golpeó con tanta fuerza los zapatos del nigromante que pensé que se había clavado en ellos. Como había sucedido antes con las mariposas de colores, esta también perdió su color y se convirtió en una mariposa negra y sin rastro de vida. Entonces comprendí lo que había sucedido. Al lanzar

el confeti por la terraza estaba pensando en Desmond y no en el nigromante. Mis sentimientos me habían traicionado.

—Aunque ya tengas escoba, sigues siendo una novata, una bruja torpe y demasiado sentimental. Esa parte tuya de mortal, tus sentimientos humanos, terminarán por destruir lo poco que se salvó de ti —gritó el nigromante mirando hacia la terraza.

Después le dio una patada a las mariposas, que volvieron a convertirse en confeti, y se alejó soltando unas estruendosas carcajadas.

Capítulo 7

Alán tenía previsto marcharse dos días después a una concentración de *area manager* que la empresa organizaba semestralmente en Holanda, la sede central en Europa. Por la mañana, antes de salir a trabajar, me dijo que estaría fuera una semana. Solía asistir solo, sin que nadie del personal lo acompañase, pero esta vez no fue así. Podía haber dejado a Azucena supliéndolo en sus funciones. Ella era la *store manager* de la tienda en la que se ubicaban las oficinas, la más adecuada y quien siempre lo había sustituido cuando él estaba fuera, pero en este viaje se la llevó con él. Tal vez era para que le sujetara el maletín durante el trayecto, le organizase los folios del programa, o comprase los tulipanes para el centro de las mesas, me dije enrabietada, porque no podía imaginarla haciendo algo diferente a su lado y, sobre todo, porque sabía que aquel viaje no era solo de trabajo.

Azucena quiso asegurarse de que yo supiese que iba a acompañarlo, pensé cuando me llamó con la burda excusa de que Alán no le respondía al teléfono ni a los mensajes de WhatsApp:

—Diana, perdona que te moleste. Soy Azucena. Estoy intentando localizar a Alán. Te llamo porque he visto que nuestro vuelo llegará media hora después de la primera reunión y creo que... —Se interrumpió. Cambió el tono de voz y en un inglés de acento exagerado, exclamó—: *Houston, Houston, we have a problem.* —Dejó escapar una carcajada hiposa y aguda.

—Creo que solo lo dijeron una vez —respondí seca y tajante, sin reírle la gracia.

—Una vez, ¿el qué dijeron una vez? —preguntó, desconcertada.

—Houston.

—Ah, no sé. Si tú lo dices, seguro que fue así. ¿Podrías pasarme con Alán? ¡Por favor! —me pidió ya en un tono más distante.

—¿Cómo es que tienes mi número de móvil? —le pregunté.

—Bueno, ya sabes, siempre hay un número en las fichas personales para temas urgentes y tu número está en la de Alán. Lo tengo apuntado en la memoria del móvil de la tienda desde hace tiempo. Espero no haberte molestado. Necesito saber si tengo que pedir a los de servicios centrales que nos cambien el vuelo.

—No estoy en casa, me pillas en el trabajo. ¿No está Alán en la tienda, contigo?

—Bueno, yo sí estoy en la tienda, pero Alán salió hace una hora y no ha vuelto. Pensé que habría ido a casa, contigo. Volveré a llamarlo. Por favor, no le digas que te he llamado o me matará.

—Ni te preocupes, de mi boca no saldrá ni un «Houston» — respondí con un deje de burla.

«Imbécil», pensé al separar el teléfono de mi oreja, y miré el aparato como si ella aún estuviera al otro lado de la línea y pudiera verme y oírme. Alán aún no me había comentado nada sobre sus intenciones de llevar a Azucena con él y era evidente que ella lo sabía; de no ser así, no me habría hecho aquella llamada. Jessica Rabbit comenzaba a reivindicar su sitio junto a mi novio, a hacerme saber que estaba ahí y que no me olvidase de que lucharía por él con uñas y dientes. A medida que pasaba el tiempo daba muestras de sentirse más segura, pero estaba equivocada: sus pretensiones se tambaleaban, pendían de un hilo porque yo jugaba con ventaja. De habérmelo propuesto, podría haber sembrado su camino de obstáculos. Peor aún, podría hacer que su historia se quedase en un limbo, repitiéndose una y otra vez, con situaciones y acontecimientos

diferentes, pero instaurada en una pausa eterna, tal y como me había explicado Claudia la noche anterior. Azucena desconocía mis sentimientos, que en aquel momento no tenían nada que ver con lo que sucedió en otro tiempo. Yo ya había llorado la pérdida de Alán, su engaño, y por eso mismo su idilio ya no me hacía daño. Lo que realmente me importunaba y lastimaba era su impertinencia, su falta de respeto hacia mí. Me moría por soltarle un sopapo verbal que le aclarase quién era yo en realidad, el poder que poseía en aquel momento sobre su vida y su futuro, pero no podía hacerlo. Todo acto tiene sus consecuencias y las que se desencadenarían después de mi reacción, de mostrar mi supremacía ante ella, serían catastróficas también para mí e innecesarias para todos. Incluso para ella, porque su único pecado era haberse enamorado como una tonta de Alán. Era tan humana e imperfecta como todos, me dije. Y me sorprendí al sentir cierta empatía por ella, una pizca de pena y compasión.

Aquel día solicité salir dos horas antes del trabajo. Tenía que recoger todo lo que había dejado sin ordenar después de la fiesta. Tras mi escapada al dormitorio después de escuchar las carcajadas del nigromante, el ático parecía una casa abandonada a toda prisa. Alán no solía colaborar en las tareas domésticas. Trabajaba más horas que yo y los días libres, cuando no salíamos fuera de casa, los dedicaba a ver series, películas, deportes o a dormitar en el sofá. En realidad, yo tenía la culpa de que todo lo relacionado con el mantenimiento de la casa recayera casi por completo en mí. Yo se lo había permitido. Y él se acostumbró a tener todo hecho, a que yo me moviese de un lado a otro mientras él escuchaba música o daba cabezazos. Para él ninguna de aquellas tareas era importante y todas podían esperar. Y, en cierto modo, tenía razón, pero yo no podía vivir rodeada de desorden y polvo, con el cesto de la ropa llena o el lavaplatos a reventar.

Mientras limpiaba y ordenaba esperé oír algún movimiento en la casa de Desmond y Ecles, pero al parecer no estaban en el

domicilio. Al anochecer, con el ático ya ordenado, bajé las bolsas de basura a la calle.

—Tú debes de ser la nueva vecina de Desmond, la escocesa —me dijo Amaya, que estaba depositando unas cajas vacías en el contenedor del cartón—. Él me comentó que también te gustan los temas de brujería. Soy la hija del dueño —dijo. Se dio la vuelta y señaló la floristería—. Me llamo Amaya.

—Diana —le respondí.

—Desmond es mi amigo. Me presta libros antiguos que hablan de remedios hechos con plantas. Algunos siguen creyendo que esos preparados son pócimas, pero en realidad son simple botica. De verdad que es un verdadero privilegio acceder a esos textos, y también que Desmond te los haya prestado. No se los deja a nadie, bueno..., a mí sí —explicó sonriendo con cierto aire de superioridad.

—Qué suerte, debes de estar contenta —le respondí, haciéndome la distraída.

Pisé el pedal del contendor de la basura para abrirlo e introduje las bolsas dentro. Ella siguió hablando, ajena a mi desapego:

—¿Cuáles te ha dejado?

—No sé, aún no los he hojeado.

—Pues te diré un secreto: esos libros tienen dos lecturas —explicó, y me guiñó un ojo al decirlo—. Míralos con detenimiento. Tenerlos, poder leerlos, es una gran oportunidad.

—¡Diana! —gritó Elda desde la entrada del portal, interrumpiendo nuestra conversación—. ¿Cómo va tu mano?

—Mejor, Elda. Ahora parece un rasguño —le respondí acercándome a la calzada.

—¿Vienes?, quiero comentarte algo.

—Sí, espera un segundo —le dije. Me di la vuelta para despedirme de Amaya, que estaba apagando las luces interiores de la tienda—. ¡Lo siento! —me disculpé, apostada en la puerta—. ¿Qué decías sobre la lectura de los libros?

—¿Qué te pasó en la mano? —me preguntó ella sin responder a mi pregunta.

—Ah, nada de importancia. —Me clavé una astilla de la puerta de El desván —señalé la tienda de Claudia y le mostré el pequeño apósito que aún llevaba en la mano—. Fue cuando los cristales de tu floristería estallaron. Con la explosión, me apoyé en la puerta. Se ve que deslicé la mano y se me clavó un trocito de madera.

—Ah, sí, la explosión. Menos mal que nadie resultó herido. No sabemos cómo pasó, pero ocurren tantas cosas que no tienen explicación que mi padre ha decidido no darle vueltas. A fin de cuentas, el seguro ha cubierto los desperfectos.

—¿Vienes? —insistió Elda desde el portal.

—No te entretengas, o la Dama Blanca se enfadará —me dijo Amaya, refiriéndose a Elda.

Ella la miró fijamente y frunció el ceño, como si hubiese oído sus palabras. Y lo más probable es que así fuera. Elda tenía un oído muy fino, recordé con una sonrisa no exenta de cierta tristeza al pensar en todo lo que me había contado cuando nos conocimos, en la otra realidad.

Crucé la calle acompañada del sonido estridente que produjo la persiana de la floristería cuando Amaya tiró de ella hacia abajo.

—No me gusta Amaya. En cambio su padre me parece un buen hombre —me comentó Elda cuando estuve a su lado—. Ya le he dicho a Desmond que esa chica no es de fiar, pero él no me hace ni caso. Piensa que estoy celosa, ¡ya ves!

—¿Y lo estás? —le pregunté sonriendo.

—Por favor, Diana —dijo mirándome de frente. Movió la cabeza, frunció el ceño y encogió su pequeña nariz en un gesto de incredulidad—. ¡Pues claro que no! Adoro a Desmond y a Ecles. Pero esa criatura no me inspira confianza. Intento protegerlos, pero ellos, los dos, se sienten atraídos por la Flor de Loto. Algunas deben

51

de tener música en las nalgas, porque no lo entiendo. —Al decirlo se contoneó con tanta gracia que se me escapó una carcajada.

—Sí, ha de ser eso —le dije, recordando a Azucena.

—Yo soy bajita y poco agraciada, pero ella es diminuta, tan blanca que me recuerda a las lechadas que se dan en los suelos de las casas para blanquear las juntas de las baldosas. Es tan minúscula y extraña que parece haber escapado de la Tierra Media. Cuando la miro no puedo evitar recordar la Comarca, donde viven los Bolsón en la historia de *El Señor de los Anillos*. No sé lo que quiere, pero tengo claro que anda detrás de algo, y no es precisamente lo mismo que Desmond o Ecles buscan en ella.

—Bueno, igual es un exceso de celo por tu parte —apunté.

—Puede que tengas razón, a veces queremos proteger tanto a nuestros seres queridos que es contraproducente —concluyó pensativa. Volvió la cabeza y la miró.

Amaya se despidió de nosotras levantando la mano izquierda. En su anular llevaba una sortija. Tenía engarzada una piedra lisa y roja, del mismo rojo que el cuenco que se formó con el líquido que encontré en mi casa, igual al péndulo del llavero de Desmond, idéntico a la tinta de aquel bolígrafo que el nigromante me ofreció. La vi porque resplandecía en la oscuridad como un faro en la costa, emitiendo destellos que iban y venían, apagándose y encendiéndose en la oscuridad que ya había tomado la calle.

Capítulo 8

En este punto fui plenamente consciente de que los acontecimientos extraños se iban sucediendo con mayor frecuencia. Parecían ir enlazados, como si fuesen eslabones de una misma cadena de sucesos que condujeran a un mismo fin. Un sentido y un desenlace que yo aún no conseguía vislumbrar. Con cada uno de ellos se generaban nuevas incógnitas, espacios en blanco, interrogantes y una sensación de soledad que se adhería a mi piel cada vez con más fuerza, porque no podía compartir con nadie lo que me sucedía. En aquellos momentos, la magia tenía la misma relevancia en mi vida que los acontecimientos cotidianos, pensé mirando a Elda mientras ella expresaba su opinión sobre Amaya.

A mí, la joven florista también me incomodaba. Había algo en ella que no encajaba, que chirriaba. Era demasiado perfecta para ser real, me dije sin dejar de observar los destellos del anillo, que desaparecieron cuando se paró frente a la entrada del metro e introdujo la mano en el bolso.

—Tampoco te hace gracia, ¿verdad? —me preguntó Elda al ver que no le quitaba la vista de encima a Amaya.

—Es extraña. Parece un personaje literario. Un ser creado en otro lugar. Demasiado perfecta, aunque he de reconocer que tiene su aquel. A los hombres les gustan las mujeres como ella, de apariencia frágil. Eso les hace sentirse más varoniles, más fuertes de lo que

realmente son. Tal vez por eso Flor de Loto tiene tanto éxito con Desmond y Ecles —le respondí sin retirar la vista de Amaya.

—Sí, tiene el aquel de *El diablo viste de Prada* —me respondió irónica Elda—. Fíate tú de las aguas mansas.

—Está claro que tienes motivos para pensar así, lo mío no es más que una sensación —repuse.

—Razones, un sexto sentido y una agudeza de oído poco común es lo que tengo. —Sonrió—. Y si a eso le añadimos una antipatía recíproca, tenemos una mezcla explosiva y perfecta para que se produzca un desaguisado en cualquier momento. Vamos, que en nuestro caso, la química solo es válida para provocar una explosión.

»Pero dejemos de hablar de ella. Si seguimos comentando y mirándola, se volverá. Te sorprendería lo que es capaz de percibir la Flor de Loto. Para mí que tiene ojos en la nuca.

—O un oído igual de fino que el tuyo —le dije sonriendo.

Y en ese instante, tal y como terminaba de predecir Elda, Amaya se dio la vuelta y nos miró fijamente, como si estuviera escuchándonos o hubiese captado nuestras miradas clavadas en su espalda. Elda se agachó y me dio un puntapié indicándome que entrásemos en el portal.

—Te lo dije —susurró bajito—. Apostaría cualquier cosa a que nos ha oído.

—No digas tonterías, ha sido una coincidencia. Parece que ha olvidado algo —expuse ya dentro del portal y con la puerta cerrada, lejos de la mirada de la florista.

—Si tú lo dices... —dijo Elda, irónica—. ¿Quieres tomar algo? Aprovecha, hice la compra ayer y tengo la nevera llena. Traje unas cervezas de esas nuevas que según dicen son artesanales. No sé qué tendrá de cierto, pero están buenísimas.

—Vale, pero nos las tomamos en casa. Así ves cómo ha quedado el ático.

—No creo que a tu chico le guste mucho verme por ahí. Ayer parecía incómodo. Ni siquiera se molestó en disimular que no le caigo bien.

—Alán no está, y siendo la hora que es, no creo que venga a cenar —le dije, mirando el reloj de mi teléfono móvil.

Elda aceptó mi invitación y subió unos minutos después. Trajo dos cervezas y al abrir la puerta me regaló una amplia sonrisa que iluminó su mirada. Cuando la vi bajo el dintel sentí como si el tiempo hubiese dado marcha atrás, como si al fin nuestros caminos se uniesen de nuevo. Su peculiar olor a pintura fresca recorrió el piso y, al notarlo, sentí ganas de llorar.

—Dime, ¿desde cuándo te pasa lo de los pétalos de rosa? —me preguntó al tiempo que levantaba varios del suelo.

—Desde siempre —le respondí, inquieta.

—Sabía que eras tan peculiar como nosotros, si no más; lo supe desde que te vi. Si no fuese así, no habrías llegado a nuestro edificio. Aquí todos somos diferentes al común de los mortales. Lo somos en nuestro físico y en nuestras percepciones. Antonio nos llama «disidentes de la realidad» y, aunque se niegue a admitirlo, él es uno más. Es como nosotros. Y tu gatito egipcio también —dijo mientras señalaba a *Senatón*, que dormía dentro de la gaveta—. Claudia tenía uno muy parecido, solo que el suyo era una hembra. Se fue el mismo día que ella nos dejó. Es una lástima que Claudia no esté aquí, habría hecho unos rosarios maravillosos con tus lágrimas —dijo dejando caer los pétalos.

Todo sucedió como la vez anterior, como la primera vez que hablamos. Me relató su encierro, cómo la encontraron y a qué se debía aquella extraordinaria capacidad suya para captar casi cualquier sonido. Quedamos en que la próxima ocasión repetiríamos en su casa, porque en la mía ella se sentía incómoda solo de pensar que Alán podía aparecer en cualquier momento. Él era diferente y no la

aceptaría, hiciera lo que hiciera, me dijo convencida, aunque con cierto apuro por cómo podía sentarme su comentario.

—Hay personas con las que jamás congeniaremos. Sé que tu novio y yo nunca nos llevaremos bien. Espero que eso no sea un obstáculo para que nuestra amistad se mantenga —me confesó mientras se levantaba—. Tengo que irme, tu chico está al llegar.

—Elda, no tienes que marcharte —le dije—. La casa es de los dos, no es solo de Alán. Además, él debe respetar a mis amistades como yo lo hago con las suyas.

—Bueno, tú tampoco respetas a todos sus amigos —contestó.

Supe que su comentario se refería a Azucena, pero no quise hablar del tema ni preguntarle cómo lo sabía. Me pareció obvio. Era evidente que había oído alguna de las discusiones que Alán y yo habíamos tenido sobre Jessica Rabbit.

—Estaré una semana sola. Alán se marcha de viaje. Podríamos quedar en esos días, así estarás más cómoda.

—Pues entonces vamos hablando. Veo que *Senatón* se ha hecho con la gaveta de Ecles. Cuando tengas que devolvérsela tu gatito lo pasará mal. Habrá que decirle a Ecles que te la regale.

—Ya me la regaló —le dije sonriendo.

—Es un cajón precioso, aunque era aún más bonito cuando lo encontraron. Tenía una piedra roja aquí —dijo, agachándose. Le dio la vuelta al cajón y señaló el hueco donde, tiempo atrás, yo había colocado el colgante que me regaló Alán—. Pero Ecles se empeñó en quitarla. No sé qué habrá hecho con ella, pero, sea lo que sea, seguro que será acertado. No todo lo que nos parece hermoso es bueno. La vista, como solía decir Claudia, suele engañarnos —concluyó mientras se erguía antes de dirigirse a la puerta.

¿Cómo no me había dado cuenta de que el pentagrama ya no estaba en la gaveta?, me pregunté mientras la despedía.

Alán llegó a los pocos minutos de marcharse Elda. Justo cuando él abría la puerta, oí el ruido de las persianas de Ecles y Desmond.

Después capté las notas de «Lost On You», interpretada por Laura Pergolizzi, una de mis canciones favoritas. Salí a la terraza. Desmond estaba en su salón, con la luz encendida y de pie junto al aparato de música. Como si hubiese notado mi presencia, se dio la vuelta, me miró, me guiñó un ojo y movió los labios sin emitir sonido alguno. Pero yo leí lo que decía: «Es para ti».

Me dio la espalda en el mismo instante en que Alán, detrás de mí, me recriminaba que aún estuviera esperándole:

—Cómo es que aún estás levantada. ¿No leíste mi *whatsapp*? Te dije que llegaría tarde.

—Tienes un pelo rojo en la camisa —le respondí, retirándolo—. ¡Qué tontería más tonta! Pensaba que hoy en día nadie se olvidaría de sacudir la ropa y borrar los mensajes del móvil —comenté con el pelo entre los dedos, mostrándoselo—. Claro que, al ser las dos pelirrojas, lo mismo has pensado que su cabello se podía confundir con el mío. Pues, querido, debo decirte que no has tenido en cuenta que hay evidentes diferencias en el tono.

No me respondió, se dio la vuelta y salió a la terraza.

—¿Podrías bajar la música? A estas horas todo el mundo está durmiendo —dijo dirigiéndose a Desmond.

—Castelar, no todos duermen, los vampiros tenemos horarios diferentes —respondió nuestro vecino, irónico.

CAPÍTULO 9

Cuando leí en los labios de Desmond «es para ti», refiriéndose a la canción que sonaba en el interior de su casa, volví a sentirme viva, como si recobrara la sensación de vitalidad y optimismo que había tenido junto a Alán durante los primeros meses de nuestra relación. Esa que transformaba la brisa en viento y desbocaba mis emociones, que me hacía sentirme deseada y, al tiempo, desearle. Que convertía cada día en una nueva experiencia, única e irrepetible. Que hacía del futuro algo deseado y no temido, que desdibujó el gris de nuestra vida y la pintó de colores intensos. La misma que le dio a nuestros labios una sonrisa tan tonta como bella y permanente. La que empapó nuestros ojos del brillo inconfundible que tiene la mirada del que está loca e irresponsablemente enamorado. Al sentir sus ojos puestos en los míos, el deseo resbaló por mi piel, y mis pensamientos se fueron junto a él sin que pudiese controlarlos.

Cuando Desmond y yo hablamos por primera vez en la otra realidad, cuando me pidió que lo llevara a volar en mi ala delta, ya me había embargado una atracción inexplicable, una necesidad irracional de abrazarme a él y de que me besara. Había sentido que quería volar junto a él y escapar de la situación que estaba viviendo. Sin embargo, en ese momento, cuando su voz, el tono de sus palabras me rozaron por dentro, me negué a mí misma que aquello estuviera sucediéndome otra vez, en el nuevo presente que estaba viviendo.

No podía volver a enamorarme, me dije, y menos de la forma en que lo estaba haciendo: tan rápido y de alguien a quien no conocía. Sin embargo, y a pesar de mis recelos, su presencia dejaba en mí una impronta que me agitaba por dentro, que no podía controlar y que cada vez me costaba más disimular.

Desmond me atraía con mucha más fuerza y pasión de lo que Alán había hecho, pero lo que sentía por él me resultaba añejo, como si la atracción que, en apariencia, sentíamos el uno por el otro ya hubiera existido y hubiese muerto súbitamente, sin un motivo y sin avisar. Aquel presentimiento me advertía de que los sentimientos que Desmond despertaba en mí no estaban exentos de peligro, y que tal vez nuestra historia, de darse, no tendría un final feliz. Y ello, el augurio inconcreto y aciago que sentía, me distanciaba de él y me impedía dejarme llevar; sentir a su lado. Aquel presentimiento era lo que en realidad temía y lo que me frenaba.

Desmond respondió al requerimiento que le hizo Alán para que bajase el volumen de la música cogiendo una copa de vino, que levantó en el momento en que la letra de la canción llegó al estribillo: «Levantemos una copa o dos por todas las cosas que he perdido de ti... Dime, ¿están perdidas en ti?». Me miró fijamente al tiempo que lo tarareaba. A punto estuve de decirle: «No, aún siguen ahí, esperándote». Porque eso fue lo que sentí y pensé, lo que resonó en mis pensamientos como un eco lejano.

De pronto, ante la mirada de estupor de Alán, Desmond señaló el firmamento, indicando el rastro que dejaba una estrella fugaz. Su luz trazó una línea violeta, desigual y efímera, que embelleció el oscuro cielo de la ciudad. Miré a Desmond.

—Ella es como tú, escocesa, no hay forma de darle caza —susurró. Aunque habló en tono muy bajo, yo lo oí como si estuviese pegado a mí, pese a la distancia que nos separaba.

Y fue en ese momento cuando dejé de ver mi terraza, a Alán y a Desmond en su casa. Abandoné el ático. Sin saber cómo me

encontré en brazos de Desmond. Estábamos en la misma cama, desnudos y llorando. Él limpiaba con la yema de sus dedos las lágrimas que me resbalaban por las mejillas, mientras yo hacía lo mismo con las suyas. Nos hallábamos en un lugar que no reconocí, en el que juraría que jamás había estado, ni con él ni con nadie. Lo miré buscando en sus ojos una respuesta a lo que sucedía, pero solo vi que él se preguntaba lo mismo que yo. Nos amábamos, tal vez demasiado, y por ello nuestro amor nos estaba haciendo daño a los dos, pensé. Porque siempre, hiciésemos lo que hiciésemos, terminaríamos lejos el uno del otro.

***

Me desperté rodeada de pétalos de rosa rojos, que cubrían parte de la almohada y de la colcha. «He debido de llorar durante el sueño», me dije. Me desarropé y, al hacerlo, algunos cayeron al suelo. En cuanto tomaron contacto con el piso, se transformaron en pequeñas bolas de cristal rojo, tan brillantes y hermosas que parecían rubís. *Senatón,* que permanecía a los pies de la cama, dormitando, oyó el sonido de los cristales caer uno tras otro, como si fuesen las cuentas desprendidas de un collar, dio un salto y, entusiasmado, comenzó a jugar con ellas. Daba brincos detrás de las que rebotaban y arrastraba con sus manitas, de un lado a otro, las que ya estaban en el piso.

Durante unos segundos intenté recordar lo que había sucedido aquella noche, después de que Alán tuviese la refriega con Desmond a cuenta del volumen de la música, pero no lo conseguí. No supe cómo llegué a la cama, ni si Alán y yo mantuvimos conversación alguna sobre su marcha a Holanda al día siguiente. Solo recordaba el contacto de la piel de Desmond con la mía, sus lágrimas y aquella manera tan especial e íntima de mirarme, teñida de dolor y de un padecimiento tan profundo que parecía no poder paliar con nada;

como si este fuese inevitable, imperecedero, casi inmortal. Eterno, pensé, volviendo a recordar cómo me miraba, y me encogí sobre mí misma. Así, agazapada bajo las sábanas, permanecí unos minutos, oyendo los derrapes de *Senatón* sobre el suelo y el ruido de las bolas de cristal rodando.

Me incorporé tras escuchar el sonido insistente del teléfono móvil. Era Samanta.

—Nena, ¿estás bien? —me preguntó, alarmada, al otro lado de la línea telefónica.

—Sí, claro. Acabo de despertarme. ¿Por qué iba a estar mal? —dije, desconcertada por su pregunta.

—Te llamé ayer por la noche y no respondiste ni contestaste los mensajes de WhatsApp. Hoy he telefoneado a Alán, pero por lo visto su terminal está apagada o fuera de cobertura. En la oficina me han dicho que ayer y hoy no has ido a trabajar.

Miré el teléfono para ver la hora. Eran las dos de la tarde y un día después del que yo creía que era al despertarme.

—Te llamo en unos minutos —le dije, y colgué sin darle tiempo a que añadiese nada más.

Consulté los mensajes del teléfono. Samanta tenía razón, había llamado y había dejado varios *whatsapps*. También tenía una llamada del trabajo. En el buzón de voz habían dejado un mensaje en el que me pedían que me pusiese en contacto con ellos lo antes posible. Y había un *whatsapp* de Alán, del día anterior, en el que daba por hecho que no había contestado porque aún seguiría dormida. Comentaba que el vuelo había llegado bien y que me telefonearía cuando tuviera un momento libre, pero que no me preocupase si no lo hacía porque tenía una agenda muy apretada.

Como era de esperar, Samanta no me hizo caso y volvió a llamar.

—Sé que me estás ocultando algo. De no ser así no me habrías colgado como lo has hecho.

—Samanta, estoy desorientada, nada más. He debido de quedarme dormida. Te he colgado para llamar a la oficina. No están las cosas para andarse con chiquitas. Si me despiden no sé qué voy a hacer, porque tampoco estoy muy bien con Alán. Lo nuestro no funciona y si a la crisis que tenemos se le añaden problemas económicos, vamos listos —le dije, omitiendo mi pérdida de memoria.

—Entonces seguís igual de mal que cuando me marché —dijo, consternada—. Te conozco, Diana, tienes voz de haber estado toda la noche llorando a moco tendido. Dime, ¿qué ha hecho Alán para que estés así?

—No es lo que Alán haga o deje de hacer. Eso ya no me importa. Ahora está más pendiente de mí que hace unos meses, es como si se hubiese tragado a Cupido, cada poco me recuerda lo mucho que le importo.

—Entonces, ¿qué sucede?

—Su presencia me incomoda. He perdido las ganas, Samanta, y además sé que está liado con una compañera de trabajo. Ahora están los dos en Holanda.

—Te dije que no te mudases, que vivir juntos era un riesgo. La monotonía es como una hiena hambrienta, se come hasta las ganas de vivir. Aparte de eso, sois muy diferentes. Lo suyo son fuegos artificiales, llenos de colores maravillosos, pero fugaces como la llama de una cerilla. Lo tuyo, en cambio, son estrellas que siempre están ahí, en el cielo, esperando eternamente a ser contadas.

—Esperando a ser contadas —repetí después de que Samanta lo dijera. Lo hice como si estuviera recordando sus palabras en vez de estar hablando con ella. Y en ese momento recordé a Desmond; la música y su pregunta, la pregunta de la canción: «¿Están perdidas en ti?». Y lo vi señalando la estrella fugaz.

Cerré los ojos y deseé estar con él. Y fue entonces cuando comprendí lo que había sucedido: mi deseo se había cumplido. No

importaba si lo había soñado, si había sucedido realmente, me dije. Lo importante es que había estado con él, con Desmond.

—¿Sigues ahí? —inquirió Samanta al ver que yo no respondía.

—Sí, sí. Estaba pensando en lo que has dicho.

—¿En lo de contar estrellas o en lo de la monotonía?

—En ambas cosas. Espero que algún día alguien me invite a contar estrellas —le dije, recordando cuando Desmond, en nuestro primer encuentro, en aquel tiempo que se fue, me ofreció contar estrellas en su DeLorean.

—No creas que eso es fácil. Por lo general, los hombres evitan ser románticos, porque cuando se ponen sentimentales pierden caché y les bajan los índices de testosterona. Y ya sabes lo importante que es eso para ellos. Yo no sé qué prefiero, si un tipo con el nivel de testosterona por las nubes o que me regalen el certificado de una estrella con mi nombre. Creo que al final la testosterona resulta más rentable. —Se rio y yo no pude reprimir una carcajada.

—Ay, nena, tú nunca cambiarás. Si te oyese alguien que no te conociera, pensaría que les tienes manía, cuando es todo lo contrario.

—No nos engañemos, los hombres son como los bombones, apetecibles, adictivos y engordan. Incluso el mío, que se sale de la norma; desde que guisa para mí, ha conseguido que los vaqueros me queden un poco más estrechos. Pero es lo que hay..., no podemos vivir sin ellos.

»Podrías venir unos días —me propuso—. Así conocerías a mi chico y le escucharías cantar versionando a Freddie Mercury. Desafina como un condenado, pero... ¡es tan sexi! Y se parece tanto a él que a veces le digo que en realidad no estoy enamorada de él, sino del espíritu de Mercury.

—Sabes que nada me gustaría más que abrazarte y, por supuesto, conocer a tu chico, pero por ahora no puedo permitírmelo. Además,

tengo demasiados temas pendientes que debo solucionar. El más importante es mi relación con Alán —le dije.

—¿Has vuelto a volar? —me preguntó.

—No he desplegado la vela desde que te fuiste. La tenemos en la terraza del ático, apoyada en un lateral, como un pájaro malherido... Charlamos durante unos minutos más. Me contó cómo iba la excavación y me hizo prometerle que la llamaría en cualquier momento si necesitaba hablar, si la soledad, la angustia o la monotonía amenazaban con vencerme. Se lo prometí, aunque sabía que no estaba diciéndole la verdad. Si aquello llegaba a ocurrir, la telefonearía solo cuando se me hubiese pasado la pena. No quería enturbiar su felicidad, que en cierto modo también era la mía, porque quería a Samanta con toda mi alma.

Después de llamar a la oficina y de justificar mi ausencia de ese día y del anterior diciendo que había sufrido un repentino cólico, revisé la casa. En apariencia, todo era normal. Mi ropa permanecía en la silla, donde la dejaba preparada todas las noches para ponérmela al día siguiente. Supuse que cuando el día anterior Alán se había marchado al aeropuerto yo estaba dormida, y así permanecí aquellas veinticuatro horas, sumida en un profundo sueño. Aquella conjetura era la más lógica, la más real y probable para cualquiera... excepto para mí. Recogí un puñado de pétalos rojos que aún estaban sobre la cama y, mientras los dejaba caer de nuevo sobre la colcha, sonreí pensando que durante ese tiempo no había estado dormida, sino que había habitado otra realidad, y lo había hecho junto a Desmond.

Capítulo 10

Al día siguiente me invitaron a marcharme del trabajo. Al salir de la oficina, pensé que era como si después de la marcha de Alán a Holanda, los acontecimientos se precipitasen uno tras otro, como si todo me condujese irremediablemente a volver sobre las circunstancias, los hechos y el presente que había dejado atrás al colocar la piedra en la gaveta. Mientras caminaba sosteniendo la caja que contenía mis objetos personales, mis compañeros se despidieron de mí, unos con abrazos, otros estrechándome la mano, y los menos dándome dos besos en las mejillas. Escuché todos los tópicos: «Te llamo», «Nos vemos», «Si me necesitas, ya sabes dónde estoy», «Hablamos pronto», «A ver si organizamos algo para vernos todos», «Son unos impresentables», «Seguro que encontrarás algo mejor que este trabajo, por llamarlo de alguna forma, no te desanimes»... Y entre aquellas palabras de despedida también se colaron algunos cuchicheos. Procedían de los de siempre, de los que se creen herederos de la empresa, de los que se sienten imprescindibles en ella y tarde o temprano terminan de patitas en la calle, con un finiquito más abultado, pero sin los honores a los que creían tener derecho.

Caminé por las calles de la ciudad en aquella mañana soleada y calurosa de agosto sin saber adónde ir. Me perdí entre el gentío. Sentí la alegría que mostraban los rostros de algunos y la estúpida prisa que impregnaba la ciudad, que empujaba los pasos de

sus habitantes, convirtiendo su caminar en una incansable y estéril carrera contra el tiempo. Por primera vez en mi vida me sentí libre, fuera de todo aquel engranaje. Y decidí vivir, solo vivir, aunque únicamente fuese por un día. Me olvidé de Alán, del pasado, de lo que pudiera acontecer entre nosotros, del trabajo, de las facturas, del día siguiente y de cómo serían los que vendrían después. Tomé el metro en la estación de Cuatro Caminos y me bajé en Gran Vía. Al apearme, dejé en el asiento la caja con todos mis objetos personales, excepto las fotografías de mis vuelos, de los lugares que había recorrido con mi ala delta. Durante muchos meses, aquellas fotos me habían permitido seguir soñando, de modo que me las llevé conmigo. En el último instante oí la voz de un pasajero indicándome que me olvidaba la caja, pero no me volví. Lo que había en ella había dejado de formar parte de mi vida; no lo necesitaba ni lo quería.

Caminé por la acera derecha de la gran avenida contemplando la vida que se abría paso alrededor. Los niños que intentaban soltarse de la mano de sus padres, los grupos de turistas fotografiando cada rincón de la ciudad, los gorriones haciéndose con las migajas que caían al suelo desde las mesas de las terrazas de los bares, las sonrisas de los empleados de los comercios, agotados, exhaustos pero amables, deseosos de una ración de sol y libertad. Los policías, las meretrices, los ladrones de guante blanco, los mendigos y los profetas que lanzaban su perorata en cualquier esquina.

Delante de mí caminaba un hombre que vestía sotana negra. Se paró de repente, levantó la cabeza y apuntó con un dedo un inmueble entre la Gran Vía y la calle Alcalá. Señalaba la cúpula del edificio Metrópolis, donde se alzaba la figura de un ángel a punto de levantar el vuelo. Yo lo había visto cientos de veces, tan inmóvil como bello, pero esa mañana, al mirarlo siguiendo la indicación del clérigo, percibí algo diferente. Atisbé un leve movimiento en sus alas que me pareció tan hermoso y frágil como irreal. A lo mejor ese

movimiento es un efecto óptico debido a la posición que el sacerdote y yo tenemos bajo el edificio, pensé restregándome los ojos.

—A él le sucede lo mismo que a usted: quiere volar pero no puede hacerlo —me dijo el sacerdote cerca de la oreja.

Bajé la cabeza sorprendida, dispuesta a dirigirme a él y preguntarle por qué me decía aquello, si no me conocía de nada. Pero el cura se dio la vuelta y comenzó a andar alejándose de mí. Seguí sus pasos durante unos minutos, pero el hombre no tardó en perderse entre la gente que caminaba por la acera.

En aquel momento, si mi ala delta hubiese estado en el club de vuelo, habría tomado un taxi y me habría ido a volar, pero no era así. Se hallaba en el ático de la terraza, desmontada y con la vela roja plegada. El sacerdote tenía razón: yo quería y necesitaba volar, pero no podía. No podía hacerlo porque yo misma me había cortado las alas, había plegado el ala roja que Rigel me regaló y también las de mi alma y mi corazón.

Estuve varias horas deambulando por las calles y decidí regresar a casa cuando el sol ya se ocultaba, dejando un rastro anaranjado de su presencia en el horizonte. Lo hice sin volver a conectar mi terminal y sin dejar de pensar en las palabras del sacerdote, que daban vueltas una y otra vez en mi cabeza.

Cogí el metro y durante el trayecto me entretuve mirando las fotos que había decidido conservar. En una de ella aparecíamos Samanta y yo abrazadas bajo el Viaducto de la calle Bailén. Nos la habíamos hecho junto a sus enormes pilares, empequeñecidas por su inmensidad. Había sido en una noche de verano como aquella, en la que el cielo era raso y el calor, sofocante.

—Más bien debería llamarse el Puente de los Susurros —había dicho yo aquel día cuando nos tomamos la foto, casi pensando en voz alta.

Samanta se volvió hacia mí.

—¿De los susurros? —preguntó.

—Siempre que vengo aquí oigo un sonido que recuerda un susurro apagado, seguramente debido al tráfico. A veces el rumor del tránsito se asemeja al del mar, sobre todo cuando es constante y lejano. Pero aquí ese ruido parece producido por voces, cientos de voces que murmuran —le respondí mirando hacia arriba e intentando enmendar mi desliz.

—A veces me das miedo —me dijo, pensativa.

—Pero ¡qué inocente eres! ¿No ves que era una broma? Me refiero a los susurros, no a la semejanza del ruido con el del mar —expliqué sonriéndole.

Sé que no me creyó. Samanta conocía tan bien como yo la historia del Viaducto, que solía recibir el sobrenombre de Puente de los Suicidas, la triste historia que vestía de luto su belleza arquitectónica y que lo había empapado de despedidas tan inesperadas como dolorosas. Ella no oía los susurros, pero algo me decía que los captaba. Sé que percibió, igual que yo, la presencia que nos acompañó aquella noche, el olor a musgo y los pasos huecos que sonaban detrás de nosotras. Y creo que también vio las huellas acuosas que las pisadas del nigromante dejaron mientras nos seguía. Aquella noche fue la primera vez que lo vi. Vislumbré su sombra intentando ocultarse en la oscuridad, como si quisiera integrarse en ella para camuflarse cuando yo miraba hacia atrás buscando la procedencia del sonido de sus pasos y de aquel inconfundible olor a humedad, a panteón, flores secas y muerte que siempre lo acompañaba. Sin embargo, por entonces yo aún no sabía quién era.

Miré la foto con detenimiento. Con ella en mis manos, sonreí recordando la cena que vino después, la música *indie* que sonaba en el local de copas y el amanecer de aquel domingo en el que despertamos dentro del coche, aparcadas junto al Retiro, con una resaca añeja y pesada que nos impedía tolerar la luz del sol.

El tren se desplazaba sobre las vías mientras yo seguía con la foto en mis manos, sin apartar la vista de la imagen y sonriendo

ensimismada, rescatando recuerdos. Continué así unos minutos, hasta que vi en la instantánea su sombra alargada, el ala ancha de su sombrero y sus manos enguantadas. Estaba recostado junto al pilar, a nuestro lado. Al verlo en la fotografía, las manos me temblaron y dejé caer la foto al suelo del vagón.

—Casi la piso —me dijo un anciano. Se agachó, la recogió y me la tendió.

Le di las gracias y volví a mirarla, con más temor si cabe del que había sentido cuando vi al nigromante en ella, pero su silueta ya no aparecía en la instantánea. Fue como si su figura hubiese resbalado por el papel fotográfico hasta salir de él, porque junto a los pies del anciano, donde antes había caído la foto, aprecié una extraña mancha negra que guardaba un extraordinario parecido con la forma del nigromante. La mácula se movía, como resistiéndose a que la engullera el suelo del vagón, que se la estaba tragando poco a poco. No le quité los ojos de encima hasta que desapareció en el piso.

No sabía qué buscaba el nigromante, qué quería de mí. De lo único que estaba segura era que no dejaría de perseguirme hasta conseguir su propósito, pensé inquieta.

Me apeé del vagón y caminé sin rumbo fijo por la estación, como si aquel lugar fuese un mundo aparte que me estuviera absorbiendo. Se diría que aquel ir y venir de personas de un lugar a otro era la antesala del cambio que de nuevo daría mi vida, tan unida a los encuentros y las despedidas como aquella estación.

Nada más salir del metro, vi que los comercios habían cerrado sus puertas. El tenue brillo de las farolas alumbraba a medio gas algunos recodos de la calle y divisé la luz que se escapaba por debajo de la puerta de El desván de Aradia. Me fijé en la sombra que proyectaba alguien que iba y venía dentro del local y con su trasiego tapaba de forma intermitente la luminosidad que salía al exterior. Era evidente que en la tienda había alguien, pensé mientras me aproximaba. Detuve mis pasos al ver un rayo de luz que se

proyectaba al exterior desde dentro del establecimiento, por una rendija alargada que había en el centro de la puerta. El haz luminoso desapareció durante unos segundos y volvió a proyectarse. Alguien intentaba tapar desde dentro aquel pequeño orificio, que guardaba un parecido extraordinario con la astilla que se me había clavado en la palma el día que se produjo el estallido de los cristales de la floristería. Sin proponérmelo, busqué la aguja dentro de mi bolso. Mientras intentaba localizarla, oí un sonido que provenía del interior de la tienda, un murmullo apagado y quejicoso.

Saqué el huso del bolso y lo coloqué sobre la rendija. Al hacerlo, se acopló a la superficie como si fuese masilla, hasta que, finalmente, la hendidura desapareció por completo. Un segundo después la puerta se abrió y la luz que salió del interior me cegó. Me llevé la mano a la frente, a modo de visera, en un intento de ver quién estaba frente a mí.

—¿Antonio? —pregunté.

Capítulo 11

—¡Diana! —exclamó—. Imaginé que podrías tenerla tú —dijo pasando la yema de los dedos por la superficie de la puerta, sobre el lugar donde unos momentos antes estaba la rendija—. Te llamé por teléfono, pero lo tenías desconectado, por eso te envié varios *whatsapps*. No los viste, ¿verdad? —concluyó en tono apurado.

—No entiendo —le respondí, aún con la mano en la frente y los ojos entrecerrados.

—Pero pasa, no te quedes ahí —me pidió, extendiendo el brazo y retirándose hacia un lado para dejarme entrar—. No te imaginas qué alivio siento ahora mismo. Pensé que no iba a poder marcharme de la tienda nunca, que jamás encontraría el pedazo de madera que le faltaba a la puerta. Estaba desesperado. He intentado taparlo con todo, incluso rellenarlo con masilla para los cristales, pero la superficie repele todo tipo de material. Es como si lo escupiera y el hueco cada vez se estaba haciendo más grande. Si no hubiese recuperado esa pieza, la puerta habría terminado partiéndose por la mitad —dijo, acariciándola—. Ha sido una suerte que te hayas dejado llevar por tu sexto sentido —me comentó ya de espaldas a mí, mientras cerraba la puerta de entrada del local.

—¿A qué te refieres? —le pregunté, ya dentro del establecimiento.

—A la capacidad que tienes para interpretar los hechos extraordinarios que suceden. Me refiero a que guardaste la astilla. Este

simple hecho ya demuestra que eres excepcional. Estoy seguro que viste cómo se movía e intentaba volver a la puerta —explicó al ver que me encogía de hombros—, y ahora la has colocado en el mismo lugar del que se desprendió después de la explosión. Elda me comentó que se te clavó en la palma de la mano. Estaba indignada conmigo por las malas condiciones en que tengo esa puerta. Lo que ella no sabe es que no hay manera de arreglarla, no se deja —apuntó sonriente.

—Has visto lo que ha sucedido y... ¿te parece normal? —le pregunté, extrañada por sus palabras y el aplomo que mostraba al hablar sobre lo ocurrido.

—¡Normal! —exclamó con expresión de asombro—. Pues... depende de lo que consideres normal. ¿O no fuiste tú quien la colocó? —me preguntó con cierta inquietud al ver mi expresión de sorpresa.

—Sí, claro que sí. La puse yo.

—Entonces no sé de qué estamos hablando —dijo, encogiéndose de hombros—. ¿Me estás tomando el pelo? —preguntó con aire burlón, mirándome fijamente a los ojos.

—Bueno, estarás conmigo en que lo que ha sucedido no es muy usual, y menos aún que los dos lo veamos como algo racional. Además, jamás habría pensado que pudieras ver lo que yo veo. No me diste esa impresión las veces que hablé contigo, más bien lo contrario. Siempre me has parecido un tanto... superficial —le espeté.

—¡Usual! —exclamó, alzando el tono de voz—. Es una palabra muy ambigua, aún más lo es su significado. Ambigua y subjetiva.

»Cuando tu novio y tú visteis el ático por primera vez —continuó—, y luego vinimos a la tienda de mi madre, no dudé en comentaros algunos trucos que ella utilizaba para protegerse. Además, ¿crees que no sé quién ese indigente que deambula por aquí? Lleva merodeando por la zona desde que llegaste, y eso que no lo veía desde que mi madre se fue. Sé que ha venido contigo, detrás

de ti. No, no eres muy normal, y yo tampoco lo soy, aunque a veces represente un papel un tanto ridículo, más que nada para protegerme. Di por supuesto que ya te habrías dado cuenta de eso, pero veo que tu intuición aún está muy verde. Soy hijo de una bruja, una bruja como tú. No tengo sus poderes, pero sí he heredado parte de su percepción. Y, como tú, no lo voy pregonando a los cuatro vientos. La gente ha perdido la fe y ahora, a los que vemos más allá de su realidad nos llaman locos. No solo tenemos que protegernos de las artes oscuras, de ese personaje que sigue todos tus pasos, sino también de las personas que no creen en la magia. Todos ellos son igual de peligrosos, créeme. Diana, yo no pretendo aparentar nada que no sea; solo me protejo.

—Lo siento —me disculpé—. Me he precipitado, pero lo he hecho por el mismo motivo que tú, para protegerme. No te conozco lo suficiente. Además, llevo un día extraño. Me he quedado sin trabajo, me han despedido esta mañana, y he pasado la mayor parte del día deambulando por Madrid. No olvides que, a fin de cuentas, también somos personas atadas a unas necesidades que debemos cubrir. Lo siento —volví a disculparme.

—Bueno, pues entonces todo resuelto. Sigamos con nuestra cotidianeidad —dijo mirando su reloj de pulsera con un gesto de indiferencia—. Se me hace tarde e imagino que tú también estarás cansada después de tanto andar de acá para allá, como me has comentado —apostilló.

—Sí que lo estoy —admití.

—A pesar de la desconfianza que has mostrado, tendré siempre presente que gracias a ti la puerta ha recobrado su forma; aún está viva. Solo por eso voy a confiarte un secreto: la puerta se hizo uniendo cientos de agujas de rueca, agujas de madera que, cuando se desprenden, parecen simples astillas. Tiene siglos de antigüedad, tantos como tu gaveta. En fin, que me siento en deuda contigo. No dudes en pedirme cualquier cosa que necesites. La vida es una

cadena de favores y cada uno está obligado a colocar el eslabón que le corresponde —concluyó al tiempo que caminaba, sin mirarme, en dirección a la puerta de salida.

—Me gustaría que me alquilases el local. Quiero regentarlo. Quiero hacerlo como lo hacía tu madre —le dije, temerosa de su reacción, porque sabía que para él ese lugar era una especie de santuario.

No me respondió. Ni tan siquiera hizo gesto alguno que evidenciara que había oído mis palabras. Levantó la mano invitándome a salir de la tienda y se dirigió al cuadro de luces. Bajó los interruptores y cerró la puerta. Yo lo esperaba en la acera, a él y la respuesta a mi petición. Pasó a mi lado y caminó hasta llegar a su coche, que estaba estacionado a unos dos metros. Abrió la puerta y me miró.

—Lo pensaré —me dijo—. Tengo que pensarlo.

Luego entró en el vehículo y arrancó el motor. Ni tan siquiera esperó una respuesta mía. Me sonrió y levantó la mano en un gesto de despedida, acompañado de un guiño y una sonrisa, que me proporcionaron cierta esperanza.

Capítulo 12

Senatón me recibió maullando. Estaba hambriento y desorientado. Había pasado demasiado tiempo solo y encerrado.

—Hola, bichito —le dije, levantándolo en brazos—. Tengo que abrir una gatera para ti, aunque me cuesta decidirme, porque lo mismo te me escapas y vuelves a deambular por los tejados. Y aunque ya estoy acostumbrada a que me dejen, me dolería mucho que tú lo hicieses —le expliqué mirándolo a los ojos y acariciándole la cabecita—. Tengo que darte una noticia: me han despedido —le dije, apoyando la barbilla en su cabeza.

Al abrir la terraza con él en brazos se revolvió, dio un salto y salió escopetado al arenero. «Quizás Jessica Rabbit tenga razón y deba poner el arenero en otro sitio», pensé. El pobre estaba que no podía más. «Cómo he podido olvidarme de él», me recriminé, mirándolo. En ese momento, al recordar las palabras de Azucena durante el incidente del arenero en la fiesta, caí en la cuenta de que no sabía nada de Alán. Saqué el terminal de mi bolso y lo conecté mientras me dirigía a la cocina para ponerle a *Senatón* pienso y agua.

Esperaba encontrarme el buzón lleno de llamadas perdidas, mensajes de voz y *whatsapps*, pero solo entraron los que Antonio me había enviado, tal como me había dicho momentos antes. Alán no me había escrito, tampoco me había llamado. Marqué su número varias veces, pero tenía el teléfono fuera de servicio. Volví a desconectar mi

smartphone y lo dejé en la encimera de la cocina. A fin de cuentas, yo tampoco lo había echado de menos, pensé mirando el aparato. Ni siquiera me había acordado de él cuando me dieron la carta de despido. No había tenido presente a Alán ni un segundo de aquel nefasto día e, inconscientemente, pensé en lo que fue, en lo que era y en lo que pudo haber sido nuestra relación. Le tenía cariño, por supuesto. Había compartido muchas cosas con él. Muchas, pero no las suficientes, me dije al tiempo que tomaba el cuenco rojo de la estantería, recordando cómo se había formado. Alán desconocía aquellos hechos, esos y muchos otros que ya formaban parte de mi vida. No sabía quién era yo en realidad y lo más probable era que no llegara a saberlo nunca, me dije mientras devolvía el cuenco al estante. *Senatón* entró en el salón y se metió en la gaveta; me senté en el suelo, junto a él, y le acaricié. Mientras lo hacía recordé la conversación que Elda mantuvo con Desmond el día de la explosión: «... tu péndulo, el material del que está hecho, se parece mucho a las cubiertas del libro rojo. Hizo bien en deshacerse de él, porque desde que lo encontrasteis no dejan de suceder hechos extraños, tal como él nos advirtió que pasaría. Y, aunque te moleste, pienso que si tu péndulo es del mismo material que ese libro, deberías hacer lo mismo que ha hecho Ecles con el libro».

Mis pensamientos fueron encadenando hechos y objetos. Primero fue el cuenco. Levanté la vista para comprobar que seguía donde lo había dejado. Era del mismo color rojo y brillante que la piedra del anillo de Amaya, como el péndulo de Desmond y casi idéntico a la cubierta de mi libro.

Me incorporé cuando oí que en casa de Desmond y Ecles empezaba a sonar una canción. La voz era de Pablo Milanés, que interpretaba «Si ella me faltara alguna vez». Me asomé a la terraza. Ecles estaba apoyado en la barandilla. Su enorme figura parecía formar parte de la oscuridad que en aquel momento reinaba en la terraza. Su salón estaba en penumbra, solo se veía una pequeña luz azul que

provenía del equipo de música. Lo observé durante unos minutos, en silencio y sin moverme, apoyada en el marco del ventanal. Él estaba quieto, como ausente, mirando la calle. Escuché que tarareaba el estribillo de la canción y que subía un poco el tono de voz al repetir: «Si ella no inundara esta ciudad todo cambiaría de color». Aunque él aún no me había hablado de Amaya, supe que estaba pensando en ella, que aquella canción le recordaba a la florista, a los sentimientos que despertaba en él la japonesa y que había compartido conmigo en otro tiempo.

—Es preciosa —dije cuando la canción terminó—. Me gusta Milanés, mucho —expliqué, caminando hacia él.

—El disco no es mío. Es de Desmond. A él esta canción le recuerda a alguien muy especial, pero no puedo decirte a quién. A mí me recuerda... —Hizo una pausa y miró hacia la calle—. Pero ¿qué haces despierta a estas horas? —me preguntó, cambiando de repente el tema de la conversación. Volvió la cabeza, me miró y frunció el ceño en un gesto claro de interrogación.

—He tenido un día... digamos que desastroso. Me han despedido y de ahí en adelante todo se ha desbaratado, incluso mi reloj biológico. No tengo ni pizca de sueño. Tampoco apetito —comenté apoyándome cerca de él, sobre la barandilla, y miré hacia la floristería.

—Me llamó «grandullón» —dijo secándose con la yema de los dedos dos lágrimas indiscretas que escaparon sin permiso de sus ojos. Habló sin retirar la vista de la calle, de la tienda—. Amaya se rio al decirlo. No lo hizo con desdén. Fue el típico chascarrillo a deshora. Sé que no hubo maldad en su comentario, pero me dolió. ¿Sabes?, nadie se enamora de un payaso; se ríe con él. ¿En qué estaría pensando cuando me fijé en ella? —se preguntó en tono apagado y con la vista perdida en algún punto del horizonte, como si estuviera pensando en voz alta.

Después se volvió y me miró fijamente a los ojos. Me pareció que esperaba que yo le diese una respuesta.

—Ya veo que tú tampoco has tenido un buen día —le dije, apoyando una mano sobre la suya—. ¿Qué te parece si nos hacemos unas pizzas? Tengo una de verduras y queso en el congelador, y dos tarrinas de helado de chocolate. Si no te gusta el chocolate, también hay de frutos rojos y yogur.

—Y tu novio, ¿no está? —me preguntó, mirando hacia la entrada de mi salón.

—Se ha ido por unos días a recoger tulipanes a Holanda.

—Creía que trabajaba en el sector textil del *retail*.

—Pues sí, pero últimamente le ha dado por la horticultura ornamental —le respondí con una sonrisa burlona.

—Ya. Entiendo.

—Bueno, ¿qué me dices? ¿Me ayudas a vengarme de él terminando con las provisiones? Sé que no te cae muy bien. Te diré una cosa, a ver si te convenzo: los helados son de él —puntualicé, guiñándole un ojo.

—No tienes que invitarme a nada para recuperar tu libro. Y deja de preocuparte por su paradero. No lo he destruido. Ni se me ha pasado por la cabeza. Además, aunque quisiera hacerlo, me sería imposible. El material del que está hecho es indestructible. Sé que es tuyo, porque oí tu nombre cuando lo saqué de la gaveta. También capté que me pedías que raspase la cubierta porque presentías que debajo había algo escrito —me dijo sin venir a cuento.

—No sé de qué hablas —le respondí, desconcertada por el giro que había tomado la conversación.

—No te asustes —me pidió—. Cuando has puesto tu mano sobre la mía, ese anillo que llevas —señaló la alianza de pedida que Alán había dejado caer dentro de mi vaso de vino la noche que me pidió que viviéramos juntos— ha tocado mi piel y, en ese momento, he visto, sentido y oído parte de lo que te he dicho; el resto lo sabía

desde el momento que encontré tu gaveta y el libro. Sé que te puede parecer extraño, incluso incomprensible, pero la vida ya lo es en sí misma. Todos somos un poco incomprensibles y extraños, pero la mayoría lo ocultan. Aunque a mí, con este aspecto de vuelto a la vida, me cuesta más esconder que soy, como tú, un disidente de la realidad. En este edificio todos lo somos... menos tu novio.

Capítulo 13

Mientras horneábamos la pizza y preparábamos la terraza para cenar, me contó, como había hecho antaño, en el otro tiempo que vivimos juntos y que él no recordaba, el accidente que sufrió. Me relató cómo perdió a sus padres y cómo heredó su capacidad para ver y sentir parte del alma y la vida que los objetos atrapaban. Aquella percepción, junto a una decena de cicatrices que marcaban su rostro, como si fuese un muñeco de trapo mal cosido, y su estatura desmedida, había condicionado toda su vida, y aún seguía haciéndolo.

—Hasta esta noche no habíamos hablado, no nos habíamos visto de cerca —me dijo Ecles, refiriéndose a su encuentro con Amaya—. Yo llevaba tiempo contemplándola desde lejos. No tenía valor para dejarme ver. Desmond y Elda siempre me han recriminado mi cobardía. Dicen que soy como el león de *El mago de Oz*, que me falta seguridad en mí mismo. Y tienen razón. Me da miedo su rechazo. No me asusta que no sienta lo mismo que siento yo por ella; eso puede darse y, aunque me dolería, no sería el mismo dolor que el que me produciría que yo la espantase, que me viese como a un monstruo. Como me vieron tus amigos el día de vuestra fiesta. Si ella lo hiciera, me dolería muchísimo más. Tus amigos me dan igual, pero Amaya me importa, lo entiendes, ¿verdad? —me preguntó.

—¡Por supuesto, Ecles! Y déjame que te diga algo muy importante: tú no eres ningún monstruo, pero si sigues pensando así,

terminarás siéndolo. Uno es lo que quiere ser, se muestra ante los demás tal y como se cataloga a sí mismo, y así es como lo ven los otros.

—Tu opinión es diferente, Diana. Tus ojos no son iguales, no ven las mismas cosas. Tu mirada es especial, diferente a la del resto. Tú ves más allá de esta realidad, del mismo modo que yo tampoco siento lo mismo que los demás cuando tomo un objeto entre mis manos. Tus ojos y tu mirada son como los de Claudia. Ella veía el alma de las personas, no su físico. No sé cómo es Amaya, si es como nosotros o como el resto de los mortales, para quienes solo cuenta lo material, lo superficial. Es probable que me haya enamorado, que haya cometido el error de enamorarme de alguien muy diferente a mí.

—No creo que sea tan diferente —le dije, recordando el anillo que la chica llevaba en el dedo anular.

—No entiendo a qué te refieres.

—Creo que compartís más cosas de las que crees. De hecho, estoy convencida de que si intentaras relacionarte más con ella, tal vez te sorprenderías.

—Si Desmond no hubiese recogido el espejo para mí, ni siquiera me habría visto —me dijo al tiempo que señalaba el gran espejo de pie que estaba en su terraza. Me fijé en que el marco estaba a medio lijar y me imaginé que Ecles lo estaba restaurando—. De no ser por el espejo, Amaya ni siquiera se habría dirigido a mí.

»Me dijo: "Grandullón, ¿ya cabes en el espejo que Desmond se llevó para ti?". Y yo, nerviosísimo, tragué saliva y me atraganté. Tosí y, en cuanto logré recuperarme de la congestión, le respondí que no, que me faltaban unos centímetros y que tenía que agacharme para verme entero. Por desgracia lo hice con un tartajeo absurdo, porque yo no soy tartamudo, y sudando como un condenado. Ella se me quedó mirando con gesto incrédulo. Seguramente pensaba que, además de feo y demasiado grande, soy idiota.

—Bueno, tampoco es tan grave—le dije, dejando escapar una risita al imaginar la escena.

—No te burles —me pidió en un tono tan imperativo y tan serio que me pareció una orden—. A mí no me hace gracia, ni un poquito de gracia. Si lo sé no te lo cuento. Eres como Elda, te burlas de mi inocencia.

—Ecles, créeme, no es para tanto. Pero lo cuentas de una forma tan gráfica que lo he imaginado y me ha parecido gracioso. En ningún momento pretendía reírme de ti, pero es que tal como has descrito la situación resultaba tan cómica... —le expliqué apoyando la mano sobre su pierna, y volví a reírme sin querer—. ¡Lo siento! ¡Lo siento! —me apresuré a decir al ver su gesto malhumorado.

Esperaba que se levantase ante mi falta de tacto o que se enfadase más de lo que estaba, pero me sorprendió cuando dijo:

—La verdad es que, si lo pienso, si me imagino tartamudeando ante ella, también me da la risa. Soy un patoso.

—Míralo de otra forma, por otra vertiente. Ya te ha visto de cerca, habéis hablado. Y sí, eres un grandullón —dije palmeando su enorme espalda, en la que mi mano pareció perderse—, un grandullón encantador. Si no le gusta tu físico, peor para ella. Pero, aun y así, puedes intentarlo, no darte por vencido. El amor muchas veces surge de la forma que menos esperamos. Ese manido «a primera vista» que todo el mundo alaba no siempre funciona, la mayoría de las veces su fecha de caducidad llega en el mismo momento en que lo empezamos a degustar. Como diría mi amiga Samanta, es un simple fuego de artificio. Precioso, lleno de colores y formas mágicas, pero efímero.

—Pero yo me enamoré de ella el primer día que la vi, y cada día me gusta más —adujo.

—Ya, pero yo no descartaría la posibilidad de que se enamore de ti cuando te conozca realmente. Nunca hay que tirar la toalla, ni tan siquiera hacer el amago de dejarla caer antes de haber luchado

con todas tus fuerzas por lo que quieres. Y, para serte sincera, parece que tú te has rendido antes de que haya comenzado el primer asalto.

»Por cierto, ¿he de descartar yo que algún día me digas dónde está mi libro? —le pregunté alzando la copa de vino y acercándola a la suya con la intención de brindar.

De pronto, una voz interrumpió nuestra conversación.

—A este paso, cuando termines de lijar ese marco, habrás crecido y al espejo le faltará más de un palmo para que tu cabeza se refleje en él —dijo Desmond desde su terraza—. Espero que no me estés puenteando —señaló en tono irónico. Me miró al decirlo y después le guiñó el ojo derecho a Ecles, que sonrió.

»Hola, escocesa, ¿dónde se ha metido tu chico? —preguntó saltando el murete de ladrillo que separaba nuestras casas.

—Recogiendo tulipanes en Holanda —le respondió Ecles, burlón.

—Genial. Entonces, ¿me invitas a una copa? —preguntó cerca de mí. Muy cerca.

Capítulo 14

Qué poco sabía de Desmond, pensé mientras me dirigía a la cocina en busca de una copa para él. Conocía la historia de Elda y de Ecles, incluso Antonio, en cierto modo, se había sincerado conmigo, pero Desmond era un completo desconocido. Sin embargo, cuando estábamos cerca, cuando le oía hablar o le miraba, tenía la sensación de que lo conocía desde siempre, que ambos formábamos parte de un mismo destino y que, incluso, habíamos vivido los mismos acontecimientos en el mismo espacio temporal. A veces imaginaba que el tiempo había gestado nuestro destino al unísono y algo nos había separado en contra de nuestra voluntad, pero que, a pesar de ello, los dos, inconscientemente, nos buscábamos una y otra vez. Mientras le servía el vino, sonreí pensando una vez más en ello, en ese algo desconocido e inmaterial que hacía que me sintiese cada vez más a gusto a su lado.

—¿Has tenido tiempo de darle un vistazo a los libros que te dejé? —me preguntó sin dejar de mirar el vino que caía en su copa, abstraído en su color rojizo y en el sonido acuoso que producía el líquido al caer dentro del recipiente de cristal. Era tal su ensimismamiento que parecía no estar allí, con nosotros.

—Le he regalado la gaveta. Bueno, se la he devuelto porque era suya —dijo Ecles, acercándome su copa para que se la rellenase.

—Si tú lo dices... —le respondió Desmond con cierto tono de ironía—. Siempre has sido muy observador, y la gaveta tiene una «D» grabada en su base que, curiosamente, coincide con la inicial de tu nombre, escocesa —dijo, mirándome fijamente.

Tras unos segundos retiró la vista y acercó su copa a la mía, que estaba sobre la mesa, y las entrechocó a modo de brindis.

—Sí, claro. Ahora me vas a venir con que también puede ser tuya porque la inicial de tu nombre es la misma —respondió Ecles con escepticismo—. No hace falta que disimules, Desmond. Diana está al corriente de lo que me sucede cuando tomo en mis manos ciertos objetos. Como sabes, no me pasa con todos, solo con algunos, y su gaveta es uno de ellos.

—¿Y tú qué crees, escocesa? ¿Ha hecho bien nuestro amigo Ecles en desvelarte su secreto? —me preguntó Desmond, mirándome de nuevo a los ojos—. ¿O se ha precipitado y ahora está en peligro?

—Mira que eres idiota —se adelantó Ecles—. ¡Qué manía tenéis de tratarme como si fuese un niño inocente e incauto! —protestó, molesto.

Lo miró ceñudo y se levantó de la mesa. Cogió la copa de vino y, moviendo la cabeza de un lado a otro, se fue hacia la barandilla de la terraza. Desmond y yo nos quedamos frente a frente.

—¿Se puede saber por qué lo has tratado así? —le recriminé—. Al menos él ha compartido conmigo parte de su vida. En cambio tú actúas como un desconocido y te tomas las atribuciones de un amigo. ¿O es que te ha molestado que me regale la gaveta?

—Solo me preocupo por él. Es demasiado imprudente en sus comentarios cuando habla sobre su intimidad. Dar a conocer algunos detalles tan personales de forma gratuita le puede acarrear problemas. No es por ti, Diana, es porque quiero que se conciencie de la repercusión que, en algunas ocasiones, pueden tener sus palabras.

—Bueno, si me lo ha contado será porque confía en mí. No sé qué tiene eso de malo. A veces también es necesario desahogarse con cualquiera, no hace falta que sea un amigo íntimo —le respondí sin mirarle mientras recogía la mesa.

Me encaminé a la cocina.

—Le gustas —me dijo Ecles bajito mientras caminaba detrás de mí con los cubiertos en la mano—. Y se pone un poco tonto cuando tú estás cerca. Desmond se siente atraído por ti desde que te vio. Estoy seguro de que solo quería que le contases algo sobre ti; quién eres, qué has hecho antes de vivir aquí. Apuesto lo que quieras a que por eso sacó a colación el tema de la gaveta. Lo hizo para sonsacarte, para que te sintieses molesta y le contases algo más de ti. Tú también quieres saber más cosas sobre él. Eso no puedes negármelo. Se nota a la legua que os gustáis —me dijo, tomando mis manos entre las suyas.

—Eso es porque te quiere mucho y sabe que al que cuenta estrellas le salen verrugas —le respondí riéndome, al tiempo que, sin saber por qué, contenía las ganas de llorar.

—Eso mismo decía mi abuela —respondió sorprendido—. Elda y Desmond se burlan de mí cuando lo digo, pero ves, ¿ves?, no soy el único que lo sabe.

Era tan grande como pequeño, pensé mirándolo y sonriendo con él. Entrañable, inteligente, pero débil en sus emociones, me dije, y me empiné para darle un beso en la mejilla, aunque él tuvo que agacharse porque, aun y así, yo no llegaba.

—Eres un sol de los que calientan y no queman —le dije al oído—. Gracias, Ecles. Muchas gracias por tu amistad.

—Quizás algún día te deje ver ese libro de cubiertas rojas tan peculiares, pero debes ser paciente y esperar a que yo esté seguro de que es el momento adecuado. No es que desconfíe de ti, créeme, pero debo ser cauto. Aún no te conozco lo suficiente. No sé las intenciones que puedes tener. En eso estarás de acuerdo conmigo.

—Sí, sí, por supuesto, a mí me sucedería lo mismo —le respondí, sorprendida por unas explicaciones que no había pedido y que en aquel momento consideré que no venían a cuento.

—Cuando Desmond y yo arreglamos el escape de agua y encontré la gaveta en el altillo, leí el texto que se ocultaba en la cubierta y también supe de dónde venía, en qué momento y lugar se creó. Ese libro no pertenece a este mundo ni a este tiempo, Diana. No quiero que te suceda nada malo. Tú eres muy especial, eres...

—Una bruja de las que no vuelan en escoba porque lo hacen en ala delta —le interrumpió Desmond, que en ese momento entraba en la cocina con *Senatón* en brazos—. Sus escobas las utilizan para decorar el dintel de la puerta de entrada de sus casas. Una bruja contemporánea. Una bruja real que nada tiene que ver con las estúpidas leyendas que nos han contado.

No le respondí. Cuando dijo «una bruja», sentí algo en mi interior que me paralizó. Mi corazón pareció detenerse por unos segundos y volví a verme junto a él en un lugar que no conocía, abrazados, llorando y maldiciendo nuestro destino.

—Trae —dije quitándole a *Senatón* de los brazos.

Cuando me acerqué a Ecles, el gatito bufó.

—La escoba que tienes sobre el dintel es de Claudia, ¿verdad? —me preguntó.

—Sí. Me la ha regalado Antonio. Le he propuesto que me arrende el local de su madre. Espero tener suerte y que lo haga, si no es así, no sé qué voy a hacer. Esta mañana me he quedado sin trabajo —expliqué.

Sonrió como si supiera que le estaba mintiendo y miró hacia la terraza. Lo hizo como si buscase la aprobación de Claudia a mis palabras, como si ella estuviera allí y él pudiera verla. Incluso pensé que ella ya le había dicho que me había dado su escoba.

—Pues no sé qué decirte, Diana —dijo Ecles—. No te hagas muchas ilusiones. Para Antonio la tienda es un santuario. Veré si

puedo echarte una mano y convencerlo para que te la alquile. Sería estupendo que se volviera a abrir y que lo hicieses tú. Hace tiempo que lo necesitamos. Cada día que este edificio pasa sin la presencia de Claudia parece morir un poco. Tal vez tú puedas devolverle la magia que está perdiendo.

—Antonio me ha llamado. Quería saber qué opinión tenía de ti —dijo Desmond, mirándome—. Le dije que lo único que no me gustaba de ti era tu chico, pero que de seguro no lo aguantarías mucho más tiempo a tu lado. No tenéis nada en común. Él no es como nosotros. Ni como tú, escocesa.

CAPÍTULO 15

Lejos de sentirme incómoda o desconcertada por todo lo que Ecles me había contado sobre mi libro y la gaveta o por el comentario de Desmond sobre que yo era una bruja, la sensación que tuve fue como si durante años hubiese llevado una pesada carga y de pronto la hubiera soltado. Al menos ellos no eran como el resto, pensé; se parecían un poco a mí, y aquello, en cierto modo, me tranquilizó.

—Gracias —le dije en respuesta a la opinión que le había dado a Antonio sobre mí.

—No tienes por qué dármelas, Diana. Es imposible que yo diga nada malo de ti o que pueda perjudicarte, no solo porque me pareces preciosa, sino también porque no sería justo —me respondió guiñándome un ojo.

—Puedes llamarme «escocesa». Me gusta que lo hagas.

—¡Qué bien! —exclamó Ecles—. Me teníais preocupado. Noté cierta tirantez en vuestros comentarios y me resultó incómodo, porque me gusta que estéis bien, que todos lo estemos. Además, Diana, quería invitarte a la fiesta del equinoccio, y si estabais enojados, habría sido violento para vosotros y para mí. O sea que lo celebraremos juntos; porque vendrás, ¿verdad? —preguntó mirándome con gesto de súplica, temeroso de que yo rechazase su invitación.

—¡Por supuesto que iré! —exclamé sin dejar de mirar a Desmond, que a su vez no apartaba la vista de mí. Me observaba tal y como lo había hecho aquel día, en el tiempo que vivimos juntos, durante la primera cena que celebramos los cuatro en mi ático. Y, de repente, como si alguien hubiese chasqueado los dedos y lanzado un conjuro, la normalidad se instaló entre nosotros. Ninguno de los tres volvió a tocar los temas de los que habíamos hablado anteriormente.

Terminamos de recoger juntos la cocina y la terraza. Reímos cuando Ecles le recriminó a *Senatón* que lanzase un bufido cada vez que pasaba a su lado. Agachado frente al gatito, le contó el porqué de su aspecto y su altura. Convencido de que este le entendía, como si estuviera hablando con un niño pequeño, le explicó que aunque él fuese grande y feo, tenía un gran corazón, y que si se hacía su amigo le protegería de otros peligros, sobre todo de la gente que es hermosa por fuera y horrenda por dentro. Le habló bajito, despacio y gesticulando en exceso. *Senatón* pareció entenderlo, porque se le acercó y restregó la cabeza contra él. Y el grandullón, nuestro grandullón, lo aupó en brazos por primera vez.

Charlamos durante unos minutos más sobre la situación económica que yo tenía que afrontar y la posibilidad de que Antonio me arrendase el local; de cómo iba a pagar el alquiler en el caso de que él aceptase mi propuesta. También sobre la florista y la falta de aplomo que mostraba Ecles. Él se molestó por nuestros insistentes comentarios sobre su actitud. Nos dio la razón, pero incidió en que le incomodaba que se lo repitiésemos tantas veces, porque pensaba que lo tomábamos por un incauto. Admitió que tal vez él fuera cobarde, pero aseguró que no tenía ni un pelo de tonto. Que quizás por ello, porque veía las cosas antes de que sucediesen, sentía temor, puntualizó enfadado. Yo le di mi palabra de que si era capaz de invitarla él mismo a la fiesta del equinoccio de septiembre, sin la ayuda de terceros, jamás volvería a tocar el tema. Lo hice porque

sabía que Ecles deseaba desde hacía tiempo que Amaya estuviese entre los invitados.

—Lo intentaré, aunque la recompensa que me ofreces no me atrae mucho, es demasiado difícil que la cumplas. Estoy seguro de que volverás a recriminarme la falta de confianza que tengo en mí mismo —expuso, convencido de lo que decía—. Si hoy he tartamudeado, cuando intente invitarla me quedaré sin voz.

—De aquí al equinoccio tienes tiempo para enmudecer, tartamudear y, si fuese necesario, hasta para aprender esperanto para comunicarte con ella. Eso sí, no vayas a mandarle un ramo de flores —le dije con cierta guasa—. Aún quedan muchos días, campeón; a por ellos, que son pocos y cobardes —concluí, dándole una palmadita en el brazo.

—¿Ellos? —preguntó sorprendido, mirándome y encogiéndose de hombros—. ¿Quiénes son «ellos»?

—Tus miedos, Ecles —le aclaró Desmond.

—No tengo miedo. No sé de dónde habéis sacado eso de los miedos. Soy cobarde, lo reconozco, pero no tengo miedo, solo inseguridad. Por supuesto que ni se me ocurre mandarle flores, y no porque sea florista, sino porque no soporto que se le robe la vida a nada.

—Pues te has enamorado de una florista. Es un tanto irónico —expuso Desmond, guiñándome un ojo.

—Amaya no es florista, lo son sus padres. Solo los ayuda en el negocio por las tardes. Tú me lo dijiste —puntualizó, mirando a Desmond—. Y ya que insistís tanto, sabed que ya le he mandado un obsequio. Le he regalado la piedra roja que encontré en el altillo del armario, la que se cayó del lateral de la gaveta, el pentagrama.

—Te dije que lo guardases junto al libro. ¿Cómo se te ocurrió dárselo a Amaya? Eres un inconsciente—le recriminó Desmond, molesto.

—La mandé engarzar en un anillo de plata y, curiosamente, le queda a la perfección, la medida es la suya —dijo haciendo un gesto con las cejas para indicar que se sentía orgulloso por ello—. No sabe que se lo he regalado yo, si es eso lo que te preocupa. Se lo envié hace tiempo, sin remite. Ahora lleva un pedacito de mí con ella. Algún día le diré que fui yo quien se la regaló. Cuando me conozca de verdad, cuando consiga que me vea por dentro —dijo, esta vez dirigiéndose a mí.

Desmond movió la cabeza de un lado a otro, pensativo.

—Ecles, la piedra no es de Amaya, no lo era, jamás lo fue y nunca lo será. Deberías haberme hecho caso y dejarla junto al libro.

Yo permanecía inmóvil mirándolos. No sabía qué hacer ni qué decir. Por unos momentos estuve a punto de decirle a Ecles que aquella piedra era mía, igual que lo era la gaveta y el libro y que no entendía por qué se la había regalado a Amaya, pero recordé las palabras de Claudia indicándome que aprovechase lo que sabía y, muy a mi pesar, callé.

—Creo que deberíamos dejar esta discusión para otro día y otra hora, ya es tarde y todos estamos cansados —los interrumpí.

—Estaría bien que nos viésemos más, aprovechando que tu chico estará unos días cultivando tulipanes —me dijo Desmond camino de la puerta—. ¡Eres tan diferente cuando no está él!

—¿Qué te pasa, vampiro? —le pregunté—. Hoy no saltas la valla de ladrillo para regresar a casa. Vuelves como un mortal cualquiera —bromeé.

—Tengo una cita ahí fuera, con el firmamento. Voy a contar unas cuantas estrellas antes de que el sol las haga desaparecer, ¿quieres acompañarme?

—No es buena idea. Estoy agotada y lo más probable es que me quede dormida durante el primer conteo —respondí sin mentirle.

Estaba desconcertada. Necesitaba descansar y, sobre todo, recapacitar, tomar las riendas de mi vida que, una vez más, parecía

desbocarse ante mis ojos. Me sentía aturdida por el hecho de conocer el paradero de la piedra. No sabía qué podía significar que la tuviese Amaya, qué circunstancias podía ocasionar ni cómo iba a recuperarla. Debía convencer a Ecles para que me dijese dónde había guardado mi libro. Meditar sobre cómo negociaría con Antonio el alquiler del local. Y, quizás, retomar la investigación sobre mis orígenes, aunque aquello ya no me importaba tanto. Tenía el presentimiento de que tarde o temprano, sin necesidad de hacer nada, los acontecimientos me llevarían a una resolución.

Mientras pensaba en todo aquello me dirigí a la cocina y cogí mi teléfono móvil. Tal vez debería hablar con Alán sobre nuestro futuro, sobre la relación que, estaba segura, él mantenía con Azucena. Aquello me parecía lo más complicado. Era arriesgado porque cabía la posibilidad de que se me escapase algún dato que no debía comentar. Si volvía a crear una paradoja, mi historia, la historia de una bruja contemporánea, como me había llamado Desmond, se volvería a repetir. Lo haría tal y como me había advertido Claudia: una y otra vez y con acontecimientos imprevisibles, pensé mientras introducía la clave para conectar mi terminal.

CAPÍTULO 16

Hablé con Alán al día siguiente, por la mañana. Me despertó temprano y se disculpó por no haber podido llamarme el día anterior. La conversación fue breve porque tenía una agenda muy apretada, o al menos eso me dijo. No le comenté nada sobre mi despido, omití lo que me había sucedido. Le dejé hablar como en un monólogo, como si mi vida y lo que me sucediera fueran un adenda sin valor que se había añadido a un contrato entre ambos ya vencido. Al final oí un «te quiero» que me sonó distante y monótono, casi impostado. Creo que mi respuesta, «yo también», fue igual de insulsa que las pocas frases que habíamos intercambiado y en las que faltó cercanía, complicidad, interés y, sobre todo, añoranza. En ningún momento de la conversación se hizo patente esa necesidad que suelen tener las personas que se quieren y están alejadas físicamente.

A pesar de todo lo que sabía, de que ya no sentía atracción por él, seguía doliéndome lo que sucedía entre nosotros. El cómo, la manera en que me estaba engañando, continuaba haciéndome daño y, aunque lo intentaba, no conseguía desvincularme de aquel dolor, de la duda de si en algún momento de nuestra relación me había amado como afirmó y manifestó en repetidas ocasiones.

Saber demasiado era peligroso y complicado, pensé mirando el terminal, imaginando a Azucena junto a él, sonriente. Y tuve que contenerme para no volver a llamarlo y decirle que nuestra relación había terminado, que ya no podía más con todo aquello.

***

Me enteré de la muerte de Duncan por Samanta. Al escucharla recordé mi primer encuentro con él en el metro de Madrid, en la estación de Cuatro Caminos. En aquella realidad paralela, me advirtió de que fuera con mucho cuidado si tenía en mi poder el auténtico evangelio de las brujas.

Samanta me llamó al mediodía, impresionada por la noticia que le había dado su amigo Andreas desde la Universidad de Glasgow, en Escocia. La llamó para informarla de que habían encontrado a Duncan sin vida sentado en uno de los bancos del metro, en la estación de Cuatro Caminos, en Madrid. Provisionalmente lo identificaron como Duncan Connor, según acreditaba la documentación que llevaba en su cartera, desaparecido en aquella misma estación de metro en 1995, hacía veintidós años.

Las pruebas de ADN aún estaban por verificar. No había familiares con los que cotejar las muestras. Tras localizar a su mujer, Virginia, en uno de los albergues de la ciudad, ella se negó a reconocer el cuerpo y a hacerse cargo de él. Alegó que su marido aún seguía vivo, vagando por aquella estación de metro. Entre la documentación que hallaron en su cartera estaba la dirección de Andreas, el amigo de Samanta y profesor de Ciencias Sociales en la Universidad de Glasgow, y eso, unido a la evidente merma de las facultades mentales que presentaba Virginia, motivó que se pusieran en contacto con él. Andreas había sido quien me remitió la documentación sobre Aradia y el evangelio de las brujas que Duncan había ido recopilando durante años.

—Mi amigo Andreas está destrozado. Viajará a Madrid para encargarse de la repatriación de los restos mortales de Duncan y para llevarse a Virginia de vuelta a su país. Según me ha contado, la pobre está muy mal. Sigue creyendo que su marido está en esa estación y afirma verlo algunos días, siempre en el mes de agosto, el mismo mes en el que desapareció. ¡Qué lástima!

»Le he dado tu dirección y teléfono a Andreas por si necesita algo. Espero que no te importe que lo haya hecho, pero lo he visto tan afectado y perdido que, al no estar yo en España, he pensado en ti, porque creo que Virginia no le será de gran ayuda, más bien al contrario, sufrirá mucho al verla. Imagina el trago que va a pasar.

La escuché sin poder articular palabra, impactada por la noticia. No podía creer que Duncan hubiera muerto, no era posible, me dije. Él no estaba en este tiempo. Se había quedado parado en aquel pasado y ahí debía permanecer, pero todo evidenciaba que no era así, que había sucedido algo que lo devolvió al espacio temporal en el que estábamos su mujer, Virginia, y también yo. Mientras escuchaba a Samanta pensé en Virginia, en su estado, en cuánto habría sufrido al recibir la noticia. Era evidente, me dije, que el amor que sentía por su marido le había robado la razón, esa lógica que le hubiera permitido reconocerle y aceptar su muerte, admitir que se había ido para siempre, que ya no volverá a compartir más viajes acurrucada como un perrillo abandonado junto a él, ante las miradas indiferentes de los demás viajeros del metro.

—Tengo que encontrarla cuanto antes —se me escapó en un susurro que Samanta no alcanzó a oír.

Me sentía muy inquieta por la noticia.

—Por supuesto que no me importa —le dije después de carraspear, intentando esconder tras mis palabras aquel pensamiento, aquel deseo de ayudar a Virginia, de dar con ella cuanto antes.

—¡Gracias! —me respondió mi amiga, claramente acongojada—. ¿Sabes?, yo no lo conocía personalmente, pero sé que era una buena persona. Andreas lo quería muchísimo, eran como hermanos, y yo aprecio un montón a Andreas. Su dolor es como si fuese mío, de no ser así, no te lo habría pedido, no me habría tomado la libertad de darle tu teléfono y tu dirección. No sabes cuánto te agradezco que te encargues de que esté bien. Eso sí, hazlo sin que te incomode en tus horarios y obligaciones laborales. Ya sé que la situación en la empresa está delicada y por nada del mundo quisiera causarte más problemas.

—Por el tiempo no te preocupes. Ahora dispongo de todo el que necesite. Ayer me despidieron —le comuniqué.

—¿En serio? No puedo creérmelo. Lo siento. Aunque... si te soy sincera, pienso que al final será beneficioso para ti. Esa empresa de poca monta es tóxica, siempre he creído que tiene algo que emponzoña la iniciativa, que convierte al que trabaja en ella en una especie de robot esclavo. Bueno, qué de tonterías digo, si los esclavos no tienen iniciativa, no les dejan tenerla, por eso lo son.

»Espero que Alán se lo haya tomado bien. Imagino que hasta que encuentres otro empleo, os alcanzará con su sueldo para manteneros, quiero decir que no tendréis problemas. Ya sabes, los problemas económicos pudren hasta la fruta de cerámica.

—Aún no he hablado con él sobre ello. Está en Holanda, en uno de esos encuentros que hacen cada seis meses. Y se ha llevado con él a su compañera, la mosquita muerta que escupe margaritas de colores chillones por la boca.

—¡Que escupe margaritas por la boca! —Se carcajeó—. Explícame eso, por favor, qué risa.

—Sí, es tan tonta, tan de plástico... Sobreactúa de una forma que solo le falta escupir margaritas de colores chillones por la boca. Te juro que cuando habla no puedo evitar imaginarme cómo resbalan por sus labios.

—Ja, ja, ja, ja. Me matas —me respondió sin poder reprimir las carcajadas.

—Sí, sí, ríete, pero la muy arpía está con él. Lo sé. Aunque Alán me lo niegue por activa y por pasiva, sé que están juntos, que ya se han liado. No sé el tiempo que voy a seguir con esto, cuánto voy a poder soportar su engaño, que es lo que más me duele.

—No te precipites, ni se te ocurra hacer o decir nada en caliente. Primero has de tener todos los cabos bien atados. En tu situación no puedes permitirte hacer tonterías. Dejarte llevar por el orgullo sería una estupidez, ellos no lo hacen. ¿Por qué crees que aguantan tanto con sus mujeres mientras les prometen a las amantes que se separarán, cuando en realidad ni se les pasa por la cabeza? Pues es por simple interés económico, nena. Y tú también tienes que velar por el tuyo. Si estás tan segura de que te es infiel con la escupe margaritas, deja que sea él quien se marche. Ni se te ocurra abandonar ese ático, que es una auténtica ganga. Y, mientras tanto, busca trabajo como una loca. No tengo la menor duda de que lo vas a encontrar...

Cuantísimo la echaba de menos, pensé mientras escuchaba su perorata de rigor, aquella arenga que tanta falta me hacía siempre, sobre todo en aquellos momentos. Algún día tendría que contarle todo lo que no sabía de mí. Samanta no se merecía desconocer una parte tan importante de mi vida, no se merecía que le ocultase nada, absolutamente nada, pero aún no podía compartir con ella todo lo que me sucedía, debía ser paciente y pragmática, tal y como ella me aconsejaba.

Colgué el teléfono con la promesa de tenerla informada de todo. Me vestí y me calcé las deportivas más cómodas que tenía, unas Adidas Ultraboost, modelo Laceless, que me había regalado Alán y que no había utilizado porque su precio me parecía desorbitado para unas deportivas y usarlas me producía cierto remordimiento. Pero aquella ocasión se lo merecía, me dije.

—Yo me lo merezco —verbalicé mientras me miraba en el espejo.

Salí a la calle en dirección al metro. Iba a buscar a Virginia y la encontraría, pensé segura de mí misma. Levanté la mano y respondí al saludo de Amaya, que ese día, contrariamente a lo habitual, estaba por la mañana regentando la floristería.

CAPÍTULO 17

Cogí la línea 6 en Argüelles y me dirigí a la estación de Cuatro Caminos, el lugar donde había visto a Virginia por primera vez. Sabía que era improbable que estuviera allí, pero tenía la esperanza de encontrarla, de que el destino o el azar volviesen a juntarnos.

Samanta no tenía datos de dónde se hallaba Virginia en aquel momento, porque Andreas no le había dado indicaciones precisas de su paradero. Sin embargo, por lo que me había comentado mi amiga durante nuestra conversación, era evidente que Andreas sabía dónde estaba la mujer. Podría haberle pedido a Samanta que sonsacara al profesor, pero fui prudente y callé. Era más seguro buscar a Virginia por mi cuenta y en el más absoluto anonimato antes de que Andreas llegase a España. De lo contrario, no lograría hablar con ella con total libertad sobre su marido y sobre lo acontecido antes y después de que Duncan falleciera. Lo más probable era que, si Virginia y yo conversábamos de todo eso delante de ellos, me censuraran por mi falta de tacto o incluso pensaran que había perdido la razón, como ya especulaban y daban por hecho que le había sucedido a la pobre mujer.

No me senté ni me quedé en un sitio fijo, sino que fui caminando de vagón en vagón durante el recorrido de cuatro estaciones que separaban Argüelles de Cuatro Caminos, buscándola

entre la gente, en el suelo, en los recodos, pero Virginia no estaba en aquel tren. Tal vez estaría en el siguiente o en los que continuarían pasando aproximadamente cada cinco minutos, recorriendo uno tras otro y sin descanso la línea 6, la circular, como gusanos dentro de un túnel. Encontrarla era como buscar una aguja en un pajar, me dije desanimada. Al llegar a Cuatro Caminos me apeé y anduve por el andén de arriba abajo durante unos minutos, mezclándome con la gente que se apeaba de los trenes o subía a ellos.

Durante aquellos breves paseos recordé algo que Virginia me había comentado: que no tenía ingresos, que había consumido todos sus ahorros en los viajes y en costearse la estancia en Madrid mientras buscaba a su marido. Si era así, y teniendo en cuenta la situación en la que se encontraba cuando la conocí, lo más probable era que estuviera alojada en un albergue, pensé. Me senté en uno de los bancos y saqué el ordenador portátil de mi mochila. Lo conecté a la red y busqué los albergues cercanos a la estación. Tendría que ir uno a uno preguntando por ella, pero no me importaba, porque el tiempo era lo único que me sobraba en aquel momento.

—Señorita, se le han caído las llaves —dijo una voz masculina a mi lado.

Al retirar la vista de la pantalla del ordenador vi las botas y el pantalón del uniforme de un guardia de seguridad del metro, que en ese momento estaba en cuclillas. Recogió las llaves del suelo y, sin abandonar su posición, todavía agachado frente a mí, me las tendió.

—¡Usted! —exclamé eufórica, como si lo conociese de toda la vida y aquel encuentro fuese una grata sorpresa.

—¿Se encuentra bien? —preguntó él, levantándose.

Imaginé que mi actitud al verlo lo había desconcertado.

—Sí, gracias. Estoy perfectamente, mejor que nunca. Le estaba buscando..., bueno, no exactamente —intenté explicarme al ver su gesto de sorpresa—. Busco a una mujer a la que usted conoce.

—¿Yo? —Se encogió de hombros y enarcó las cejas.

—Es una indigente. Se llama Virginia y, por lo que vi un día, usted suele invitarla a desayunar churros. Hace unos días su marido falleció aquí, en uno de estos bancos.

—¿Es usted periodista? —me inquirió en un tono que me pareció reprobatorio.

—No, no, para nada. Usted no me recordará, pero hace un tiempo, no puedo decirle si han pasado días o semanas, Virginia me estaba pidiendo unas monedas y usted se la llevó.

—No la recuerdo. Pero... ¿para qué quiere localizarla?

No supe qué responderle. Todo lo que podría haberle contado, dados los acontecimientos, le parecería extraño, fuera de lugar, y desconfiaría aún más de mí, pensé. Me quedé en silencio, mirándolo, y en ese instante dos mujeres se situaron entre los dos e interrumpieron nuestra conversación. Cada una llevaba una escoba, ambas artesanales y burdas. El mango estaba confeccionado con la rama de un árbol y las cerdas eran ramitas secas atadas con una soga de esparto.

—La voy a colgar sobre el dintel de la puerta, como nos ha dicho la bruja —le dijo una a la otra sacando la escoba del papel en el que estaba medio envuelta—. Ya sé que puede parecer una tontería, pero esta escoba tiene algo especial, lo noto. No es como las demás.

—Yo me la voy a llevar a la oficina y voy a mandar a la «genia» de mi jefa a barrer un desierto. Somos meigas, querida, habrá que hacer uso de nuestra condición —le respondió la otra. Al decirlo, se volvió y me miró fijamente durante unos segundos.

—A barrer un desierto —murmuré, y recordé a Azucena sacudiéndose la arena que *Senatón* le lanzaba sobre los pies.

Cerré los ojos y visualicé al vigilante del metro dándome los detalles que sabía acerca de Virginia, sonriéndome y estrechándome la mano como si fuésemos viejos conocidos y estuviera encantado de prestarme ayuda. «Soy una bruja y puedo hacer uso de mi condición», me dije.

—Desde que encontraron a su marido, no la he vuelto a ver por aquí. Gracias a Dios que aquel día ella no estaba en la estación. Yo no estaba de turno, pero me enteré de todo; aquí las noticias corren como la pólvora. Se revisaron las grabaciones para verificar los movimientos del hombre. En ellas se le ve salir del vagón y sentarse en el banco, como si estuviese agotado, exhausto. Debía de encontrarse mal, eso está claro. Luego no hay nada más de importancia, solo lo de siempre: la indiferencia. La gente pasaba a su lado, incluso hubo quien se sentó junto a él sin percatarse de nada. Seguramente ya había fallecido. Parece algo normal, un suceso que, desgraciadamente, se da con más frecuencia de lo que la gente cree, pero para mí esta historia es muy extraña.

—¿A qué se refiere?

—A lo que contaba Virginia. Ella creía que su marido viajaba en uno de los vagones de esta estación. Él desapareció aquí hace veintitantos años..., no sé si lo sabe —comentó. Asentí en silencio—. En ese momento fue Virginia quien denunció su desaparición. Incluso estuvo vigilada. Era la primera sospechosa. ¡Pobre mujer! Y ahora, de repente, él aparece, veintidós años después y en la misma estación de metro, con la misma ropa, los documentos que llevaba en aquel momento y un periódico de entonces. ¿No le parece extraño?

—Sí, un poco raro sí que es —admití.

—Virginia es una mujer extraordinaria. ¿Sabe?, le tomé cariño.

—¿Tiene idea de dónde puedo localizarla? Algún albergue, una zona determinada o a una hora en la que frecuente algún lugar

concreto. Un parque, una salida de metro o parada de autobús —le pregunté.

—Que yo sepa, el último sitio en el que estuvo fue el Centro de Acogida San Isidro. Está en el Paseo del Rey, 34. Es uno de los mejores que hay. Ofrecen cuatro comidas diarias, camas y asistencia sanitaria, que ella solía necesitar casi a diario. Se lo consiguió un sanitario del Samur Social, un chaval muy majo. Movió Roma con Santiago porque, ya sabe..., las plazas, por desgracia, son limitadas en estos sitios. Pero no puedo asegurarle que siga allí. Con todo este jaleo, a lo mejor Virginia ha decidido volver a su país. O quizás algún familiar ha venido a por ella.

—¡Ojalá esté bien! —exclamé.

—Para ir al centro de acogida, ahorrará tiempo si cambia de andén, porque tiene que bajarse en Príncipe Pío y, si continúa en esta dirección, recorrerá todas las estaciones de la circular hasta que dé la vuelta el tren.

—Muchísimas gracias —le dije, y le tendí la mano.

—De nada, señorita. Menos mal que estaba aquí y he visto que se le caían las llaves. El llavero es muy bonito y la gente, hoy en día, roba de todo. Tenga cuidado y no deje su mochila abierta o al alcance de cualquiera. —Señaló la bolsa que yo tenía abierta sobre el banco y volvió a su trabajo.

Después de aquello no me cupo la menor duda de que ya estaba preparada para mandar a Jessica Rabbit a barrer un desierto de los de verdad. Si esa arpía volvía a escupir margaritas de colores chillones y envenenadas delante de mí. o si se atrevía a repetir que *Senatón* era pelón, buscaría en el atlas uno bien grande, lo más árido posible, y la mandaría a barrerlo.

—Ha sido un placer refrescar tu memoria, meiga —oí que decía una de las mujeres que ya estaba dentro del vagón del metro que en esos momentos estaba a punto de partir.

Me levanté dispuesta a coger el tren para hablar con ella, aunque el convoy se dirigía hacia Nuevos Ministerios, en dirección opuesta a la que me había recomendado el vigilante. Sin embargo, aunque me incorporé con rapidez, no me dio tiempo a subirme. Vi que la desconocida levantaba su escoba e interpreté el gesto como un saludo de despedida. Claudia, Koldo y Antonio tenían razón, pensé mientras observaba el tren adentrándose en el túnel. Mi mirada es diferente a la del resto de los mortales, es la de una bruja, pero no soy la única que ve otras realidades, la única que cree en la magia. Somos muchos, muchos más, y cada día que pasa estoy más cerca de ellos, de los que son como yo.

CAPÍTULO 18

Uno de los funcionarios del centro de acogida me informó de que Virginia llevaba varios días sin aparecer por allí. Por suerte, llegué un poco antes de la hora del almuerzo, de modo que coincidí con las personas que, aunque no pernoctaban en las instalaciones, iban allí a comer. Muchos de ellos conocían a Virginia por el apodo de la Escocesa. Sus rasgos físicos, su marcado acento, la forma de hablar y sus modales refinados no pasaban desapercibidos. Tampoco su historia, que casi todos sabían.

—Sí, sí. Conocemos la historia del fantasma de Cuatro Caminos —me dijeron dos mujeres que afirmaban haber acompañado a Virginia en alguna ocasión y que me juraron haber visto a Duncan en el vagón del metro.

Me relataron como el hombre aparecía cuando el tren llegaba a la estación o salía de ella.

—Solo lo vimos en esa estación, en ningún otro sitio; por eso creemos que es un fantasma. Volvimos más veces con ella, pero solo lo vimos un día —puntualizaron.

Se sorprendieron al descubrir que su relato me parecía interesante y que consideraba que no le faltaba rigor, que las creía. Y, animadas por el respeto que mostré hacia sus palabras, me describieron a Duncan con todo lujo de detalles.

—Están locas —dijo un hombre que pasó a nuestro lado mientras yo hablaba con ellas—. Si acepta un consejo, no crea nada de lo que le cuenten estas dos arpías —finalizó, mirándolas con una expresión de resquemor.

No le presté atención porque sus palabras me parecieron una falta de respeto hacia las mujeres y, por ello, ni tan siquiera le miré. Ellas callaron durante unos segundos, parecían acostumbradas a aquel tipo de comentarios, pero, aun y así, por sus gestos y su silencio entendí que las palabras del individuo les disgustaban.

En la acera de enfrente, apoyado en la tapia de ladrillo que separaba la calle de las vías del tren de cercanías, un hombre delgado, alto y bien parecido nos observaba. Permanecía inmóvil, como un perro guardián que estuviera esperando cualquier movimiento extraño para arrancarse a morder. Tenía la boca cerrada y los labios comprimidos, como si estuviera apretando las mandíbulas con fuerza. Mantenía la mirada fija en mí. Aunque lo miré varias veces directamente a los ojos y le sonreí, él no movió ni un solo músculo de la cara. No dejó escapar ni una expresión que evidenciara algún tipo de emoción o sentimiento. Sus ojos negros y aquella extraña mirada tan fija en mí me sobrecogieron. Se me antojó que intentaba decirme algo que yo no conseguía descifrar.

—¿Quién es ese hombre que está ahí enfrente, mirándonos? —les pregunté a las mujeres.

—Ah, sí —me dijo una de ellas—. Es amigo de Virginia. La primera vez que lo vimos fue unos días después de que ella se instalase en el centro. No sé cómo ni cuándo pasó, pero se hicieron muy amigos. Salían juntos algunas veces. Él no utiliza las instalaciones, se ve a la legua que tiene posibles. A mí no me gusta, no me parece de fiar. Quizás haya venido buscándola, como ha hecho usted.

—A veces se nos va la cabeza y no atendemos a nada, pero creo que ese sujeto está más ido que Virginia o que cualquiera de nosotros —continuó la otra mujer, mirándolo de soslayo—. A veces no

es cuestión de si se tiene dinero o no. A veces la soledad o el desamor nos juegan malas pasadas, y él tiene pinta de estar un poco extraviado —dijo, llevándose un dedo a la sien derecha y girándolo—. De no ser así, ya me dirá usted qué hace un hombre joven y tan guapetón con Virginia. Además, no es de nuestra clase social. Ya le digo yo que aquí hay gato encerrado.

—Bueno, bueno, para un poco, que cuando arrancas no hay quien te frene —le recriminó la compañera—. Lo mismo estamos equivocadas en todo, no se tome nada de lo que le hemos dicho al pie de la letra.

»Si encuentra a Virginia, dele recuerdos de parte de Anita y Angélica —dijo, señalando a su compañera y después a ella—. Dígale que la echamos de menos. Nos gustaba escuchar las historias que nos contaba sobre Escocia y las investigaciones que seguía su marido sobre las brujas, las auténticas brujas, no las que quemaron en la hoguera. ¡Qué interesante era todo! Parecía tan real que daba escalofríos escucharla. Sobre todo lo de ese viejo evangelio en el que, según nos dijo, se encuentran escritas las trece leyes sagradas para cualquier bruja. Era la obsesión de su marido y el motivo que lo trajo a Madrid. Quería encontrar el evangelio de las brujas.

—A mí todo lo que tenga que ver con parapsicología me atrae muchísimo, por eso creo que el hombre que murió en el metro no era el marido de Virginia. ¡Qué va! Nosotras lo vimos en ese vagón y, créame, era un fantasma. Una persona no puede morir dos veces, ¿o sí? —me preguntó Anita. Yo me encogí de hombros—. Eso creo yo —se contestó a sí misma—, que también es posible morir dos veces si lo hacemos en tiempos y épocas diferentes.

—Anita, ¡para ya! —le exigió Angélica—. ¿No ves que la vas a volver loca? Además, tendríamos que ir entrando, es tarde ya —concluyó, mirando su reloj de pulsera.

Ya me disponía a ir al metro cuando el hombre cruzó la acera y se dirigió a mí:

—No sé qué le habrán contado de mí esas dos alcahuetas, pero nada de lo que hayan podido decirle es cierto, estoy seguro. Todos cambiamos la realidad y creamos la nuestra propia, que a menudo poco tiene que ver con la de los demás. Me llamo Farid —se presentó, tendiéndome la mano.

—Diana —le respondí, devolviéndole el saludo y extendiendo la mía, que él estrechó con fuerza—. Nunca había oído ese nombre —comenté.

—Tal vez sea porque es de origen árabe. Aunque es uno de los más comunes, vendría a ser como aquí Paco o Manolo —me respondió con una sonrisa, mostrando unos dientes blancos y bien alineados.

—Entiendo —le dije, y pensé que no podía ser de otra forma, porque sus rasgos se parecían mucho a los de los tuaregs; solo le faltaba el pañuelo azul añil en la cabeza para ser idéntico a uno de ellos.

—La vi hablando con el vigilante del metro y oí las explicaciones que él le dio sobre lo que ocurrió con el marido de Virginia. No sé cómo logró que el vigilante le contase todo lo que sabía y pensaba. ¿No será usted periodista? Lo digo porque parece tener mucha mano para conseguir información —comentó. Yo no le respondí—. Bueno, pues si lo es, no hallará nada de interés en esta historia, créame, nada más que añadir a lo que le han contado las dos alcahuetas con las que ha estado hablando, y eso ya lo sabe media ciudad. No deja de ser parte de una leyenda urbana.

—¿Me ha estado siguiendo? —le pregunté.

—¿Hay motivos para que tenga que hacerlo?

—Usted sabrá. Lleva apoyado ahí —señalé la tapia— desde que he llegado. Desde el momento que salí del albergue. Y no me ha quitado la vista de encima ni un solo momento. Juraría que estaba esperando a que saliese para acercarse a mí. ¿Me equivoco?

—No, en eso no se equivoca, pero sí en pensar que la he seguido, porque no ha sido exactamente así —me respondió—. La vi en el metro, en Cuatro Caminos. Caminaba por el andén arriba y abajo. Me llamaron tanto la atención sus paseos como a usted el hecho de que yo estuviera observándola desde la otra acera —apostilló con una sonrisa irónica.

—Bueno, una cosa no tiene que ver con la otra —le dije, sonriendo también.

—Estuve sentado a su lado en el metro. Esperaba la llegada del siguiente tren, pero usted andaba tan abstraída que no se dio cuenta de mi presencia. Entonces el vigilante le dio un manojo de llaves y usted comenzó a preguntarle acerca de Duncan y Virginia. Por eso la seguí; me intrigaron sus preguntas, el interés que mostraba por la historia de mi amiga Virginia. ¿Es periodista? —insistió.

—No, no lo soy. Pero conozco a Virginia. He sabido de la muerte de su marido y tengo que hablar con ella. Un amigo del matrimonio viene a España a buscarla y a repatriar los restos mortales de Duncan, que ella no ha querido reconocer. Creo que necesita ayuda. Si usted es su amigo, debería saberlo.

—Es curioso que Virginia no me haya hablado nunca de usted, ¿no cree? —respondió en tono mordaz.

—Esta conversación empieza a ser un poco absurda —le dije, molesta—. Ni usted se fía de mí ni yo de usted. Llegados a este punto será mejor que lo dejemos estar. Encantada de conocerle. —Le di la espalda y comencé a andar.

—Sé dónde se encuentra Virginia —dijo en un tono de voz más alto de lo habitual—. Si realmente quiere ayudarla, la llevaré hasta ella.

—¿Cómo dice? —pregunté, dándome la vuelta, y me planté frente a él.

CAPÍTULO 19

—La vida está llena de recovecos, de esquinas, de claroscuros, sonidos, luces y cientos de personas a las que casi no prestamos atención. A veces ni siquiera nos percatamos de que existen, pero, si nos faltasen, originarían un caos, una paradoja que cambiaría radicalmente la dirección de nuestros pasos. Virginia lo hizo conmigo, cambió la dirección de mis pasos y, a juzgar por lo que he visto, a usted le pasó lo mismo —me dijo y, acto seguido, levantó el dedo índice indicándome que esperase.

Sacó del bolsillo interior de su chaqueta el teléfono móvil y cargó una aplicación. Vestía traje negro de seda y camisa cuello Mao del mismo tejido y color que el traje. Era atractivo, mucho, pensé mirándolo de arriba abajo, y al hacerlo me fijé en las sandalias de cuero marrón que calzaba. Le daban un toque desenfadado y muy personal que me gustó. Calculé que rondaría la cuarentena, esa edad en la que los hombres, no todos pero sí algunos, suelen tener el cerebro asentado y un físico maduro y joven al tiempo. La edad del bocadito en los labios antes del beso, así la definía Samanta. La mejor edad para hacer el amor con un hombre, solía comentar cuando alguno con aquel aspecto físico y más o menos esa edad se paseaba por la oficina.

—¡Perdón! —se disculpó mientras guardaba el terminal—. Como le decía, usted y yo tenemos un vínculo y creo que un objetivo similar. Si me acompaña verá que no la engaño y se dará cuenta de que tengo razón.

—¿Dónde está Virginia ahora? —le pregunté—. Eso es lo único que me importa... por el momento —puntualicé.

—En mi tienda. Voy a reunirme con ella en unos minutos, en cuanto llegue el taxi que he pedido. Si quiere, puede acompañarme.

—Su tienda —dije encogiéndome de hombros y haciendo un gesto de incomprensión con las manos.

—Sí, mi tienda. Soy anticuario.

—¡Quién lo diría! Más bien le imaginaba sentado tras una gran mesa de madera de nogal, en un despacho de paredes acristaladas en lo más alto de la Torre Picasso, en plena City. Los pocos anticuarios que he conocido son mayores y demasiado clásicos —expliqué, mirando sus pies.

—Mi abuelo fue el precursor del negocio del que hemos vivido y gracias al que hemos prosperado toda la familia, el primero que se dedicó a ello. Comenzó vendiendo en el Rastro muebles, libros y todo tipo de objetos que traía de Francia y de Egipto. Finalmente estableció el negocio en el barrio de Salamanca y, aunque seguimos frecuentando el... inquietante Rastro madrileño —dijo haciendo una pausa para enfatizar el adjetivo—, la tienda no es solo un negocio, es nuestra jaima. Yo conservo uno de los pisos del mismo edificio y ahí es donde se encuentra ahora nuestra amiga. No se preocupe, no la perderé en la ciudad ni iremos a la periferia; en todo momento estará en un lugar conocido —me explicó, y me tendió la tarjeta de visita de la tienda.

—¿Cuándo conoció a Virginia? —le pregunté y, tras mirar la tarjeta, la introduje en uno de los bolsillos exteriores de mi mochila.

—La pregunta adecuada más bien sería cómo la conocí —me respondió, mirándome fijamente—. Si algo nos ha unido ha sido Virginia y la forma en que la conocimos ambos; el motivo por el que tú la buscas y el que a mí me ha hecho protegerla e intentar ayudarla. Cuándo sucedió es lo de menos.

»¿Cómo la conociste tú, Diana? Y ¿qué motivos tienes para querer volver a verla? ¿Por qué quieres ayudarla? —me preguntó, tuteándome con la más absoluta naturalidad, como si lo hubiera estado haciendo en todo momento.

—Por ahora eso es asunto mío.

—Bien, entiendo tu prudencia, ella puede evitar que pierdas la cabeza. No olvidemos que ¡solo puede quedar uno! —exclamó irónico, y me guiñó un ojo.

—¿Tengo que reírme, o es solo un chascarrillo de mal gusto?— le espeté.

—No. Es un guiño a ti y a *Los inmortales*. Me gusta la historia y he pensado que a ti, siendo escocesa, te gustaría aún más que a mí.

—No soy escocesa y, por favor —dije levantando la mano frente a él—, no lo digas, no digas que lo parezco. Estoy harta de escucharlo.

—Siento si te ha incomodado mi comentario. Solo pretendía romper el bloque de hielo que parece haber entre nosotros. No tengo ninguna intención de engañarte. Por mi parte, estoy dispuesto a confiarte todo lo que sé sobre Virginia y su marido, y me atrevo a aventurar que es mucho más de lo que tú sabes. Lo voy a hacer porque estoy convencido de que nuestros destinos se han cruzado por un motivo muy concreto. Nada es casual, no lo es en este tiempo que vivimos, ni lo ha sido ni lo será en ningún otro.

Levantó la mano y el taxi que había pedido se detuvo a nuestro lado.

—Y bien, qué me dices, ¿me acompañas? —me preguntó, tendiendo el brazo en dirección al vehículo.

Mientras subía al taxi, agachó la cabeza ligeramente y se llevó el dedo índice a los labios indicándome que guardara silencio. Durante el trayecto él permaneció sin hablar, consultando su teléfono móvil. Yo hice lo mismo. Saqué el portátil de la mochila y lo conecté a internet para buscar el nombre de la tienda que figuraba en la tarjeta que momentos antes me había dado. Revisé la información que había sobre el anticuario y comprobé que los datos relativos a la tienda eran reales.

—¿Y ahora qué? —le pregunté cuando nos bajamos del vehículo, ya frente al establecimiento.

—Antes de que veamos a Virginia, es importante que hablemos nosotros dos; no querría que volviese a las condiciones de confusión en que la encontré —me dijo mientras abría la puerta del local y me cedía el paso.

Entramos en el establecimiento, atiborrado de objetos de todo tipo. Lo atendía un hombre vestido con un traje negro y camisa blanca, que saludó a Farid y habló un momento con él antes de salir por una puerta que había tras el mostrador.

Podría haberme detenido junto a cualquiera de los artículos que estaban en venta, porque todos y cada uno de ellos eran piezas únicas e irrepetibles: los muebles auxiliares, las lámparas de techo o de pie, los sillones de piel marrón que, como el rostro de las personas, mostraban las arrugas que el paso del tiempo había dejado en su piel. Las máquinas de escribir y las de coser, los libros que parecían esperar los ojos de un lector para que sus historias volvieran a cobrar vida, incluso algunas joyas que, imaginé, no serían de mucho valor, porque permanecían expuestas sobre las bandejas de alpaca que había encima de los muebles. A pesar de que los artículos eran antiquísimos, todos estaban en unas condiciones extraordinarias,

como si acabasen de ser confeccionados. Podía haberle preguntado por cualquiera de aquellos objetos únicos, porque todo me llamaba poderosamente la atención. Pero no lo hice. Me detuve frente a un retrato que presidía la pared izquierda del local, rodeado de varios óleos de paisajes y bodegones. Nada más verlo, mi ritmo cardiaco se aceleró. Intenté moverme, dejar de observarlo para que Farid no percibiese el desasosiego que sentía en aquel momento, pero no pude retirar la vista de él.

—No hay ni un solo cliente que no se detenga a mirarlo, como has hecho tú —dijo Farid—. No está en venta, pero son muchos los que han intentado comprarlo. Hay ofertas desorbitadas, tanto que, por seguridad, el cuadro no duerme en la tienda. Aparte de su valor real, astronómico, pertenece a la colección privada de la familia. Está datado en el siglo XVI y la técnica utilizada es muy similar a la de *La Gioconda*, pero mientras que Da Vinci empleó madera de álamo como base para su óleo, este retrato —lo señaló— es un óleo sobre madera de haya negra. Como imaginarás, el color del material dificulta la ejecución, pero el artista consiguió una obra maestra. Eso, unido a su antigüedad y al hecho de que es el único retrato que hay de él, hacen que esta pieza alcance un valor incalculable. —Hizo una pausa y me miró—. Perdona, creo que no te he dicho que el retrato es de un vampiro escocés. Está rodeado de una leyenda demasiado hermosa y bien hilada a través de los siglos como para no ser real. La superstición que arrastra el personaje le confiere un valor que, al menos para mí, supera con creces el aspecto económico.

El personaje del retrato guardaba una semejanza con Desmond tan extraordinaria como, según había manifestado Farid, la técnica empleada para realizar aquel majestuoso óleo de un metro y medio de alto por uno de ancho. Sin embargo, el estado de conservación en el que se encontraba me llamó la atención. No parecía tan antiguo y, a decir verdad, tampoco me dio la impresión de que estuviera

confeccionado en madera de haya negra. Ese detalle me hizo dudar de la veracidad de las palabras de Farid.

—A mí no me parece tan antiguo como dices y, además, la madera parece de pino. No creo que sea haya negra —dije recordando mi gaveta, que sí era de esa madera. Me acerqué y lo miré con más detenimiento.

—Para no tener conocimiento sobre antigüedades eres una gran observadora. Lo que estás viendo es una copia. El original se encuentra a buen recaudo. Sería un riesgo excesivo e innecesario tenerlo en la tienda.

—No he dicho que no esté al corriente sobre antigüedades, solo que los anticuarios que he conocido no tienen mucho en común contigo. Las antigüedades me fascinan. Pero soy una aficionada de clase baja que no puede permitirse nada de lo que hay en tu negocio. Los precios no solo sobrepasan mi nómina mensual, sino que algunas de estas piezas ni siquiera podría comprarlas con el sueldo de todo un año.

Lo miré fijamente y, tras unos segundos, continué en tono seco y distante:

—No me gusta que me mientan o intenten tomarme el pelo. Lo digo porque hace unos segundos me dijiste que era el original y que no dormía en la tienda.

—¡Lo siento! Nada más lejos de mi intención que ofenderte, y menos que pienses que te he mentido. No ha sido así, solo he intentado que vieses el cuadro como si realmente estuvieras ante la obra original. Si te hubiese dicho que no lo era habría influido en tu punto de vista.

»No pienses que me rodeo solo de eruditos para adquirir, valorar o encontrar tesoros, obras de arte u objetos únicos; también me gusta contar con la opinión de los que no son expertos en la materia. Su mirada, su punto de vista, suele detectar detalles que pasan desapercibidos para muchos expertos. Me ha sorprendido mucho que

de un simple vistazo hayas sabido que no era el original. ¿No serás una bruja? —me preguntó esbozando una sonrisa.

—No entiendo a qué viene esa tontería.

—Mi abuelo conoció a una meiga que vivía en una aldea gallega. Ella le relató que la mirada de las brujas tiene el poder de embaucar y que, además de enamorarte, ven más allá que cualquiera de nosotros. Le aseguró que las brujas, las auténticas, no necesitan hechizos ni pócimas para crear magia o para ver las otras realidades que se mezclan con la nuestra, porque su mirada es capaz de viajar de una realidad a otra. Me refiero a las múltiples realidades que, según algunos, existen a la par. Poseer ese poder debe de ser lo más impresionante que nadie pueda imaginar, ¿no crees?

—No sé. Solo de pensar en ello me bloqueo. Ya tengo suficiente con una realidad como para haber de bandearme en más de una. Tengo la suerte de que no me sucede nada de lo que has contado, por lo que deduzco que no soy bruja —le respondí con una sonrisa, intentando disimular el desasosiego que me estaban produciendo sus palabras.

—Muchas lo son y aún no lo han averiguado. Otras renuncian a serlo toda su vida.

—¿Me estás hablando en serio? —le inquirí con un gesto de incredulidad, porque su insistencia ya me parecía excesiva.

—Por supuesto que sí. Creo en los vampiros, en las brujas y en muchas otras criaturas. —Señaló el cuadro—. El vaticinio que la meiga le hizo a mi abuelo constaba de muchas y diferentes predicciones que fueron cumpliéndose a través del tiempo. Solo queda una que aún no se ha realizado. Le aseguró que el destino de nuestra familia estaba unido al de una bruja, pero en mi familia no hay ninguna... aún, por eso sigo buscándola, porque creo que su augurio, como sucedió con el resto de los que hizo, se cumplirá —declaró sin dejar de sonreír.

»Podrías volver a analizar el cuadro y decirme si ves algo más en él que te llame la atención.

—¿No cree usted, señor anticuario, que es un poco ridículo? Este cuadro es una copia —le respondí con sorna.

—La copia y el original son idénticos. No quiero tu opinión sobre el material o la técnica, solo que lo vuelvas a examinar como lo hiciste antes. Tu mirada, cuando lo observabas, no era la misma, incluso tu iris cambió de color. Te juro que tus ojos me parecieron verdes.

—Dijiste que es el único, la única imagen que existe de él —expuse. Él asintió con un movimiento afirmativo—. Tal vez sea el único porque es un autorretrato.

Volví a mirarlo y pensé que, sin lugar a dudas, aquel hombre de ojos azul añil y piel blanquísima, de labios perfectos y pómulos marcados, era Desmond. Recordé los óleos que él tenía en su casa, también el que me regaló, y aquel comentario de Ecles sobre la maestría que Desmond poseía para el realismo. Una técnica que, según Ecles, se negaba a utilizar. Solo pintaba abstracto, excepto el dibujo de un ala delta roja que hizo sobre el cabecero de mi cama con pintura acrílica durante aquel pasado que, en esos momentos, me parecía lejano e irrecuperable. También pensé que Farid sabía mucho más de lo que aparentaba. El significado de sus palabras y aquel vaticinio que aún estaba por cumplir me intranquilizaron.

Me volví y lo miré inquisitivamente. Quise buscar en sus ojos un atisbo de duda, un gesto en su rostro que diese muestras de un posible engaño, porque, si no me equivocaba y Desmond era el personaje del retrato y también su autor, era posible que él y Farid se conocieran. Pero el anticuario seguía contemplando el óleo a la espera de que le dijese algo más. Sus ojos continuaban fijos en la pintura como si contemplase la obra original. Era evidente, pensé, que aquel retrato ejercía una atracción ineludible sobre el anticuario

y sobre todo aquel que lo contemplase. Farid permaneció unos segundos sin percatarse de que yo le estaba mirando, ensimismado y sonriendo, hasta que, de repente, se volvió hacia mí.

—¡Extraordinario! —exclamó alzando un poco el tono de voz—. Efectivamente; es un autorretrato. He investigado durante años sobre este personaje y sobre el autor del cuadro. Varios eruditos sostienen la misma teoría que tú; afirman que es un autorretrato de uno de los vampiros más enigmáticos y desconocidos de Escocia. Su nombre es Desmond.

Cuando oí el nombre del vampiro tuve que controlar mi mirada, mis gestos, e incluso hube de tragar saliva para poder replicar su comentario.

—Bueno, si era un vampiro, no sé cómo pudo ser el autor. Dicen que los vampiros no se reflejan en los espejos. Entonces, ¿cómo se autorretrató? —respondí, irónica.

—Tal vez hayan mentido sobre ello. La mentira solo intenta ocultar la verdad. No tiene otro cometido, esa es su única razón de ser. En ese caso, lo más probable es que los vampiros se reflejen en los espejos, no duerman en ataúdes ni necesiten un puñado de su tierra natal para descansar. Quizás todo eso sea un adorno estúpido para ocultar su verdadera esencia y no dejarnos ver que son más poderosos de lo que creemos, igual que las brujas. —Me sonrió de nuevo.

—¿Por qué te interesa tanto la historia de este vampiro?

—Porque aún vive y voy a encontrarlo —me respondió, volviendo la mirada hacia el óleo.

Al escuchar sus palabras y el tono de voz que utilizó, al ver cómo fijaba la vista sobre el retrato, aquella mirada obsesiva y casi aterradora, me preocupé aún más.

—¿No íbamos a ver a Virginia? —le pregunté con la voz un poco quebrada, intentando desviar sus pensamientos del cuadro y,

con ello, salir de aquel lugar que parecía habernos encarcelado a los dos.

—Sí, sí, claro. Lo había olvidado... —Hizo una pequeña pausa—. ¿No te habrán inquietado mis palabras? —me preguntó.

No le respondí, solo esquivé su mirada—. Está bien, porque no quiero que tengas miedo. Le busco porque su rastro me conducirá hasta una pieza de un valor aún mayor que su retrato. Algo impagable: el evangelio de las brujas, el auténtico.

—En realidad lo que te interesa son las brujas. Quieres encontrar a esa que, según la meiga, había de formar parte de tu familia y su destino. Es eso, ¿verdad?

—No del todo. Si realmente la meiga tenía razón, no tengo necesidad de hacer nada para que la bruja entre en nuestro círculo familiar. Estoy seguro de que lo hará. Me interesa más su evangelio, porque en ese texto tienen que estar recogidas las claves para viajar en el tiempo. Y está claro que ese vampiro las tiene. Existen crónicas que hablan de su presencia en diferentes siglos.

»Hasta que conocí a Virginia —prosiguió— no tenía nada más para seguir investigando sobre el paradero de ese libro, estaba perdido. Mis investigaciones habían llegado a un punto muerto. Cuando la conocí se abrió ante mí un nuevo horizonte, una nueva vía. Su marido seguía muy de cerca el rastro del evangelio. Iba tras él como lo he hecho yo, y creo que ella sabe mucho más de su paradero de lo que dice. Si no fuese así, no conocería detalles relevantes de su contenido y la forma en que durante siglos han conseguido ocultarse las brujas adoradoras de la Luna, las auténticas brujas. Si Virginia no supiera más sobre el texto, no afirmaría, como lo ha hecho, que su marido no ha muerto y que sigue vivo en esa estación del metro.

—Entonces, según tus investigaciones, ¿qué es lo que une al vampiro con el evangelio? —le pregunté.

—Según dice la leyenda, él estará donde esté el evangelio. Como si la existencia del libro y la suya fuesen una condena o no pudieran darse el uno sin el otro. El último dato sobre él, sobre su existencia, lo encontré en unos textos de la época victoriana. Según unos documentos, se le enterró en el cementerio de Greyfriars, en Edimburgo. En un *mortsafe*, una tumba enjaulada.

—Jamás había oído nada sobre los *mortsafes*. Una jaula sobre una tumba, ¡es aterrador!

—Las construyeron para que los vampiros, o los mortales convertidos en vampiros, no escapasen. También para proteger los cadáveres en general, porque los maleantes los robaban y luego los vendían a los médicos.

»La cuestión es que su cuerpo desapareció —añadió—. No fue robado, porque no hallaron excavaciones subterráneas bajo la tumba, que era como procedían los ladrones de cadáveres. Todo estaba intacto. Algunos investigadores afirman que jamás estuvo en aquel ataúd y que todo fue una artimaña para simular su muerte. Dicen que el vampiro era un impostor, un escapista que se ganaba la vida como embaucador. Yo me inclino por pensar que sigue vivo, que escapó de su encierro y sigue entre nosotros.

—Tengo que reconocer que la leyenda es digna de una película de terror.

—Y que lo digas —coincidió, y movió la cabeza de izquierda a derecha—. Te mostraré el material gráfico de que dispongo. Te dejaré consultar toda la documentación que he reunido sobre el vampiro, incluso sobre otros temas, todos relacionados con la parapsicología. A cambio, te propongo un trato. —Hizo una pequeña pausa, como si necesitase tomar aire, y continuó—: Quiero que me ayudes a buscar el evangelio. Por supuesto, recibirás una importante compensación económica, tanto si lo hallamos juntos como si no lo encontramos. Creo que tú puedes conseguir que Virginia recuerde más de lo que lo ha hecho conmigo. Incluso puedes percibir si te

miente o no. Tienes una mirada diferente, eso no puedes negármelo. Eres muy observadora.

—Y el vampiro, ¿también vamos a buscarlo?

—No hará falta. Si encontramos el verdadero evangelio de las brujas, que es un incunable, y si él, tal y como dice la leyenda, sigue vivo, no estará muy lejos del libro.

Capítulo 20

Intenté disimular ante Farid la emoción que sentía. Era la primera vez que tenía ventaja, que la posibilidad de realizar un jaque mate estaba en mis manos. Mis piezas estaban mejor situadas en el tablero. Siempre, durante toda mi vida, había jugado con desventaja. Había sido un simple peón sacrificado en cada partida por el bien de los demás. Había dado palos de ciego una y otra vez, pero en aquel momento sabía más que ninguna de las personas que me rodeaban. Incluso tenía más información que Farid. Él parecía haber pasado gran parte de su vida siguiendo el rastro de Desmond para llegar al evangelio, a mi evangelio, y yo tenía las dos cosas al alcance de la mano; solo necesitaba convencer a Ecles para que me dijese el paradero de mi libro, dónde lo había escondido.

Volví a mirar el retrato y pensé que, tras aquella supuesta alergia al sol de mi amigo Desmond, se escondía otra realidad, una verdad aún más grande y tal vez tan terrorífica como lo que me había contado Farid sobre los *mortsafes* escoceses, las tumbas enjauladas. Desmond era un vampiro perdido, como yo, en una ciudad ruidosa y sin alma, un ser que deambulaba y malvivía en un siglo que no le correspondía. Si era así, dejarse ver, descubrir su verdadera identidad, era un suicidio, porque nadie lo creería. Si se exponía, todos pensarían que había perdido la razón, como le había sucedido a

Virginia, y los pocos que lo creyesen intentarían destruirlo o aprovecharse de él, como evidentemente pretendía hacer Farid. Desmond, al igual que yo, no podía arriesgarse a perder la cabeza. Debía pasar desapercibido, como uno más, aunque no lo fuese. Yo también debía mantener la mía sobre los hombros, no perderla dejándome llevar por los sentimientos que él me inspiraba. No sabía el motivo real por el que mi amigo estaba unido al destino del evangelio, pero tenía claro que así era, tal y como Farid me había relatado. De no ser el caso, Desmond y yo jamás nos habríamos encontrado.

Mi vida podía estar en peligro junto a él, pensé entristecida, y al hacerlo sentí una punzada en el pecho. Al imaginar que Desmond tal vez solo me estaba utilizando y que no era como yo creía, que acaso ni siquiera sentía una pizca de atracción hacia mí, me sentí desfallecer. Debía jugar bien la partida; observar, ser paciente y esperar a que los demás movieran sus piezas antes de hacerlo yo con las mías. Si lo conseguía, si llevaba a cabo una buena estrategia, por fin encontraría el significado de la gaveta, hallaría mis orígenes y descubriría por qué me dejaron en la puerta de aquel mísero hospicio perdido de la mano de Dios, pero, sobre todo, averiguaría cuál era mi vinculación con aquel texto y verificaría su autenticidad.

—Trato hecho —respondí y le tendí la mano, que él estrechó con fuerza, como cuando nos habíamos presentado hacía apenas dos horas—. Pero no me pidas que presione demasiado a Virginia, no está bien y no quiero acrecentar su pena.

—Por supuesto que no. Aunque no me creas, a mí también me preocupa su estado, y no solo por mi interés en encontrar ese libro, sino también por ella, me cae bien. Es una buena persona.

—Espero que cumplas tu promesa y me dejes ver la documentación de la que dispones sobre el vampiro y la existencia de ese evangelio del que hablas.

—No dudes de mí, soy un hombre de palabra. Virginia está en mi casa, arriba —dijo, señalando la puerta que había tras el mostrador—. Si te parece bien, subimos a buscarla y almorzamos los tres juntos; es ya tarde y a este paso vamos a tomar el té antes del almuerzo —me dijo, extendiendo la mano para indicarme el camino.

Asentí en silencio y lo seguí hacia la puerta que estaba detrás del mostrador y que, según supuse, conducía al piso superior. Sin embargo, el empleado nos salió al paso:

—Si va en busca de la señora Virginia, no está en casa. Salió hace unos minutos. Quise advertirle a usted de que se iba, pero ella me lo prohibió. Insistió en que no le molestase, ya que usted estaba ocupado —comentó el dependiente, mirándome de soslayo.

—¿Dijo adónde se dirigía? —le preguntó Farid.

—Ya sabe... —le respondió el otro, un poco apurado, bajando el tono de voz—. Al mismo sitio de siempre; en busca de su marido. Se marchó por la trastienda. —Y señaló la puerta hacia la que nos dirigíamos Farid y yo cuando él nos paró.

Por lo visto, además de conducir al piso superior, aquella puerta también daba a la calle, pensé.

—Debería haber cerrado la tienda hace una hora —le dijo Farid a su empleado al tiempo que consultaba la hora en su reloj de pulsera—. ¿Cómo es que sigue aquí?

—Me quedé por si necesitaban algo —le respondió el dependiente.

—No, no es una clienta —dijo Farid, sonriendo—. Puede marcharse ya. ¡Es tardísimo!

El hombre no se demoró ni un minuto en despedirse de nosotros y salir del establecimiento.

—¿Y ahora qué? —le pregunté a Farid, encogiéndome de hombros—. Si Virginia se ha ido no podré hablar con ella, y esa era y es mi prioridad. No olvides que por eso estoy aquí.

—No te preocupes por Virginia, volverá. Siempre lo hace. Estará en el metro hasta media tarde y regresará antes de que caiga el sol. Mientras tanto, si te parece bien, podemos almorzar juntos. Después te enseñaré parte de la documentación, lo más relevante. Dártelo todo sería absurdo, es una cantidad ingente de documentos y notas. Solo necesitas saber cómo y qué debes preguntarle a Virginia para que, si sabe dónde se encuentra el texto, nos conduzca hasta él.

—Estás muy seguro de que ella sabe dónde está —comenté mientras salíamos de la tienda.

—Pues sí, y desde que te vi lo estoy aún más. Tengo un presentimiento, una sensación de euforia que nunca antes había sentido. Soy muy intuitivo. Mi madre siempre dijo que yo era diferente, que tenía un don porque lloré en su vientre. Ese don es para mí la intuición. Si te contase algunas cosas que me han sucedido, cómo he encontrado algunos de los objetos únicos que tengo, te sorprenderías. Estoy seguro de que no me creerías —me dijo, mirándome de una forma diferente a como lo había hecho con anterioridad.

—Inténtalo, lo mismo eres tú quien se sorprende de lo crédula que soy yo —le respondí, esbozando una sonrisa que ocultó mi ironía.

—¿Conoces El paraguas? —me preguntó. Yo negué con la cabeza al tiempo que recordaba el paraguas rojo de la portada de *En un rincón del alma*, la novela que me regaló Alán en los comienzos de nuestra relación.

Farid era atractivo; alto, con estilo, culto e inteligente, quizás demasiado inteligente. Joven y, en apariencia, con una posición económica y social muy acomodada, pensé. Era fácil enamorarse de él, casi tan fácil como lo fue para mí enamorarme de Alán.

—Espero que te guste. Es un sitio con encanto y la cocina es espectacular, como sus caldos y su repostería. Iremos caminando.

Está muy cerca de aquí, en Jorge Juan esquina con Lagasca, a la altura de los callejones de Puigcerdá...

***

Salieron del restaurante unos segundos antes de que nosotros llegásemos a la puerta. Él no me vio, pero yo sí los vi a ellos. Fue su risa lo que me hizo buscarla; aquellas carcajadas estúpidas no podían ser de otra persona. Al verla me detuve en seco, a unos metros del restaurante. Farid me preguntó qué me pasaba. Yo agaché la cabeza y escondí mi mirada dentro de la mochila.

—Creo que ha sonado mi teléfono —le dije, haciendo el ademán de buscarlo.

Vi que Alán le abría la puerta del taxi y que ella subía al vehículo sin dejar de reírse, escupiendo margaritas de colores chillones por la boca. No lo imaginé, en aquella ocasión vi las flores saliendo de su boquita de piñón, de labios barnizados de rojo carmín, porque, como dijo Farid, las brujas tenemos una mirada diferente, especial y mágica. Aunque no queramos, siempre vemos más allá. Y él, Alán, le sonreía con cara de estar idiotizado por su risa y por sus contoneos sensuales y premonitorios de lo que seguramente él deseaba que sucediese después.

Capítulo 21

Farid no estaba equivocado: su intuición funcionaba. Se inclinó y, sin disimular, me preguntó:

—¿De verdad buscabas el teléfono? Porque, si era así, mirabas en un sitio equivocado. Creo que iba en aquel taxi —dijo, señalando el vehículo que ya se alejaba.

Le respondí con una sonrisa teñida de rabia y tristeza, un malestar que comenzó a llenar de pétalos rojos parte del interior de mi mochila y que oculté cerrando la cremallera lo más rápido que pude para que Farid no los viese.

—No sé si mi indumentaria es apropiada para este sitio —le dije, intentando desviar la conversación a otro tema.

—No te preocupes por eso. Es un almuerzo, no una cena. Ya sabes…, la etiqueta y el protocolo dependen mucho de la hora del día y, de todas formas, estás estupenda. No a todo el mundo le sientan tan bien los pantalones vaqueros. No te agobies, ni por eso ni por ese taxi y quienquiera que fuera en él. Si te fías de mi intuición, y debes hacerlo, creo que no es importante para ti. Quizás lo único relevante es que te encontrases con ellos, o con él; que los vieses, nada más —afirmó, seguro de sí mismo.

—Era uno de mis jefes. No he ido a trabajar, dije que estaba enferma. Imagina si llega a verme —repuse.

—Deberías practicar más, mientes fatal —dijo mirándome a los ojos—. Sería interesante que dieses unas cuantas clases de oratoria política, es lo más eficaz para que la gente crea en tus palabras aunque estés contando una flagrante mentira. Y si la política no es lo tuyo, como me sucede a mí, te invitaré a jugar unas cuantas partidas de póquer, ni te cuento lo que se aprende jugando al mentiroso...

Si lo hubiese conocido antes, tal vez aquel almuerzo habría sido una cita cargada de deseo, sueños y algo más, me dije mirándolo mientras él hablaba con el dueño del local. ¡Era tan culto, atento y observador! Tenía muchas de las cualidades que siempre me habían atraído en los hombres, pero había aparecido en mi vida a destiempo para aquellas cuestiones tan humanas.

Durante el almuerzo no hablamos de los asuntos por los que estábamos juntos. La tensión que momentos antes reinaba entre nosotros se suavizó nada más tomar asiento. La desconfianza pareció licuarse, desaparecer absorbida por el ambiente cálido y acogedor del restaurante. Sonreí mientras él me sugería lo que debía probar y, por unos momentos, pensé hasta qué punto nos asemejábamos en aquellos momentos a la pareja que Alán y yo habíamos formado en los comienzos de nuestra relación, cuando ambos íbamos a la caza de eso que a veces llamamos amor.

Consiguió que me evadiese, que olvidase por qué estaba allí, con él. Lo hizo explicándome la composición y elaboración de los platos que íbamos a degustar, que no comer, apuntó, porque una cosa difería mucho de la otra, no era en absoluto lo mismo, me dijo. Sonreí al escucharle y pensé que tenía razón, y mucha.

Uno a uno, los platos del menú fueron pasando por nuestra mesa cargados de aromas, colorido, una exquisita elaboración y una bella presentación, que trajeron a mi memoria el fragor de las olas al chocar contra los acantilados, su olor y sabor; el sabor del mar. Sentí el aire limpio del Cantábrico y el de las verdes tierras de Asturias junto a mí.

—Esto ha sido una auténtica experiencia para mi paladar. Gracias, Farid, lo necesitaba. Necesitaba desconectar de la realidad, del día a día.

—No tienes por qué dármelas, al contrario, yo soy quien debo agradecértelo. Tu compañía es el maridaje perfecto. Ya sabes, las viandas y los caldos toman más sabor, color y olor dependiendo de con quién se compartan y en qué lugar se haga. Este es uno de mis restaurantes preferidos, pero solo traigo a personas especiales, como tú.

Levantó la copa de vino y la acercó a la mía para brindar.

—Pero... no te fíes de mí —añadió, sonriéndose y mirándome fijamente a los ojos—. Tal vez mis pretensiones no se queden en la relación de dos socios en busca de un incunable. Eres una mujer muy interesante y yo un donjuán por naturaleza. ¿No has pensado que quizás, tras mi invitación a almorzar, haya una intención oculta, un propósito que nada tenga que ver con incunables ni reliquias extraordinarias?

—¡Venga ya! —le respondí, rozando mi copa con la suya, e hice un gesto de despreocupación, como si sus palabras fueran una tontería, aunque estaba segura de que no lo eran porque, al decirlo, su tono de voz y su mirada cambiaron.

—¿Cuándo me vas a contar lo que te une a Virginia, cómo la conociste? —dijo después de que el camarero se alejase tras dejar los cafés y el licor en la mesa.

—Hay poco que contar. Tú tampoco me has hablado de ello, solo dijiste que lo más importante no era cuándo, sino cómo la conociste. Ya ves que tengo muy buena memoria.

—La conocí en la tienda. Vino buscando libros antiguos que hablasen sobre las bases más antiguas de la Wicca, unas creencias que permanecieron ocultas durante más de diez siglos.

—Pero tu tienda es un anticuario —le dije sorprendida—. No he visto que tengas muchos textos. Solo algunos libros que no parecen tener demasiado valor, repartidos sobre los muebles.

—Este tipo de negocios, como todos, tiene sus bambalinas, sus pasadizos ocultos y sus claroscuros. Dispongo de mucha documentación que no está a la vista. También de objetos que te sorprenderían. Son las reliquias que se guardan para aquellos que no quieren ceñirse al estricto tutelaje de la ley. No te asustes, solo soy un «conseguidor», algo parecido a un bróker, además de anticuario —puntualizó, como si esta última actividad le restase gravedad a lo anterior—. Te enseñaré algunos cuando regresemos.

—¿Para qué quería Virginia documentación sobre la Wicca?

—En sus más remotos orígenes, es la región que profesaban las brujas adoradoras de la Luna. Su diosa se llamaba como tú: Diana. —Me miró sonriente—. Dicen que, entre muchos otros poderes, esas mujeres tenían la capacidad de viajar en el tiempo, lo que casi las convertía en inmortales. Y eso es lo que buscaba Virginia, el rastro de las brujas. Me comentó que su marido era un estudioso de los orígenes de las brujas y que había conseguido viajar en el tiempo, como lo hicieron ellas. Quería seguirle los pasos, volver con él, donde ahora se hallaba. Es evidente que él lo consiguió, porque tuvo en sus manos el evangelio. El resto creo que ya lo sabes. Si tienes un amigo común con Virginia o con su marido, debes saberlo.

—No del todo —le dije, intentando hablar en un tono convincente y no gesticular demasiado para que no se diese cuenta de que le ocultaba información.

—Mientes mal, muy mal, ya te lo he dicho antes —comentó con una sonrisa—. Pero no me importa, solo quiero que me ayudes. Tenemos un trato, y te advierto que cerrar un acuerdo con un hombre como yo, con poder, es como hacerlo con el diablo. —Me pareció que su mirada se endurecía y sus pómulos se afilaban.

—Farid, no me gusta que me amenacen. No me gusta nada —
le dije molesta, ocultando el miedo que, por unos momentos, sentí.

—No es una amenaza, es un simple aviso. Me agradas, Diana.
Me agradas incluso por encima de lo común, ya te lo he dicho antes,
pero para mí encontrar ese evangelio es muy importante, pasa por
encima de cualquier cosa. Ha sido mi prioridad durante años. Solo
quiero que tengas claro ese punto. Respeto tu intimidad, y te doy
mi palabra de que seguiré haciéndolo mientras dure nuestra relación
profesional. Hemos cerrado un contrato verbal. Te has comprometido a colaborar conmigo para dar con ese evangelio. Solo te pido
que no me engañes, que si sabes algo sobre ese libro, no me lo ocul-
tes —dijo tajante, cambiando su tono varias veces mientras hablaba.

—No —respondí con determinación, y lo miré con aire desafiante—. Me he comprometido a ayudarte con Virginia, a intentar
conseguir la información que ella pueda tener sobre el paradero del
evangelio, nada más. En ningún momento hemos hablado sobre
los datos de que yo disponga, ni de la obligación de dártelos para
encontrar ese libro. Solo de Virginia.

—Entonces, ¿tienes información sobre el libro y no me lo has
dicho?

—Tengo la misma que tú. Sé que Virginia acompañaba a su
marido en las investigaciones, que este desapareció y que ella cree
verlo en el metro. Nada más. Quiero localizarla porque se niega a
reconocer el cuerpo de su esposo. Un amigo del matrimonio viene
a España para repatriar los restos mortales de Duncan y no sabe
dónde está Virginia. Ha intentado localizarla, pero le ha sido imposible. Da la casualidad que soy amiga de una alumna suya y ella es la
que me lo ha pedido directamente. Me contó lo que le sucedía, en
qué condiciones estaba, y se me ocurrió que el sitio más idóneo para
empezar a indagar sería en el metro.

—Pero al vigilante le dijiste que ya la conocías.

—Me lo inventé para que él me contase si la había visto. Esa vez sí supe mentir —le dije irónica.

Pedimos la cuenta y nos la trajeron enseguida. Farid se quedó pensativo, ensimismado, dando vueltas entre sus dedos a la tarjeta de crédito. Finalmente la colocó junto a la factura y me miró.

—Discúlpame, no estoy muy acostumbrado a fiarme de nadie, es una de las claves del éxito de mi negocio. Soy un embaucador y siempre temo encontrarme con alguien como yo. ¡Lo siento! Vayamos a la tienda y olvidemos nuestra conversación. Volvamos al comienzo, será más productivo que estar desconfiando el uno del otro. ¿Te parece?

—Farid, ¿para qué quieres ese libro? —le pregunté al tiempo que nos levantábamos de la mesa.

Me miró en silencio, ya de pie. Se acercó a mí y me dijo bajito, pegado a mi oreja:

—Lo consultaré, me beberé sus páginas, la información que hay en ellas, y luego lo destruiré.

CAPÍTULO 22

Jamás se me habría ocurrido que Farid quisiera encontrar el evangelio para destruirlo. Al escucharle, recordé las pintadas que encontré en mi antiguo apartamento, donde vivíamos Alán y yo antes de mudarnos al ático de Argüelles. También pensé en la destrucción de la documentación que me envió Andreas desde Escocia con todo el material sobre Aradia y las conjeturas sobre el paradero del evangelio de las brujas. Rememoré el estado en que me encontré el apartamento: los folios hechos añicos, repartidos por todo el piso del salón, y aquel líquido rojo que, al verterlo en la tartera, se adhirió a ella y la convirtió en un cuenco del mismo color y consistencia que las cubiertas de mi libro.

Nada más salir del restaurante, el teléfono móvil de Farid sonó. Levantó la mano en un gesto de disculpa y se retiró unos metros de mí. Hablaba en francés, bajito y pegado a la pared del edificio contiguo al restaurante. Yo le esperé a la sombra de uno de los árboles que había en la acera porque, a pleno sol, el calor a aquella hora de la tarde comenzaba a ser insoportable.

Aquel hombre tan atractivo, culto e inteligente, que aparentaba ser un materialista, que en un principio me había hecho creer que lo único que le importaba era encontrar una pieza de valor incalculable, ahora decía querer destruirla. Algo no encajaba en todo aquello, pensé mientras las dudas sobre sus intenciones respecto a

mí comenzaban a surgir de nuevo. ¿Y si Farid fue quien entró en mi apartamento y pintó aquella luna de sangre?, me pregunté. Tal vez había mentido, como lo había hecho yo. Podía haber estado tras mi pista desde que vivía con Alán en el piso de Manuel Becerra, que curiosamente estaba muy cerca de su tienda, en el barrio de Salamanca. Quizás no era tan intuitivo como había dicho y ya conocía a Alán, de modo que al verlo con Azucena en aquel taxi supo el motivo de mi reacción. Si mis conjeturas eran ciertas no podía hacer nada, debía continuar con la misma actitud frente a él y no levantar sospechas. Estaba en un callejón sin salida, pensé aterrada.

—¡Discúlpame! —me dijo—. Sin duda la tecnología tiene muchas ventajas, pero también nos ha hecho más esclavos. Debería haber desconectado el teléfono. Siento que hayas tenido que esperarme.

Le sonreí con desgana, aún inmersa en mi desconfianza.

—¿Pasa algo? —me preguntó al ver que caminaba sin mirarlo y en silencio.

—No, no. Es este calor tan seco. Me mata, como la ciudad. Aunque amo Madrid, ya sabes: hay amores que matan.

—Eso lo solucionaremos enseguida. El aire acondicionado de la tienda es un milagro, y en el sótano la temperatura es estable, ni frío ni calor. Ahí tengo toda la documentación que quiero enseñarte. También guardo el original del cuadro del vampiro, en una caja fuerte. Es más pequeño que la copia, pero aún más real, si cabe. —Sonrió—. Te sorprenderá. El estilo me gusta tanto como la pintura de Antonio López. Ese hombre es diferente al común de los mortales, ¿lo conoces?

—Desmond —dije pensando en voz alta.

—Me refiero al pintor, Antonio López García, no al vampiro. ¿Seguro que te encuentras bien?

—Sí, sí, perdona, no sé en qué estaba pensando —dije, intentando enmendar mi desliz—. Conozco los cuadros de Antonio

López, son un prodigio, igual que sus esculturas. No creo que el cuadro de tu vampiro le llegue ni a la suela de los zapatos —le dije con cierta ironía, enfatizando el posesivo.

Al escucharle hablar sobre el cuadro, mis conjeturas se desbarataron. Farid no conocía a mi amigo Desmond, me dije. Por su actitud, por todo lo que me había comentado sobre él y las investigaciones que había llevado a cabo en torno a su vida, era evidente que no se habían visto. En ese caso, era evidente que tampoco me conocía a mí, pensé recuperando parte de la calma perdida.

—Mira —me dijo nada más cruzar el umbral de la puerta de entrada del local—. Como te dije, ese cuadro ejerce una extraña atracción en todo aquel que lo contempla —me comentó mirando a un cliente que, parado frente al óleo, lo observaba estático, ensimismado en la pintura—. Eso sucede con la copia, ni te cuento la sensación que produce ver el original, tenerlo frente a ti...

Accedimos al sótano tras abrir una puerta acorazada, algo que me resultó tan extraño como imprevisible. Pensé que aquel habitáculo sería más pequeño, de dimensiones y estructura comunes. Lo había imaginado como el típico trastero o almacén en el que Farid guardaría algunos objetos de un valor relativo, con la característica caja fuerte de pared y un espacio destinado para una mesa de despacho. Tras ella estaría la tradicional estantería llena de archivadores de cartón a rebosar de facturas y albaranes de entrega. Pero, una vez más, me sorprendió. El sótano, que a simple vista ocupaba una parte considerable del bajo del edificio, tenía las paredes aisladas con láminas de metal que iban del suelo al techo. En dos de ellas había varias librerías de puertas acristaladas que guardaban cientos de libros, y no me cupo la menor duda de que eran piezas únicas. Había grandes cajas de madera repartidas por el suelo, algunas ni tan siquiera habían sido abiertas. Vi sellos de las aduanas de diferentes países, pero predominaban los de El Cairo, y la mayoría eran antiquísimos. La temperatura era estable y controlada por un

sensor. Me sobrecogió tanto la cantidad de objetos, lienzos, joyas y libros que había en aquel recinto que no pude evitar pasear por él, ensimismada en la contemplación de cada pieza.

—Impresiona, ¿verdad? —dijo Farid, sentado en el sillón de piel marrón que tenía junto a la mesa—. Este es mi reino, en el que solo entran personas de mi confianza. Todas y cada una de estas piezas están vivas; tienen alma. A veces solo bajo para escuchar lo que cuentan. Ese y no otro es su verdadero valor, lo que le da sentido a mi búsqueda: encontrarlos para después protegerlos.

—Entonces, es curioso que quieras destruir el evangelio —comenté sin poder reprimir mis pensamientos.

—Créeme si te digo que me dolerá hacerlo, pero no tengo alternativa. Lo que haga con el libro es cosa mía, y eso incluye los motivos para destruirlo. Te recuerdo que nuestro trato no va más allá de encontrarlo —puntualizó.

No quise preguntar más, porque su mirada me resultó aún más tajante que sus palabras.

—He recapacitado sobre todo lo que me has comentado y no entiendo qué relación puede haber entre el evangelio y el vampiro. No se me ocurre qué vinculación pueden tener.

Sonrió y, con un gesto de la mano, me indicó que lo siguiera.

Farid se situó frente a una de las paredes que estaban vacías. Sacó un llavero del bolsillo interior de su americana, similar a los aparatos que desconectan las alarmas de las casas; plano, de metal y con una piedra de cristal verde en el centro. Se dio la vuelta y, de espaldas a mí, lo acercó al tabique. Sin tocar la pared comenzó a trazar en el aire una espiral. Cuando dejó de mover la mano frente al tabique, la lámina de metal se abrió hacia nosotros como si fuese una puerta. Tras ella estaba la caja fuerte.

—¡Increíble! —exclamé—. Lo que tienes aquí montado es sorprendente. No sé qué puede tener más valor, si lo que guardas en este recinto o esta especie de habitación del pánico.

—Sin lugar a dudas, lo que guardo —expuso, girando la rudimentaria rueda de la caja fuerte.

—No entiendo que tengas una caja fuerte tan elemental. Comparada con las demás medidas de seguridad del recinto, es como si utilizases máquina de escribir con papel de calco en vez de emplear un ordenador con tratamiento de textos.

—En el fondo soy un romántico. —Sonrió—. Aunque no lo creas, esta bestia —dijo, dando una palmada sobre la caja fuerte— es mucho más segura de lo que aparenta. La electrónica tiene muchas puertas traseras, pero este dinosaurio es casi inviolable.

»Date la vuelta —me pidió—, quiero que lo veas de una vez, sin que aprecies antes ni un ápice de la pintura.

El retrato poseía un realismo sobrecogedor: el azul añil de los ojos, la textura y expresión de los labios, los poros de la piel, visibles y de una apariencia tan real como escalofriante. Parecía estar vivo. Al mirarlo, la sensación fue turbadora, tanto que desbarató mis pensamientos y creo que, por unos momentos, hasta mi raciocinio. Parecía que era él, el vampiro, quien nos estaba contemplando, y no al revés.

—Es tan real y hermoso que duele mirarlo; es sobrecogedor —dije sin apartar la vista del cuadro, con dificultad, como si mis palabras también me hiciesen daño al ser pronunciadas.

—La belleza es peligrosa. Es como un canto de sirena: escucharlo durante un segundo resulta inocuo, pero si le dedicas más tiempo de atención puede ser perturbador, muy peligroso. Por ello hay que dosificar la contemplación de esta obra. Igual sucede con la mirada de las brujas, que pueden captar cualquier cosa que pretendas ocultarles y, lo más temible, enamorarte —explicó una vez más en tono irónico, con el cuadro sujeto entre sus manos—. Ya te dije que era muy especial. Como ves, no exageré. Es extraordinario, tan perfecto y enigmático que cuesta retirar la vista del rostro y prestar atención al resto de la obra. Intenta fijar la mirada en su cuello, y

si lo consigues, porque muy pocos lo logran, dime qué ves. Te costará hacerlo. No te asustes si ves que no te es posible, es algo que le sucede a todo aquel que ve la pintura original.

Tal y como Farid me advirtió, me resultó difícil dejar de contemplar sus ojos, aquella mirada violeta que parecía entrar en mis pensamientos, que me desbarataba por dentro, igual que hacía la de Desmond.

—Un colgante —le respondí.

—Eso es lo que une a nuestro vampiro con el evangelio de las brujas. Según mis investigaciones, esa piedra roja que cuelga de su cuello formó parte del incunable.

Capítulo 23

A medida que iba averiguando más datos, la posibilidad de que el vampiro del cuadro fuese Desmond cobraba más sentido. Y si no lo era, tenía que ser un antepasado suyo con el que guardaba un parecido genético increíble, similar al de los gemelos idénticos, y del que hubiese heredado aquel colgante rojo con forma de péndulo que pendía de su llavero. Porque el péndulo que el padre de Amaya había sujetado el día de la explosión y que, según había dicho el florista, evitó que los cristales le cayeran encima, era idéntico al colgante que exhibía el retrato. Tenía la misma forma, el mismo color y parecía metálico.

—Pero... en la copia el colgante no aparece. O al menos yo no lo recuerdo —dije sin retirar la vista del óleo.

—El pintor que realizó la reproducción no vio la piedra en el cuello del original. A pesar de tenerlo frente a él, fue incapaz de apreciarla y pintó el retrato sin ella. En varias ocasiones he hecho una prueba: he mostrado los dos juntos, el original y la copia, y solo unas pocas personas, muy pocas, notan la diferencia. Es asombroso, ¿no crees?

—Sin duda —le respondí, atónita.

—Este cuadro es un auténtico «expediente X». Sabes a lo que me refiero, ¿verdad? —preguntó, y asentí en silencio—. Terminas de ser partícipe y fiel testigo de una vivencia que no tiene una explicación

racional. Este retrato es una prueba más de que no todo se puede explicar a través de la ciencia. —Hizo una pequeña pausa en la que cerró los ojos como si estuviera retomando un pensamiento perdido.

—Tendré que creer lo que me dices, no me queda otra porque no puedo cotejar tus palabras con nadie —comenté en tono burlón.

—No te miento, Diana. No tengo ningún interés en mentirte en esto. Según los documentos que he ido recuperando de archivos ocultos en monasterios, bibliotecas personales y lugares tan recónditos e insospechados que no imaginarías jamás, la piedra que cuelga del cuello es parte de las cubiertas con las que fue confeccionado el evangelio —me explicó mientras introducía el cuadro en la caja fuerte.

—¿Me estás diciendo que las cubiertas de ese evangelio son como la piedra?

—Sí, y están confeccionadas con una aleación desconocida —aseguró.

Dio un último giro a la rueda de la caja fuerte y, al hacerlo, un ruido fuerte, seco y metálico sonó en su interior. Fue como si algo hubiera chocado contra la puerta con fuerza, estampándose contra ella.

—¿Qué ha sido eso? —pregunté dando un respingo hacia atrás, asustada.

—El cuadro —respondió él con voz serena, como si aquello no tuviese la más mínima importancia—. Sucede cuando lo devuelvo al interior. Es como si se precipitara contra la puerta una y otra vez. No te asustes, en breve lo dejarás de oír.

—No hablarás en serio... —le dije con evidente preocupación.

—Sí, completamente en serio. He intentado buscarle una explicación, pero no lo he conseguido. Si ahora abriese la caja, el cuadro estaría en la misma posición en que lo dejé; sin embargo, es evidente que se mueve y golpea el interior. No hay nada más que pueda producir ese ruido.

Hizo una pausa, me miró, levantó el brazo y me indicó con el gesto que nos dirigiéramos a su mesa.

—Será mejor que olvidemos el retrato. Le estamos prestando demasiada atención. Voy a pasarte los datos de los que te hablé. ¿Te parece bien que lo haga en un *pendrive*? Así te resultará más fácil llevártelos y podrás consultarlos con calma. Espero que los analices tal como has hecho con el cuadro original. Estoy seguro de que a mí se me ha escapado algo y, con toda probabilidad, tú lo verás, como ha sucedido con el colgante, porque es evidente que tienes la mirada de una bruja. —Hizo una pausa y me miró sonriente—. Aunque no lo seas —puntualizó al ver mi expresión de enfado.

—Si tú lo dices... Creo que solo soy observadora. En cuanto a los documentos, si dices que mi mirada es especial, ¿no crees que sería más efectivo que me dejases ver los originales? —le pregunté, mirando de soslayo la lámina de metal que ya cubría de nuevo la caja fuerte. Los golpes, como me había dicho Farid, eran cada vez más tenues, menos audibles.

—Te pasaré solo lo imprescindible. Los datos que te doy son los mismos, resumidos pero exactos. Será lo mejor para ti y para mí, créeme. No soy el único que busca ese texto, hay muchos más que van detrás de él, y no todos son como yo ni usan los mismos métodos. Si te sucediese algo no me lo perdonaría... Me gustas, Diana. Eres una buena persona.

Aquella declaración sonó diferente y estuvo acompañada de una mirada que, por unos segundos, lo alejó de la búsqueda incansable y obsesiva de mi evangelio.

—Farid, debes disculpar mi desconfianza —le pedí. Callé un segundo, tomé aire y, mirándolo a los ojos, le dije—: Pienso que no me dices la verdad. Creo que en realidad no buscas ese libro, sino al vampiro.

—Durante mucho tiempo lo busqué a él con la esperanza de que me condujera al evangelio, y no he abandonado del todo esa

idea, no voy a mentirte. Si tomamos todos los datos que tengo y que tú podrás ver cuando consultes la documentación que te he dado, todo lleva a pensar que si el vampiro tenía esa piedra, también estuvo cerca del evangelio, por no decir que el libro estuvo en su poder y que tal vez sigue estándolo. Pero no sé dónde está ese vampiro, que es más escurridizo que una anguila. Sin embargo, ahora que he encontrado a Virginia, mi búsqueda ha cambiado de dirección, por el momento —puntualizó.

Pero no lo creí. Había algo en su mirada, en sus gestos y en el tono de su voz que me decía que mentía, que lo que realmente pretendía era encontrar tanto al vampiro como el evangelio, y que tal vez quisiera destruirlos a ambos.

Apenas tardó unos minutos en pasar al dispositivo electrónico la documentación de la que me había hablado.

—No puedo decirte cuánto tiempo voy a tardar en revisarlo —le dije, tomando de su mano el *pendrive* dorado—. Ahora mismo tengo muchos temas pendientes y, para serte sincera, este asunto me está superando; me parece surrealista.

—Tómate el tiempo que sea preciso. Yo estaré fuera lo que queda de mes, de vacaciones, así que la tienda también estará cerrada. Cuando regrese, iré a París sin pasar por España. Nos vemos a mi vuelta, que será sobre el veintitrés de septiembre, más o menos. En pleno equinoccio, una fecha tan mágica como lo es nuestra investigación, ¿te parece bien? ¿Crees que para entonces habrás tenido tiempo de revisarlo?

—¿Te vas? —le pregunté sorprendida—. ¿Y Virginia? Pensé que te apremiaba que yo hablase con ella.

—Y me urge, pero no por ello voy a precipitarme. Llevo demasiados años con esta investigación como para ahora tirarlo todo por la borda. Además, ahora cuento con una socia —añadió con una sonrisa—. Mientras yo descanso y soluciono los temas pendientes que tengo, tú estarás dándole un repaso a la documentación,

revisando, cotejando y sacando tus propias conclusiones, que, dicho sea de paso, me interesan más de lo que te puedas imaginar. El que hayas visto la piedra en el cuadro es una garantía de que si hay algo en esa información que yo no haya visto, tú lo detectarás. Estoy seguro de ello.

—Parecías tan interesado en Virginia que me sorprende que ahora te marches. Y si me dice dónde está el evangelio, ¿qué harás entonces? —le pregunté, a sabiendas de que aquella posibilidad era inviable, porque Virginia no sabía que el evangelio, en aquellos momentos, estaba en manos de Ecles, al que ella ni siquiera conocía.

—Si consigues que lo haga, en el caso de que ella lo sepa, lo pospondré todo e iremos juntos a buscarlo, de eso no te quepa la menor duda. Lo más probable es que Virginia solo nos lleve a más pistas que, unidas a los datos que yo te he dado —señaló el dispositivo—, pueden conducirnos a su paradero. Y eso, créeme, no será cuestión de una semana, sino de mucho más tiempo. Este no es un trabajo que se pueda realizar a destajo. Si hubiera sido así, el evangelio de las brujas ya estaría en mis manos hace tiempo. Cuando revises estos datos, te darás cuenta de que todo conduce una y otra vez al mismo sitio, es como un gran laberinto. El objetivo es encontrar la salida o su centro. Allí, en uno de esos dos puntos, debe estar el texto. Pero aún no he logrado llegar a ninguno de los dos, aún sigo perdido dentro de él, enterrado en la infinidad de datos de que dispongo.

—Farid, no tengo muy claro si me compensa seguir en esto. Si tú no lo has conseguido, no creo que yo sea capaz de hacerlo —dije levantando el *pendrive*—. Además, siento que si sigo adelante estaré firmando un contrato sin fecha de vencimiento, y eso es lo que más me asusta.

Aunque ante él me había mostrado incauta, no lo había sido. A medida que fui recabando datos y supe lo que se proponía Farid, sus verdaderas intenciones, me sentí más insegura. Participar en aquella investigación podía acarrearme problemas, y no solo a mí, sino

también a Desmond. Comprendí que para estar a salvo, Farid debía seguir ignorando mi verdadera identidad, mi vida y, sobre todo, el lugar en el que residía, algo que seguramente sería imposible si mantenía el trato con el anticuario.

Tal vez él estuviera jugando las mismas cartas que yo en aquellos momentos, me dije. Quizás supiese quién era yo en realidad y me estuviera utilizando para llegar al libro y a Desmond. Cuando nos encontramos en el albergue, mi intención era únicamente encontrar a Virginia, ayudarla y averiguar qué le había sucedido a Duncan, pero las casualidades nos habían unido en una búsqueda con objetivos diferentes, y en ese momento me sentí atrapada.

Lo miré y, por unos instantes, tuve miedo, miedo de él. Sin duda Farid era un hombre poderoso, capaz de muchas cosas para alcanzar sus objetivos, pensé recorriendo con la vista los objetos que allí atesoraba. Era muy improbable que, después de haberme revelado todo aquello, me dejara ir sin más. Sin darme cuenta, me había metido en un callejón sin salida.

—Firmamos un contrato verbal, ¿lo recuerdas? —inquirió.

—Sí, claro que sí, pero ahora que sé todo lo que conlleva, no lo tengo claro. Lo siento, pero no me veo capaz —le dije, tendiéndole su *pendrive*.

—Diana, debo admitir que te he mentido. Ninguna de las personas a las que les he mostrado el cuadro original del vampiro pudo ver el colgante. Hasta ahora, solo tú y yo lo hemos visto. Por eso creo que si hay algo que se me ha escapado en esos datos —dijo mirando el dispositivo— únicamente tú serás capaz de encontrarlo.

Durante años, Farid había estado buscando a alguien capaz de ver en el óleo el colgante que el vampiro llevaba en el cuello. Me explicó que había mostrado el cuadro a las personas que tenían alguna relación con su investigación, aunque sin dar a conocer sus fines ni motivos, omitiendo sus investigaciones y objetivos. Quería asegurarse de que la piedra realmente estaba en el original, porque

nadie más que él la veía, y aquello le llevó a pensar que su obsesión por encontrar el evangelio le estaba produciendo algún tipo de alteración mental. Su objetivo al llevarme a la tienda no solo era que yo hablase con Virginia, también quería comprobar si yo podía ver el colgante. Por ello no mostró desconfianza ni tomó precauciones al mostrarme el cuadro y el lugar donde lo guardaba, algo que a mí me pareció extraño considerando que no nos conocíamos de nada, pero que dejé pasar por alto cuando él me explicó que buscaba el evangelio. Ambos teníamos intenciones ocultas y nos estábamos aprovechando de la ignorancia del otro. Para Farid, que yo hablase con Virginia era lo de menos, porque la mujer ya le había dicho prácticamente todo lo que sabía sobre el evangelio. Y ella tampoco había visto el colgante.

—Es una buena persona, como tú. Me ha contado todo lo que sabe y no puedo pedirle más. Cuando me dijiste que un amigo de su marido venía a buscarla, me alegré. De hecho, ya tenía pensado ayudarla para que volviese a su país. Creo que aquí corre peligro.

—¿Por qué no me lo dijiste? Todo habría sido más fácil —le recriminé.

—No me habrías creído. La verdad muchas veces es tan peligrosa como la mentira. Ahora te ruego que creas en mis palabras. Mi único interés es encontrar ese libro, y quiero que me ayudes. Has visto el colgante, y si lo has hecho es por algo. Todo, absolutamente todo, tiene un sentido, nada sucede por casualidad, y menos en este caso. Llevo años buscando a alguien como tú, que tenga la misma percepción que yo para lo paranormal. Incluso has oído los golpes en la caja fuerte. Te aseguro que nadie los capta; si quieres, te lo demostraré. Aunque quizás estemos locos los dos —añadió con una expresión que me sobrecogió—. Dicen que la locura es contagiosa y que no es extraño que el dinero y las obras de arte conduzcan a ella.

»No quiero que tengas miedo de mí —me aseguró—. Te protegeré, siempre lo haré. Te doy mi palabra que así será, pase lo que

pase siempre estaré a tu lado, ¡te lo prometo! —exclamó, tan seguro de sus palabras que, aunque su intención y significado eran lo contrario, volvieron a atemorizarme.

Aquel «Te protegeré, siempre lo haré» me produjo una sensación extraña e inquietante que pareció rodearme, envolverme en una especie de bruma que se quedó pegada a mi piel y mis sentimientos. Por unos segundos viví un *déjà vu* que no aventuraba nada positivo.

—Estás pálida, ¿te encuentras bien? —me preguntó.

—Estoy saturada, eso es todo.

—Dejaremos que el tiempo corra, él es el dueño y señor de nuestras vidas. —Hizo una pausa—. No olvides mi oferta, es una cantidad considerable que pude permitirte llevar una vida acomodada dedicándote solo a investigar para mí. En realidad no me preocupa mucho lo que pueda suceder, porque sé que si tenemos que volver a encontrarnos, lo haremos, ya sea en esta realidad o en otra.

El teléfono de línea interna que tenía sobre la mesa sonó. Me indicó con un gesto que le perdonase y lo descolgó. Habló unos segundos en francés, colgó y volvió a mirarme.

—Hace unos minutos he tenido un *déjà vu* —me confesó—. Estoy seguro de que estamos unidos por algo que desconocemos pero que ha hecho que nos encontremos, y no creo que sea solo el evangelio.

»Virginia está ya en la tienda. Nos espera —dijo, cambiando el tema de conversación—. Vayamos a hablar con ella, si aún quieres hacerlo —me propuso, y yo asentí—. Quédate el *pendrive* y piensa en lo que te he dicho, es un buen trato. Si decides continuar, hazlo sin más. No tienes que darme una respuesta ahora. Toma —dijo, y me entregó un teléfono móvil—. Utilízalo solo si es estrictamente necesario. Este es mi número y este el apartado de correos donde debes mandar el dispositivo y el teléfono en el caso de que decidas no seguir con la investigación. Si es así, no te molestaré más, te doy

mi palabra —aseguró al tiempo que me tendía una tarjeta, pero diferente a la que me había dado en el albergue, pues solo figuraba el apartado de correos y un número de móvil—. En cuanto me haya marchado no tendrás otra forma de ponerte en contacto conmigo.

Cuando regrese, te llamaré a ese número —dijo, señalando el teléfono que me había dado y que yo tenía en mis manos.

CAPÍTULO 24

Me sorprendió el aspecto físico que tenía Virginia. De habérmela encontrado en la calle no la habría reconocido, pensé mientras la miraba de arriba abajo. Vestía unos pantalones anchos y tobilleros de color marfil que parecían confeccionados en seda, y una blusa del mismo tejido y de corte también amplio. Llevaba unas sandalias marrones, muy similares a las de Farid. Tenía un aspecto pulcro y elegante, con el pelo limpio y recogido en un moño bajo. Iba ligeramente maquillada y olía a un perfume que no identifiqué, pero que por su fragancia supuse que debía de ser muy caro. Estaba en la entrada de la tienda, charlando animadamente con el dependiente.

—¿Es Virginia? —le pregunté a Farid desde el fondo de la tienda, mientras la observaba quieta, casi estática, sin dar crédito al aspecto de la mujer.

—Por supuesto —me respondió Farid—. Necesitamos muy poco para revivir. Somos como la vegetación. Basta un poco de agua y un rayo de sol para que volvamos a la vida. Eso le ha sucedido a ella. Solo tuve que darle los libros que venía buscando y demostrarle que creía en ella, en lo que le sucedía, para que el milagro se produjese. De este modo recobró la esperanza, únicamente fue cuestión de que volviera a creer, a tener fe.

—Entonces fue así como la conociste, vino a tu tienda buscando unos libros. Pero ¿qué libros? Tú no estás especializado en ese tipo de artículos.

—No de cara a la galería. Comercio con muchos objetos, tú misma lo has visto —explicó con una sonrisa azorada.

—¡Ya! —respondí irónica.

—A veces perdemos la memoria sin saber por qué motivo y la recobramos del mismo modo. Eso le sucedió a Virginia. Estuvo durmiendo en el escalón de la tienda una noche entera, esperando a que abriésemos. Mi empleado no la dejó entrar, pero ella siguió ahí, sentada en el suelo, apoyada en la pared. Le dijo al dependiente que buscaba un libro antiguo que hablaba sobre la existencia de universos paralelos y le aseguró que no se iría de allí hasta que no se lo mostrase, porque ese texto podía ayudarla a encontrar a su marido. Le explicó que su esposo se había perdido en una dimensión paralela a esta. Que necesitaba ese tratado no solo para ir en su busca, sino también para encontrar el evangelio de las brujas, ya que ese incunable era el motivo de la desaparición de su cónyuge. Él, al escuchar el título que le daba la mujer, me llamó.

—Pero ¿cómo supo ella que tenía que venir a tu anticuario? —le pregunté, desconcertada.

—Me contó que uno de los policías de la Científica le dio la dirección de la tienda. Le dijo que si encontraba el evangelio para él, la ayudaría en la búsqueda de su marido. Eso fue después de que Duncan muriese en uno de los bancos del metro y tras localizarla para que identificase el cadáver. La acompañé a buscar al agente, pero en el departamento nadie lo conocía, y aunque nos atendieron muy bien, no le prestaron mucha atención debido a la extraña actitud de Virginia antes y durante el intento frustrado del reconocimiento del cuerpo de Duncan. Y el resto ya lo sabes. La ayudé y aún sigo haciéndolo. No pienses que me mueve solo el interés, también

lo hago porque es una buena persona y se lo merece, como todos los que se hallan en una situación extrema.

—Ahora me vas a decir que eres un ángel —repuse con cierto sarcasmo.

Sin responderme, comenzó a caminar hacia la entrada de la tienda. El sol ya había caído y el dependiente miraba de soslayo su reloj de pulsera.

—Ya me encargo yo de todo —le dijo Farid—, ya puedes irte. Gracias por tu paciencia y tu tiempo, Ígor.

—No tiene por qué dármelas, señor —le respondió el hombre, y se marchó.

—Virginia, esta es Diana. Diana, Virginia —dijo Farid a modo de presentación.

Ambas nos saludamos con un beso en la mejilla y repetimos casi al tiempo el cortés «Encantada».

—Diana también está interesada en la teoría de la existencia de mundos paralelos y en la relación que esta pueda tener con la desaparición de tu marido y el paradero del evangelio de las brujas, pero además conoce a un amigo de tu marido. Me gustaría que le dijeses, igual que hiciste conmigo, todo lo que sabes sobre ello. Es posible que pueda ayudarte.

—¿Conoces a un amigo de mi marido? —me dijo con un brillo de desconfianza asomando a sus ojos.

—Bueno, es que Farid no se ha explicado del todo bien. No conozco a Andreas personalmente, es una amiga mía quien lo conoce y fue ella quien me pidió que lo atendiese mientras esté aquí. Viene a España para repatriar los restos mortales de Duncan y a buscarte por si necesitas ayuda o quieres regresar a Escocia con él.

—Duncan no ha muerto —me respondió ella enfadada, en un tono seguro y firme—. El hombre que encontraron no es mi Duncan, no el que vivió conmigo. Ese vino de un universo paralelo.

No lo conozco, ni siquiera sé si he llegado a vivir en algún momento con él.

Farid intervino para que la conversación no se enrareciera, porque yo no supe reaccionar a las palabras de Virginia; su seguridad en lo que decía y el tono imperativo que empleó me dejaron muda y algo incómoda. El anticuario le explicó que mis intenciones no iban más allá de comunicarle la llegada de Andreas y que él me había contratado para ayudarle en la búsqueda del evangelio. Ella siguió mostrándose distante, como si no creyera del todo sus palabras, pero cambió su discurso y el tono.

Cuando subimos al piso comprobé que Farid me había mentido: él no vivía allí de asiduo. En todo caso, utilizaba aquel espacio como lugar de consulta e investigación, pensé mirando asombrada alrededor. La vivienda era un *loft*, no había más tabiques que los dos que separaban el baño y la cocina americana del resto de la estancia. Las paredes del apartamento quedaban completamente ocultas por unas estanterías que iban del suelo al techo, repletas de libros. Muchos de los volúmenes estaban colocados en diferentes posiciones, tapando otros que quedaban detrás de ellos. No había lugar para cuadros, adornos ni ningún objeto decorativo. Solo algunas lámparas de pie proporcionaban luz al gran espacio que componía aquel *loft*, tan extraordinario como su propietario. Los ventanales tenían miradores de cristal con marquetería y no había ningún tipo de estor o cortina que impidiese ver desde la calle el interior de la vivienda. En una esquina, cerca del ventanal más grande del apartamento, había un tocadiscos y, junto a él, un gran número de vinilos apilados en diferentes montones. En el centro destacaba un sofá profundo y largo que, según imaginé, habría hecho las veces de cama para Virginia el tiempo que llevaba allí residiendo.

—Me dijiste que vivías aquí —comenté.

—No, seguro que no te dije eso. En todo caso te habré dicho que la casa me pertenece y que mi familia vivió aquí. De hecho, esta

fue la residencia de mi abuelo y mis padres. Yo solo lo utilizo cuando estoy en la tienda. Y ahora sirve de alojamiento para Virginia —dijo, y sonrió al mirarla.

—Espero que sea por poco tiempo. Necesito recuperar mi vida —comentó ella.

—Es tarde —dije al darme cuenta de que el sol ya se había puesto—. Si te parece bien —propuse, dirigiéndome a Virginia—, podemos vernos otro día con más calma.

—Si tú no tienes prisa, yo prefiero que hablemos hoy, no dispongo de mucho tiempo en estos momentos y, si te soy sincera, te atiendo por Farid. No me gusta hablar con nadie sobre lo que me ha sucedido —contestó ella, indicándome con un gesto que me sentase en el sofá.

—Voy a pedir unos canapés y bebidas —intervino Farid, cogiendo su teléfono móvil—. ¿Qué os apetece?

Virginia no me contó nada que yo no supiera, a excepción de su teoría sobre la desaparición de su marido:

—Dejé de verlo en el metro el mismo día que apareció ese otro Duncan sentado en el banco de la estación. Algo tuvo que suceder para que él dejase de frecuentar el tren. Después, los de servicios sociales me localizaron. Tras ellos vino la policía y los del juzgado. Sé que mi Duncan encontró la forma de volver al año en que desapareció y que ahora está ahí, esperándome. Tal vez te resulte difícil creer lo que te digo, pero es tan cierto como que ahora estamos aquí. Junto a nosotros hay más realidades que existen a la par, y en una de ellas está mi Duncan, el que ha vivido conmigo. Esa estación de metro es una puerta, una entrada a otra dimensión, posiblemente a muchas más, y yo voy a regresar a la que me pertenece en el mismo espacio temporal en el que él desapareció. Encontraré la forma de hacerlo y, cuando lo consiga, lograré que mi Duncan deje esa maldita investigación y volveré a vivir con él. Cambiaré su destino y el

mío, porque el tiempo no existe, se repite una y otra vez, solo que no lo percibimos.

—¿No piensas encontrarte con Andreas? —le pregunté.

—Con el Andreas que viene a España no. Lo haré con el que conocí junto a mi marido, por supuesto —me dijo, absolutamente convencida de que iba a encontrar esa puerta por la que llegaría al pasado, a su pasado.

Y yo la creí, porque ya había vivido esa experiencia. Sin embargo, temí por ella, ya que el pasado, el presente y el futuro eran demasiado inestables, proclives a cambios imprevisibles, algo que Virginia ignoraba, pensé recordando las múltiples paradojas que podía causar en su regreso, situaciones que podían cambiarlo todo o conducirla al mismo lugar una y otra vez.

—Si Andreas se pone en contacto conmigo le diré que no te he visto. Imagino que es lo que tú prefieres, que no sepa dónde estás.

—Así es. Te lo agradezco —me dijo con una sonrisa.

Nos despedimos ya entrada la noche, después de que ella me enseñara varios libros que la habían ayudado a entender la posibilidad de la existencia de universos paralelos, de múltiples pasados, presentes y futuros que existían de forma simultánea, la misma teoría en la que Rigel creía ciegamente y en la que me había adoctrinado, de modo que había podido asimilar y entender lo que me había sucedido también a mí.

—Piensa en mi propuesta —me dijo Farid mientras abría la puerta del taxi que había pedido para mí—. No olvides que estaré fuera hasta septiembre, pero que cualquier suceso urgente, que consideres importante, puedes comunicármelo a través del móvil que te he dado. —Y con estas palabras, me tendió un sobre cerrado que cogí.

Me despedí de él pensando que al día siguiente le devolvería el dinero que había en aquel sobre junto con el dispositivo electrónico y el teléfono. Lo enviaría al apartado de correos que me había

facilitado. Sin embargo, algo me decía que, aunque lo hiciera, aunque intentase desvincularme de él, no lo conseguiría.

Farid tenía razón: había algo que nos unía, algo que se escapaba a nuestro raciocinio y a nuestra voluntad. Yo, como él, sabía que, quisiéramos o no, volveríamos a vernos, en esa o en otra realidad, pensé mientras por el cristal trasero del taxi lo veía levantando la mano para despedirse de mí.

Capítulo 25

Llegué a casa a media noche. En el ascensor recordé que *Senatón* había estado solo prácticamente todo el día. Desde el momento en que conocí a Farid, mi abstracción había sido tal que olvidé mi vida, mi cotidianeidad, a *Senatón* y a Alán. Incluso mi situación económica, mi reciente despido, pasaron a un segundo plano y dejaron de ser importantes. Puse el sobre, el teléfono y el *pendrive* sobre uno de los estantes del salón y me dirigí a la cocina, donde *Senatón* maullaba reclamando su pienso. Lo acaricié mientras me disculpaba con él y le llené el comedero. Dentro del ático el calor era insoportable, de modo que abrí todas las ventanas y me dispuse a darme una ducha. Necesitaba relajarme, pensar qué iba a hacer. Tenía demasiados frentes abiertos. En poco tiempo todo parecía haberse confabulado, como si el destino, una vez más, jugara conmigo a su antojo, y lo peor no era aquello, lo más inquietante era que no sabía adónde me conducirían los cambios que se avecinaban en mi vida.

Antes de meterme en la ducha sonó mi móvil. Era un mensaje de voz de Alán. Me decía que me echaba de menos y se disculpaba una vez más por no haberme llamado. No había tenido ni un momento de respiro, aseguraba. Finalizaba con la promesa de recuperar el tiempo perdido a la vuelta de su viaje de trabajo, que tanto le estaba estresando, me explicaba con voz cansada, y se despedía con su típico: «Te quiero, brujita». Dejé el teléfono, cerré el grifo

de la ducha y me dirigí al dormitorio. Bajé las maletas que había en el altillo, las coloqué sobre la cama y fui descolgando toda su ropa para meterla en ellas. Después hice lo mismo con sus colonias, cremas y sus zapatillas de marca, una cincuentena de pares que no me cupieron en las maletas, por lo que las introduje en las bolsas que solía guardar para esos casos. No paré hasta no dejar rastro de su presencia en el ático. Lo coloqué todo en la entrada de la casa y, cuando finalicé, me senté en el suelo, rendida, al lado de los bultos y rompí a llorar.

Me sentía una imbécil, una incauta, una estúpida y no sé cuántas cosas más. Y allí, rodeada de pétalos de rosa rojos que no paraban de cubrir el suelo, oí que Ecles me llamaba desde su terraza.

—Diana, ¿estás bien? —me preguntó preocupado, porque había escuchado mi trajín de un lado a otro de la casa y, cuando este cesó, mi llanto desconsolado que, poco a poco, pasó a convertirse en un quejido lleno de rabia e impotencia.

Me restregué los ojos intentando despabilarme, tomé aire y le contesté, aún congestionada:

—Sí, Ecles, solo estaba dejando escapar un puñado de sentimientos que me hacían daño.

—Yo a eso lo llamo llorar a moco tendido —respondió él con la elegancia infantil que le caracterizaba—. Tengo helado de chocolate, tabletas de chocolate y galletas con chocolate. Te invito a darte un buen atracón. El azúcar es el mejor antidepresivo que conozco, aunque engorda y, según dicen los nutricionistas, es un veneno para el páncreas si se abusa de él. Y digo yo: si te estás muriendo de pena, ¿para qué quieres un páncreas sano?

No pude evitar reírme. Me levanté y salí junto a él.

—Eres un cielo —le dije acercándome y, como dice la letra de la canción de Sabina, le planté dos besos, uno por mejilla.

—No creas —respondió él, cogiendo mis manos entre las suyas—. Yo también tengo mis prontos, solo que tú eres mi amiga

y uno, con los amigos, debe guardarse el mal temperamento. Dime qué te traigo —me pidió, haciendo ademán de ir a buscar algo de lo que me había ofrecido.

—Nada, con tu compañía es más que suficiente.

—Pues entonces tendrás que contarme qué te pasa. Solo hay dos opciones: o sueltas lo que te preocupa o te das un atracón de chocolate. Algo tenemos que hacer para barrer esa pena.

Y se lo conté. Y él me escuchó. Lo hizo como un amigo, como alguien que te quiere y sabe que por el mero hecho de escuchar lo que te sucede, encontrarás cierto alivio en tu pena, porque tienes con quién compartirla.

—Me he dejado llevar por la ira, lo sé —le dije—. No estoy enamorada de él, pero le tengo cariño, y su engaño ha hecho que me sienta insignificante. Eso es lo que más me ha dolido; su mentira. No me lo merezco, y no puedo soportar la rabia y la tristeza que me causa.

—Querer es fácil, pero dejar de hacerlo cuesta lo indecible —explicó pensativo—. A ver, ¿qué piensas hacer con sus cosas?

—Pedirle que venga a recogerlas. No sé cómo se lo tomará, pero no me importa. Quiero que se vaya. No soportaría volver a verle.

—Si necesitas que te eche una mano, no tienes más que llamarme y vendré. Estaré contigo el tiempo que necesites.

—Gracias, Ecles, pero no creo que sea necesario. Supongo que tendrá un poquito de dignidad, que aún le quedará algo de eso y no intentará contarme otra mentira. Es capaz de decirme que no era él y que sigue en Holanda.

—Espero que no te vayas del ático. No me gustaría que lo hicieras, a ninguno nos gustaría. Te apreciamos mucho los tres.

—Yo también lo espero, aquí me siento muy bien. Ya veremos cómo va todo.

Estuve a punto de decirle que, si me separaba, yo también habría de abandonar el ático. No tenía ingresos y si Alán se marchaba, si

dejábamos de compartir gastos, mi situación económica rozaría la pobreza. Sin embargo, recordé el sobre con el dinero que me había dado Farid y respiré. ¿Qué podía pasar si lo utilizaba, si esperaba un tiempo para devolvérselo? Tenía hasta septiembre para pensar qué hacer, mientras tanto actuaría según creyese más conveniente. Charlamos unos minutos y volvió a insistir en que lo llamase en cualquier momento si lo necesitaba.

—Desmond y yo estaremos durmiendo, pero si Alán se presenta antes de tiempo, o si decides quedarte a esperarlo, o si te sientes incómoda en algún momento, tú llámanos. ¡Prométeme que lo harás!

Pasé la mayor parte de la noche en vela, repasando todo lo que había sucedido. Pensé en Desmond mientras miraba hacia la terraza, sentada en la cama del dormitorio. Levanté la mano y la llevé a la pared del cabecero e imaginé que aquel dibujo de la vela roja que él pintó para mí estaba ahí, sobre la pared. Sentía una extraña atracción hacia él, un sentimiento que nunca antes había experimentado y que no podía ni quería controlar. No tenía la menor duda de que el vampiro del cuadro era él. Si yo era una bruja, él podía ser un vampiro; todo cabía en aquella realidad que estaba viviendo, me dije. Un vampiro diferente en modos, costumbres y cualidades a lo que nos habían contado, del mismo modo que yo era una bruja que nada tenía que ver con aquellas de las que hablaban las leyendas populares. Me quedé dormida esperando que él cruzase la terraza para ir a casa de Claudia, pero no supe si lo hizo, si en algún momento se asomó a mi ventana abierta y contempló mi duermevela, si protegió mi descanso como yo deseaba que lo hiciese.

Nada más despertar conecté el teléfono móvil y comprobé si tenía mensajes o llamadas perdidas, si Alán había intentado ponerse en contacto conmigo al ver que no le había respondido, pero no había nada. Desayuné con calma, bajo el sol de aquel agosto que a mí, en aquellos momentos, me parecía vacío, solitario e incluso frío.

Dejé comida y agua para *Senatón* y, cuando ya estaba preparada para salir, le mandé un mensaje a Alán través del WhatsApp:

Ayer os vi salir del restaurante, a ti y a Azucena. Es triste que me hayas mentido de esta forma. Creo que no me lo merezco.

He hecho tus maletas. Quiero que te vayas. Está todo en la entrada de casa. Por favor, pasa a recogerlo y deja las llaves dentro. Si me aprecias un poquito, si alguna vez me has querido de verdad, hazlo cuanto antes. No quiero volver a verte, es lo único que te pido. Creo que, después de lo que has hecho, al menos me merezco que respetes mi decisión de no verte más.

El encuentro con Farid el día anterior había sido interesante y, aunque al principio mi intención había sido darle pábulo para que me condujese hasta Virginia, su poder de convicción y persuasión sobre mí me había hecho olvidar mi objetivo prioritario, que era hablar con Virginia a solas. Había querido acercarme a ella sin máscaras, sin artificios, y contarle parte de lo que sabía sobre aquella estación de metro, pero no tuve oportunidad de hacerlo. Tampoco pude confiarle que no era la primera vez que nos veíamos ni recordarle las circunstancias en que nos habíamos conocido, porque debía evitar que Farid descubriera mi mentira sobre Virginia y sobre mis intenciones.

Farid me había dicho que ya no estaría en Madrid, que se marchaba al día siguiente y que el local estaría cerrado, por lo que decidí que era el momento idóneo para visitar a Virginia. No debía esperar, ya que ella podía tomar una decisión inesperada en cualquier momento. Debía verla cuanto antes, a ser posible anticipándome a la llegada de Andreas, que, con toda probabilidad, desbarataría mis planes.

Al coger las llaves de la estantería para salir de casa vi el sobre, el teléfono y el *pendrive*, y no pude evitar pensar en lo imprudente que había sido. Había aceptado el sobre sin mirar lo que contenía, sin saber qué cantidad comprendía la realización de aquel trabajo. Asombrada una vez más por la sugestión que Farid había ejercido sobre mí, cogí el sobre, lo abrí y conté el dinero. Había doce billetes de quinientos euros, seis mil en total.

No podía creer que aquella cantidad de dinero fuese parte del pago por un trabajo que todavía no había aceptado, ni que Farid me lo hubiese entregado sin saber si se lo devolvería o desaparecería con ello, que podía ser lo más probable. Miré los billetes, aún incrédula, pensando que todo era demasiado extraño, que aceptar aquel sobre, sin mirar lo que contenía, había sido una irresponsabilidad por mi parte. Volví a meter el dinero en su interior y volteé el sobre. Al hacerlo, vi escrito una serie de números y, debajo, una frase de Farid:

2234

Esta es la clave de acceso del teléfono móvil.
Si aceptas el trabajo, introdúcela cuando necesites ponerte en contacto conmigo. A mi regreso te llamaré a este número. Mientras tanto, recuerda: no estaré disponible. Farid.

El pulso me tembló y el sobre cayó al suelo. ¿Y si Farid me había puesto un localizador en el aparato?, me pregunté aterrorizada, sin poder quitar la vista del móvil que aún estaba en la estantería, junto al *pendrive*.

Sin pensarlo, salí al rellano y golpeé con los nudillos la puerta de Ecles. No quise pulsar el timbre para no sobresaltarlos, porque imaginé que Desmond también estaría en casa, durmiendo.

—¿Estás bien? —me preguntó Ecles nada más abrir la puerta, soñoliento y preocupado.

—Sí. Siento haberte despertado. Verás, tengo que salir y no voy a estar en todo el día. Antes de irme quería pedirte un favor. No te lo pediría ni te habría molestado a estas horas si no fuese importante.

—Adelante —dijo, restregándose los ojos con un bostezo.

—Ayer me propusieron desarrollar una investigación. Pero, aunque el trabajo está muy bien pagado y no creo que sea complicado llevarlo a cabo, no termino de decidirme. Desconfío de la persona que me lo ha propuesto. Me dio este teléfono para comunicarme con él... —Hice una pausa y lo miré a los ojos—. Quizás creas que es una estupidez por mi parte, pero se me ha ocurrido que el teléfono puede tener instalado un localizador o algo así. ¿Tú podrías comprobarlo?

—Por supuesto, destripar artefactos electrónicos es lo mío. ¿Te dio algún otro dispositivo?

—Un *pendrive* con los documentos que debo revisar. Imagino que escaneados. Aún no lo he abierto.

—Pues dame los dos. Eso sí, no sé lo que tardaré, porque si quieres estar completamente tranquila, tendré que pasar tanto el teléfono como el *pendrive* a un compañero que trabaja en el departamento informático. Es un auténtico *hacker*. Él comprobará si hay algo instalado en los programas de los dos aparatos y, si lo encuentra, lo inutilizará.

—Gracias, Ecles. Voy a por ellos.

Cuando tuvo el teléfono en su mano sus ojos adquirieron una expresión extraña. Se me antojó que él, mi amigo, había abandonado su cuerpo, que estaba en otro lugar, lejos, muy lejos de mí.

—¡Demasiadas almas! ¡Demasiadas vidas! —exclamó de repente y sin mirarme, con los ojos aún puestos en el terminal—. No sé quién es el propietario de este aparato, pero está rodeado de infinidad de espíritus —explicó con voz hueca y quebrada.

—Debí avisarte. Olvidé tu extraordinaria percepción con los objetos; perdóname —me disculpé—. Es un anticuario. Es lógico que hayas tenido esa apreciación. Si entrases en su tienda...

Él levantó la mano para interrumpirme.

—No puedo entrar en un anticuario, Diana. Ya has visto lo que ha sucedido cuando he cogido el teléfono. Si entrase en un lugar de esas características, me volvería loco. Lo más probable es que perdiese la razón, no lo soportaría.

»Te diré algo en cuanto mi amigo lo revise...

Capítulo 26

Cuando llegué a la tienda comprobé que, contrariamente a lo que me había dicho Farid, el establecimiento permanecía abierto. Y no solo eso; para ser tan temprano, el local estaba muy concurrido. El hecho de que se hubiera reunido tanta gente en un anticuario tan elitista se debía a una subasta que iba a realizarse al mediodía.

Llevada por la curiosidad y un poco molesta por la mentira que me había contado Farid, decidí entrar en el establecimiento antes de ir al *loft* para hablar con Virginia.

Recorrí el local abriéndome paso con cierta dificultad entre la gente que esperaba a que diese la hora en que comenzaría la pequeña subasta. Mientras lo hacía no pude evitar pensar en lo injusto que era el mundo; cómo era posible que hubiese tanta gente con tantísimo dinero mientras que otros vivían sumidos en la pobreza. Me dio la impresión de que algunos de los allí presentes captaron mis pensamientos reprobatorios, porque me miraron y murmuraron entre ellos. O tal vez solo se debió a que mi atuendo resultaba fuera de lugar, al lado de sus joyas y sus perfumes, pensé.

Busqué la copia del cuadro del vampiro para volver a verlo, pero no estaba. En su lugar había un óleo de una manzana roja por cuya piel resbalaban dos gotas de agua. Era tal el realismo de la pintura que las gotas parecían moverse. Ígor se acercó al lienzo acompañado de un hombre mayor que renqueaba apoyándose en un bastón

con empuñadura de marfil. El dependiente me miró de soslayo y comenzó a hablar con el posible cliente en francés.

Esperé a que terminase para dirigirme a él.

—Buenos días —le dije.

—Buenos días, ¿en qué puedo ayudarla? —me preguntó en un tono y una actitud que me parecieron distantes, lo que me sorprendió.

—Veo que aún no cierran por vacaciones —comenté con cierto retintín—. ¿Podría decirle a Farid que estoy aquí y que me gustaría hablar con él?

—Disculpe, pero no sé de quién me está hablando —me respondió en un tono tan neutro y formal que me recordó a un mayordomo inglés.

—Pregunto por Farid, el dueño de este establecimiento. Ayer estuve aquí con él, no venga a decirme ahora que no me recuerda —le solté, molesta.

—Le aseguro que no sé a quién se refiere. Tampoco recuerdo haberla visto antes. Lo mejor será que no nos precipitemos. Si es tan amable, espere aquí un momento mientras voy a llamar a mi jefa. Ella la atenderá y seguro que puede solucionar su problema —me explicó en el mismo tono comedido, bajito y sin apenas gesticular.

Vi que desaparecía tras la puerta trasera del local.

El dependiente no tardó en regresar con una mujer que debía de andar por los sesenta y cinco años, aunque no aparentaba más de cincuenta. Tenía el pelo blanco recogido en un moño, y en su fina tez resaltaban sus ojos grises. Vestida con un modelo de alta costura de diseñador francés, caminaba hacia mí despacio, al tiempo que saludaba a algunos clientes con gesto amable y una sonrisa destinada a mostrar la satisfacción que le producía el hecho de verlos allí.

—Buenos días —me dijo sonriente. Se quitó las gafas de presbicia y me miró a los ojos—. ¿En qué puedo ayudarla? —me preguntó en tono cordial, como si yo fuese una posible clienta que se

hubiera dejado caer por allí de casualidad—. Ígor, mi empleado, me ha dicho que pregunta usted por Farid, pero aquí no conocemos a nadie que responda por ese nombre.

—Pues ayer mismo estuve aquí con él. Es el dueño del anticuario, e Ígor, aunque afirme lo contrario, también se hallaba presente.

—Mucho me temo que debe de haber un error. La propietaria soy yo. Le reitero que no conocemos a nadie que se llame Farid. Es posible que se haya equivocado usted de tienda —insistió—. En cualquier caso, tal vez pueda ayudarla —añadió con una sonrisa—. Quizás la pieza que anda usted buscando también la tengamos aquí.

La miré y arqueé las cejas. No daba crédito a lo que la mujer me estaba diciendo, a su descarado cinismo. Ella seguía sonriendo y yo, incrédula, sin apartar la vista de su sonrisa, creí percibir un rastro genético medio oculto bajo el carmín rosa a juego con el esmalte de uñas. Una diminuta seña de identidad que me recordó a Farid.

—Dígale a su hijo que no me gusta que se burlen de mí —repliqué, devolviéndole la sonrisa—. Por cierto, ¿dónde está el cuadro del vampiro? —inquirí desafiante, señalando la pared donde estuvo colgado.

—No tengo descendencia —respondió en tono tajante. Su rostro abandonó la expresión afable y la sonrisa desapareció de sus labios—. Si no está interesada en adquirir alguna de nuestras antigüedades, le ruego que me disculpe. Tengo mucho que hacer. —Se acercó a mí, me tendió la mano y, aprovechando el ademán, se pegó a mi oreja. Muy bajito, casi en un susurro para que el resto de los clientes no la oyesen, dijo—: El cuadro al que se ha referido no existe. No vuelva por la tienda a no ser que él se lo diga. —Elevó las cejas y me miró fijamente—. La discreción es el pilar en el que se sostienen estos negocios, ¿estamos? —me inquirió con gesto adusto.

No hubo opción de intercambiar ni una sola palabra más. A una señal de la mujer, Ígor se acercó a mí y me acompañó hasta la calle.

—*Bonjour, mademoiselle* —me dijo ya fuera del local.

—Han retirado el cuadro de la tienda. ¡Qué hábiles! —exclamé irónica.

—*Peut être* —dijo sin poder reprimir un atisbo de sonrisa, aunque manteniendo en todo la compostura ortopédica que había mostrado desde que lo vi por primera vez.

Acto seguido, se dio la vuelta y entró de nuevo en la tienda. Permanecí unos minutos en la acera mirando el interior del anticuario. Después me dirigí a la entrada del portal que se asentaba en los bajos del edificio. Si no recordaba mal, el piso de Farid se ubicaba en él. En el rellano, a la derecha, estaba la garita del conserje.

—Sí, sí, sé de quién me habla —dijo el hombre en tono amable y servicial cuando me dirigí a él para preguntar acerca de Virginia—. Se refiere a la invitada de la señora Fischer. Pues verá, se marchó esta mañana y no creo que regrese, porque llevaba su equipaje. Pero... si quiere saber algo más, acérquese al anticuario; la señora Fischer está hoy en la tienda porque van a celebrar una subasta. Seguro que estará encantada de atenderla. Es una mujer encantadora, ojalá esta fuese su residencia habitual. Ella y su sobrino Gerald son los vecinos más amables que tengo.

—¿Son alemanes? —le pregunté.

—Pues no sé qué decirle, creo que sí —me respondió, y se quedó unos instantes en silencio, como si estuviese meditando lo que le había dicho—. Al menos creo que los nombres sí lo son, aunque como hablan en varios idiomas, pues tengo mis dudas.

—Muchas gracias.

—No hay de qué. Para servirla.

Virginia podía haberse dirigido a cualquier lugar, pensé. Su cambio físico y de actitud no significaba nada; su estabilidad emocional podía seguir siendo la misma, me dije al recordar lo que había comentado durante la cena y en la sobremesa, los libros que me había mostrado y su intención de volver con Duncan, al tiempo

que ambos habían compartido. Lo más probable era que hubiese regresado a aquella estación de metro, a Cuatro Caminos. Aunque también cabía la posibilidad de que se hubiese marchado con Farid, o Gerald, como le había llamado el conserje, pensé con una sonrisa agria. «¡Esta me la va a pagar!», me prometí, rabiosa.

Mi teléfono móvil sonó justo antes de que entrase en el metro. Me detuve, lo saqué de la mochila y me retiré de la entrada para no obstaculizar el paso de los viajeros, cada vez más numerosos.

—Hola, nena, ¿cómo vas? —me preguntó Samanta a través de la línea telefónica.

—Pues no muy bien. Tenía pensado llamarte esta noche —le respondí.

—¿Y eso? ¿Qué sucede?

—He cortado con Alán. Me mintió. El viaje a Holanda es una farsa. Ayer lo vi saliendo de un restaurante, aquí mismo, en Madrid. Fue de casualidad. Iba con esa tipa que escupe margaritas. He puesto su ropa en las maletas y he salido. Espero que lo recoja todo antes de que yo regrese, porque no quiero verlo ni de refilón.

—Lo siento, por ti, claro está. Él que se las apañe. ¿Te encuentras bien? Quiero decir, no estarás hundida, ¿verdad? Dime que no lo estás.

—Pues no lo sé. Tengo sentimientos encontrados. Sabía que estaban juntos, ya te lo dije, pero verlos ha sido duro, y más después de que mintiera. Creí que estaba en Holanda, te lo juro.

—Lo imagino, ya sabes..., Murphy trabaja todos los días y a veces lo hace muy bien, a conciencia. Esta vez creo que se ha esmerado. Es un mal trago, sí, pero a mí me hubiera gustado pillar a más de uno con el carrito del helado, cielo. Míralo por esa vertiente. La duda, nena, es peor que la realidad más cruda.

»Y dime, ¿qué tienes pensado hacer? ¿Te vas a quedar en el ático? Ya sabes que puedes disponer de mi casa cuando quieras.

—Me han ofrecido un trabajo de investigación, aunque la verdad es que aún no tengo claro si voy a aceptarlo. El hombre que me lo propuso es un anticuario y no me inspira mucha confianza, qué quieres que te diga.

—Ningún anticuario inspira confianza —apuntó con una carcajada—. Suelen oler a naftalina y, aparte de mayores, son demasiado clásicos y encorsetados.

—Este es atractivo, alto, joven y está podrido de pasta.

—Entonces, ¿cuál es el problema? Te llevas el coche para regresar a casa cuando quieras y todo solucionado.

—No vas a cambiar nunca —respondí.

—Está bien, perdona, dime cuál es el problema, por qué no confías en él.

Le relaté lo que había sucedido aquella mañana al regresar a la tienda. Omití todo lo referente al cuadro y a Virginia, y le dije que la investigación era sobre el paradero de un incunable.

—Además, la cantidad de dinero me parece exagerada, y más sin haber visto resultados y sin saber si voy a devolvérselo o desaparecer con ello, que sería lo más común, lo que haría la mayoría.

—Bueno, tú no eres como la mayoría, doy fe de ello. De lo contrario, no estarías planteándote ese punto, ya te habrías fugado con esos seis mil euros, que, tal y como está todo, no sirven para nada, nena. Además, para él será una propina, seguro. Si estuvieras en su lugar, pensarías que es una cantidad ridícula.

»En cuanto a lo que te ha sucedido esta mañana —prosiguió—, es más común de lo que crees. Ese tipo de negocios suelen llevarse con mucha discreción, más aún si estás buscando un incunable, que seguramente no quiera dar a conocer y que formará parte de su colección privada y oculta por los siglos de los siglos. En estos negocios, como sucedía en la monarquía hispánica del siglo XVII, siempre se tiene un valido para que ejerza en nombre de uno. Lo más probable es que esa señora, la tal... —Hizo una pausa.

169

—Fischer —respondí.

—Esa —dijo en tono despectivo—. Estoy segura que no tiene nada que ver con él y que ejerce de valido. Recapacita si te interesa el trabajo, si lo consideras bien pagado, y sí es así, no le des más vueltas. Eso sí, yo que tú le pediría más pasta. Teniendo en cuenta lo que me has contado, no sabes cuándo lo puedes concluir, el tiempo que te va a llevar. Nena, ya somos muchos los mal pagados para que ahora tú te sumes a la lista, más aún teniendo la oportunidad de conseguir más beneficios económicos. Y, créeme, si se ha tomado tantas molestias para que no se le localice así como así, es que está muy interesado en esa pieza, quizás roce la obsesión. Aprovéchalo, no seas ingenua.

—No sé, hay algo que no termina de convencerme. Ya veré —le dije—. Y tú, ¿qué tal va todo en esa orilla del Nilo?

—Muy bien. Mi Freddie Mercury sigue deleitándome en todas las facetas, es un crac. En cuanto a la excavación, pues ya sabes..., mucha tierra y un sol de justicia, nena. Pero no te llamaba para hablar de mí, sino de Virginia. Esta mañana se ha puesto en contacto con Andreas y le ha comunicado que ella se encargará de todo lo concerniente a la repatriación de los restos mortales de Duncan. Según me ha comentado, Virginia estaba en perfectas condiciones. Hablaba de forma muy sensata y su aspecto era impecable. Nada que ver con lo que le habían dicho.

—¿Su aspecto? —le pregunté sorprendida—. ¿La ha visto? ¿Andreas ya está en España?

—¡Qué va! Iba a tomar un vuelo esta tarde. Después de la conversación que han mantenido por FaceTime con Virginia lo ha cancelado. Quería que lo supieras para que ya no estuvieses pendiente de si te llamaba o necesitaba algo...

CAPÍTULO 27

No podía comentarle a Samanta que había sido testigo del estado en que se encontraba Virginia antes de conocer a Farid, ni confiarle mi convencimiento de que su extraordinario cambio se debía a la ayuda emocional y económica que le había prestado el anticuario. Tampoco podía contarle que había estado compartiendo cena e información con ella la noche anterior y que lo más probable fuese que ella, al tener conocimiento por mi parte del viaje de Andreas y de las intenciones que este tenía al llegar a España, hubiese decidido llamarlo para evitar que él interviniera en sus planes y los trastocase. Unos propósitos que, deduje, posiblemente no había compartido con nadie a excepción de Farid.

Tras colgar el teléfono, recapitulé todo lo que había sucedido en tan solo un día. Los acontecimientos habían hecho que mi vida volviese a dar un giro de ciento ochenta grados. De tenerlo todo en la palma de la mano, había pasado a encontrarme en el punto de origen. La información que había obtenido sobre Virginia y Duncan, sobre el evangelio e incluso sobre Desmond, no variaba sustancialmente de lo que ya sabía antes de conocer a Farid. Estaba segura de que ni siquiera el *pendrive* contendría ninguna información que yo no tuviera, a excepción de alguna curiosidad histórica sobre los vampiros escoceses o las brujas, probablemente basada en leyendas urbanas o en supersticiones populares o creencias religiosas.

Evidentemente, no tendrían nada que ver con la realidad mágica que yo conocía; la verdadera magia.

Por un tiempo, mi objetivo prioritario fue encontrar a Virginia, ayudarla y que ella me ayudase, pero la esposa de Duncan se había esfumado ante mis ojos, y algo me decía que había encontrado la forma de regresar con su marido, de alcanzar aquella realidad que la devolviera a un tiempo en el que él, Duncan, aún estaba con vida. Virginia había desaparecido como lo había hecho Farid, pero a él lo volvería a ver, estaba segura de ello.

—En esta o en otra realidad —verbalicé mientras bajaba las escaleras que me conducían a la estación de metro.

Al hacerlo, al pronunciar aquella frase, no pude evitar recordar a Rigel y lo mucho que lo necesitaba, en lo diferente que habría sido mi vida si él no se hubiera ido.

Tomé el metro en Manuel Becerra con dirección a Argüelles. No sabía si Alán habría pasado por el ático. El WhatsApp me indicaba que mi mensaje había sido visto, pero no tenía ninguna respuesta. Y aunque temía encontrármelo en casa, decidí volver. Solo allí podría poner en orden mis ideas, enderezar mi vida, recuperar el control de los acontecimientos y decidir qué iba a hacer a partir de ese momento.

Esperé la llegada del tren sentada en uno de los bancos mientras observaba a la gente que llegaba a la estación y a la que ya aguardaba en el andén. La mayoría de las personas me parecieron insólitas, fuera de contexto. Eso no me inquietó, porque ya me había sucedido con anterioridad. Este fenómeno, que yo solía denominar «coincidencia astral», hacía que personas con un rasgo común, pero completamente desconocidas entre sí, se encontraran en el mismo lugar y crearan una atmósfera peculiar, a veces más propia de un escenario cinematográfico.

Había un sacerdote que vestía hábito negro y levita, con una Biblia vieja y deslavada en la mano derecha y, en la izquierda, un

maletín negro de piel; su aspecto regio y expresión adusta recordaban a la clásica figura de un exorcista. Cerca de él, un prestidigitador disfrazado de arlequín lanzaba al aire varios objetos con la forma de las piezas del ajedrez. Una mujer pequeña y esmirriada, con los labios y los pómulos pintados de rojo carmín, caminaba arriba y abajo por el andén con un cestillo de mimbre lleno de violetas apoyado en la cadera. Al fondo, cerca de las escaleras de acceso a la estación, un anciano menudo y de apariencia frágil sostenía con visible dificultad una cuerda atada a una veintena de globos de colores que se elevaban y casi rozaban el techo, amenazando con arrastrarlo en su vuelo. Por unos momentos pensé que todos formaban parte de la comitiva de un circo. Sonreí al contemplar aquella maravillosa diversidad y tomé el tren junto a ellos. Al entrar en el vagón me percaté de que en él viajaban personas aún más extrañas y peculiares que aquellas con las que, segundos antes, había esperado en el andén.

Cuando el convoy se detuvo en Cuatro Caminos, todos se bajaron en tropel y el vagón se quedó vacío. Miré con estupor alrededor, sin entender qué estaba sucediendo, y, desconcertada, volví la vista hacia el andén. Entonces los vi. Virginia y Duncan caminaban cogidos del brazo, charlando y riendo. Duncan estaba tal y como yo lo conocí, incluso su chaqueta y su maletín tenían el mismo aspecto. Ella era veinte años más joven que la noche anterior, cuando cenamos juntas en el piso de Farid. Quise apearme del vagón para ir tras ellos, pero una mano se apoyó en mi hombro y me detuvo.

—¡Diana! Hija de Aradia, descendiente directa de la diosa lunar, ¡ni se te ocurra! —me ordenó—. No debes interferir en sus vidas.

Era una mujer mayor, vestida de negro riguroso. Junto a ella se encontraba una de las mujeres con la que, días atrás, me había cruzado en el metro. Llevaba la misma escoba que entonces y, a diferencia de la mujer enlutada, que me miraba enfadada, ella me sonreía.

—¿Hija de quién? ¿A qué se refiere? —le pregunté mirándola fijamente, desconcertada.

—Bien lo sabes, Diana. Siempre has sabido quién eres, aunque durante un tiempo te hayas negado a aceptarlo. No es necesario andarnos con subterfugios absurdos. Ellos —dijo, señalando a Virginia y a Duncan— son seres normales. Debes dejarlos estar donde y como se hallan. Si interfieres, los volverás locos. Nuestro tiempo, nuestra vida y todo lo que conlleva forma parte de otra dimensión. En ella todos los tiempos son uno e infinitos a la vez.

—Señora, le aseguro que nunca he sabido quién soy. Llevo toda mi vida intentando encontrar un rastro de mis orígenes —le dije alzando el tono de voz—. Pero ella —señalé a Virginia— puede darme las respuestas que llevo buscando toda mi vida, y además puedo ayudarla a que no cometa el error de seguir el mismo camino que casi la condujo a la locura —concluí desafiante.

—Eso no es cosa tuya. Deberías ocuparte solo de tu vida, cada día pareces más mortal, ¡siempre inmiscuyéndote en asuntos ajenos! ¡Como si no tuvieras bastante con lo tuyo! Porque, dime: ¿cómo has podido perder el libro y el pentagrama? Muy a mi pesar, al final tendré que admitir que Salomón, el nigromante, tiene razón: eres una novata, una bruja torpe y sin escoba, descendiente de un estúpido mortal. Si sigues con esa obsesión, amando a ese vampiro majadero, al final acabarás aniquilando nuestra Orden —expuso, mirándome con rabia. Al oír su alusión a Desmond, recordé aquella visión en la que aparecíamos los dos juntos y llorando en un lugar y un tiempo que no reconocí—. Por tu estúpida inconsciencia, por tus caprichos, terminaremos siendo descubiertas y perderemos lo que siglo tras siglo hemos protegido en el más absoluto secreto: nuestra inmortalidad. Tú céntrate únicamente en encontrar el evangelio y el pentagrama, en protegerlos y perpetuar tus dones, conocimientos y descendencia. Si te empeñas en enamorarte de nuevo de ese vampiro de poca monta que se hace pasar por mortal, volveremos al principio de nuevo.

El tren arrancó de golpe y me tambaleé. La luz del vagón pareció sufrir una bajada de tensión y el interior se quedó a oscuras. Sentí el murmullo de gente, alguna que otra risa, y vi que muchos utilizaban la linterna de sus teléfonos móviles. El vagón volvía a estar repleto de pasajeros, pero ya no eran los mismos que me habían acompañado en aquel recorrido extraño y, tal vez, perteneciente a otra dimensión, pensé recordando las palabras de la mujer enlutada. Cuando la luz volvió, comprobé que ella seguía allí, pero ya no estaba de pie, sino sentada frente a mí. La miré fijamente y ella me sonrió.

—Perdone, joven —me dijo—, ¿sería tan amable de ayudarme a bajar en la próxima estación? El vagón se tambalea mucho y temo caer.

—Madre —dijo la otra mujer—. No moleste, yo la ayudaré. ¿No recuerda que he venido con usted?

»¡Discúlpela! —exclamó dirigiéndose a mí con una sonrisa azorada—. Es la memoria, que a su edad cada día le falla más.

La reprimenda de la mujer y sus comentarios sobre Desmond y el nigromante se quedaron en mis pensamientos como si fuesen un eco que se repetía una y otra vez. Ella sabía quién era Desmond, conocía el nombre del nigromante, estaba al corriente de que yo había perdido el evangelio y el pentagrama, y, lo más importante, conocía mis orígenes. Antes de que se levantase del asiento quise volver a hablar con ella. Necesitaba que me revelase más datos, que me explicase de una forma menos expeditiva a qué se refería y por qué hablaba de aquella manera tan ofensiva de Desmond, asegurando que me enamoraría de él. Sin embargo, por más que lo intenté no fui capaz de mover un solo músculo. No pude vocalizar una sola palabra y, no solo eso, mi mano permaneció adherida al asa que colgaba de la barra del vagón y mis pies, pegados al suelo.

—Qué maleducada, por Dios, ni siquiera ha contestado a la hija cuando le ha pedido disculpas. ¡Qué vergüenza! —oí decir a un hombre que estaba sentado cerca de la anciana enlutada. Miró a los

175

ocupantes del vagón esperando una muestra de complicidad hacia sus palabras, pero nadie abrió la boca.

Intenté responderle, pero fui incapaz. Finalmente, cuando vio que nadie en el vagón reaccionaba a su comentario y que en apariencia yo seguía indiferente, el hombre retiró la vista y pareció olvidarse de mí.

Respiré aliviada al ver que había dejado de ser el centro de las miradas de los pasajeros del vagón, pero mis inquietudes no remitieron, porque todavía era presa de aquella especie de parálisis que parecía tener origen en los ojos de la anciana enlutada, que no dejó de escrutarme ni un solo instante. Al salir del vagón, las dos mujeres pasaron a mi lado como si yo no estuviera allí y jamás hubiesen intercambiado palabra alguna conmigo. Cuando ambas se bajaron del tren, recobré mis movimientos.

Aún me quedaban tres estaciones para llegar a Argüelles, estaba en Guzmán el Bueno. Recorrí despacio los vagones hasta encontrar asiento. Necesitaba descansar. Cuando al fin pude sentarme, cerré los ojos y, de nuevo, pensé en lo que me había dicho la anciana. Debía recuperar el evangelio y el pentagrama, me repetí una y otra vez, sin poder pensar en nada más hasta que el tren llegó a mi estación. Tenía que recuperarlos para así hallar una respuesta a todo lo que me estaba sucediendo, pero no sabía cómo iba a persuadir a Ecles para que me dijese dónde lo tenía o qué había hecho con él. Recobrar el pentagrama sería aún más arduo, porque lo tenía Amaya engarzado en su anillo.

CAPÍTULO 28

Cuando salí de la estación ya había anochecido, sin embargo no tenía conciencia de haber pasado tantas horas dentro del suburbano. Miré la hora en el teléfono móvil y comprobé que eran más de las once de la noche. Había vuelto a suceder: me había internado de nuevo en un agujero de gusano que, como una goma elástica, se había ido estirando para luego encogerse de golpe sobre mí y devolverme a mi tiempo. Me había lanzado de un lado a otro como si yo fuese la piedra de un tirachinas manejado por la voluntad de la anciana, porque estaba segura de que había sido ella quien propició aquel viaje en el tiempo solo para reprenderme e intentar fijar mi atención en la recuperación del evangelio y del pentagrama, a los que ella daba una importancia vital.

La pantalla de mi teléfono me indicaba que tenía un mensaje en el WhatsApp y otro de voz. Decidí escuchar primero el de voz, que era de Antonio. Me decía que había resuelto alquilarme el local de su madre, El desván de Aradia, y me pedía que me pusiese en contacto con él si aún seguía interesada.

—El desván de Aradia —dije, pensando en voz alta.

—Está allí —me respondió una mujer de facciones asiáticas—, justo enfrente. El letrero no se ve muy bien porque lleva mucho tiempo cerrado —explicó, señalando la puerta.

—Lo sé, solo hablaba conmigo misma. Vivo en ese bloque, pero muchas gracias.

—Yo también lo sé. —Sonrió con timidez y yo la miré con gesto de no entender lo que quería decirme—. Sé que vive ahí, con los otros seres extraños. Soy la dueña de la floristería, la madre de Amaya, y llevo esperándola toda la tarde y parte de la noche. Conoce a mi hija, ¿verdad?

—Sí, por supuesto. ¿Le sucede algo? —le pregunté acercándome a ella, porque noté que su tono de voz había disminuido al pronunciar el nombre de su hija.

—Estoy muy preocupada por ella. Me he quedado aquí, a esperarla a usted, porque necesito pedirle un favor.

—¿De qué se trata?

—Quiero que le devuelva el anillo al Frankenstein. Él se lo regaló a Amaya —expuso la mujer mientras me tendía una cajita—. Está ahí dentro. No he querido tocarlo más de lo necesario, no puedo hacerlo. Las veces que lo he tenido en mis manos he visto cosas rarísimas, que me asustan. Desde que mi hija lo recibió, la tienda se ha convertido en un lugar extraño, como si fuera una conexión con otro mundo. Hay un hombre al que no conocemos, y al que no podemos dirigirnos, que entra y sale de nuestro negocio cuando quiere. Con el calor que hace estos días, él lleva gabardina, sombrero y guantes de piel, como si estuviera helado. Mi marido y yo creemos que es un *yūrei*, un fantasma atormentado que ese anillo ha arrastrado hasta nuestra pequeña floristería. ¡Por favor! ¿Podría devolvérselo al Frankenstein?

—Se llama Ecles —le dije, molesta por la reiteración de la mujer— y es amigo mío. ¿Cómo sabe usted que el anillo es de él?

—Después de la extraña explosión que hubo en la tienda, mi marido recordó el anillo, porque la piedra que tiene engarzada es muy parecida a la que el albino, el basurero, lleva colgada de su llavero. De hecho, cree que las dos piedras son iguales y que tienen

las mismas energías. Él piensa que la piedra del llavero impidió que los cristales de la explosión le cayeran encima, pero también notó a su alrededor una fuerza extraña que no le gustó y que lo aterrorizó como nunca antes en su vida. Tiene miedo, por eso pidió a sus amigos que le ayudaran a descubrir quién había efectuado el envío a mi hija. Cuando un regalo está cargado de energías negativas, hay que retornarlo a la persona que te lo obsequió. De no ser así, las energías seguirán rondándote siempre, no se irán.

—¿Amaya sabe que usted tiene el anillo y que me lo va a entregar?

—Sí. Al principio se negaba a devolverlo porque pensaba que el albino..., no recuerdo su nombre —dijo pensativa.

—Desmond —respondí.

—Eso, estaba convencida de que Desmond se lo había mandado. Aunque es casi igual de extraño que todos los que viven ahí, es un buen hombre, le deja libros para consultar y le da consejos. No nos parece el hombre apropiado para ella, pero Amaya se siente muy atraída por él, y hasta ahora su padre y yo le hemos dejado hacer porque sabemos que él no está interesado en nuestra hija, al menos no como ella lo está en él. Cuando su padre le mostró de dónde y de quién procedía el anillo, aceptó dárnoslo para que se lo devolviésemos a su amigo.

—Podían habérselo enviado por correo —le dije—, aunque lo más apropiado sería que ustedes mismos se lo hubiesen devuelto, o ella, su hija.

—Tenemos miedo, por eso queremos que usted se lo entregue y que le pida que, por favor, deje en paz a nuestra hija. Nuestra pequeña no es para él.

—Lo haré, no se preocupe —dije, cogiendo la cajita—. Le devolveré el anillo. Espero sinceramente que a partir de ahora la tienda recobre la normalidad que, según usted, ha perdido. Pero, de todos modos, déjeme que le puntualice una cosa: Ecles es una

excelente persona y estoy convencida de que su hija sería muy feliz con él, aunque su apariencia no sea la de un joven samurái —declaré—, que de seguro es lo que ustedes quieren para ella. Sus guerreros, en la actualidad, solo sirven para decorar un salón, señora —recalqué, enfatizando el apelativo.

Los faros de un coche que permanecía aparcado unos metros más allá de donde estábamos nosotras se encendieron.

—Siento mucho si la he molestado. Le agradezco su favor —dijo, y se inclinó frente a mí. Después comenzó a caminar en dirección al coche donde la esperaba su esposo.

En ese momento Desmond salió del portal y cruzó la calzada.

—¡Vaya, escocesa! Debes de haberle hecho un gran favor a la madre de Amaya, porque un *teineirei* no se hace a la ligera —me dijo mientras se acercaba a mí.

—¿Un qué? —le pregunté cuando ya estuvo a mi lado.

—Es una reverencia y muestra del agradecimiento que siente hacia ti. También se emplea para pedir perdón por un error, pero imagino que la mujer no habrá cometido ninguno, sino que tú, bella escocesa, le habrás hecho un servicio importante. De no ser así, los padres de Amaya no estarían aquí a estas horas —dijo señalando el vehículo que salía del lugar donde había permanecido estacionado.

No esperaba encontrarme con Desmond, aunque en realidad no habíamos coincidido por casualidad. Él había salido a buscarme.

—¿No trabajas hoy? —le pregunté al tiempo que introducía la cajita que me había dado la madre de Amaya en uno de los bolsillos exteriores de mi mochila.

Él no perdió de vista lo que hacía y siguió el movimiento de mi mano hasta que la caja estuvo a buen recaudo.

—No, libro hoy y mañana. Estaba en la terraza y te he visto llegar. La madre de Amaya y su marido estuvieron toda la tarde en la tienda, luego cerraron y esperaron en el coche. Su hija no ha venido

hoy. Pensé que estaba enferma, pero veo que en realidad querían hablar contigo.

—Vaya, has estado toda la tarde y parte de la noche preocupado por la ausencia de la joven japonesa. Igual sus papis no la han dejado venir para que tú no sigas cortejándola —le dije irónica—. Creo que no les gustas. Eres un poquito mayor y demasiado blanco para ser el yerno con el que han soñado mientras la educaban y pagaban sus estudios en colegios de moral encorsetada y elitista. Un consejo, cuando vuelvas a verla, cántale: «Tu madre no lo dice, pero me mira mal. "¿Quién es el chico tan raro con el que vas?"». Creo que ella no sabe la opinión que tienen sus padres de ti, de todos nosotros —apostillé mirando nuestro edificio.

—Me gusta Loquillo, y esa canción es una de mis preferidas. Pero estás equivocada si piensas que he cortejado a Amaya en algún momento.

—Por si se te ocurre, no está de más que sepas que sus padres sí lo creen y que no les caes bien; ni tú, ni Ecles y creo que tampoco yo.

—Te ha devuelto el anillo con la piedra, ¿verdad? —me preguntó. Por toda respuesta, me limité a dirigirle una mirada desafiante—. Si lo ha hecho, Ecles no debe saberlo. Mañana mismo se dará cuenta de que Amaya no lo lleva, claro, pero será incapaz de preguntarle a ella. Hará mil cábalas, pero jamás imaginará que ella se lo dio a sus padres y ellos a ti. Es mi amigo y cualquier cosa que le haga daño me lo hace a mí. Si no me equivoco y te lo ha dado, por favor, no le digas nada a él.

—Pues podrías haber tomado esas mismas precauciones con Amaya. La japonesita bebe los vientos por ti y lo sabes; sin embargo, no has hecho nada por quitarte de en medio para dejarle el camino libre a tu amigo, con lo mucho que dices quererle.

—No sé qué te pasa —dijo con una expresión seria que recorrió sus ojos y les robó la luz que tenían—. Sabes que Amaya no me

atrae. No soy responsable de los sentimientos que pueda inspirar en los demás. Tú, sin ir más lejos, pasas de mí, aunque yo me dejo el alma en cada gesto o palabra que te dedico.

—No estamos hablando de mí —le respondí.

—Yo sí, y si he bajado ha sido para invitarte a tomar una copa de vino y a contar unas cuantas estrellas conmigo. Me lo debes, aunque a lo mejor ese novio de cartón piedra que tienes no te deja salir de casa con extraños.

—Eres un poquito imbécil, ¿lo sabes? —le espeté—. Para que te enteres, ya no estoy con él, pero si lo estuviera daría igual, no me tomaría una copa contigo a solas jamás.

—Leí una novela en la que la protagonista decía que «jamás» era una palabra muy mentirosa. Te demostraré que tiene razón; lo es.

—Quizás otro día, hoy estoy muy cansada. Necesito darme una ducha, cenar algo y ver cómo está *Senatón*. Lleva solo todo el día —me excusé.

—Si cambias de opinión, estaré en casa, escuchando música. Ya sabes que soy un ave nocturna, no consigo dormir por la noche. Piénsatelo, voy a comprar unas cosas y regreso en un rato.

Me tendió la mano para cruzar de acera, pero no la acepté porque, aunque me moría de ganas de hacerlo, tenía miedo de sentir más de lo que ya sentía por él.

—Sé cruzar la calle sola, gracias —le dije mientras empezaba a caminar.

—No pretendía ayudarte a cruzar la calle, quería cruzarla contigo..., de tu mano —puntualizó—. Mira, creo que ya va siendo hora de que dejemos de actuar como idiotas. He sido muy directo y claro desde que te conocí, pero comienza a cansarme esta especie de baile absurdo que pareces ensayar solo conmigo. Si no quieres que te vuelva a dirigir la palabra, dímelo y no te molestaré más.

—Lo siento —me disculpé—. Últimamente mi vida se ha puesto patas arriba. He perdido mi trabajo, he roto con Alán y no tengo claro qué voy a hacer a partir de ahora. Reconozco que estoy un poco irascible —le comenté, sincerándome con él.

—A veces los acontecimientos suceden en cadena, uno tras otro. Darle vueltas o encerrarse en lo que nos pasa no sirve de nada. Por el momento no pienses en qué vas a hacer, es mejor que te tomes unos días de descanso.

»Date esa ducha que has dicho —añadió a continuación—, ocúpate de *Senatón* y, si después de todo eso el sueño no te vence, te espero en mi terraza.

Se marchó no sin antes rozar mi mejilla con la mano, la misma que me había ofrecido hacía unos segundos. Lo hizo como al desgaire, en una caricia escurridiza que me erizó la piel. Sus ojos se clavaron en los míos y de nuevo me asaltó aquel presentimiento que me abordaba sin previo aviso y me decía que, quisiera o no, terminaríamos juntos.

Capítulo 29

Después de atender a *Senatón* y darme la ducha que tanta falta me hacía, me serví un vaso de leche fría y me senté en el salón. Saqué el anillo de la caja y contemplé el pentagrama. Me llevé la mano al cuello y toqué la cadena que, desde que quité el pentagrama, estaba vacía. Tomé el anillo y lo volteé varias veces, intentando ver la forma de separar la piedra sin que esta sufriese ningún desperfecto. Quería colgarla de nuevo en la cadena, pero la piedra parecía haber sido engarzada a conciencia, porque no se movía ni un milímetro, como si no hubiese un solo hueco entre la plata del aro y ella. Lo dejé sobre la mesa sin dejar de pensar en cómo sacarla sin que se rompiese. *Senatón* comenzó a remolonear a mi lado.

—¿Qué pasa, bichito? ¿Quieres mimos? Has estado demasiadas horas solo, ¿verdad?

Me miró tan fijamente que llegué a pensar que entendía mis palabras y soltó un maullido largo y lastimero que me hizo sonreír, porque me pareció una respuesta a mis preguntas. Luego saltó sobre la mesa y comenzó a jugar con el anillo, empujándolo por la superficie con sus patitas. La sortija fue saltando de una garra a la otra hasta que por fin la piedra se desprendió. Como si supiese lo que estaba haciendo desde que comenzó a jugar con el anillo, en cuanto se desprendió la piedra, *Senatón* se sentó, me miró y volvió a maullar.

El pentagrama estaba intacto, incluso conservaba el pequeño orificio donde iba el aro que luego permitía introducirlo en la cadena. Me levanté como un resorte y fui a mi joyero para buscar entre los colgantes un arito similar. Me llevó unos minutos desenganchar la nueva argolla y colocarla en el pentagrama. Después lo deslicé por la cadena y me la colgué al cuello.

Respiré aliviada. Con la piedra entre mis manos, cerré los ojos y deseé que todo volviera a la normalidad. Estaba saturada de tanta información, de tantos cambios, de aquel huracán que parecía ir desbaratando toda mi vida a su antojo. Agobiada por el cansancio, por la sucesión de todos aquellos acontecimientos que aún no comprendía, desee ser una persona normal, que la magia abandonase mi vida. Justo en ese momento oí en la calle las carcajadas del nigromante, de Salomón, como lo había llamado la anciana vestida de negro. Salí a la terraza, me acerqué a la barandilla y miré hacia la acera de la floristería.

—Si quieres dejar de ser una bruja, yo puedo ayudarte. Te dije que esto no era para ti, tienes más de mortal que de criatura del otro mundo. Mira, aún conservo el bolígrafo. Déjame subir y te ayudaré a deshacerte de la magia que tanto te estorba —dijo, levantando la mano para mostrármelo.

Sin perderlo de vista, pasé las manos por la barandilla y las palmas me quedaron recubiertas del polvo rojo de ladrillo. Después las saqué hacia fuera y palmeé, mirándolo con aire desafiante. Las partículas fueron precipitándose como una cascada fina, casi incorpórea, pero especial y extrañamente visibles, resplandecientes como la purpurina. El viento que soplaba en ese momento las arrastró sobre él y, al caerle encima, su figura desapareció.

Aún permanecía apoyada en la barandilla, mirando hacia el lugar donde Salomón se había esfumado, cuando oí que Ecles hablaba dirigiéndose a mí.

—Diana, ¿cómo te ha ido el día? ¿Estás más tranquila? —me preguntó desde su terraza—. ¿Alán vino a buscar sus cosas? ¿Te llamó?

Desmond apareció en la terraza de su casa.

—¿Te animas? —preguntó, sacando una botella de vino de la bolsa de papel en la que traía la compra—. También hay tarta de zanahoria, cuatro raciones. —Me guiñó el ojo derecho al pronunciar el número de raciones que había comprado—. Elda subirá en unos momentos. Anda, acompáñanos.

No le respondí. Tenía a Ecles frente a mí, mirándome fijamente el cuello sin parpadear siquiera. Lo observé con atención porque me pareció que estaba palideciendo por momentos, que algo le sucedía.

—Ecles, ¿qué ocurre? ¿Estás bien? —le pregunté alarmada.

—Esa piedra es la que le regalé a Amaya —afirmó, señalando el pentagrama que colgaba de la cadena en mi cuello.

—No, Ecles, te equivocas. Es mía —aseguré, acercándome al murete que separaba nuestras terrazas para mostrársela—. Me la regaló Alán hace años. Se parecerá, pero no lo es.

Cogió la piedra y me miró.

—Sí que lo es, Diana. ¡No vuelvas a mentirme! —gritó mientras se le humedecían los ojos.

Al instante me recriminé por haber sido tan inconsciente, mientras seguía con la vista las dos lágrimas que caían por sus mejillas.

—¡Lo siento! —me disculpé, pero mi voz quedó empequeñecida por su grito—. No te he mentido, Ecles. La piedra es mía —dije, sincerándome.

—Yo la encontré y se la regalé a Amaya, de modo que era de ella. Hice lo mismo que con la gaveta, te la regalé a ti. Al menos espero que no vuelvas a cometer el mismo error que antaño —dijo mirándome fijamente, con una expresión en sus ojos que no había visto antes.

—No entiendo, ¿a qué te refieres? —le pregunté, sopesando la posibilidad de que, al encontrar la gaveta, la piedra y el evangelio en el altillo del armario, hubiera visto más de lo que había dicho.

—Tienes muy mala memoria para lo que te interesa —me respondió en el mismo tono de voz agudo y elevado, con una ironía que no era propia de él.

Era tan extraña e inusual su actitud que, por un segundo, creí estar frente a otra persona. Fue como si mi amigo se hubiese ido justo en el momento en que vio la piedra en mi cuello, colgando de la cadena.

—Ecles, Diana no tiene la culpa de lo que ha sucedido. Siempre puedes darle a Amaya otra sortija con una piedra que tenga más valor que esa. Ya sabes que todo sucede por algo. Nada se debe al azar, porque hasta el azar sigue unas pautas —le dijo Desmond, que apoyó una mano sobre el hombro de su amigo en un intento de calmarlo.

—No me vengas ahora con tonterías, vampiro —respondió, retirando la mano de Desmond de su hombro y apartándose de él—. Tu postura es muy cómoda, siempre lo ha sido. Eres el menos indicado para dar lecciones. Aún no le has dicho nada a ella, ¿verdad? ¡Qué inocente soy! Claro que no lo has hecho, no necesitas hacerlo. Dame tu péndulo y le haré un nuevo anillo a Amaya con él —le dijo desafiante, extendiendo la mano.

—¡Tranquilízate! —le gritó Desmond, y sus ojos parecieron clavarse como dagas en los de Ecles.

Saqué la piedra de la cadena y se la ofrecí a Ecles, quien, tras el grito de Desmond, se demudó y pareció encogerse sobre sí mismo.

—Toma, en casa tengo la sortija. Ahora te la doy y la engarzas de nuevo. Nuestra amistad vale mucho más que una piedra. Solo te pongo una condición: quiero que se la des tú mismo a Amaya. Nada de envíos anónimos. —Alargué la mano, ofreciéndole la piedra sobre la palma.

Como salido de la nada, *Senatón* saltó sobre el murete y se colocó junto a nosotros, me dio un zarpazo en la mano y la piedra cayó al suelo. El gato fue tras ella, la empujó con sus patitas, se la introdujo en la boca y salió corriendo como un condenado ante nuestro asombro.

Ecles se dio la vuelta y regresó al interior de su casa. Desmond tampoco pronunció palabra alguna, ni tan siquiera se le escapó un gesto de sorpresa o de alarma ante lo que terminaba de suceder.

—Voy a buscarlo. Seguro que está debajo de la cama, donde suele esconderse. Habrá creído que es un juguete. ¡Siento mucho lo sucedido! —exclamé, dirigiéndome a Desmond.

—Te dije que fueras prudente, Diana, y no me has hecho caso —me respondió sin mirarme, con la vista y la atención aún puestas en el recorrido de *Senatón* durante su huida con la piedra.

—Desmond, esa piedra siempre fue mía, al igual que la gaveta y el libro que encontrasteis, y yo diría que Ecles es consciente de ello —le dije, molesta por la actitud que mostraba en aquel momento hacia mí—. Esa capacidad que tiene para ver el alma de los objetos, como él lo define, va más allá. Lo acaba de demostrar con sus palabras. Me pidió que no le mintiese más, pero él me ha mentido a mí. Nos ha mentido a todos, y durante mucho tiempo. No tengo ningún problema en devolverle la piedra si él es capaz de enfrentarse a sus miedos, a sus demonios, y vencerlos, pero, ya puestos, como mínimo me merezco que me diga dónde está mi libro, qué ha hecho con él. A mí tampoco me gusta que me quiten lo que me pertenece, lo que ha sido mío desde siempre. Ese libro lo es, y Ecles lo sabe, del mismo modo que sabe que el pentagrama también me pertenecía.

Capítulo 30

—Veo que aquí nadie pierde el tiempo —dijo Alán mirando a Desmond. Había entrado en casa, pero yo estaba tan enfrascada en lo que sucedía que no me había percatado.

—¿Qué haces aquí? —le pregunté sorprendida, y entonces recordé que tenía un *whatsapp* suyo que aún no había mirado.

—Estoy en mi casa, ¿o se te ha olvidado que el alquiler del ático está a nombre de los dos? —dijo con aire desafiante y mirando a Desmond, que en vez de marcharse se había apoyado en el muro que separaba nuestras terrazas y lo observaba esbozando una sonrisa irónica y provocativa—. Te he mando un mensaje al mediodía. Aún estoy esperando una respuesta.

Entré en casa y él me siguió. Desmond no se movió; se quedó allí, con la vista fija en la puerta de la terraza, que dejé abierta.

—¿Y bien? —le dije sin mirarlo a la cara.

—Y bien, ¿qué? —contestó él.

—Espero que hayas venido a recoger tus cosas —le dije, esta vez mirándolo a los ojos.

—Diana, a mi regreso iba a decirte lo que estaba sucediendo. No me has dejado tiempo para hacerlo bien.

—Sí, sí, ya sé —lo interrumpí—. Que si unas cervezas después del trabajo, una cena de empresa, los viajes que hacías para dejarla en su casa todos los días, lo sola que está. Esos «Qué obsesión tienes,

Diana, al final vas a conseguir que Azucena me guste» —dije imitando su voz y sus gestos—. ¡Venga ya!

—Pues sí —me contestó, sentándose a mi lado—. Es difícil que me creas, soy consciente de ello, pero te quiero, Diana, te quiero mucho, y precisamente por eso quería que nuestra ruptura fuese lo menos dolorosa posible para ti. Sé que cuesta entenderlo, pero estas cosas suceden. Me he enamorado de Azucena. Ha sido algo inevitable.

—¿Cómo puedes tener ese estómago? ¿Cómo has sido capaz de falsear un viaje a Holanda? Te has reído en mi cara, Alán. Tú no me quieres ni un poquito. Si me quisieras habrías sido sincero, sin más. Tu mentira me ha herido más que el hecho de que estés enamorado de Azucena, si es que lo estás, porque a lo mejor solo es otro capricho más, como lo he sido yo.

»Ya estás tardando en recoger tus cosas y marcharte —le dije, señalando la entrada de la casa.

—Verás, la cosa es que he pensado quedarme en el ático. A ti nunca te ha gustado y a Azucena le encanta; además, el precio es lo que siempre busqué, ya lo sabes. Te daré la parte que te corresponde de lo que hemos pagado juntos y, si quieres, te ayudo a buscar otro piso y me ocupo de pagar la fianza y el primer mes de alquiler.

—¡Vete! ¡Sal ahora mismo de aquí! —grité desaforada.

Pero él no se movió del sofá, ni siquiera pareció inmutarse.

—Piénsalo. Creo que es una buena opción para los dos —insistió despreocupado, como si mi estado de ánimo no le afectase lo más mínimo.

—He dicho que te vayas. ¡Márchate! —volví a gritar, y señalé la puerta de la calle.

—¿No has oído lo que ha dicho? —le preguntó Desmond, que había saltado el murete y ya estaba en mi terraza.

—Ahora va a ser que el vampiro tiene patente de corso —respondió Alán con sarcasmo, y se puso en pie.

—¡Lárgate! —le ordenó Desmond, esta vez mirándolo tal como lo había hecho hacía unos minutos con Ecles.

—Hablaré con Antonio. Esto no va a quedar así —amenazó Alán, dirigiéndose a Desmond.

—Pues claro que va a quedar así —le respondió este—. Antonio es mi amigo. Ya estás tardando en poner tus nalgas en otro sofá —concluyó, señalándole la salida.

—Me llevo las maletas, pero volveré, y no solo a por el resto de mis cosas —dijo, señalando las bolsas con las deportivas—. Volveré a poner todo esto en orden.

Cogió las maletas con la ropa y las sacó al rellano antes de cerrar la puerta de golpe. El estrépito retumbó en todas las habitaciones.

—¡Vaya tela! —exclamó Elda desde la terraza de Desmond tras el portazo de Alán—. Yo que venía dispuesta a tomarme un vinito y un pedazo de tarta, escuchar música y echarme unas risas... y me encuentro con semejante movida. Ecles también se ha marchado. Me ha dicho que iba a la obra, pero hoy no trabaja. Le noté triste y solivantado al mismo tiempo. Luego subo y me encuentro con esto. ¡Dios, qué estrés! Bueno, ¿alguien piensa explicarme qué ha pasado aquí?

—Su novio, que es idiota —respondió Desmond—. Se ha pasado tres pueblos y dos capitales de provincia, y ya me conoces..., a mí los listos me hacen inteligente.

—Qué lástima no haber estado un poco antes en casa, lo habría oído todo, pero el metro se paró más de quince minutos. Seguro que fue una avería, pero el caos que ha originado el parón ha sido tremendo. Acabo de llegar, ni me ha dado tiempo a cambiarme, he subido directamente —dijo pasándose la mano por el mono blanco de trabajo. Nos miró a la espera de una respuesta, pero ninguno abrió la boca—. Bueno, ya me contaréis lo que ha sucedido.

»¡Dios! Casi lo olvido —dijo, dirigiéndose a mí—. Ecles me ha dado un mensaje para ti, Diana. Ha dicho que tu libro está en la

Biblioteca Nacional. Por lo visto, no recuerda en qué lugar exacto lo dejó, pero me ha comentado que seguramente tú lo encontrarás. Ah, y ha añadido que él no se queda con nada que no sea suyo y que si no te lo devolvió fue solo para protegerte. Sí —dijo rascándose la cabeza con aire pensativo—, creo que me debéis una explicación. Los dos —puntualizó.

Desmond saltó el murete y regresó a su terraza, rodeó con sus brazos a Elda y le susurró algo al oído. Ella me miró y me lanzó un beso llevándose la mano a los labios, después los dos entraron en la casa y yo me quedé allí sola, mirando hacia la puerta por donde Alán se había marchado, aún sin digerir ni dar crédito al comportamiento que había tenido, a lo que me había pedido sin el más mínimo reparo. No dejaría que se saliese con la suya, pensé indignada. Hablaría con Antonio por la mañana, me dije, lo haría sin perder ni un solo minuto, a primera hora, y de paso cerraría el arrendamiento de El desván de Aradia, pensé mirando el sobre que me había entregado Farid. Había decidido utilizar el dinero, ya vería cómo me las arreglaba para devolvérselo si al final no aceptaba el trabajo de investigación.

Estaba en el punto de partida, en el sitio al que había deseado volver: rodeada de mis amigos, como antes de que colocase el pentagrama, la piedra roja, en el lateral de mi gaveta y, al hacerlo, el tiempo volviera hacia atrás separándome de todo. Sin embargo, nada había sucedido como imaginé que pasaría. Había perdido la gaveta y mi libro. Me había encontrado con personajes irreales que no paraban de darme pautas, amenazarme o exigirme que hiciese tal o cual cosa y, lo peor de todo, mis amigos Ecles, Elda y Desmond comenzaban a mostrar sus claroscuros ante mí. Tenía el presentimiento de que ocultaban tanto o más que yo, y sospechaba que en el fondo éramos unos desconocidos luchando por un fin que, tal vez, tuviese más en común de lo que yo había supuesto. Todo aquello me inquietaba.

Muy a mi pesar seguía siendo una bruja torpe, aunque ya tuviese mi escoba, y, como me habían dicho Salomón y la anciana vestida de negro, demasiado mortal, pensé al oír la voz de Desmond llamándome desde la terraza y sentir que el corazón se me aceleraba.

—Escocesa, ahora que por fin nos hemos librado de tu novio, podríamos ir juntos a contar un puñado de estrellas. Hagámoslo antes de que el amanecer nos sorprenda. Venga, dime que eres capaz de dejar de pensar, de abandonarte aunque solo sea por unas horas —dijo desde su terraza.

Pero aunque me estaba muriendo de ganas por compartir algo a solas con él, aunque deseaba escapar de aquella realidad y abandonarme, como él decía, no le contesté ni me levanté del sofá.

—¿Por qué no lo haces? ¿Por qué no te dejas ir? Ninguna bruja que no esté enamorada podrá regentar mi desván, y yo sé que quieres hacerlo —me dijo Claudia, que de pronto estaba frente a mí.

Su presencia ni siquiera me sorprendió; ya había aceptado quién era y lo que mis ojos podían ver. Ya no me hacía preguntas sobre la existencia de esta u otra realidad, simplemente las aceptaba.

—¿Es que no me has oído? —inquirió—. No puedes rendirte, aún te queda mucho camino que recorrer, solo estás en el comienzo. Tu historia acaba de empezar. Es importante que El desván de Aradia vuelva a abrir sus puertas. Es más importante de lo que crees. Solo puedes hacerlo tú y, para eso, antes de nada debes enamorarte de él, de Desmond —concluyó, señalando la terraza.

—Es que ya lo estoy, Claudia. Estoy enamorada de él, pero tengo miedo —respondí recordando la visión en la que Desmond y yo permanecíamos juntos en el mismo lecho, arropados por cientos de pétalos de rosa rojos.